wa] **look. "Did you**

you have no idea. orgetting for the mom...

She glided toward him, though her eyes reflected bewilderment at his tone. "Have I done someth—"

"No, but I hope you will." Cort swept her close, uncaring that she could not help but be aware of his arousal.

Lexi gazed up at him, golden eyes startled. Then, a slow smile curved her full lower lip. "And what do you hope that I will do?"

"This." He took her mouth in a blatantly sexual kiss. Hungry, hot, his lips flowed over Lexi's, demanding a response. No need to demand. She yielded with exquisite sweetness, melding her generous mouth to his.

Her slender hands feathered up his neck, thrust into his hair, stripping away the leather thong that confined it. Loose strands drifted free and held at the edges of their heated mouths.

Did she sense, he wondered, all that he offered, all that he was? Power. Control. Tenderness. Danger.

Praise for Diane O'Key

"Diane O'Key's debut novel, *CHERISH THE KNIGHT*, has it all: an enchanting Saxon vixen, a Norman knight to die for, humor, danger, and mutual attraction as Lexi and Cort's secrets unravel in Medieval England."

~Joyce Henderson, award-recognized, multi-published author of Promise the Moon

~*~

"Talk about a knight to remember! Diane O'Key's debut novel, with its lush background and gripping characters, will have you begging for more. *CHERISH THE KNIGHT* is truly a keeper!"

~Lynnette Hallberg, multi-published author of Moonlight, Motorcycles and Bad Boys

~*~

"A rich visual tapestry, castle intrigue and romance, *CHERISH THE KNIGHT* has the right ingredients for a savory read. Diane O'Key has her finger on the pulse of medieval romance!"

~Jaime Rush, New York Times bestselling author

Cherish the Knight

by

Diane O'Key

This is a work of fiction. Names, characters, places, and incidents are either the product of the author's imagination or are used fictitiously, and any resemblance to actual persons living or dead, business establishments, events, or locales, is entirely coincidental.

Cherish the Knight

Contact Information: info@thewildrosepress.com

Cover Art by *Arial Burnz*

The Wild Rose Press, Inc.
PO Box 708
Adams Basin, NY 14410-0708
Visit us at www.thewildrosepress.com

Publishing History
First English Tea Rose Edition, 2012
Print ISBN 978-1-61217-282-8
Digital ISBN 978-1-61217-281-1

Published in the United States of America

Dedication

First, to the other two-thirds of The Three Musketeers, my incomparable critique partners, Joyce Henderson and Lynnette Hallberg. I wouldn't be here without your support and well-deserved kicks-in-the-pants. Love you, sisters of my heart.

~

To my fabulous agent, Nicole Resciniti, for your encouragement and belief in me. There are no words....

~

To Michael Joy, my techie-savior, for both your friendship and selfless giving.

~

To Bud Leavitt, the other half of The Odd Couple, history teacher extraordinaire and dear friend, just because I love you.

~

And first, always, in my heart, my two favorite men in the world: my son, Colin, kind heart, good soul, superb artist: you are a gift and the joy of my life.

Best for last, my husband, Dennis... extraordinary "ordinary" hero. Your integrity, generous spirit, and unconditional love are my anchors—priceless. Thank you for giving me the space to be who I am. Forever, you are my own cherished knight.

Chapter One

Avonly Manor, The Cotswolds, England, 1071

He should be dead. On his way to his parents, his corpse draped over his shield. Naught but his own stupidity to blame. Yet by the grace of Odin and incredible luck, he was instead immersed up to his chin in a steaming bath. It seemed the gods did, indeed, protect fools.

Cort Dornogard heaved a self-disgusted sigh, closed his eyes, and relived that morning's battle...

Cort cursed, thrusting his kite-shaped shield high as the spiked flying mace whipped within inches of his unprotected head. Impossible to reach the helmet that swayed from his saddle's pommel. For his shield occupied his right arm. His sword, Deathwright, his left hand.

Across the small glade, Dane whirled his flare-bladed ax above his head, its song a deadly *thrum*. On the crisp morning air rode a wounded horse's shrill scream, the clang of metal on metal, a man's cry. Flying grit stung Cort's eyes. He inhaled the salty-sweet odor of fresh blood, the sour stench of sweat, the incongruous fragrance of spring flowers. Behind the shield, his aching right shoulder absorbed yet another blow from the mace.

A pained cry drew his gaze. Geoffrey, whose assailant wrenched a sword from the young knight's chest, then turned toward Guy.

"Falcon!" Cort roared over his shoulder. "See to your back!" But already engaged in a frontal attack, Guy made a hapless target for the enemy intent on skewering him from behind.

"Whoremonger!" Cort spat. "To work, Deathwright!"

In his rush to take Guy, the knight spurred close to Cort's left side. Not the first man to make that mistake.

Cort swung Deathwright high and level. The powerful cut took the bastard at the base of the throat. His mouth opened and closed; his sword clattered to the ground even as he tipped from the saddle.

But the impact and momentum of Cort's sword pulled him upward, and he lowered his shield as a counterbalance. The opening his opponent needed.

A strange whistle sounded to Cort's right, another behind him, but they barely registered. With sickening clarity he watched the bronze-knobbed mace aglitter in the sun. Descending to smash his skull. Instinct snapped his head sharp left, though he never took his eyes from the lethal weapon. A blurred streak whistled within inches of his neck, followed by a fleshy thud.

The attacker's mace wavered, then struck Cort's right shoulder with stunning force. His arm numbed. His shield slid to his fingertips. He doubted he'd live long enough to feel any pain.

Cort's gaze sliced to his opponent's face. Instead of the victorious sneer he'd expected, the man sat rigid, his expression a frozen agony, a stone embedded in his left eye. Dead. With a clink of metal links, the corpse pitched to the ground.

"Slingers! There be fuckin' slingers in the trees!"

Even as the crude language told Cort at least one of their assailants was Anglo-Saxon, the small rebel band fled. Hooves thundered, sunlight glancing off mail hauberks and conical helmets.

Cort grunted, taking in the wounded and dead comrades deserted by their fellows. "What the hell's become of chivalry?"

The bloodlust of battle ebbed, its pulse now a slow heaviness in his blood. Though his shoulder's blessed numbness was wearing off, Cort surveyed his own contingent. With the exception of Geoffrey, several others appeared to have sustained only minor injuries. Relieved, Cort wiped sweat and dirt from his face with his tunic, then sheathed Deathwright.

Slingers replayed in his head. No doubt, he owed them his own life, probably several of his men's as well.

He scanned the surrounding trees, saw nothing. Who were they? Where had they come from, and where had they gone?

Across the alder grove, a lean figure in mottled brown and green, wide hat pulled low, dropped lightly from a branch. A leather sling dangled from the thong-wrapped right wrist.

Cort offered an appreciative salute. The stranger returned it, then disappeared among the trees. Seconds later, pounding hooves receded into the distance. An eerie silence settled.

A single slinger, a brief glimpse of a shadowed face, the impression of light-splintered eyes.

Chapter Two

Voices, bleats, barks from the courtyard below drifted through his second-floor chamber window and drew him back to the present. Water surged as he pushed himself up and jarred his abused shoulder. He cursed ripely. It ached like a bitch, but he had a hundred things to see to.

"Odin's eyeless socket!" This day he'd awaited for almost five years had not gone as expected. He'd anticipated resistance upon arrival at Avonly, the estate promised him by King William, but not the attack en route. Right now, he had no time to ponder the source. He needed to speak with Guy, with Lord Graham, Avonly's former Earl, check on Geoffrey...

Cort groaned with pleasure as he allowed the water's heat just one more minute to seep into his abused muscles. The chamber pleased him. Comfortable, lacking affectation, both neat and tasteful. Its raised-dais bed, with a thick hunter-green coverlet over several dark furs, flanked by a tall oak cupboard and leather-bound chest. Several large rush mats covered the wood planks between the tub and far wall. Only the sizeable tapestry on the near wall and the high-backed chair beside the stone hearth hinted of luxury.

A sharp rap sounded on the door.

"Enter!" Surely the sumpter horses had been unloaded by now and 'twas Philip, his temporary squire—another problem to be addressed, dammit—come to deliver his clothes coffer.

Aware of the now-cooling water, Cort snagged the rough cloth and herb-scented soap from the stool beside the tub. Working up a lather, he scoured himself with his left hand, avoiding his bruised and swollen right shoulder. Knees thrust skyward, he slid beneath the water, then pushed himself upright with his feet.

The chamber remained empty. Had whoever knocked not heard him? “Enter!” he called again.

Releasing the cloth, he lathered his dripping hair. Eyes closed, he felt for the stool and replaced the cake of soap before working vigorous fingers against his scalp.

“*Dieu*,” he muttered, spitting suds as he wiped his eyes. The bucket of rinse water sat on the floor to his right. His shoulder ached too abominably to even consider lifting it.

Soft footsteps sounded behind him.

“Philip? Dump this bucket over my head, would you?”

In response came a soft sloshing. A moment later, warm water sluiced from the crown of his head down over his shoulders. With a low, pleasured moan, Cort tilted his head back. A soft drying cloth descended on his hair. Strong yet gentle fingers massaged his scalp, then toweled most of the wetness from his shoulder-blade length mane.

“My thanks, lad.”

As the cloth slid away, Cort surged to his feet and grabbed it to dry himself. A sharp gasp was followed by a husky, though most feminine, voice. “Stop this instant! Ah—Ah—Don—!”

“Beg pardon?” Cort inquired, stepping out of the tub. The towel now held strategically in front of him, he turned to face the young woman.

“I wasn’t speaking to you.” Her blunt response was tempered by its brimful-of-laughter tone.

“Oh?” He tilted his head as his eyes scanned the room, empty but for the two of them. “Art a witch who converses with spirits, then?”

"Nay." Head angled away from him, she seemed to inspect something over her shoulder. "With Athene, sir."

Following on the heels of her previous comment, that response prompted Cort to step back. Though less superstitious than most, a twinge of unease stirred.

"Blood of Odin," he murmured. "She speaks not with spirits but with goddesses."

The girl must be touched in the head. Sweet Christ! She could well have bashed him over the head with the bucket and left him to drown! Who was responsible for allowing her access to his chamber?

"She won't bite," the young woman assured him. "Nor will I."

She turned her head at last to look at him.

Cort's breath snagged in his throat. Late afternoon sunlight streamed through the long, narrow windows set in the parapet wall, outlining her in misty gold. Surely it must be God's own jest that one so beautiful should be so addled.

"Why look you so, my lord?" The soft-spoken query held equal parts confusion and curiosity.

Torn as he was between her suspected madness and her unearthly appeal, Cort's voice failed him. A sheer, amber-laced headcloth did little to conceal the midnight fall of her hair, which swayed all the way to the backs of her knees as she tipped her head to study him in turn. But it was her eyes that riveted his attention, their color unlike any he had ever seen: deep, tawny gold in the hazy light, like multi-faceted gems. Offset by lush lashes and elegant eyebrows as inky as her hair. Skin as translucent as the sun-shot petals of a white rose. A generous mouth moist and pink as strawberries.

If she were indeed mad, he would gladly taste of that madness...

Seeming discomfited by his unblinking stare, the girl's gaze plumbed the cause of his disconcertion. Then her golden eyes twinkled with mischief. "Did you think, when first I spoke, that I was too overcome by your appearance to complete the thought?" She laughed lightly. "I must have sounded the veriest simpleton."

Caught off guard as much by the change in topic as the girl's coherent comments, Cort's memory raced to retrieve her first words. All the while, she merely stared at him, patient as a mother awaiting her child's first steps.

He offered a tentative, "Stop! A-don?" It sounded as absurd now as it had then.

Her laughter was like the tinkling of bells. "Close enough. You thought I spoke to you, did you not? That I was, mayhap, calling you...Adonis?"

Whipping the thick towel about his waist, Cort cursed the unwelcome blush that heated his face. "Nay, I... Nay!" He stuffed the loose end of the towel into the fabric snugged about his waist. Because what he wanted, really wanted, more even than he wanted to breathe, was to toss the towel, then her, onto the bed. And follow her down. Feel her long, lush body beneath his. He swallowed the lump that had erupted into his throat. "I thought no such thing!"

"Did you not?" Her brazen gaze assessed him from head to toe. As if she intuited his thoughts, a too-knowing smile curved her full lips, but she said only, "Surely others before me have commented on your comeliness."

"Comeliness?" Unsure whether he felt more taken aback by her unexpected candor or her description of him, Cort again found himself reduced to staring.

"You are most handsome, sir, but Adonis is not what I meant to say." The girl seemed unperturbed by his shock. "My comment was directed to Athene, and well she knows it." She lifted a hand to the back of her neck. "Though I do not call her such unless I am angry. I prefer Thene. And she responds more readily to one-syllable commands."

Loki's own! If he had ever engaged in a more inane conversation, Cort could not recall it.

"Do you, I wonder?" he muttered to himself, deciding to test the thought. His voice no less fierce for its softness, he growled, "Stop!"

Raising his left hand to his temple, he massaged it with his fingertips and narrowed his eyes, pinning the girl with a glare. "I *am* speaking to you."

Though her eyes widened, she remained prudently silent.

"Now." Cort bit back his temper. "Perhaps you will be kind enough to explain what you are doing here. I made it clear I needed no assistance with my bath."

The girl shook her head slightly, as though she were the one dealing with a person whose wits had gone begging. "Actually, you did."

His scowl stopped her cold, and she changed tack.

"I did not come to bathe you, though I would certainly have done so had it been requested. 'Tis only common hospitality, after all. Yet I was glad enough to help with the bucket, my lord, and if—"

"Stop!" Cort again ordered through clenched teeth, extending his left hand as if he might physically halt the flow of words. "A simple answer, wench, if you can manage it. What are you doing here?"

"My uncle said you have need of my services," she answered.

"Have need of— I said no such thing!" Cort exploded.

"Art not wounded, sir?" Her gaze moved with

grim assessment over his swollen and discolored shoulder.

"Yes, but..." Words faded as the truth dawned on him.

"I am both Lord Graham's niece, sir, and Avonly's healer. If you will permit, I can bring you some measure of relief." With a graceful movement of her hand, the girl directed him to the bench set before the hearth.

Still unsettled by their initial conversation, Cort pulled the bench at a right angle to the fire to allow the girl better light. The harsh screech of wooden legs against hearthstone had no sooner ended than a strange, breathy cry, much like that of a baby bird, sounded close by, in conjunction with the tinkling of bells. Whirling, Cort's eyes swept the chamber, then swung back to the girl, who had moved up beside him.

Eyes flashing, she scolded, "Loud noises frighten her! You must be more careful, my lord."

"Would you tell me what in Hades is going on?"

A sudden stirring within the girl's midnight hair sent Cort scooting backward. His calves collided with the end of the wooden bench. Had she not grasped his wrist and tugged him upright, his backside would have been as damaged as his pride. But at the moment, naught seemed as important as the herb-and-rose fragrance of her hair, or the tingling warmth where she touched him.

Once more steady on his feet, Cort forced himself to reclaim his hand and watched warily as the girl reached into her pocket and withdrew...a berry? She raised her hand to her left shoulder and crooned softly.

A flat, furry face peeped from behind her neck, its pink- and-black nose sniffing the fruit. A glimmer of needle-sharp teeth flashed in the instant before a tiny tongue flickered out to draw the berry into a wide, lipless mouth.

"Athene, I assume," Cort allowed.

"Who else?" The girl grinned. "I am far more likely to converse with her than with witches or pagan goddesses, I assure you."

He forced his gaze away from her mouth and focused on her eyes, pale topaz now in the thin afternoon light. Their clear, honest depths concealed nothing, nor attempted to, and Cort knew he had never in his life seen eyes more sane than hers. With a secret grimace at his own foolishness, he subsided onto the bench.

"What is that thing? What sort of animal is Athene?" Cort studied the curious little beast with its dark bandit mask, small triangular head, dainty paws capped in slender but lethal-looking claws.

"A ferret, my lord. Have you ne'er seen one before?"

He shook his head, still-damp hair brushing his jaw and shoulders. "Is't a rodent?" He extended a tentative finger in Athene's direction.

As though she understood the insult, the ferret arched her back and emitted another of those breathy screeches, backpedaling into the cover of her mistress' hair.

"Now you've hurt her feelings," the girl teased. "What an abysmal thing to say. She is of the otter family, though grateful I am that her fur is too thin and coarse to appeal to the more fashionable. She is bright and clever and inquisitive—'tis why I named her Athene—and deserves better than to adorn the collar or hem of someone's garment."

"You are fierce in your defense of her," Cort noted. "Is her belled collar for protection or merely a pretty vanity? Perhaps you take her hunting with you and toss her into the sky like a peregrine, bells singing from her neck rather than from jesses?"

Laugh throaty, the girl turned impish eyes to

him. "No, though your image of a flying ferret is amusing. Athene wears the bells so I can locate her should she wander off. When she's not riding my back or shoulder, I oft cage her. She could easily become lost or trapped in some cranny or other, and if she ventured out of doors, I fear I'd never find her again. When I allow her to run free in my chamber, the sound of the bells signals she is well. She moves with total silence otherwise, and can squeeze into the most unlikely spaces."

The girl retrieved her basket from beside the tub, where she must have set it down to rinse his hair. Returning, she sank to her knees beside Cort.

Athene now observed him from her mistress' shoulder, intelligent black eyes wide with curiosity. Making gentle kissing sounds, the girl bent her head toward the animal, which inched farther from cover. Its tiny tongue flicked her lips in answering affection. Then, retreating once more, Athene draped herself about the girl's neck and settled into sleep.

Clearly accustomed to the animal's movements, the girl sorted through an array of leather bottles and clay jars, extracting several. Silence descended as she arranged the medicines, then rose to place a shallow earthenware bowl at the fire's edge. She dropped a pinch of grayish-green powder into the dish, added water from the ewer on the washstand, and stirred the mixture. With a satisfied nod, she returned to Cort's side.

"Have you a name, mistress?" The question dropped softly into the quiet space between them.

"*Certes*, sir. Alexis. Alexis Fallon." She raised her eyes momentarily from her task. "Though I prefer Lexi, my lord. 'Tis what everyone calls me."

"Lexi." He weighed the sound on his tongue. "A pretty name, though Alexis is pretty as well."

"Thank you, my lord." She returned her attention to the assortment of herbals and ointments. "Yours is pleasing also, though rather unusual. Court Dor...Dorn... How do you pronounce it?" Lexi again raised her eyes to his.

"Dornogard." He shifted his gaze toward the fire.

"Norse?" she persisted when he said no more.

"You needn't chatter to distract me."

"I don't chatter. I'm curious."

He huffed. "Yes, Norse. My forbears sailed from Bergen, Norway after Charles the Simple ceded Northern France to Cnut the Dane in 911. They swore fealty and were absorbed into the Norman culture."

"Normandy. Land of the Northmen. 'Twas wise of Charles to secure the peace by granting them what they'd already conquered."

Cort nodded. "The Vikings' reputation as fierce warriors is well deserved."

"As we English have good cause to know," she said dryly.

"And since they chose to blend with the French culture rather than change it—" Cort ignored her comment rather than disturb the casual ease between them—"both benefited greatly from the compromise."

Apparently equally unwilling to become involved in political discourse, Lexi dipped her fingers into a wide-mouthed pot and raised them to his injured shoulder. A pungent odor wafted around Cort's head, overpowering her sensual, earthy scent. Nostrils flared, he shifted away from her.

"What have you there, mistress?"

"Eye of spider, tongue of lizard, scale of beetle, bile of worm," Lexi chanted in an ominous, sing-song cadence. She lifted dancing-with-laughter eyes to his.

"Bile of worm?" He lifted a dubious eyebrow. "I was not aware... Though mayhap English worms..."

She laughed briefly at his dry humor, growing

instantly serious as her fingers massaged the ointment into his damaged shoulder. "Truth, 'tis a mixture of several healing herbs distilled with fish oil, comfrey leaves, and henbane. The most effective I have found for bruises, my lord. First used by the ancient Greeks, who referred to comfrey as knitbone. I have found no other poultice its equal for soothing broken skin or bones or rashes."

The pressure of her fingers was firm and rhythmic, yet so gentle it did not cause additional pain. Again, warmth tingled down his arm, then up his neck, into his chest at her touch. Somehow, both soothing and arousing. He gritted his teeth, determined to ignore the latter.

"You have a light touch, lady." Cort's eyes drifted shut beneath her tender ministrations.

"I have no wish to hurt you, my lord." As the soft words drifted over him, he experienced the strange sensation that they were layered with double meaning.

The light rustle of fabric and almost instant withdrawal of her fingers tore the thought. When he opened his eyes, Lexi was rising to her feet. Lithe, lovely. "You are fortunate not to have sustained far more serious damage, Lord Dornogard. More often than not, a flying mace crushes bone and muscle and results in permanent injury."

Cort's hand shot out to grasp her arm, his sleepy gaze of moments before now sharp and suspicious. Lexi gasped, her wide eyes dark as amber—shock or guilt?—as he drew her face to within inches of his own. Close enough to see the inky ring surrounding that incredible amber. Close enough to kiss that sensual, pink mouth. Lust knotted his belly. Dammit. "How know you I sustained this bruise from a mace?" he growled. "Unless one of my men...?"

For just an instant, or had he imagined it? Cort

thought Lexi would pounce on the offered excuse. Instead, she shook her head and turned her face toward his shoulder. Her shuddering breath could as easily have been a reaction to his implied physical threat as to guilty knowledge.

"The wound itself tells me so." She winced when his fingers tightened. "Its center is the most badly damaged, but smaller bruises radiate from it, dark marks such as a knobbed mace would leave. Look for yourself, sir."

Cort tipped his head to the side, studied his shoulder at length before releasing his grip on Lexi's arm. Her words were true. Yet that she'd quaked beneath his hand gave him pause.

He said only, "'Tis as you say."

Lexi shrugged, her smile tremulous as she backed up a step. "No harm." She lifted her elegant hands in a vague fluttering motion.

He grunted. Instinct warned this was not the time to pursue his suspicions, though he would not forget them. Odin help her if she'd had aught to do with the attack, with Geoffrey's injury. For now, he flexed the hands that wanted to fist and curbed his anger.

"Nevertheless, 'twas poor payment for your aid. Already the pain eases." He inched his injured shoulder in first a small circle, then a larger as he realized, with some amazement, that 'twas true.

In what he assumed an attempt to dispel the tension that had risen between them, or to divert his mind from the reason for it, Lexi returned the conversation to an earlier topic. "Court is indeed an unusual name. Like Lexi, a shortened form of your full name, is it not? Let me guess."

This should be interesting, Cort thought, returning her steady regard only with great effort. He splayed his hands beside his thighs on the bench and stretched his long legs, preparing to enjoy himself.

"Courtney" was her first guess.

He shook his head.

"Cortland."

"Nay."

"Courting?" she asked in disbelief.

This time his mouth quirked while his eyes told her no.

"Cort—ege!" she announced, sounding proud of her knowledge of the French word, one of many introduced into English as a result of the Conquest.

Cort released a short bark of mirth, but nothing more.

"Toad's tongue." Lexi scowled her frustration. "Is't some strange Nordic name, then?"

"Nay. My parents like it." Cort could not control the laughter beginning to rumble from his chest.

"Ah," she breathed after several moments, mischief in those coin-gold eyes. "Mayhap...Courtesan?"

It was too much. Unable to contain himself any longer, Cort threw back his head and roared with delight, more so when he caught the stunned expression on Lexi's face. Color rode high on her cheekbones, and her eyes dilated to an impossible roundness in her delicate, heart-shaped face. Whether appalled by her own temerity or his reaction to it, Cort could only guess.

When he at long last regained his composure, Cort rubbed away the moisture that had gathered in his eyes and said with deliberate casualness, "Cortland and cortege are closest, I suppose. At least their first syllables are correctly spelled: C-O-R-T."

"Well?" Lexi demanded at length, arms crossed beneath ample breasts. "What is it?"

"What?" he asked, the picture of innocence.

"Your name. Or art you as addled as you earlier thought me, *Cort*?"

To speak to him thus bordered heavily on insolence, but she smelled so good, *looked* so good, and he was enjoying himself too much to take offense. "That's it, my lady. All there is. Cort."

"But you said..."

"No, lady." Because it pleased him, he tested the ebony satin of her hair with light fingertips. "*You* said there was more."

"Ooooh..." She spun on her heel and stalked with grave dignity from the room, taking her furry little beast and the sound of his amusement with her.

A moment later, however, her dark head reappeared around the edge of the door, chin angled in defiance. "Should you have need of it, the dish on the hearth holds a distillate for pain. Drink it. Like salt, 'tis not advisable to rub it in."

Chapter Three

Distillate for pain.

"Geoffrey," Cort rasped in guilty disbelief, running taut fingers through his still-damp hair. "I never asked after him." Self-directed anger shot him to his feet.

With a curse that would have made even the outspoken Lady Lexi blush, he realized his coffer of clean clothing had not yet arrived. Whipping the bath sheet from his waist, he flung it to the floor and scooped up his stained chausses. He gritted his teeth as he pulled them up his legs and over his hips, fastening only those leather points necessary to satisfy decency. Without thought for footwear or a shirt, he wrenched open the door with his left hand, stepped back from its inward swing. An instinctive movement he'd learned early and well in a right-handed world.

Cort pounded down the spiral wooden staircase, still cursing himself as a lackwit. Leaping from the third step to the slate entryway, he absorbed the shock with bent knees and turned in the same motion toward the hearth at the hall's far end.

Christ on the cross! How could he have forgotten? Lady Lexi might not converse with witches, but he found himself again wondering if she was one. Not once had he thought to inquire about Geoffrey. He'd been too busy with important things like playing name games and discussing the intellectual merits of ferret ownership! With wondering how the lady's mouth would taste, how her lithe body and full breasts would feel pressed against... By Odin and his Aesir!

Cort covered the distance to Geoffrey's prone form with long, purposeful strides, careless of the startled expressions of those around him. He dropped to his knees beside Geoffrey and laid a tentative hand on his forehead.

The young knight's skin was waxen and clammy, his face lax. Dead? Then a stark moan issued from the boy's dry lips, and the vise around Cort's chest relaxed a fraction.

A rueful smile touched his mouth. The *boy* was scarce three years younger than he, yet worlds behind in experience. He had earned his spurs and offered Cort his services only last winter. Since then they'd fought but a handful of minor skirmishes, devoting their energies instead to supervising skilled forced laborers at the stone castles under construction by order of William, King of England.

Though not the *glorious* introduction to knighthood Cort suspected Geoffrey had wished, he never complained. Cort had responsibilities. The Conqueror had chosen him as one of a select few to oversee the peace and stability of England's Southern coast. If he was willing to work alongside serfs, cotters, and gruff stonemasons, Geoffrey seemed content to follow his commander's lead.

Cort had assured him more than once he would see enough bloodshed in his lifetime. Geoffrey's enthusiastic response to that prompted his lord to say, "Foolish lad, you were not at Hastings."

The remembered conversation tore at Cort as he studied the deathlike mask of his now truly-blooded knight. And he wondered if the boy at last understood his own lack of battle fervor. Skill in combat and love of it were two very different things. He prayed Geoffrey would not pay the ultimate price to learn that lesson.

Around Cort, conversation resumed. Banked

flames crackled upon the hearth. Burning oak and herb-sprinkled rushes scented the air. He closed his eyes and sucked in a fortifying breath. A gentle hand lighted on his bare shoulder. He raised his face to the giant towering beside him.

"Have you been watching over him, Dane?" Cort asked his huge, enigmatic knight.

"Yes, m'lord. I only l-left for a moment. To relieve m-myself." Anxiety etched the man's features.

"No need to defend yourself, my friend. I know you would not desert Geoffrey when he most needs you. But there is little we can do for him at the moment. Get some rest. I'll stay with him."

"Oh, no, m'lord. The lady said I'm to b-bathe him with a cool cloth. And w-watch for fever."

"Mayhap the lady should be doing that herself."

"She did, m'lord, t-to show me how." Dane's earnest gaze moved to Cort's damaged shoulder. "H-how is your own wound?"

At the moment, he could not afford to remember the jolt of her touch, the spreading warmth. "Better. The lady rubbed in a salve and gave me a draught for pain."

"Aye, L-Lady Lex. She was very g-good to Geoff." The giant smiled.

Lady Lex. Geoff. That quirk in Dane's intelligence, to which Cort had grown accustomed, was often mistaken for insolence by those who did not know him. With names of multiple syllables, Dane chose the one he apparently found most appealing and ignored the rest. Cort's lips tipped in a wry smile. Had the lady told Dane her full name, 'twas fortunate he had not chosen to call her Al.

Another moan from Geoffrey erased any hint of mirth. Cort moved aside as Dane hunkered down to wring out the cloth floating in a bowl of clean water. The boy's expression eased as Dane cleansed sweat from his face, then bathed his forehead and neck, careful to avoid the bleached linen bandage wrapped about his right shoulder and upper chest.

Renewed wonder and respect grew in Cort. An incredible warrior, Dane yet cared for Geoffrey with the tenderness of a mother for her babe, his gigantic, battle-scarred paws now as gentle as they were brutal when wielding ax or sword.

A cool gust of air from the entry hall heralded Guy's arrival, and Dane moved to protect Geoffrey from the draft. Squeezing the giant's shoulder, Cort rose to greet his second-in-command. When, after several seconds, Guy's startled countenance registered, Cort became aware that the serfs and knights in the hall also studied him with peculiar expressions.

"Is your garb what the fashionable new Lord of Avonly wears these days?" Guy visibly struggled for a neutral tone and a straight face.

"Amiton," he muttered, ignoring Guy's misplaced humor.

"What?"

"Amiton," Cort repeated. "Never mind." Looking down at himself, he fought an unwelcome blush. Dammit! He'd learned to master his temper—most of the time. Why could he not control that? Still, he refused to rise to the bait or excuse his dishabille. He cast a covert glance at his audience. It wasn't as though these people had never seen a bare-chested, barefoot man before.

Still, he was their new lord. Oh, hell.

He shook his head. "I'll explain later." Gathering his dignity about him in lieu of the absent shirt, he said curtly, "Come with me. We have things to discuss."

Wisely, Guy abandoned the topic of his lord's attire, or lack thereof, and followed him up the stairs.

****

"Not the *castle* you envisioned?"

"Castle?" Cort snorted. "'Tis built of wood. Small wonder Graham surrendered so quickly four years ago."

"Still, his stewardship since swearing fealty to William seems to have been prudent. The manor and lands flourish."

Cort wandered to the open casement to survey the manor. Situated on the River Avon, meadows rolled green and fertile, their verdant beauty patched with tilled fields and orchards. Thick forest bracketed the North and East. The river wound a sparkling path through the valley below. Having traveled the better part of four years along England's rocky Southern coast, *this* area struck a responsive chord of home: Normandy.

His brow furrowed at the realization of how close he and his men had come to never arriving at all. The fact that the attack had occurred but one league distant. The too real possibility that their assailants resided in the very manor he'd come to claim. To which he'd sent a messenger a sennight past to presage their arrival. Though he was not suspicious by nature, these people could not welcome that claim, and only a fool would disregard logic and common sense.

Guy moved up beside him. "Wonder if they'd have aided us or our attackers?"

"Thor's hammer! How do you do that?" Cort demanded, only half-amused.

"Do what?"

"Know what I'm thinking."

"Years-long friendship, countless battles." Guy grinned. "Besides, by your solemn expression, I vow Dane could have scried it."

Cort nodded. For all the giant might be slow-witted, none was more fierce or loyal. Dane was his man as few would ever be. Likewise, he knew Guy appreciated the man's worth and intended no unkindness.

His second-in-command gazed out the window, eyes narrowed. "That hill northeast of the manor would be ideal for a stone keep."

"You're doing it again." Cort scowled. "My exact thought. But first we must see what information we can glean from our two prisoners. Where are they?"

"Tied up, secured in a room, a guard at the door."

"Good. Until we know more, we cannot discount treachery. 'Twas not a chance attack. Those men were waiting for us. I would know why and who leads them."

Guy turned a hooded gaze to Cort. "We go on, then, as planned?"

"I see no current advantage, only possible harm, in doing otherwise. Best to play it close until we're sure which way the wind blows."

His friend switched topics with a bland smile. "Some think her beautiful."

Cort shrugged to disguise his body's carnal response to the mere thought of the girl, winced when his shoulder rebelled. "Perhaps. For now, let's concentrate on Graham and the manor's residents, knights to peasants."

Despite his words, Lexi's face surfaced. *Beautiful.* He shut down the image.

Cort wandered to the carved side table and poured wine from an ornate silver ewer into two embossed goblets. He extended one to his friend, then rested his hip against the raised bed frame and sipped his own.

"You were there when the Lady Alexis treated Geoffrey?" Cort tucked his right arm close to his side to ease the ache.

Guy eyed his arm and shoulder but didn't

comment. “Aye.” From his seat on the wooden bench, he stretched out sturdy legs. “Not that she noticed, except to issue orders that I hand her this or that.”

Cort, who could well imagine the scene, smiled in empathy.

“Authoritative wench,” Guy grumbled. “But skilled. Not an ounce of fear in her, either. Surrounded by unfamiliar, armed knights, you’d think she’d be nervous. Hah!” He wagged his dark head. “We might have been invisible. The only one she paid any attention to, other than Geoffrey, was Dane. As though they understood each other. Strange.” He took a deep swallow of wine.

Strange, indeed. Again Cort wondered if witchery played a part in the lady’s effect on him, this inexplicable attraction—

“But she’s gifted, Cort. Truly gifted. *Jesu!* Accustomed as we are to barber-surgeons on the battlefield, ’twas amazing to watch her. Imagine! She actually washed her hands. Poured wine into the wound and over the stitching needle. Mentioned Hippocrates or some such.” Guy again drank from his goblet and stared into the blue-orange flames of the fire.

At the mere mention of the lady’s hands, Cort again felt them, gentle yet provocative, against his skin. Blood surged hot in his veins. He stifled a curse at his body’s wayward response. *Concentrate.* Who, in Loki’s bag of tricks, was Hippocrates? Male, female, sorceress, wizard, what? Cort flexed his fingers and after a long moment of silence, asked, “What did she say? About Geoffrey’s condition?”

“Not much. That he’d lost a lot of blood. Gave him something to slow further loss. Dane had to pry the lad’s jaw open to get it in him, then again for a posset of willow bark and nightshade before she closed the wound.”

Cort’s throat tightened. His fingers splayed so

that he almost dropped his goblet. "Nightshade—belladonna?" Belladonna could kill.

Guy nodded. "Offered to drink some herself *after* she finished treating Geoffrey. Said she didn't wish to fall asleep in the middle of sewing up the hole in his chest."

Cort grunted in reply. He remembered the waxen texture and cool temperature of Geoffrey's skin. If he died without developing a fever... Cort's grip convulsed around the stem of his goblet. "Did she offer aught else in regard to his condition?"

"Only that he be kept warm and his wound cleansed regularly, the dressing changed twice each day. As he should sleep for some time, she ordered a quiet chamber prepared for him. She seemed quite confident of his recovery, Cort."

"Lady Lexi had best be right," he said through clenched teeth. "Belladonna, by all the saints."

"Naught in her manner indicated she wishes Geoffrey harm," Guy soothed.

"She said as much about me, yet, I don't know. A feeling. She knows more than she's telling. Not a threat so much as..." Cort pushed away from the bed and slammed his goblet down on the oak chest.

"Loki's diseased liver! While my head warns caution, my gut says differently. Won't be the first time I've followed my instincts, will it?" He paused. "Still, she bears watching."

"I don't need to tell you, at this juncture they all need watching. While Graham appears cooperative and competent, what is real, what is appearance has yet to be determined."

Cort forced a cool smile. "True. We both know how deceptive appearances can be, do we not?"

"Aye." Guy's green gaze held Cort's hard one.

Silence hung heavy while the men drained the remainder of their wine. When it became clear Cort meant to add nothing more, Guy rose with a casual salute, set his cup on the hearth, and strolled toward the door.

"Send Graham to me, Guy. I would speak with him at length, myself, before this evening's meal."

"Of course. Oh, I told him to have his personal things moved from this chamber to one down the hall beside his daughter's and Lady Lexi's. There'll be serfs in and out, but it shouldn't take long. I thought it best he do so as soon as possible."

"Exactly right. Thank you."

Nothing was exactly right. He could not afford this fist-to-the-gut attraction to a woman he neither knew nor trusted. Yet her unforgettable, earthy scent filled his head still; her delectable mouth challenged him to plunder. Odin help him...

Change. Reality. Appearance. As the portal clicked shut behind his friend, Cort's gaze lighted on the shallow, untouched bowl the lovely, fascinating—possibly duplicitous—Lady Alexis had left on the hearth stones. For him.

Chapter Four

Cort descended the stairs several hours later to a great hall awash with light and sound. Jewel-toned tapestries fluttered against planed-oak walls. The cavernous hearth's flames cast leaping shadows on the rush-strewn floor and high, arch-beamed ceiling. Soft music drifted from the hidden alcove at the far end of the room, all but drowned by the bustling kitchen serfs and the conversations and robust laughter of knights and men-at-arms gathered for the "welcome" feast. Rushlight torches added their golden glow to the charged atmosphere. Before the others noted his arrival, Cort's gaze swept the room. Pleasure swelled in him at the obvious care taken in the eve's preparations.

Richard Graham's gaze found Cort's. Gray at the temples with a pleasant face, Graham approached him and offered a formal bow. "We are prepared to dine as soon as it pleases you, my lord."

Cort stepped into the hall. The noise level diminished, then ground to silence.

Aware Graham's people would take their cue from him, Cort recalled his mother's admonition that honey caught more flies than vinegar. "I did not mean to keep you waiting. But with Philip having to serve both myself and Sir Guy... Were it not for this wretched shoulder, I'd have dressed myself."

During their conversation that afternoon, Cort had mentioned the need to replace his squire, Thomas, who'd contracted a sweating-sickness in Cornwall and would return to Normandy to serve one of Cort's younger brothers. Graham had hesitated, suggesting Cort consider all candidates before making such a weighty decision. The training and responsibilities of a squire were serious, his skill and bravery in battle carrying literal life or death consequences.

Assuming Graham had given consideration to the problem in the intervening hours, Cort now listened to the man with care. "There's a lad I think would suit as your squire, my lord. My nephew, Stefan. Though he has completed his training as a page, I've requested he serve us tonight. He began his duties as squire several months ago, thus has some rudimentary knowledge. Stefan's an able lad and quite intelligent."

Cort's brow furrowed in concern. "Who fosters him now? I'd not take him from the man who has already spent time and expense on his education." And possibly make an enemy in the process.

Graham's eyes conveyed suppressed amusement. "He's mine. Or was. Nay." He waved aside Cort's attempted objection.

"In truth, you'd do me a favor. I choose now to fight only under duress. I took the boy only as a favor to my sister's husband. Stefan's training will be more rigorous, his future far more secure with you. It is the best possible choice for all concerned, my lord."

Cort weighed Graham's offer. "Introduce us, and let's see what the lad thinks. If he is amenable and appears to suit, I shall undertake his fostering."

Graham smiled, then grew serious. "I'd not have you think me a toady, sir, but I am reminded of our conversation this afternoon. You've an honest concern for others." He motioned toward the crowded hall. "Few knights consider their social inferiors' feelings. I believe you possess a generosity of spirit that bodes well for Avonly. As well as a practical, instinctive intelligence about human nature."

"What I possess is a desire to live. A squire whose loyalties to his master are torn or forced is not the ideal choice for defending one's back on the battlefield."

Graham turned toward the dais, directing Cort ahead of him. A long table set on the raised platform constituted the top of a double-legged T, its base two rows of parallel trestle tables for the knights and men-at-arms. They continued to mill about, their resumed conversations desultory, their expressions wary.

Cort made a thorough survey of the gathering as he approached the dais stairs and knew he'd been wise to forbid weapons within the hall. Even his own men appeared tense. *All these men are now mine*, he reminded himself. *And tonight, I must make them believe that.*

Reaching the raised platform, he saw Guy and Dane at the far end, engaged in conversation—but not with each other. Indeed, from Cort's perspective both appeared to be addressing thin air. Then his steps and Graham's vibrated through the wood planking, and the two knights turned to greet them.

Dane's expression was unusually animated. Guy's eyes danced with deviltry. The former delighted Cort; the latter put him on guard. In a moment he understood both. Half hidden behind Dane's massive bulk stood a slender figure garbed in muted-gold velvet, her face averted as she spoke to a serf. But Cort knew that dense ebony hair and luscious form, the piquant beauty of the face momentarily concealed from him. Remembered Guy's comment about the odd communion between the blond giant and the lady.

Lexi. Somehow, she had reached Dane as no one else ever had. Cort needed only to look at the man's face to know that. His heart constricted with tenderness for this man-child who had come to expect either pity or ridicule—not true offers of friendship—from those around him. Unless the lady's kindness was a ruse...

As if privy to his thoughts, the girl turned and raised her face to Dane's. Again, Cort experienced that unprecedented, unwelcome slap of heat, the almost uncontrollable need to take her. Then Dane rumbled something Cort could not decipher, and Lexi smiled up at him, placing her hand on his brawny arm. Dane nodded. She tightened her grip for an instant before allowing her hand to fall away, and Cort relaxed. For now, he would rein in his damnable desire, but as he'd told Guy, allow instinct to guide him. The light in Lexi's eyes shone like warm amber. And foolish or not, he wished they would shine so for him. "My lord," Guy said, drawing Cort's attention. "I do not believe you've met Lord Graham's daughter." His voice a subtle rebuke, Cort realized with chagrin that his preoccupation with Lexi had blinded him to the presence of the young woman beside her.

Spit and hellfire! From the corner of his eye, he caught Lexi's gamin grin as she watched the damnable blush spread up his throat to heat his cheekbones. Impudent wench. Pretending his face was not scarlet as a radish, he bowed from the waist and raised the other girl's tiny hand to his lips. "I am honored, Lady..."

"Melissande." Shoulders proudly set, Graham stepped into the breach. "Lord Cort Dornogard," he said to his daughter.

Cort managed, barely, not to wince at the hopeful gleam in the man's eyes. A matchmaking father was the last damn thing he needed. Now, a matchmaking uncle, with Lexi as the prize…

"Lord Dornogard." She removed her trembling hand from his, her voice so soft, her face so pale, Cort sensed she felt either an immediate aversion to him or was scared to death. He had but a momentary impression of delicate features and pale blue eyes before she bent her head. He was left gazing at her filmy headpiece and a wealth of hair even paler than his own. The girl's eyes remained downcast as Guy seated her, preventing Cort from reading their expression. But clearly, and thankfully, he decided, she did not share her father's marital aspirations.

Graham indicated Cort's seat, that of the rightful overlord, at the center of the table. The one that had, until today, belonged to Graham himself. But as he settled Lexi to Cort's left and then sat beside her, he did not appear resentful.

As if in answer to Cort's mute observation, Graham leaned behind Lexi and shrugged. "Things are as they are. I meant what I said during our earlier discussion, my lord. Make these people yours, and I shall be content."

Each encounter with Sir Richard left Cort more impressed, the man's quiet wisdom a soothing balm on potentially raw wounds. While Cort was neither naïve nor foolish enough to accept men's actions at face value, something about Graham paralleled his father and, more tangentially, his uncle. His father's advice about being fair, giving others the benefit of the doubt, echoed in his mind. Content for the moment with his assessment, he would nevertheless remain alert. While life presented more than enough problems without looking for those that might not exist, this morning's attack cautioned against trusting too easily. If at all.

Once the head table settled, the knights and foot soldiers sought places along the diagonal benches, which extended half the hall's length. As both the old and new lords of Avonly had anticipated, Normans sat at one table, Saxons at the other. Too much to hope they'd willingly mingle. It would take time and tolerance for the two cultures to blend, to see each other as individuals, to learn to like or dislike according to personal merit rather than birthplace.

But it would come. It *would*. Cort had to believe that. For himself. For all of them.

****

They dined on stewed venison and roast boar, pullets seasoned with rosemary and sweet violet, mutton steeped in a savory sauce. There was cabbage cooked with onions and leeks, fresh spring peas, and fine white bread, hot and crusty. Ale flowed freely from ewer to mug to mouth, though with Cort's permission Graham had cautioned the serfs to alert him if any of *his* men appeared to overindulge.

Cort understood. "I appreciate the loyalty of these men who have served you all their lives, Sir Richard. But you realize, as do I, that 'twould not do to have them begin their tenure under me with an ale-induced display of misplaced fealty."

Rich burgundy wine was served to those at the head table. Cort savored its fine bouquet and full-bodied flavor and thought of the vineyards in Normandy. He must see to importing some of his own stock. Mentally, he added that item to the already long list of tasks he planned to begin on the morrow.

Melissande, who sat to his right and shared her trencher with Guy, appeared totally engrossed in her food, returning only monosyllabic answers to either man's attempt at conversation. After several unsuccessful efforts, Cort turned his attention to Lexi and Graham.

Lexi, however, seemed no more prone to converse than her cousin. Cort wondered if she was still miffed with him or merely distracted. Either way, her lack of attention allowed him to quietly study her. In addition to her lovely face and form, she possessed an innate elegance that contrasted with yet emphasized her lively spirit. While appearing delicate and feminine, her husky voice and clear, hearty laugh bespoke strength, as did her precise, economical gestures. She accepted with relish every choice tidbit he selected for her from their shared trencher, but drank sparingly of the wine, preferring the cool well water provided at her request.

Contrasts. Layers. Soft but strong. Amusing, then serious. Intelligent but down to earth. A challenge…without meaning to be. A Siren…without knowing she was. And, because of that, irresistible.

When her responses to Cort's renewed attempts at conversation were polite, but clearly of less interest to her than her uncle's, Cort retreated.

Welcome to Avonly, my lord.

Popping a final bite of venison into his mouth, he chewed slowly and contented himself with snippets of their discussion of mundane affairs.

"John's leg is on the mend, though..."

"...soon be up and about."

Lexi laughed low. "If his wife has anything to say...not...whack him with her broom."

"...enough herbs?" Graham's brow furrowed.

"For now. Though I'll need more fennel and willow bark..."

Cort's interest in their conversation waned as he watched the men seated below. Though wary glances and several heated looks passed between the tables, he saw no sign of overt hostility. When asked for permission to remove the trenchers and serving platters, Cort readily agreed.

Once the tables were cleared, Melissande waved to a sweaty, heavyset woman who hovered in the archway leading from the hall to the courtyard. Moments later, a lengthy procession of scullions marched through the hall, bearing silver dishes of subtleties. A rare treat reserved for only the most august occasions, the dessert's appearance heralded much foot stomping and rousing cheers of delight. That the treats had been prepared in honor of his arrival was not lost on Cort, though the company in general seemed more concerned with consuming them than what they symbolized. Delicate pastry shells cradling a whipped blend of honey and marzipan, they smelled as good as they tasted.

For the first time since the meal began, Lexi appeared to be enjoying herself. She closed her eyes as she spooned the confection into her mouth. Cort could have sworn she purred with pleasure as the gooey sweetness slid over her tongue and down her throat. He watched as she swallowed, then followed with his eyes the path of her tongue as it licked an errant drop of the honeyed mixture from her bottom lip.

A sudden, inexplicable urge to trace that same path with his own tongue tightened Cort's groin. He shifted his legs to ease the discomfort. A futile attempt, and now painful, as tight went to hard and throbbing.

Right forearm pressed in his lap, Cort managed a soft, "You like it."

"What?" Lexi jumped.

Cort's gaze moved to her plate. "The subtlety."

"I've always appreciated subtlety. Oh, the dessert." She tossed her hand. "Yes, it's one of my favorites."

"Are you still angry with me?"

"Angry? Whyever would you think that, my lord?" Lexi asked, bewildered.

"Well, my initial reaction to you this afternoon was not all it could have been," he admitted, his tone droll. "Next, I frightened Thene, and then frightened you when you guessed the source of my wound. And

I laughed at your most inventive attempt to rename me."

In response to his arched brow, Lexi raised her own. "Considering your list of offenses, you do not seem overly contrite."

"I'm not, though I hope you will forgive me anyway. As Guy will tell you, I've a somewhat irreverent sense of humor."

"You are forgiven, then, my lord, for I've been known to have an irreverent thought or two myself."

"I'd never have guessed," he muttered.

Lexi ignored him. "I was never really angry with you. Considering the situation, I understand why you acted as you did, and the name game was my own fault. I hope I am not so petty as to become angry about such things."

"When you seemed averse to speaking with me during dinner, I—"

"Forgive me, sir. I did not mean to ignore you. But I saw little of my uncle today and needed to discuss some household matters. I am concerned as well about Sir Geoffrey and considering the use of several herbs I've not yet tried. If his condition worsens—"

That fast, Cort's desire cooled; his mood flashed from congenial to severe. Lexi blinked as his hand clamped on her forearm. He leaned toward her and growled, "It had best not."

"Better not."

"Pardon?"

"You said, best not, which is incorrect. 'Tis *better* not."

Cort's nostrils flared. "What in Hades are we talking about here? I'm discussing Geoffrey's chance of survival, and you're correcting my English?" His fingers bit into the bones of her wrist.

She winced. "Bad habit. But I was discussing his treatment before you interrupted me. Besides, there is no question of life or death. I changed his poultice before I came down, and there is no sign of putrification or fever. My main concern is that the muscles heal well so that his arm not be crippled."

Cort studied her, then nodded. "'Twas crass of me not to allow you to finish your thought. Still, as I said, you had bes—better—be right."

"If I'm not?" Lexi challenged, raising her chin and narrowing her eyes. "Will you do as they did to that poor physician in Normandy whose incorrect prognosis resulted in his patient's death? Throw me in the river and watch me drown?"

"It bears considering."

"Hah!" She sniffed with disdain.

When he did not respond, Lexi focused on his set jaw, perhaps seeking to analyze his mood. At length she said, "I think you use your temper as my brother often does, to mask a deeper emotion."

She sighed. "Is it that you are suspicious of my skills? My intent? Or that you feel responsible for Geoffrey's injury?"

Disarmed that she had hit so close to the truth, Cort answered simply, "Both."

"I understand. Were I in your position, I'd feel the same. Accompany me this evening when I tend your man's wound, sir. Ask as many questions as you like about what I do and why. You may even learn something."

Cort quirked a brow at her tone. *Tread lightly, lady, or* you *will soon learn what I ache to teach you.* "I shall."

"Good. Now, if you will kindly give me back my hand, I'd like to return to my...subtlety."

Unaware until that moment that he still held her wrist, Cort snapped his hand back as though bitten. "I know where I'd like to plant my hand," he muttered. "Subtlety be damned."

Lexi tossed him a quelling look as she retrieved

her spoon and enjoyed the last of her dessert—then magnanimously offered to finish his. "Since you appear to have lost your appetite," she said with a bland smile.

Chapter Five

Cort rose to his feet shortly thereafter. Instantaneous silence gripped the hall. All eyes turned to him. He met the stares of those who appeared hostile or wary as directly as those that offered trust or encouragement.

"Know you the Roman village of Elton?" he began, satisfied with the silent nods of response. "'Tis after Elton I would fashion our new, larger town here."

Only Guy did not look surprised, though until that moment he couldn't have been sure Cort would settle upon Avonly as his chosen holding. While it had seemed the most promising of those proffered by the king, their discussions had outlined imaginary parameters of a someday-in-the-future town, weighing both the strengths and weaknesses of available settlements.

Until today, Cort had not been inclined to settle in one place. He'd moved on to each new location along the Southern Coast as soon as possible and felt no regret at leaving the previous one. He had decided quickly, almost instinctively, that Avonly would be the site of his primary estate.

Cort noted Guy's sidelong glance at the petite woman to his right and smiled to himself. His friend did not seem to object. A rumbling from the lower tables claimed his attention. He frowned at the ill-concealed guffaws and critical mutters of a group of Graham's men. Amused by Cort's plan, and making no effort to hide it, several gestured their contempt. One actually threw his head back and roared with mirth.

Cort stood passively throughout the display, expression calm, eyes steady. Aware at last that he laughed alone, the man choked down his mirth and glared at his new lord. Graham leaned forward as if to rise; Cort halted him with a slight motion of his hand. Graham might mean well, but Cort knew he must fight his own battles were he to win these men to his side.

"Is it me you think incapable? Or yourselves?" He homed his deliberate gaze on those who had expressed disbelief. No response. "You do not yet know me well enough to judge my abilities, or I yours. But I am not accustomed to failure. What I would do here is both reasonable and progressive—as those who are willing to listen will hear." He raised his left hand. "Those who are not are free to leave. I release you, without condition, from your bonds of fealty—and wish you success. Elsewhere."

Punctuated by Lady Melissande's gasp, a stunned silence fell. None, Cort realized, had ever heard the like. Though an occasional villein might purchase his freedom from his master, he was legally regarded as chattel, like a horse or a cow. A lord did not relinquish his property without recompense. It contradicted everything these people knew. He gauged their expressions, which ran the gamut from awe to disbelief, and spoke accordingly.

"This manor house itself will remain as it is and retain the name Avonly. But the stone castle I intend to build, and the surrounding lands the king cedes to me, will be known as Amiton. *Ami*, French for friendly, and *ton* the Norse equivalent of town."

Guy's approving nod told Cort he recalled the word from earlier that afternoon.

"The name will symbolize what I wish for us here: peace, hospitality, friendship. Strife will not alter that goal, but it *will* cause delay and harm those willing to work for the general good. We cannot succeed unless we work together. Any here who chooses to oppose our success I would see gone. He is of no value to me. Or to anyone at Amiton."

A response to Cort's stern tone was not long in coming. Over the babble of voices, he picked out random comments.

"Our lands are not so vast as Elton's."

"We've not the population to develop such a place."

"A stone castle costs a fortune and years of labor."

"'Tis what I'd expect of a Norman," the man who had laughed with derision commented. "Strange ideas, impossible goals. The desire to move backward rather than forward. 'Tis a thousand years old, Elton."

"And still standing!" Lexi shot to her feet. "As are many of the Roman buildings—and the only decent roads in all England." Hands pressed upon the table, she leaned forward for emphasis.

"'Twas our own Anglo-Saxon ancestors, not the Normans, who drove out or destroyed the native populations of Elton and numerous other thriving towns. Our own who obliterated much of what they achieved during the Roman occupation. Listen, and think, before you speak again, Donald." Her eyes blazed golden fire.

"Your pardon, my lord." Lexi grimaced up at Cort as she resettled her gown about her on the bench. "I should not have interrupted."

Blinking back his astonishment at her defense of him, as well as her logic and knowledge, Cort could not find it in himself to chastise her for speaking out of turn. In truth, those flashing gold eyes were magnificent, that soft, mobile mouth...titillating. He managed a bare nod for her apology, then once more faced the lower tables.

"I understand your doubts and will answer all reasonable questions, for I have given this plan much consideration." He riveted cold eyes on Donald and warned, "But know I will tolerate neither interference nor insubordination."

His Norman knights nodded, acknowledging their experience of that truth.

"Have you a bailiff, Lord Graham?" Cort asked.

"Of course."

"Make him available to me on the morrow after we break our fast. Should any wish to leave rather than serve me, he will draw up the appropriate documents for my seal. My offer of freedom stands. There are sufficient enemies without the walls. I will have none within Amiton."

"As you say, Lord Dornogard." Graham cast a censorious glance at Donald and his cohorts. "I have devoted my life to maintaining the honor of my name and my home. I would not see it shamed by the discontent." Point made, he folded his hands on the edge of the table.

"There is much to be done," Cort said. "As we begin early tomorrow, I would see the hall set to rights and you men retired as soon as possible." He inclined his head toward his second-in-command. "Report to Sir Guy for your orders. Any problems are to be brought to me. Sleep well. And know that from this moment, unless it be by your own denial, I consider all of you, every man, woman, and child, *my* people and will treat you accordingly."

His move to the rear of the dais was a dismissal. The serfs made quick work of clearing the lower tables. Placing them against the walls, they spread pallets to accommodate those who would sleep in the great hall.

Cort turned to the dais steps and found himself face to face with Stefan, whom Graham had introduced briefly at supper. "Good eve, my lord. I understand you wish to speak with me." The boy's greeting was stiff, his gaze locked with Cort's.

With all else occupying his mind, Cort had forgotten about the youth. Now, he took a moment to assess him. Impossible to miss his resemblance to his sister. That same glossy ebony hair, those aristocratic features. While Stefan's square jaw and thinner mouth saved him from prettiness, his lashes were as long and thick as Lexi's, his eyes as arresting. But crystalline gray, not gold, so light they appeared almost colorless in the flickering light of the wall-set flambeaux. Tall and slender, with shoulders just beginning to fulfill the promise of maturity, he was a handsome lad in his dark green tunic and buff hosen.

An elusive memory niggled at the edges of Cort's mind. But he needed to focus on the boy and let it go for the moment. "Your uncle has offered you to me as squire."

"Aye." Stefan's tone told Cort nothing.

"What think you?"

The boy looked taken aback by the question at first. Then his lips tugged up slightly at the corners.

Cort could almost see his mind replaying the words Cort had just spoken to his new subjects, wondering if he really meant them. He watched Stefan struggle with and lose his battle against testing his new lord.

"That you will not allow me to refuse," the lad said flatly.

"Think you I want a squire I cannot trust? Life is more valuable than misplaced pride."

Stefan seemed immobilized by Cort's candid gaze and the realization that Cort had recognized the challenge for what it was—and answered with honesty rather than anger.

"Truly, you would allow me to choose, my lord?" The first evidence of emotion moved in the youth's eyes.

"I would not otherwise have asked."

Before Stefan had a chance to respond, Graham moved up beside them. "What think you?"

Unaware he was repeating Cort's very words to his nephew, he directed the question to the man. But it was the boy who answered. "I would serve this man, Uncle, if it please you both."

Graham nodded satisfaction of his nephew's acceptance before bowing deferentially to Cort. "The final word is yours, Lord Dornogard."

"Nay. I promised it to the boy, and he has given it." Inclining his head to the pair, he bade them good night. "Your duties begin at first light," he advised Stefan in parting.

"Aye, my lord." Cort heard the bemusement in the boy's tone and smiled to himself.

He had just begun to climb the stairs when he heard his name. Turning back, he saw Lexi hurrying from the hall. Several steps above her, Cort awaited her approach.

"Do you still wish to look in on Geoff with me? 'Tis late, I know, and you have had a long day."

Cort slapped his hand to his brow in self-disgust. He'd forgotten Geoffrey...again. He must be more tired than he realized. "Nay, I would see him. Just as I would thank you for your defense of me against Donald."

"I was not defending you so much as taking him to task for his stupidity."

Caught between a groan and a laugh, Cort tipped his head to hide his reaction. Ah, the value of honesty.

"Cort!" Guy's voice drew his gaze. "May I speak with you before you retire?"

"Of course." Turning again to Lexi, Cort said, "I will be along momentarily."

"Around the corner, third door on your left, my

lord." Her voice drifted over her shoulder as she moved briskly down the hallway toward the rear of the keep.

"Well, what think you of her?" Guy's voice held a vague dread.

Cort forced himself to drag his focus from the spot where Lexi had disappeared, trim hips swaying. He faced his friend and shrugged. "She is beautiful."

"Aye." Guy sighed. "Think you to offer for her, then?"

"Offer…I—" Cort stammered to a halt. "I scarce know the girl."

"But she is of the nobility, and the match would irrevocably bind her and these people to you. 'Twould please the king greatly, I think."

"I will please myself in this, not the king. I've given up near five years of my life to serve as he requested. I'll not give away the rest. Nor would he ask it of me. My marriage will be as he promised, when and to whom I wish, be she lady or peasant." He raked his fingers through his hair. "And I have too much else on my mind at present to even think about such."

Was he not already pulled in enough directions? This *lord of the manor* was no easy role.

Guy took a step forward. "But you noticed she is lovely."

"I am busy, not blind."

"Have you ever seen such hair? And those eyes..."

"Extraordinary. Yet I desire more than mere beauty in a wife."

"We have been friends a long time, my lord."

Struck by the strange tone of Guy's voice and the seeming irrelevance of his remark, Cort looked closely at him for the first time. His features were almost pained. Disturbed and confused, Cort descended the steps and laid his hand on the man's arm. "What plagues you, Guy?"

"I would know if you decide you want her, Cort." His earnest gaze knotted Cort's belly. "I'll not press my own suit if 'tis so."

"Thor's hammer! You've only today met the girl. Are you so soon besotted?" *Pot, kettle,* he thought. A female between them was the last thing he needed, yet Guy's miserable expression was answer enough.

"I'd not considered her as a potential wife," Cort mused, "though I cannot deny I find her desirable. But I must first know her better, be sure of her loyalty, trust her. And there is no better time than now to begin."

With a thoughtful smile, he dropped his hand from Guy's arm, then stepped around him and strode down the corridor.

"Where go you?" Guy's head snapped around to follow Cort's progress.

Cort halted in mid-stride to peer back at his friend. "To further my acquaintance with the lady."

"But she's—"

"With Geoff. Were you not standing here when she said so?"

Guy's eyes widened almost comically, and he began to laugh. A full minute passed before he found sufficient breath to gasp, "We h-have been speaking at cross purposes, I think."

"What?"

"You thought I...I meant—"

"Lexi, of course." Cort scowled impatiently.

"Forgive me." Guy was still trying to control his laughter. "But I spoke of Lady Melissande."

"Melis—" Recalling that lady's initial reaction to him, Cort's lips thinned. "Rest easy on that score, my friend. I have no more interest in her than she has in me."

Obviously startled by the conviction in Cort's tone, but seeming encouraged by it, Guy's grin broadened as he saluted his commander. "We both had the right of it, I think. Different as night and day they may be, yet each a beauty in her own way."

Less than honest, perhaps, but rather than hurt his friend's feelings, Cort nodded agreement. Melissande couldn't hold a candle to Lexi's vivid loveliness. Guy was welcome to the pale little thing. Cort pivoted on his heel and strode down the shadowy corridor.

****

Once around the corner, Lexi leaned against the wall and breathed, slow and deep. Her heart tripped in her breast and warmth curled in her stomach as it had when she'd opened her eyes at the table and found the new lord's gaze fastened on her mouth. When his eyes shifted slowly upward to meet hers, she'd had to command herself to remain still rather than lean into him.

Bless the saints, he had the most incredible eyes. Concentrating on his shoulder wound this afternoon had taxed her willpower, for all she'd wanted to do was sit and stare at him. She had, thankfully, been able to turn her blurted "comeliness" into apparent teasing, but the truth was, she'd never meant anything more. He was the most beautiful man she'd ever seen. Had Athene not been there to provide a distraction, Lexi feared she'd have made a total fool of herself.

She'd seen many Normans since the Conquest, some fair, some dark. Her own countrymen's looks oft proclaimed Scandinavian heritage. But never had she seen a man like Cort. She was no stranger to the male body, having bathed numerous knights who sought Avonly's hospitality as well as those she'd treated for wounds and illness. Yet no man before today had affected her as Cort did.

Hand pressed to her throat, Lexi thought the Roman physician Galen, who'd believed medicine's progress relied upon understanding human anatomy, would have loved to get his hands on Cort Dornogard. *She* would love to get her hands on... Oh, my. She really had to stop this.

But she couldn't help thinking of how he'd looked at supper. Even richly garbed, there was no disguising those long Nordic bones. Add the strong, lean hands, the sharp, flaring cheekbones and straight nose...

Naked, he had been awe-inspiring. Clothed, he surpassed magnificent. Dark gray hosen delineated muscular legs. The brilliant crimson tunic embroidered with King William's golden lions rampant emphasized the massive width of chest and shoulders. The snowy, full-sleeved shirt complemented his tanned skin and drew attention to the white, even teeth in his sensual mouth. His brows, like his long lashes, were several shades darker than his winter-wheat hair. And those eyes of purest aquamarine reminded Lexi of a sun-spangled forest pool blending blue sky and emerald leaves. Incredible.

Until they'd darkened as they had earlier today when she mentioned the cause of his wound. And he'd more than frightened her. For an instant, she feared he meant to tear her limb from limb to learn what she might know of the attack on his men. While she knew naught of the assailants, what she *did* know was that to reveal *what* she knew and *how,* would, undoubtedly, turn her life upside down. Her secret. To keep it hurt no one. To reveal it would destroy both her pleasure and her freedom. Lexi calmed her breathing and pushed the dark shadow from her mind.

Determined to focus solely on Geoffrey, she continued down the rear passage. But a sound behind the second doorway caused her to pause and listen. She could have sworn she'd heard... A weak moan drifted through the slightly ajar portal.

She stepped closer, peering through the crack into the blackness beyond. Though she knew it to be a large storage room for linens, there was no question the sound had come from within. Inching the door wider, she stepped from the murky light of the hallway into the pitch darkness of the closet. She could see nothing.

"Who's there?" she called softly. "Where are you?"

A pitiful groan sounded to her left. Determined to help whoever it was, realizing she might well need light to do so, Lexi turned and retraced the few steps to the door, intent on retrieving one of the hall torches. A sudden rustling to the right arrested her movement just within the doorway. She instinctively stretched her hand in that direction. Her fingers contacted plush velvet, beneath which she could feel the yielding warmth of flesh.

"Art all ri—"

Something hard slammed against the side of her head. Stars burst behind her eyelids. Lexi sagged to her knees, then slumped to the floor, her hair spilling out into the hallway.

"Traitor," hissed a distorted voice against her ear.

Fabric brushed Lexi's face as her assailant stepped over her. Then darkness swallowed her.

Chapter Six

His leather-soled right boot shot out from under him so quickly, Cort barely had time to throw his arm against the wall for support. Then his left boot skidded to the side. He slammed against a doorframe, shoulder screaming, as his fingers scrabbled for purchase. Forehead pressed to well-planed wood, he found his balance and blinked at the floor.

Two, he thought, disgruntled. After rounding the bend in the corridor, he'd been counting doorways instead of watching his step.

As he looked down now in the uncertain light, he saw—and felt—beneath his still-sliding boots what looked strangely like black ice. His first thought was that someone had spilled pitch, or something equally disagreeable, and failed to wipe it up. But as he narrowed his eyes against the dimness and followed the stain's dark path into the closet, he recognized the outline of a body. Clothed in gold.

Cort's breath left him in a hiss. He lifted his feet together and jumped backward, shoving himself from the wall, then fell to his knees beside what he belatedly realized was Lady Lexi's hair. Slick as jet, it pooled about his calves.

"Guy!" His voice thundered off the walls. "To me!"

Pounding boots at once echoed in the passage.

"Cort!" His second-in-command slid to a halt behind him. "What—God's bones," he whispered, then raced down the hall and wrested a torch from its bracket. He raised the flambeau above his head as he returned and pushed the door fully open.

Even as the men watched, bloody ribbons seeped from beneath the lady's head into the rough wood of the closet floor. Exchanging a quick look of confusion with Guy, Cort rose, stepped into the cubicle, and slid his arms beneath her inert form. He gritted his teeth against the pain as her head fell to his bruised shoulder, then straightened and hurried toward the foyer. Guy raced ahead, calling for assistance.

"My lord?" Stefan stood at the entrance to the great hall.

"Where is your sister's room?" Cort moved past Guy, his gaze fixed on the boy. He dared not allow himself another look at the girl's white face and blood-matted hair.

Stefan reached shaking fingers to his sister's cold cheek. "Lexi." His voice shook as he raised bewildered silver eyes.

"No time," Cort said. "Show me to her room. Then go find Melissande."

His gaze moved to Guy. "Find Graham."

He negotiated the stairs with care and followed Stefan past his own second-floor chamber down a narrow hallway with four doors. Opening the last, the boy stepped aside so Cort might precede him. Cort covered the short distance to the bed, laid Lexi gently atop the coverlet, and turned to her brother, whose eyes begged for answers.

"Get Melissande," he ordered. "Now. Your questions can wait."

Stefan stared blankly for a moment, then spun on his heel and sprinted through the door.

Alone, Cort eased himself onto the side of the bed and gingerly touched Lexi's bloodied temple. The translucent skin was already discolored, a hard lump above her ear hot beneath his fingertips. "Ah, lady." He sighed, smoothing her hair over the pillows. "Who would do such a thing?"

By the time help arrived, he had asked that question once too often, and within him had grown a focused determination unlike any he had ever known to find the answer.

Graham was by turns distraught and enraged, Melissande pale and anxious. When water, towels, and herbals had been delivered as she ordered, Cort took Graham aside to explain what he knew of the situation. Which was far too little for either's peace of mind.

Cort saw his own helpless anger reflected in the older man, along with an equal determination to find the culprit. A possible link between Lexi's attack and his own assumed secondary importance. He wanted the person who'd hurt her. To ambush armed soldiers was one thing; to ambush a woman, something else entirely. It had coward written all over it. And few things sickened him as much as cowardice.

As he spoke with Sir Richard, Cort watched Melissande cluck and coo and flutter about Lexi like a nervous pigeon. When she dabbed at the wound as though it might bite her, her mouth twisted with distaste, he could not control a disgusted growl.

"Gently!" he barked, moving toward the bed.

Melissande cast him a quick, frightened glance.

Graham stayed Cort with a hand on his forearm and cast his daughter a censorious glance. She blanched, but applied herself to her task without further mincing. Satisfied, Cort moved aside once again at Graham's urging.

"She lacks her cousin's knowledge and instinct for healing." The man's eyes offered an apology—and, again, that hopeful, discomfiting gleam as he added, "But she assumed her duties as chatelaine, at which she excels, four years ago when my wife died. She will make a fine wife for some lucky lord."

Not this lord.

When Cort did not react, Graham continued. “Her mother taught her the broad use of simples and trained her to care for Avonly’s people, and she did so, until Lexi’s arrival. Without a qualm she yielded that duty to her cousin, whose instinct for the healing arts far exceeds Melissande’s.”

He shrugged. “Lexi was eager to contribute her knowledge and her ceaseless energy, Melissande more than content to concentrate on household concerns. I’m sorry she is not more adept, my lord. But she will do her best.”

Cort managed a brusque nod and turned back toward the bed, not trusting himself to speak. This unaccustomed feeling of helplessness left him surly. He abhorred that while he’d had no reason to suspect Lexi was in danger, he’d nevertheless failed to protect her. To see this vital, stunning woman harmed—in his own home—raked his insides. Only the realization that he could do no better kept him from ordering Melissande from the room.

Dane’s entrance was a Godsend. It seemed Guy had told him about Lexi and that she would be unable to tend Geoff again that night. The giant had left his friend’s side to see if he might help. As tender with her as he was with Geoff, he nudged Melissande aside and again cleaned the wound. Next, he applied a periwinkle salve, the same one Lexi had used on Geoffrey to retard bleeding. Lastly, he fashioned a poultice of yellow mold.

“The lady told me it speeds healing and pr-prevents festering.” Dane’s face worked as he struggled to recall Lexi’s exact words as she’d worked over Geoff’s wound. “I d-don’t think we should give her a sleeping draught. Mayhap some water wh—when she wakes.” Clearly ill at ease with his limited knowledge, he shifted from foot to foot and looked to his lord for reassurance.

“You did well, Dane. Thank you.” Cort gripped

the man's forearm. "The lady will thank you herself, I'm sure, when she's better. Care for Geoff in her absence, and she will be more than pleased."

Dane answered with a shy smile and a nod, then cast a soulful look at the still form on the bed as he departed. "Poor L-lady Lex."

****

"Not...traitor."

Cort's head shot up from his chest. He rubbed the heels of his hands against his eyes as he moved from the chair in which he had fallen asleep to Lexi's bedside. A wick floating in a pool of wax illuminated her pale profile.

"What?" His hand settled on the crown of her head.

"I'm not a...traitor," she rasped through dry lips.

Cort thought that a ridiculous statement, but recalling their first meeting, reserved comment. He was too glad to hear her voice. Instead, his response was a reasonable, "Of course not. Who would say such of you?" Yet a small doubt niggled at the back of his mind even as he denied it.

"Wh-whoever hit me." Lexi slowly opened her eyes, their golden irises almost swallowed by the blackness of dilated pupils. As though even the meager glow of that single taper was painful, she moaned and at once lowered her lids.

Sensing the cause of her distress, Cort dipped a cloth in the bowl of cool water on the bedside table, wrung it out, and laid it over Lexi's closed eyes. She sighed her pleasure. A smile wisped over her mouth.

"Thirsty?" Cort asked after several silent minutes.

"Hmmm."

Cort poured water from a ewer into an earthenware cup. Wedging his arm beneath Lexi's shoulders, he raised her slightly. Her head sagged back against his wound, and he swore.

"Oh!" She struggled to sit. "Your bad shoulder."

"No harm," he assured, though he slid in behind her so his chest might absorb her weight. The side of her breast, full and warm, pressed against his arm as he lifted the cup to her lips. He damned his instant arousal and allowed her a few small sips before replacing it on the table.

"Dane said you are to have only a little at a time."

"I know that. But my head is still...clouded, and my throat is so dry."

"Physicians do make the worst patients."

Lexi raised a hand to the cloth covering her eyes and lifted a corner to glare at him.

A good sign.

"Well, they do." He placed his hand over hers, so delicate and small, and resettled the damp fabric. "But now is not the time to discuss it. Sleep, lady. I won't leave you."

If his presence here made anyone uncomfortable, none would dare gainsay the new lord. And fortunate—though naught about Lexi's attack was fortunate—'twas night rather than day, when his attentions would have been required elsewhere.

"Nay," she murmured. "What of Geoffrey? And you must need seek your own rest, my lord."

"Aye," he said, though he had no intention of doing so. *Unless I may lie beside you.*

As now was not the time for that, Cort stepped away from the bed and dragged his chair closer. Lexi's thoughts were coherent, her show of spirit reassuring. "Do not worry about Geoff. Dane is with him and says he is as comfortable as can be expected."

"Glad." She slipped again into healing sleep.

Cort wished he could do the same as night waned toward morning, but Lexi's admission of having been called traitor and the identity of her attacker plagued him. Had she been harmed because of her defense of him at supper? Or because she had treated his wound and those of his men? Mayhap both.

Then again, might one of his own men suspect she'd been somehow involved in the attack? Not directly involved, but with foreknowledge? The possibility that anyone under his command would harm a woman left him half-ill.

While he could not yet afford to trust her, Lexi was compassionate as well as intelligent, a healer by nature. But someone had hurt her, likely for that very reason. Another puzzle to solve, along with the motivation for and perpetrators of the attack his own men had suffered. Were the two events related? And there was still the mysterious slinger who'd saved them. Something...there was something he should remember. But he was too tired, even to sleep.

He dropped his head back against the chair he had dragged from his own chamber—Graham's chair, which he'd correctly guessed would be a tight fit—stretched his long legs and yawned. Because he had no answers to the weightier issues, he let his mind wander for a time over lighter things. The contrast between Lexi and Melissande, the latter's obvious aversion to him. It disconcerted him as much now as it had at supper, and not because it was a matter of pride.

Well aware for most of his adult life that women found him attractive, he was occasionally pleased by that fact, sometimes cynical, but most often amused. Not that it wasn't convenient at times. Yet the resultant experiences had taught him that while much could be said for physical pleasure, it was fleeting. Relationships based solely on desire were shallow and ultimately unsatisfying. Only when the need burned strong did he avail himself of a willing woman, despite his peers' light ridicule of the many golden opportunities missed.

Certainly, he was unaccustomed to women treating him as Melissande did. Not in the least attracted to her, it was nonetheless disturbing to have her shy from him like a spooked filly, especially when he'd given her no cause. Loki's balls! Did she, like Guy, like Graham, think he might consider her as a potential wife? Never. Still, another irritant, however minor, that must be dealt with. Tactfully.

His mind veered to Dane's earlier care of Lexi. Recalling that scene now, many hours later, it occurred to Cort that Lexi's kindness and patience had done more to build Dane's confidence in one day than his own friendship had in years. Never before had he seen the man assert himself, except on a battlefield, nor speak more than three or four words at a time. Yet twice within a matter of hours they had conversed, if only briefly, and Dane had shown himself quite capable of thought outside the realm of combat. Who would have guessed? More to the point, how, after all these years, could he not have known?

Unfamiliar guilt stirred within Cort as he acknowledged that, despite his years of acquaintance with and feelings of protectiveness toward the blond giant, he had always, however unintentionally, treated Dane with condescension. As though he were a lesser being. For a man who prided himself on his sense of justice, the realization was both humbling and enlightening.

Cort opened gritty, exhaustion-blurred eyes, and after several attempts managed to focus on Lexi. Visible now in the early morning light, her face appeared less pale, her breathing deep and even.

From belowstairs came the faint stir of human activity as the serfs prepared for the new day. A light breeze, rife with the scent of dust and wildflowers, lifted the hair along his temples. Cort shoved stiffly to his feet and rotated his aching shoulder as he approached the bed.

A tinkling of bells dropped into the dawn silence. He turned toward the sound, unable to suppress a smile at the sight of Athene on her hind legs, front paws gripping the metal bars of the cage as she peered between them. A cute little face, he was forced to admit.

A bowl of berries tucked into the corner beside the cage drew Cort's eye. He removed two, then held one between his fingers and cautiously offered it to the ferret. When she reached for it, his courage deserted him. He jerked his hand back, and the berry pinged off the wall behind him. For a man who did not shy from war horses...

Steeling himself, Cort extended the other fruit. After an experimental lick with her tiny tongue, Athene speared the berry with her needle-like teeth and proceeded to munch contentedly. When Cort offered another, she nudged his hand and licked his finger before accepting it.

If he hoped to get close to Lexi, he must accept—No. He shook his head at the absurd truth. This little rodent would have to accept *him.* He caressed her head with his finger, at which she arched her neck like a cat. Encouraged, he unlatched the cage door and extended his hand.

Curling her body around the edge of the opening, Athene dropped to her belly and inspected him with those oddly intelligent, dark eyes. Cort clicked his tongue at her as he had heard Lexi do. She canted her head but did not move farther into the room. Nose and whiskers twitching, Athene raised herself up to gaze about. At the sight of Lexi stretched upon the bed, she bounded across the floor, back arched like an inverted U. It was one of the most comical sights Cort had ever seen, and a spontaneous bark of laughter escaped him.

Ignoring the new lord of Amiton's reaction, Athene leaped at the edge of the coverlet and clawed her way to the top of the bed. She hopped onto her mistress' familiar shoulder, reached a slender paw to Lexi's cheek, and looked down at her still face.

When light flicks of her tongue also failed to elicit a response, Athene retreated to the curve between Lexi's neck and shoulder and curled up there. She blinked several times, then folded her paws across her chest and closed her eyes.

"She'll be glad to see you when she wakes," Cort whispered.

He approached the pair, careful not to disturb the ferret, and drifted the backs of his fingers down Lexi's cheek, which truly was as soft as the rose petals to which he had yesterday compared it, and reassuringly warm. Unable to resist, he leaned toward her, inhaled her unique scent of spring-fresh herbs, and buried his face in that mane of glorious raven hair.

Cort pressed a kiss to Lexi's forehead, another to her lovely mouth. Full, warm, moist. He wondered, had she been awake, if she'd have kissed him back or slapped his face. And decided the possible slap would have been worth the risk.

He wanted her. Badly. But even more than that, he wanted her safe. A smile of rare tenderness slanted his mouth. He straightened and headed for his chamber.

Though he'd spent an all but sleepless night, Cort thought it a small price for the insights he'd gained. He only regretted the knowledge had come at such a price to Lexi.

Absurdity dispelled his somber musings as he recalled his last words in Lexi's chamber. "I talked to a rat," he muttered, shaking his head. "A flat-as-an-oatcake, hopping rat."

Chapter Seven

Despite several visits to his sister during the night, Stefan awaited Cort in his chamber. The squire began to empty steaming buckets into the tub before Cort even closed the door. That chore completed, he moved to where Cort had sunk onto the fireside bench and removed his lord's boots, then lifted his tunic and shirt over his head, careful not to jar his wound.

Hands stretched high, Cort refused to give in to the stiffness in his right shoulder. He counted to ten, then lowered his arms and stood. Stripping off his chausses, he dragged himself to the tub and sank gratefully into the hot water.

"Just what I need, lad," he murmured as his head fell back against the curved wooden rim.

"It seemed reasonable, my lord, after your all-night vigil, that you'd wish to refresh yourself. Though I thought you might prefer to sleep."

"I cannot afford to lie down now. Much needs doing today. This bath will set me to rights."

"Lexi is improving?" Stefan asked after a moment.

"Quicker than we'd hoped. She woke briefly after your last visit and spoke quite rationally. Aside from a painful lump and probably worse headache, I expect she'll do very well." What, Cort wondered, would Stefan think had he seen him with his face buried in Lexi's hair? If he knew how Cort ached to touch and taste every inch of her lush body? Instantly hard, he cursed under his breath, quirked an eyebrow, and forced his attention back to his squire. "Not a vaporous sort of female, is she?"

Stefan dropped down beside the tub. "You noticed."

He grasped the washing cloth and soap from the hearthside stool, dipped them in the water, and began to lather Cort's back with a rhythmic pressure. Careful to avoid his injured shoulder, the boy worked his way around to Cort's arms and chest, then down his torso and legs.

He paused to rinse the cloth and asked, "Would you have me wash your face? Uncle Richard always preferred to do his own."

Loath to open his eyes, yet knowing he dared not relax too long, Cort forced himself upright and took the square of linen from Stefan's hand. Staring at the boy from beneath heavy lids, he said, "I would rather do it myself. Is there enough clean water to rinse my hair?"

"Yes, my lord. If it pleases you, I'll wash it. No sense in straining your shoulder." Stefan hesitated. "'Tis I who owe you thanks." His eyes shone with gratitude. "If you'd not found Lexi—"

"No thanks are necessary for doing what anyone else would have done, lad."

"Nay, my lord. You need not have overseen her care at the expense of your own rest. It was...difficult to see her thus."

Indeed. Though Cort would not have foregone those final, delightful moments with her for all the wine in Normandy. He scrubbed his face, then splashed it with water from his cupped palms, allowing Lexi's brother time to regain his composure. As though he had not noticed the tremor in the boy's voice, he commented with a casualness he was far from feeling, "Helpless, you mean? Strange, perhaps, but I've always felt more protective of strong women than of weak ones. And the little I know of your sister leads me to believe she prefers to rely on her own strength rather than others'."

"Aye." Stefan's tone was both proud and frustrated. "She will not ask for help even when she needs it, and often demands too much of herself. I am forced to covert watchfulness to avoid accusations of *hovering*."

The snort that punctuated the remark was typically male, and Cort felt some of the tension within him loosen. "Her word, I assume, hovering?" He winked when Stefan nodded. "Take heart, squire. You are not alone. I understand completely, and you have my sympathy."

"You have a sister?"

"Three. And an indomitable mother who taught them well. Not the middle one, perhaps. She enjoys playing the damsel in distress. Lacking the privileges of the eldest and the attention lavished on the youngest, I think Julianna has felt a greater need than the other two to devise her own identity. She's rather good at it, actually. My brothers fall all over themselves to please her, and I imagine by now she has suitors doing the same." Cort chuckled at the thought.

"When did you last see her?"

"Almost five years ago."

"I would miss Lexi much in that time."

"As I have missed Julianna and her escapades. But she usually drops the facade with me since it gains her naught but my amusement. If her temper when I ignore her antics is an indicator, beneath that fragile demeanor, she has an iron will."

"I have seen *your* temper as well, my lord." Stefan swallowed audibly and rushed on. "You have brothers also?"

Cort narrowed his eyes. "You have yet to see my temper, squire. Nor do you want to." At Stefan's jerky nod, Cort relented. "Aye, three brothers also. I am the eldest."

"Holy Mother." The boy whistled in awe.

"Two others, a boy and a girl, died in infancy." Cort caught the sadness in his voice and continued in a practical tone. "But my parents are fortunate to have seven living children. They are very happy together. And obviously busy."

Stefan's lips twitched at the droll humor. "You come by your fortitude honestly, then, my lord."

"I hope so." He dragged his hands down his face. "The water cools, and I have many duties this day. Best we finish here so I may be about them, lad."

"Aye." Stefan lathered Cort's scalp without further comment.

****

Only three people presented themselves in the hall to request release from service at Avonly. To Cort's surprise, Donald was not among them. He debated whether that was cause for hope or concern.

The first petitioner, a man-at-arms, professed to have an ill son in the North; the second, a female scullion, claimed a dying mother in London; the third, a young knight, had a girl in his Welsh birth village whom he desired to wed. Without argument, Cort granted their petitions.

As the three made to depart, he said, "Should you wish to return, know you are welcome here."

Pulling forelocks and drooping kerchief, blank amazement on their faces, they bowed and curtsied from the hall.

"These people will either bless your kindness or flee the place *en masse*," Guy drawled from his place across the table. "Care to lay a wager either way?"

Expression bland, Cort pivoted on the bench to face his friend. "You know me better. If life's taught me anything, it's to expect the unexpected. Which means I never bet, even on a *sure thing*."

Cort motioned the serfs spreading fresh rushes from the otherwise empty hall. All knights and men-at-arms were occupied with myriad tasks about the manor.

Guy turned the conversation to more serious concerns. "How is Lady Alexis this morning"?

"Well enough that I had to tell Dane to watch her. When I looked in on her before coming down, she was awake and insisting she be allowed to check on Geoff and our prisoners." Though he'd ached to take her in his arms, she'd looked too fragile to touch. "I told her Dane would care for Geoff, someone else could worry about the two prisoners, and ordered Dane to tie her to the bed if necessary to keep her there." His lips twitched. "She was furious. I find that most encouraging."

Guy laughed outright at his lord's smug demeanor. "I doubt she'll thank you for your concern."

Cort shrugged. "But she will obey me."

Though his second-in-command's expression said he thought that was yet to be seen, Cort shifted topics. "I've made a list of things requiring immediate attention. Graham's cooperation is essential. So far, he's made some useful suggestions and given me the names of those he feels will be most helpful."

Guy retrieved a narrow, leather-bound volume from the seat beside him and slid it across the table. Cort unsnapped the clasp and flipped to the first page. His bold, precise script enumerated, by chronology and importance, the many tasks that faced him and his people if Amiton were to become a reality.

"We're going to be busy." He cast Guy a tight smile. "It did not seem quite so intimidating when we began planning a year ago."

"'Tis always hardest to begin. But the men are already organizing those who will expand, subdivide, and work the fields. Many of Amiton's knights won't be happy with the tasks assigned them, but we'll need every strong back available."

Cort scowled. "If our men can *lower* themselves, so will they."

Guy rested his elbows on the table and steepled his fingers. "I made that clear. Also, I've sent Kevin and Henri to London to collect the rest of your retinue, as well as your stonemason and his crew. Outriders left this morn to carry the news you seek tenants and tradesmen. It but remains for you to notify the king you've chosen Avonly—Amiton—" Guy's eyes twinkled, "as your permanent residence and petition for the surrounding lands promised you."

Cort shook his head in awe. "Were you up, too, most of last night?"

"Just before sunrise, eager to implement the dream."

"You, sir, are a wonder."

"Now that's God's own truth," Guy drawled without an ounce of humility.

Laughing green eyes bright with purpose, mouth curved in a pleased smile, he reached across the table to grip his commander's forearm. "It's unfolding, my lord, just as we believed. No goal is without obstacles, but there's the challenge. And no one loves a challenge more than you."

Fatigue and uncertainty dropped away from Cort like a doffed mantle. He surged to his feet with renewed energy and threw his arm about Guy's shoulders as he rounded the bench. Hopeful and determined, they left the hall to survey the activity in the bailey, then mounted their destriers to inspect the countryside.

Of the thirty-nine stone castles King William had commissioned in 1066, Cort was proud to have supervised the initial construction of three. The Conqueror's strategy to build and garrison a fortress in every major town and city had discouraged rebellions and ensured English loyalty. Though the plan came dear in both time and coin, widespread insurrection would be more so, as well as a drain on his military forces.

Cort accepted that his flair for design and architecture had made him a natural overseer for strategic strongholds. That he'd have preferred not to spend these years following the conquest serving his country in that particular manner he kept to himself. He had inherited his artistic bent from his father, who appreciated its pragmatic application in William's scheme.

But Cort was more than satisfied to at last be released from the obligation to pursue more personal goals. This last year, especially, had seemed long and arduous. Perhaps because his own dream had focused with the discovery of Elton. It had sparked an imaginative fire, fed by Guy's shared enthusiasm.

Together they'd discussed logistics of size and location, argued the strengths and weaknesses of Cort's proposals, laughed at the irony of *regressing* to Roman concepts of irrigation and layout, which had been ignorantly dismissed with the ascendance of Angle and Saxon invaders. Another truth his father had taught him: *Often, the best way to move forward is to first move backward.* Cort had not understood at the time what his father meant. He understood now.

During yesterday's conversation with Graham, he'd been careful to avoid personal comments, explaining his plans and plying the former lord with questions about stone and slate quarries, supply transport, and available craftsmen. Sir Richard had compiled lists, somewhat grudgingly it seemed to Cort, relevant to each major point of their discussion.

This morning, after allowing their horses to

gallop along the forest verge for a time, Cort and Guy drew rein to survey the land spread before them. Sweeping meadows, undulating hills sprinkled with pink and yellow wildflowers, hundreds of acres crowned by thick woodland, a blessed source of both timber and game. And through its center the peaceful River Avon, silver-blue promise of life-giving water, and supply and trade accessibility.

"You've chosen wisely, my lord," Guy said after a lengthy silence.

"I hope so." Cort glanced back toward the manor house, face clouded with doubt. "The hill just north of Avonly is an ideal site for Amiton's castle, the countryside well suited to farming, grazing, and hunting. Far enough from London to prevent involvement in court intrigue, close enough for convenience when we're required at court or have need of the city's resources. And the river is an invaluable asset. But 'tis neither landscape nor location that concerns me, as I think you know."

His second-in-command responded with a troubled nod. "'Tis the human element. Though I expect it's too much to ask that all the people be accommodating, we would be equally suspicious if they were. Naught's perfect."

"Aye. But the incident with Lady Lexi makes me uneasy. It was a coward's work, Guy." Lovely despite her injuries, Lexi's ashen skin and blurred eyes haunted him. "I could better handle an attack upon myself."

"I spoke of it with Sir Richard this morn. He seemed as baffled as we. Somewhat disconcerting since he's known these people all their lives. But I truly believe he knows naught about what happened last night."

Cort's hair wafted about his face in the early morning breeze. He pushed it back over his shoulders and breathed deeply of the scents of primrose and new grass. "I agree. He strikes me as an honest man, more peacemaker than aggressor. Is it possible someone from outside Avonly was in the manor last night? Someone connected with the attack on us? If so, that person had to know the lady treated our wounded, and/or defended my views at supper. It would not otherwise make sense to call her traitor."

"True. Graham was most upset by that." Guy's brow furrowed in thought. "Perhaps the assailant is an outsider with an inside informant?"

"Possibly. There are too many *possiblys*." Cort narrowed his eyes in frustration. "What say you? Is't *possibly* time for us to have a meaningful discussion with our two prisoners?"

He did not wait for a reply to his unspoken command, but spurred Tyr down the gentle incline toward Avonly. Guy thundered in his wake.

Chapter Eight

Cort kept his posture casual, his expression anything but. The two men he faced refused to meet his gaze. Hard, pitiless, as he thought of Geoffrey and the potential slaughter of his men during yesterday's attack.

Standing awkwardly, hands and feet shackled, the prisoners glanced up, then away. Cort could almost smell their fear. As the silence stretched, he expected they might choke on their quick, anxious breaths.

They'd been sitting on the floor when he entered and had risen as much in defensive respect, he guessed, as because they sought to put themselves on more even footing. Cort sneered. They were not the first to assume his height was an illusion rather than an uncomfortable reality. Even on their feet, he towered over them. He wore a padded gambeson and belted tunic to add width and breadth to his already massive physique. The captives swallowed audibly and shared mutually frightened glances before dropping their gazes to the floor.

"I am Lord Dornogard." He keyed his voice so low they had to strain to hear it. Experience had taught him control was somehow more fearsome than a shout. And he tried hard to remember it. To fight back the temper that bade him roar. "Who are you? And what do you know of the man—or men—behind yesterday's attack?"

The older of the pair, whose leathery skin, work-worn hands, and rough attire attested to the life of a peasant farmer, lifted wary eyes. "I be known as

John Goodland," he said, unable to disguise the tremor in his voice. "I know naught of the attack but that I were paid to join in."

Without comment Cort turned his attention to the second man. Boy, actually. "Look at me." The lad raised his head with apparent reluctance. "Answer me."

A hint of defiance darkened light blue eyes. "Tom. Tom Dray. And I don't know nothin' either."

"Is that so?" Cort infused the almost casual drawl with patent disbelief. He exerted deliberate pressure on the bandage tied just above Tom's elbow. The boy flinched but made no sound.

A hard smile curved Cort's mouth. "I wonder what it would take to make you know something. Enough pain might loosen your memory—and your tongue."

The older man had begun to sweat, while the younger one stiffened and returned him stare for stare. Those responses told him something of each man's character, and he would use them accordingly.

"How fares your leg, John?" Though the wound was not visible, Cort had asked the guard, one of Graham's knights, about the prisoners' injuries. Always best to know an adversary's weaknesses in advance. "Took a wound in the thigh, did you?"

John's face drained of color. He swayed. So, the brief exchange with Tom hadn't gone unnoticed. *Not one for pain, eh, John?* He would be the easier of the two to break. Cort wanted—needed—information, and fear was a powerful weapon. He meant to exploit it.

He balled his hand into a fist and drew it slightly back, level with the man's upper leg. His smile nasty, he prayed he had judged Goodland accurately and asked in a soft voice, "Are you still sure you know nothing of the attack?"

"Please, my lord," the man whined, shuffling

backward out of reach. “I-I’ll tell ye what I know, but it ain’t much.” Sweat dripped now in a steady stream from his temple to his jawline.

“Very good, John.” Cort slowly unclenched his hand.

The boy snorted his disdain of the proceedings, fiery eyes declaring Cort would not break him thus.

Turning languidly in his direction, Cort emitted a bored sigh. “A bit premature, don’t you think? Your contempt. I’ve not yet begun with you, lad.

“Ah, Guy.” Cort turned as the door clicked open and his second-in-command entered. “Your arrival is most timely. Find another cell for this brave young fellow, will you? His friend John and I have things to discuss, but he has no wish to join us. Yet.”

Guy grasped the boy by the shoulder and pulled him forward, his features as harsh as Cort had ever seen them. “Move,” he growled, prodding the door wide with his booted foot.

“Tom.” Cort spoke as though the comment were an afterthought in the second before the prisoner disappeared from view. “I do applaud your physical courage. In fact, it makes me wonder how well the rest of your family handles pain. And how long you could bear to watch them suffer.” His voice dropped to a whisper. “Do you doubt my ability to locate them?”

It was a stab in the dark, innuendo couched in silken menace. But the horror on the boy’s face before he managed to mask it told Cort how accurate the thrust had been.

He nodded with bleak satisfaction. Right again.

****

“Curse Loki’s bones, I feel like we’re chasing our own tails!”

“One step at a time, my friend. It’s a start.” Guy’s calm response provoked a scowl from Cort as he sank onto the settle beside him.

Almost an hour had passed since they'd parted company. Cort allowed his shoulders to momentarily sag with fatigue. The hall was quiet, deserted but for a lone serf on the opposite side of the room, who sprinkled herbs among the rushes. Two dogs nosed along behind him. Scanning the area with wary eyes, Cort drew in a long breath and expelled it slowly before answering the question his friend had not asked.

"John Goodland was a veritable font of information, very little of it useful. But I've no doubt he told me all he knows of the attack. Unfortunately, that *all* would fit on my toenail."

Cort shot Guy a humorless glance. "The man doesn't have a firm bone in his body. I kept expecting him to dissolve into a glob of pudding at my feet."

Guy grimaced his disgust, then rose to draw cups of ale for both of them. "So." He returned to press a drink into Cort's hand. "What did this *quivery* fellow have to say?"

Cort could not resist a smile at the too-apt description. "He's a farmer, as I thought, unfamiliar with weapons other than a hoe or scythe. An odd choice for an assault on armed knights. He's from Kenilworth, just northwest of here, and has a large family to support.

"Apparently, they endured a hard winter, and our friend, along with several neighbors, was approached by a man he says had the look and speech of English nobility. Now there's a surprise." Cort pinched the bridge of his nose. "Goodland swears he never saw him before, and as the man was clad as a knight, helm and all, the farmer remembers only that he had brown eyes and was of medium build."

"That certainly narrows the field." Guy's raised brow mirrored his sarcasm.

Cort glowered. "He offered John and several of his villein friends enough gold to buy freedom from their lord, who is Baron Riveaux, by the way."

"A niggardly man, but not unbearable."

"That is neither here nor there. The point is we can now be certain it was a planned ambush. And whoever financed it had the means to do so." Cort swore beneath his breath. "Goodland received half the promised payment in advance. So did his cohorts. The strategy, it seems, was to overwhelm us by sheer numbers. Though both my opponent and Geoffrey's were trained knights. Probably yours, as well."

"Yes." Guy's hands curled into fists.

"I saw no point in telling John that he and his fellows were no doubt hired merely as distractions. While they might have struck a blow or two, I expect their main purpose was to harry us. Make us easier targets for our trained adversaries." He dragged his hands over his face. "Nor is there any question most were supposed to die during the skirmish. Those who survived were likely skewered afterward by the very knights they'd fought beside."

Cort shook his head in disgust. "Most lords consider their own serfs and villeins less valuable than animals. If John and his colleagues didn't even belong to the man responsible for paying them, he had little to lose save the meager sum it cost to initially lure them. Had things gone as our unknown schemer planned, I'm certain there'd have been no trail for my father or my men to follow. Dead men don't talk."

Guy nodded strong agreement with Cort's analysis. "Did he say nothing of motivation? Other than coin. Surely the *noble* lord who paid him offered some reason to attack us?"

"From Goodland's somewhat garbled explanation, I gather he and the others were led to believe we'd recently been freed from service with those quelling the rebellions in the North. We'd planned to visit some of our righteous anger on these shires farther south."

Cort lifted a sardonic eyebrow. "The lord who hired them said our purpose was to punish the English in this area whom the king suspected of aiding their Northern countrymen. Plausible enough, I suppose."

"Aye. A clever manipulator, whoever he is." Guy laid a hand on Cort's shoulder. "I expect you're exhausted, my lord, but...while I expect his story will be much the same as Goodland's, when you feel up to it, Tom Dray wishes to see you. Seems your parting remark made an impression."

Cort pressed his fingers to tired eyes, then ran his hands through his hair. "So, *now* he wants to talk? No!" He grunted with sudden resolve. "Mayhap on the morrow. Let our young friend stew a bit."

He pushed himself to his feet and looked down at Guy. "At the moment, I've a need to cleanse my mental palate. I must check on Geoff. And see how successful Dane has been in keeping the lady abed."

Instantly, he colored at the image his careless phrase had conjured. Guy, who knew him well, burst into laughter. "Go on, then," he choked, waving him out of the hall.

Without conscious intent, Cort ran up the stairs. To Lexi's room, not Geoff's. Unaware, he'd naturally gravitated to the unusual blend of spice and sweetness that was Lexi.

She wasn't there. Anger and anxiety churned a nasty mix in his gut.

When he retreated down the stairs and stormed past the hall into the corridor that led to Geoffrey's chamber, Cort ignored his friend's laughter. Perturbed with himself, Cort slammed open Geoff's door.

He didn't know what he'd expected. Certainly not what he found. Athene, fast asleep, was curled on Geoff's bandaged chest, and Lexi, gowned now in a soft green kirtle, sat on the floor across a backgammon board from Dane.

"Have a care, my lord." The girl spoke without looking up from the game. "Geoffrey needs rest and quiet, not noise enough to wake the dead."

Cort bristled at the reprimand. Refused to be drawn in by his body's heated response to her proximity. His gaze flew to Dane, whose face reflected chagrin, then confusion, as he looked from his lord to Lexi and back again. But there was no doubt where his loyalty lay. He leaped to his feet with a smart salute. Cort nodded curtly before returning his attention to Alexis.

"My lady." His voice sounded as gritty as sand.

She raised guileless eyes to his, then stood slowly to face him and brushed off her skirts.

"What do you here?" he asked through clenched teeth.

"Dane did not wish to leave Geoff unattended, but he could not be in two places at once, could he?" Lexi's biting tone told him she was unfazed by his anger. "I assured him I was quite well enough to come down, so he need not run back and forth between us. Besides, I wished to check on Geoffrey myself."

"So you completely disregarded my orders."

She straightened her spine. "I did not do so to anger you, my lord. But I could not stay abed with nothing to do. I thought as long as I was with Dane—"

"'Tis not the point, lady, as I think you are aware. You were told to rest today. When I give an order, I expect it to be followed."

Lexi's eyes flicked to Dane, who now stood shamefaced. Gaze truly contrite, she said, "Do not be angry with Dane, my lord. He only did what he thought best." She met his unblinking gaze with her own.

"Are you now giving me orders?"

"A request. If anyone should suffer your temper, 'tis I."

"My temper? Under the circumstances, I think my control admirable. You've yet to witness my temper, Lexi." He narrowed his eyes to slits. "But be assured you will if you again disobey me. Nor do I think Dane requires, or appreciates, your defense of him."

"I did not mean to offend..." Her voice trailed to a whisper, no doubt in response to the giant's proud stance and stony expression.

"He is a man, well able to care for himself. You are not."

Lexi stiffened. Eyes wide, mouth tight, she looked ready to explode. "Why is it men always think women helpless, incapable of watching out for themselves?"

"Because they generally are?"

Cort took his cue from her expression and held up a hand. "Enough. I did not come here to argue. 'Tis clear, though, despite your still-pallid complexion and vividly bruised temple, your spirit is returning."

"Last night's incident was an aberration. I assure you, I am more often than not quite capable of caring for myself."

"Mayhap. But as a member of my household, you are under my protection. As such, you will live by my rules. Had you a need to see Geoff, you should have come to me for permission."

"I am not accustomed to asking permission every time I—"

"Then become accustomed," Cort snapped. "Until I know who attacked you last night, and why,

I'll not have you running about so I do not know where you are."

As he'd more than half-expected, her sharp tongue at last got the better of her. "Must I be escorted to the garderobe? Chaperoned when I collect my herbs?"

Cort raised a censorious eyebrow. "If need be to assure your safety."

"To so curtail my freedom will smother me, my lord. I cannot, will not live so."

He gentled his voice at the plea in her eyes. "'Tis not my intent, lady. But I would rather you feel smothered by me than have you strangled by someone else."

"Impossible man."

Her comment startled a muffled exclamation from Dane, who was watching the exchange with obvious fascination.

"Stubborn woman." Though he tried to suppress it, a corner of Cort's mouth quirked. He brushed her hair from her bruised temple, let his fingers linger for a moment on her slender throat. "You will do as I say, Lexi. For your own good."

Lexi shivered at the contact, but set her jaw at a stubborn angle, and Cort thought for a moment she meant to contradict him, or at least further argue her cause. But good sense prevailed, and she did neither. Just regarded him at some length with somber eyes before relenting with a bare nod.

"Good. Now, Dane will stay with Geoff, and I will take you back to your room. You've still too little color. I'm glad you've not forced me to indulge my sudden wayward impulse to knock you on the head." He allowed a slight smile meant to show his good humor had been restored.

"I do seem to have that effect on people lately."

Cort shook his head before following her out the door. While Lexi might have fooled Dane with her veneer of obedience, Cort knew better. He had not lived through numerous battles and on-site construction conflicts without learning to gauge human behavior. He understood too well that both her militant step and flippant remark said he could issue orders till the sky fell.

She would do as she damn well pleased.

Chapter Nine

Even fatigue loved his face. It had been Lexi's first impression when she'd seen him belowstairs. Now, as he followed her into her room and she turned toward him, she affirmed that truth. Sleeplessness had etched Cort's features with a fine-drawn edge they had lacked upon his arrival at Avonly. A hard strength that appealed in a different way from yesterday's more youthful handsomeness. His vivid aqua eyes were less bright, the line of his mouth more strained. But he was no less beautiful than she'd originally thought him.

Inwardly, Lexi sighed. How foolish, this strange, undeniable pull she felt. And hopeless. Should Cort decide to take a wife from among his people, Melissande was the most logical choice—and surely far more pleasing than she. Delicate, fair, and demure, a competent domestic, the former Earl of Avonly's daughter was everything a man could desire.

As honest with herself as she was with others, Lexi had acknowledged long ago that her unusual height and dark hair fell far short of the conventional standard for beauty. Just as her love of learning, her sometimes suspect skill in the healing arts, her natural candor set her apart, and repelled men more often than not.

But she couldn't be other than she was, had never really wanted to be. Until now.

Conqueror or no, this man attracted her as none other. Looking up into his serious face, she again delighted in his towering height, which made her feel small and feminine, a rare experience in her life. His massive shoulders and chest, the sleekly muscled arms evident even beneath linen chainse and soft wool tunic, seemed to Lexi to emphasize her own slenderness.

A secret smile touched her mouth, and Cort's expression shifted from bland to curious. "What, lady?" He regarded her expectantly.

"Nothing," she whispered, turning her head sharply away. And was at once sorry.

Pain lanced through her temple, behind her eyes. She swayed with the unexpected force of it as her lids slid closed. Before she could reach out to steady herself, Cort scooped her into his arms and headed toward the bed. She reveled in his easy strength, the hard, warm chest pressed against her suddenly sensitized breasts.

"I'm fine," she muttered against his shoulder. His shoulder!

"Your injury, my lord. You must not overtax—"

"Or?"

"I will be forced to use leeches to reduce the swelling."

"Charming."

"Making faces at me will not change my mind. It is you who are in need of atten—"

"Would you gainsay me again this day?" Cort's voice was gruff against her ear.

"I—"

"Hush," he warned, settling her against the pillows. "You're pale as new-fallen snow, your skin nearly as cold."

Until she felt the heat of his hands chafing hers, Lexi had not realized how very chilled she was. Residual pain throbbed along the injured side of her face. She lifted shaking fingers to the bruise.

Cort eased her hand back to her side. "Let me."

With a tenderness she'd not dreamed possible in

such powerful hands, his fingertips lightly massaged the area around the bruise, then drifted to her forehead, across her eyelids. The motion, beyond soothing, had her purring low in her throat.

"You are a magician, sir."

"And you are a witch."

Though she noted the thick tenor of his voice, his touch generated such pleasant sensations, Lexi paid it little heed. Eyes closed, she found her other senses doubly acute, attuned to the subtle fragrance of sandalwood and Cort's own unique scent, the whispering slide of cloth, the tiny sparks of fire that moved along her skin wherever he touched. When he at last removed his hands from her face, she felt somehow bereft.

Her eyes fluttered open. And gazed directly into Cort's, mere inches away. Darker than Lexi had ever seen them. Hot. She didn't know where that knowledge came from, just that it was so. Hot with intent as they moved from her eyes to her mouth and back again. As though he waited.

Slowly, he raised his hand and drew his knuckles down her cheek. Lexi turned instinctively into his touch and pressed her lips against the backs of his fingers. Shocked at her boldness, her gaze flew to Cort's, but his eyes were shuttered, impenetrable. Mortified, she turned her head into the pillow.

Strong fingers captured her chin and forced her face back to his. "Where is the courageous girl I know? My honest, dauntless champion?" Despite his teasing tone, his eyes remained avid.

Caught in his stare, Lexi could think of nothing clever to say. But he did not seem to expect a response. He lowered his head by small degrees, as if to allow her time to turn away. She did not, could not. Seemed capable only of watching the slow descent of his mouth toward hers, knowing she had never wanted anything as much as she wanted to know the taste of him.

His lips as they took hers were firm and warm, neither tentative nor possessive. They simply settled, seeming content merely to make contact. For a moment. Then he leaned into the kiss, molding his mouth to the contours of hers, and was still no longer.

Long, lean fingers tunneled through her hair, pressed into her scalp as he urged her mouth more fully against his. Lexi fell into a world of taste and touch, uncaring of anything save the sweetness of Cort's wine-warm breath and the velvety texture of his wide, mobile mouth. Untutored as she was, she gladly followed his lead, opening her lips to the insistent probing of his tongue, glorying in the slow heat that dripped through her blood like thick honey.

A low moan escaped her as he abruptly withdrew his mouth. Lexi heard his harsh breathing before she raised weighted lids to watch him. Cort's jaw was rigid, his lips compressed over clenched teeth. For a moment, she thought him angry. Then her passion-dazed eyes found his, and Lexi wondered if he'd been as affected as she.

"Don't," she whispered around the tightness in her throat.

"I-I'm sorry. I did not mean to..." He turned away and pushed up from the bed.

"No." Lexi grasped his forearm and pulled herself to a sitting position. "Don't. Don't leave me." Emotions churning, helpless tears welled along her lower lashes. Her bottom lip trembled as she gazed into his set face.

Cort's body stiffened as though he fought some inner battle. Lexi loosened her grip. Perhaps she had misread his reaction, and he truly did regret the kiss. If so, she'd not further humiliate herself, or him, by pleading that he stay.

She had barely removed her hand from his sleeve when Cort's arms closed around her, easing their descent as he pressed her down into the bed furs.

"Sweet Christ," he groaned against her mouth as his chest crushed her beneath him. His hands skimmed the sides of her breasts. His lips trailed kisses over her eyes and cheeks. Then he reclaimed the mouth she so readily offered.

Need surged, demanded, spawned a hunger Lexi had never dreamed, did not begin to understand. Dizziness engulfed her, but it was a sensation quite unlike what she'd felt earlier. This was a vortex with Cort at its center, a compelling whirlwind that moved her to his will. That coaxed and pleasured and melted her bones until she burned from the inside out. No innocent to castle gossip, she'd oft overheard lustful remarks, but 'til this moment, never truly understood.

If Cort's hands were as adept with a sword as on a woman's body... Conscious thought spun away as his left hand cupped the underside of her breast, his thumb sweeping the crest. Lexi arched her body mindlessly upward. His hand kneaded the lush flesh in appreciative response. His mouth retreated a degree so that his tongue might play over her teeth, dip behind her lower lip, sweep the contours of her kiss-swollen mouth.

"Dear Freya." With obvious effort, Cort pulled his lips from Lexi's and dropped his sweat-dampened forehead to her shoulder.

"You *are* a magician, my lord," Lexi whispered when her breathing slowed enough to allow speech. "You have just revealed another person inside me I never knew existed."

Her fingers sifted through his long gilded hair as he raised his head to look at her. "Is't so, lady?" He offered a tentative smile.

"You know I do not lie. Even when it would benefit me to do so."

"Such has been my experience of you," he agreed, brushing tumbled hair from her bruised temple.

"Do you often do that, my lord?"

"Do what, lady?"

"Mix religion and mythology."

Confusion clouded his features, and Lexi laughed. "First you took our Lord's name in vain, then called on Freya. A Norse goddess, is she not? Mayhap your senses were as scattered as mine."

"Mayhap." He pushed himself upright and gave her a pained look. "I did not bring you here for this. Truly. It just... I'm sorry—"

"Are you, my lord?" She made no attempt to hide the disappointment that colored her voice. "I, too, am sorry then, but only that you feel the need to apologize. For myself, I would not change a moment just passed."

His mouth twisted. "Truth be told, neither would I."

"But you stopped," she accused.

"'Twas time to stop, Lexi," he said through gritted teeth. "If you knew aught of men and women..."

"I know a great deal." Her chin jutted with defiant pride. Which only made him want to claim her mouth once again and push to see how much she truly knew.

"But you said—" His face darkened with suspicion. "I mean... Damnation! You said you'd discovered another person within yourself. I thought you—"

"Lack of experience does not equate with ignorance. I am sixteen, my lord, and have eyes and ears, you know."

"So you have." The tension drained from his face

and shoulders as he kissed those eyes and ears. Then he gifted her with a rogue's smile and touched gentle fingers to her mouth. "Lips, also, that taste as good as they look."

Cort leaned forward, replacing his fingers with his mouth in a lingering kiss. "I, too, am honest. When I can be." His smile turned enigmatic. "Sleep. Just for a while. I will see you at supper."

"Yes, my lord." Surprised at how lethargic she felt, Lexi did not argue.

"Good girl." Cort pulled the fur over her legs. "And Lexi," he said as her eyes drifted shut, "though I expect I should be, I am *not* sorry."

****

Throughout the day, the people of Amiton watched their new lord with obvious interest. They commented among themselves that his furious energy, which rivaled that of three men, would set the pattern for the ensuing months. Cort smiled when his men relayed these snippets of conversation. By the end of the workday, none would doubt his sincerity or determination to implement the plan he'd revealed at dinner the previous evening. Through his own sweat and blood as well as theirs, he would build an estate like his adored father's.

While his role would gradually evolve into strict supervision, Cort knew the importance of his personal involvement in the initial tasks he'd set these people. The more quickly he earned their loyalty and trust, their acceptance of Norman possession, the more productive they would be. Dissension was counterproductive, taxing both physical and emotional energy. Cooperation was the key, and the best way Cort knew to encourage it among others was to practice it himself.

As expected, Guy had handled the preliminaries. When he arrived at the chosen castle site, Cort found work crews already unloading large stones from ox-drawn carts. The thud of axes echoed from the forest north of the hill on which the castle would be built.

Turning west, satisfaction surged through him at the activity along the riverbank. Work sleds hauled and dumped pruned tree trunks, which men roped together to form sturdy barges that would carry slate and rock from quarries too distant for practical land transport.

Though actual layout and construction would not begin until the stonemason and his hirelings arrived, the intervening time would be used to haul raw materials and prepare the site. The years Cort and Guy had spent supervising castle construction had taught them invaluable lessons. Ones they now planned to employ for their own benefit.

Kevin and Henri should return in a few days from London with Karl Demming, the stonemason. He and Cort had met when King William had referred Cort to him for advice on the fortress under construction at Portsmouth. Built within the existing walls of a ruined Roman fort, Cort had encountered problems in repair of the old stonework. Demming had provided clever answers to the dilemma, and they'd parted on a note of mutual respect. Now more than ever, their meeting seemed a stroke of good fortune.

Demming had recently completed Warwick Castle, less than ten miles north, and was thus both free to accept another commission and familiar with the area's resources. The coincidence reinforced Cort's belief that his choice of estate was a wise one.

Perversely, that thought recalled the doubts and problems he had already encountered here. Lexi not least among them. His body cried out for release from the passion she had kindled earlier. Hoping to alleviate the lingering tension, he stripped down to chausses and boots and labored like a man driven. It seemed the wisest option of the three that appealed, the other two being picking a fight for the hell of it, or throwing Lexi down and ravaging her.

Without a word, Cort first joined the group of men unloading stone from the carts. When they'd emptied the wagons, he nodded tersely to those who'd worked beside him and headed down the hill to assist the men assembling the barges.

As he grappled with the rough logs, a courageous churl approached and offered him a pair of heavy leather gloves.

"My thanks." Cort donned the gloves and returned to his task.

"Welcome, m'lord." The man trudged back to rejoin the others who aligned logs and lashed them together.

Along with several sturdy villagers, Cort dragged the remaining felled trunks into position beside the makeshift boat builders, then helped push two completed barges to the river's edge.

"Good work, men." He stripped off the gloves and handed them to the man who'd lent them to him. "Again, my thanks, sir."

"Evan, m'lord. M'name's Evan."

"Evan, then. I thank you."

"We thank ye for the help, m'lord."

"We'll help each other, eh, Evan?" Before the man had a chance to respond, Cort turned and strode up the embankment toward the trees from which sang the sounds of ax and saw.

His wounded shoulder rebelled when he attempted to swing an ax two-handed. Recalling Lexi's threat to use leeches to reduce any future swelling, he contented himself with hacking limbs from already-felled trees, an easy task with his good left arm. When Guy called him from the chore an hour later, Cort noticed for the first time how low the sun rode in the West.

"A good first day's work, my lord."

"What were you doing while I labored like a peasant?" Cort's grin took the sting from his words.

"I rather like you covered in grimy sweat. Good for your image. Salt of the earth and all that."

Cort huffed, flexed his shoulders, and marched down the incline to the foot of the castle site to retrieve the clothing he had earlier discarded.

"Where's Deathwright?" Guy's eyes scanned the ground as he moved up beside Cort.

"In my chamber."

"You came out here unarmed?"

"Spare me the outrage, Guy. What did you expect, that the villagers would fall on me *en masse* and bludgeon me to death?"

"The point is we don't know what to expect. I doubt these men would risk a group hanging, but what of the band who attacked us yesterday? Who's to say it won't happen again? We cannot be sure they're not still close by."

"I'm not sure of anything right now." Weary, Cort wiped the sweat from his brow with his forearm. "Except that I don't want these people to see me as an enemy. Since my purpose today was to earn their trust, not threaten them, I thought it wiser to leave my sword behind. I noticed, as well, that you stationed guards against intruders." He arched a brow at his second-in-command.

"*Naturellement*. That still doesn't mean you should go about unarmed."

"I have a blade in each boot. Not Deathwright, but better than naught.

"Now, what word from the patrol you sent back to the scene of yesterday's debacle?"

Guy knew when to leave well enough alone. "Clean as a picked carcass. If not for the torn ground, they'd never have known 'twas the right spot. Not a scrap, much less corpses."

"Damn! If their horses hadn't followed the others and Geoffrey been badly wounded... I was so sure they wouldn't have the courage to return for the bodies."

"I doubt they volunteered. My guess is whoever planned the attack either forced them to return or sent another group after the dead."

"Whichever, they're out of reach, along with any clues they might have provided, and that's an end to it."

Guy nodded, then turned toward the tree line and whistled.

His destrier, *Intrepide*, cantered down the hill toward them.

"Unlike you, I played lord of the manor today and rode among the fields to oversee the clearing of new acreage. Care to ride back to Avonly?"

Cort shook his head. "I'll walk. See you at supper."

"Your men will see you safely home." He swept his arm toward the guards stationed about Avonly's perimeter, then vaulted into the saddle and returned a casual salute to Cort's tight nod.

The need for sentries rankled, at odds with his hopes for a peaceful welcome, but unquestionably necessary. The ambush, Lexi's attack. He must not for one moment forget either.

****

"They keep c-coming, my lord! More and more each day."

Cort shared Dane's delight as they sat their mounts side by side in the cool wood and watched the activity below. His call for tradesmen, farmers, any and all able-bodied men and women had reaped a harvest far greater than expected.

"Only two weeks since we arrived, a bit more than one since Kevin returned with the royal deed ceding me the vast acres about Avonly. Hard to believe the progress we've made in so short a time."

Dane frowned. "Many are sad at first."

"Victims of the Northern Rebellion. Most lost their homes and belongings, a loved one or an entire family." Cort watched the newest contingent of bedraggled arrivals plod down the road toward the manor. A part of him ached for them while another, more practical, part recognized their misfortune as his gain. "Come winter, many would have starved or frozen to death."

"Now, there's no n-need." Dane smiled, his gaze fixed on the keep rising from the hill. "Master D-Demming keeps them busy."

"We're lucky to have such a skilled stonemason and his journeymen and apprentices. But as you say, he needs all the common labor he can get."

Dane nodded, clearly fascinated with the swarm of laborers. Some shoveled lime and sand into huge, water-filled troughs; others mixed mortar or drove stone-laden ox carts up the incline. "Hard work," he said succinctly.

Cort marveled at the man's understatement. He'd lost track of the hours Dane had spent at the site, lifting, hauling, performing tasks most of the knights considered below them. With never a complaint or expectation of thanks. It was one of the reasons he'd requested his friend's company today. But not the most important one. Though Dane did not relax unless forced to it, Cort found himself enjoying the man's company as never before. Because of Lexi.

Stunning, fascinating, frustrating Lexi. She had made him see that if Dane spoke little, he listened well—and understood. And she'd drawn him out as no one else had ever been able to do. Because he'd established himself as her main protector, they spent much time together. Often Cort would see them from a distance, strolling the meadows, wandering the wood in search of herbs and flowers. Or hear their laughter in the great hall, their discussions of strategy over one of their frequent board games. And wish he could join them.

Lexi. From the moment he'd laid eyes on her, her beauty and wit had stunned him. The kiss they'd shared had staggered him. In the two weeks since, she'd managed to avoid being alone with him. And because he deemed it safer, he'd let her. Except for sharing the evening repast, she deftly skirted his days. And as a result, haunted his nights. His entire body ached to finish what they'd begun that day in her chamber.

Yet he could not dispel his initial suspicion that she hid something. While he'd believed her when she said she did not lie, shadows moved in Lexi's usually clear golden eyes as she pressed for more freedom at every available opportunity during their evening discourse. What need had she, or any woman, for such? Even his independent mother and sisters accepted their men's protection without question.

That Cort knew he did what was best for Lexi didn't make the wanting any less. Yet to succumb to it might be the biggest risk of his life.

He gritted his teeth and put spurs to Tyr, waving Dane to follow. As the destrier leaped forward, Cort cursed fate, free will, and the king's promise that he might select his own bride.

Of all the women in Normandy and England, he had to desire the one woman he did not wholly trust. Dared *not* choose.

Chapter Ten

"Knothead!"

There had been no further threats against her or anyone else, yet His Mighty Thick-Headed Dornogard continued to insist she be guarded outside the manor house. Despite her frustration, Lexi took care not to crush the cluster of periwinkle she laid beside the mugwort in her basket.

"Dolt!" She kicked up moss with the toe of her leather shoe and wished it were Cort's shin instead. However discreet her protector, the freedom and privacy she'd always enjoyed while gathering medicinal herbs and flowers had disappeared with the knowledge she was being watched. As she was now, by Brian, her most frequent bodyguard when Dane was otherwise occupied. She'd like to tell his Almightiness what to do with his "It's for your own good!"

And she just might. If she could ever get him alone. He was always surrounded by others, whether at supper or during the day.

Her breath hitched as she recalled how Cort had looked this morn at the site of the new keep. As had become their habit, she and Dane rode the boundaries of the estate after they broke their fast. Upon their return, Cort, shirtless and sweat-streaked, that glorious mane of golden hair pulled into a long tail, already labored alongside the villagers. Massive chest and arm muscles bulging, he and two other men she did not know wrestled an uprooted stump away from newly leveled ground.

Lexi's blood hummed at the memory. Her pulse

scattered. Need curled through her to run her hands over Cort's wet, powerful torso, to rake the leather thong from his hair and wrap herself in its thickness.

It took every ounce of control not to reveal, every time she looked at him, her overwhelming fascination. Wanting to throw herself into his arms, feel again that rock-hard chest against her breasts, even when he infuriated her. As she'd done that afternoon of the mind-numbing kiss. How could she trust such a deep, immediate attraction? This bewildering sense of intimacy far beyond Cort's physical appeal?

She didn't trust herself around him.

Trust. How, she wondered, might he respond to complete honesty? Brow furrowed, Lexi shook her head. Based on his attitude thus far, not well. Though she feared her deception might hurt them both, she believed it necessary. She would not be less than what she was.

She pushed aside the yearning, willing her mind back to the present. Watching Brian shave the bark from the willow on the riverbank as she'd shown him, Lexi sighed. The incredible kiss she and Cort had shared might have been a figment of her imagination. If she didn't know better, she'd think he was running from the feelings she'd sensed in him that day. But after watching him at work and meals for over a fortnight, she couldn't imagine him running from anything. Least of all, her.

Granted, both were busy with separate tasks, but he'd made no effort to seek her out. Even her brother, who spent a great deal of time with his new lord, could shed no light on the situation. In fact, according to Stefan, Cort never spoke of her at all.

A cool breeze ruffled the River Avon's surface, casting diamonds upon the undersides of elm and alder leaves. Sun-splashed grass and colorful wildflowers dipped and swayed about Lexi's feet, but their subtle perfume failed to entice her. A thrush warbled above her and its mate answered.

The natural world was as it had always been. Her world would never be the same.

"This pouch is full, my lady," Brian called as he loped up the bank. "Are you ready to return?"

"I suppose." She forced a smile, reminding herself it was not Brian's fault he accompanied her. Yet while he or Dane forever watched her, she'd never have the chance to—

Brian cleared his throat, curtailing her self-pity.

"You've better things to do, I'm sure, than whittle bark from trees—or dance attendance on a woman who does not need your protection."

"I don't mind." He gave her a shy smile. "My ribs still ache from the trouncing Lord Dornogard gave me yesterday. And I'd rather you not need my protection than take the chance you might, my lady, and I not be there."

Though Lexi wanted to scream her frustration, she nodded as they moved side by side from the shady woods into late spring sunshine. Rolling green meadows gave way to the earthy smells of new-plowed fields and a purposeful cacophony as they approached the manor. She wondered if she'd ever grow used to the now-constant activity and noise. She had never heard such incessant droning nor seen so many people.

She had never felt more alone in her life.

All at once, Lexi longed for the parents she'd not seen in almost two years, far to the north. She shuddered at the thought of their fate had her father not recognized the futility of the Northern revolt and refused to participate. Many, less wise, had been burned out, their lands and families devastated, livestock slaughtered or confiscated.

It seemed to Lexi that from the day Kevin and

Henri returned from London with the rest of Cort's contingent, the manor and countryside rang with the sounds of swordplay, axes, orders, and laughter. For as Avonly's natives realized Cort expected as much of his Normans as he did of them, tensions eased. While some still resented the conquerors' presence, mutual goals bonded them ever closer.

Brian hailed a hunting party riding toward them. As the horsemen veered into the woods, he called, "Bring back a deer for the midday meal. I'm famished!"

Lexi recognized Kevin at the head of the group. He flashed white, uneven teeth, saluted, and rode on.

"With the fish and eels netted daily by the hundredweight from the Avon, I doubt you'll go hungry," she teased her companion. Though a portion of each catch was salted or pickled and preserved for winter, or traded with inland manors for grain and vegetables, the meals at Avonly more than sufficed.

Brian and Lexi spoke briefly with women and children headed toward the trees to forage for wild herbs and edible roots. Baskets swinging, they sang as they moved on.

"I sometimes feel I'm the only one without an assigned task," Lexi grumped.

"You?" Brian turned startled eyes to her. "You're always busy, my lady!"

Lexi wrinkled her nose in dissatisfaction. "True, some days it seems the men are more intent upon severing their own limbs than the trees', and stomachaches and fevers are common. But I feel I should be contributing something... tangible."

She swept her arm toward the now-sprawling village beyond Avonly's walls. Tents and recently erected thatch-roofed huts dotted the landscape west of the hill under excavation for the stone keep. "The town Lord Dornogard plans is taking shape."

Together they studied its common, a central hub from which the streets radiated like wheel spokes. Lexi admired the design's symmetry, the precise plots outlined behind each new structure. "Yet I do naught but watch from a distance."

"You care for the sick. You mend the wounded. Is that not a tangible contribution?" Blue eyes serious, Brian adjusted the pouch's shoulder strap.

Rather than answer, Lexi shrugged and asked, "Have you been with your lord long?"

She studied the young knight. Handsome, not much taller than she, but lean and wiry and known for his skill with a mace.

"We did not know each other at Hastings, though I saw him there. I sought him out afterward, when he was recruiting men to build the king's coastal fortresses."

"You preferred such duty to battle?"

"Yes," he said without hesitation. "Like my lord, I would rather build than destroy." His look challenged her.

Lexi grinned and shook her head. "I'm not impugning your honor or courage, sir. In truth, I applaud your choice. So many young men think war glorious. Only those who've fought one understand its brutality."

Respect dawned in Brian's eyes as he gauged the sincerity of her words. "I couldn't agree more, mistress."

Geoff hailed them as they entered Avonly's bailey. Skirting a goose girl and her honking flock, he crossed the flat paving stones that bordered the tiltyard. Though Lexi had warned him not to tax his injury, he spent an hour each day limbering his damaged muscles through light exercise. She had to admit he looked the picture of health with his ruddy cheeks and bright eyes.

"Good day, my lady. Brian."

"Good day, Geoffrey. You look well." Lexi smiled.

"Better and better, thanks to you." His hazel eyes held a wealth of gratitude.

"And Dane," she added, sloughing off the compliment.

Geoff nodded agreement. "I've a message for you. Our lord wishes you to join him in the solar after supper this eve. Something about plans for the new castle donjon."

Lexi glanced toward Brian, then back to Geoff's expectant gaze. "Me?" Her eyes widened in disbelief. "Surely you misunderstood him."

Geoffrey's expression shifted to curious. "Why should he not want to see you, lady?"

"I... It's just that... You're sure he meant me, not Brian?" Lexi's mind whirled in speculation.

"Unless you and Brian now share the same name, he asked for you."

Bewildered, she nodded. "Thank you, Geoff. I'll be there."

After all but ignoring her for almost three weeks, Cort now requested to see her? A shiver of apprehension seized Lexi. She knew nothing of castle design.

He wanted something. What?

****

"...the greatest knight in all Christendom. His horse shines like copper, and his chain mail of gold glitters like the sun." Stefan's eyes kindled with admiration.

Cort huffed, not even deigning to look up from his perusal of the plans spread before him. "Take care with Deathwright's grip, lad. Rub in the oil with slow, circular strokes."

"Aye." After a moment Stefan added, "'Tis a thick hilt, my lord. Cumbersome." He held the sword before him, inspecting it in the firelight. "You should have a new haft made, a metal one. Like—"

"Don't say it," Cort warned with a quick glance in the boy's direction. "No doubt this great warrior you speak of has a sword whose blade is chased with gold, its pommel encrusted with gems."

"How did you...?" Stefan's voice trailed off at Cort's raised brow.

"Deathwright's hilt is a perfect fit for my hand. Don't tamper with it, Stefan. Leave be." Cort's tone and look were as stern as Lexi had ever known them.

She sighed when her brother continued, unable to leave the subject alone. "Surely you've heard of him, my lord. The Golden Dragon of Normandy is legend."

"Exactly. Legend. Golden mail," Cort scoffed, skewering his squire with those bright turquoise eyes. "The man wears iron mail like every other knight."

"You know him, then? What's he like, my lord?" Stefan's enthusiasm appeared undimmed by his master's disdain.

Lexi absorbed the conversation as she slipped onto a bench to the left of the hearth, just out of Cort's field of vision. His attention on her brother, she was sure he had not seen her enter the solar. As intrigued as anyone else by the numerous stories of the Golden Dragon, she waited in silence for Cort's reply.

"A man, Stefan. He's only a man, with strengths and weaknesses like any other."

"But there are fantastic tales about his feats of heroism," her brother continued in a disappointed tone, returning his attention to Deathwright's shimmering blade.

Cort's expression softened in the ruddy glow of the two candles set upon the table. "Listen to your words, boy. *Legend. Fantastic.* No man can be more than flesh and blood. No man is invincible. If you expect him to be, you'll be disillusioned."

"Yet some men are extraordinary," Stefan ventured, seeming loath to relinquish the dream.

Cort's mouth tipped in a lopsided grin that curled Lexi's toes. "Aye, lad. But rare. Most *heroes* are made through circumstance and opportunity, not intent."

"Shatterer of dreams," Guy's voice chastised from the shadowed corner behind Lexi.

She almost slid to the floor in shock, unaware until that moment of his presence.

"Nay," Cort said, his gaze still on Stefan. "A realist. Personal knowledge has taught me most legends are overrated."

Guy's dark chuckle prickled Lexi's spine. "Jealous?" he goaded.

As Cort turned toward his friend with a jaundiced glare, his gaze locked with Lexi's. For a lightning moment, something flared in his eyes. Gone in a heartbeat, she wondered if her own yearning had imagined it there. His expression now reflected only that hurtful, casual indifference.

"Eavesdropping, my lady?"

Lexi stiffened, but met his cool gaze with her own angry one. "I was invited, my lord. By you." She was proud of the haughty tone that disguised her emotional turmoil. For despite his obvious lack of interest in her, Lexi could not deny her increasing fascination with him. His about-face treatment of her rankled and bewildered. What had she done to—

"So you were. Though I do not appreciate you sneaking up on me in such a way."

It was a challenge Lexi could not resist. "Sneaking? I but came in quietly so as not to disturb your conversation." That wasn't exactly true, she thought, but she hadn't been sneaking, either. "If I wished to sneak, you'd not catch me. As if I could, guarded as I am every moment from some imagined danger of your fevered mind. Forbidden solitude even to gather herbs or mix medicines. Think you I've not noticed your guard dogs prowling about in the passageway outside the herbal?" Her hands fisted at her sides as she half rose from the bench.

"I was right," Cort said with a brittle smile, seeming unaffected by her tirade. "Someone should hit you over the head on a regular basis."

Pain lanced through her, swift and bittersweet. He was not teasing as he had been the last time he'd said those words.

Cort ignored her answering sputter as he lifted his gaze beyond her to Guy. "Look at these final changes before I send them to Demming, will you? Come here, Lexi. Join us." It was not a request, but his focus was again on the parchment before him.

"I know nothing of castle architecture, my lord," Lexi objected. Still, she moved up beside him.

Footsteps sounded in the hall, and her uncle hurried into the solar.

"Forgive me for interrupting, my lord." His gaze swept down to the tunnel-and-underpinning plans for the stone keep, then lifted to Cort. "One of the stonemason's apprentices is below. Herr Demming has a question he needs answered before they continue work in the morning."

Cort gusted a sigh. "Have him wait in the hall. I'll speak with him when I'm finished here."

Graham nodded and retreated down the stairs.

Cort smoothed a second rolled parchment over the first, and Lexi found herself impressed by the clean, fluid lines of the drawings Cort indicated. "Oh. They are beautifully done."

His smile was possessive.

"You drew these?" she asked, amazed.

He shrugged. "I seem to have a talent for it. Inherited from my father."

She had never thought about his family, his past. But now did not seem the time for such questions. Instead, she asked, "Why show them to me?" She studied the plans, absorbing the outlines of the donjon and curtain wall. "I've no interest in—"

"Even the women's solar?" Cort interrupted. "And what of the new herbal I've designed?"

Though a contrary voice urged her to refuse the bait, Lexi's eyes were drawn to Cort's hands, their long, sturdy but graceful fingers tracing the perimeter of her future workroom with its large window opening. A bright, airy space at least twice the size of her present herbal, she guessed. With a Southern exposure, to make the most of the natural light.

Cort's hand slid up the parchment to the top floor of the donjon. Atop the herbal, a bank of windows spanned the outer wall of a wedge-shaped solar to the right of the stairs. Again, he had made good use of space and sunlight.

Cort turned his hand to the side, flexing his fingers. Lexi thought it an unconscious gesture, yet it drew her like a child to a forbidden sweet. A warrior's hand. An artist's hand. A lover's hand. Too well she remembered the tender caress of those fingers. On her face, her mouth, her breast.

"You approve?"

Lexi almost jumped out of her skin, then realized Cort could not possibly know what she was thinking. "Y-yes, my lord," she stammered, praying he could not read the longing in her eyes. "It was...is...I..." Damn these memories she could not control! "Perfect, my lord. Just perfect."

From the corner of her eye, she took in Stefan's concerned frown, but could do nothing to reassure him. Knowing she must escape before her desire to touch Cort's tanned cheek, trace the dimple beside his mouth, run her fingers through that beautiful, gilded hair overwhelmed her, Lexi fled.

Several long minutes of silence passed before Cort turned to Stefan. "Squire, return Deathwright to my chamber and await me there."

"Aye, my lord." He hefted the heavy blade and disappeared down the hall.

"That was time well wasted."

Cort grunted but said nothing.

"There was a purpose?" Guy persisted when his friend remained silent.

Cort slammed his hand on the table in frustrated temper. With Stefan gone, he felt free to vent his disgust. "My intent went awry," he admitted with a scowl.

"Ah." Whatever the hell that meant.

"Damn it, Guy. I'm in no mood for your sarcasm. Almost three weeks are gone by, and we're no closer now than we were the day of the ambush to finding the perpetrators. Or Lexi's attacker."

Guy left his stool in the shadowed corner to straddle the bench on which Cort sat. Facing him, he apologized. "I did not mean to make light of things. But where the lady is concerned, you are hardly acting the Lord of Amiton."

"I have no choice, Guy. You, if anyone, should understand that. Though she draws me like a Siren, I dare not allow her close to me 'til I'm sure."

"Has she done aught to rouse suspicion?" Guy tensed, his voice tight.

"Nay, nor to soothe it. 'Twas my purpose in inviting her tonight. I'd hoped to ask her, with Stefan present, about the slinger. To watch the two of them react. A look, a gesture—anything that might reveal they know more about the ambush than they will admit."

"You don't trust Stefan?" Guy's wide-eyed surprise almost made his lord smile.

Cort shook his head. "I've no reason not to,

though I'll put my faith in no one fully until we discover the truth. It's myself I don't trust. Not around her."

Shoulders hunched, he slid the heavy pewter cups from the top corners of the plans still spread before him and watched the parchment curl upon itself. "As for Stefan, he's not yet been forced to make a choice between me and his sister. If that time comes..."

Guy placed a comforting hand on Cort's shoulder. "It may never come. The girl is pained by your treatment of her. It hurts me to look at her when you're in the same room. Perhaps if you were kind to her, as you were at first, it would yield better results. You know what they say of catching flies with honey rather than vinegar."

Wondering if he looked as weary as he felt, Cort stared into the flickering candle flame. "I cannot. She has not sought me out alone, and I almost feel she wishes to avoid me." He shifted his sad gaze to Guy. "I remember too clearly the day we met, her knowledge of what caused my wound. Though her explanation made sense, her eyes and body told a different story. I'd bet Tyr she was scared to death and knows more than she's telling."

"That doesn't mean she approved of the attack or was somehow involved in it."

"I know that." Cort's hands fisted as he dropped them to his thighs. "But I also know enough to trust my instincts. And you heard her tonight. Why does she chafe so at her lack of freedom? She's allowed to do anything she wants, just not alone. Her comments about *sneaking* were almost a challenge. I dare not risk it," he repeated.

Guy grunted in understanding, though his expression told Cort he remained dubious. "Mayhap if you told them the truth about..." His words trailed off at the hard look Cort leveled at him. "Just a thought."

His hand gripped Cort's shoulder, then fell away. "This is as hard on you as a pitched battle, isn't it?"

"Harder, my friend. Much, much harder."

Chapter Eleven

"Who's the knothead now?" Lexi flopped backward onto her bed, arms splayed like a crucified angel. *Don't just give the man something to chew on, stuff it down his throat. Don't ease his suspicions, heighten them. And be sure to point him in the right direction. Tell him you can sneak if you must—and how much you resent your lack of privacy.*

"Blood of the martyrs," she muttered, draping an arm across her eyes. "I let him rile me and ran off at the mouth like a drooling idiot."

There was no hope for it. She couldn't take back her words, only pray Cort thought them but angry ravings. When bulls grew teats. She sighed. The man was too smart by half.

Not for one minute did Lexi believe tonight's purpose had been her approval of his plans for the new castle. Did he think her a dunce? Cow dung! The man drove her to distraction without even trying. But he did have the most beautiful eyes. And hair. And hands.

Lexi snapped upright. Damn her attraction to him. She had more important things to worry about.

What would he do if he knew the truth? Hang her head on a pike as an example to all womanhood, no doubt. At the very least, curtail what little freedom she still had.

Yet he might come to trust her if she told him the truth. And at the bottom of it all, that was the crux, she thought again. Trust.

What if he didn't believe her? Even if he did, the result might be the same. Her deception harmed no one. It was a simple matter of self-preservation. She shuddered at the idea of being imprisoned in her room—or worse. She could not risk it.

Though Cort's treatment of his people was fair, even kind at times, she knew firsthand his cold, inflexible side, and his interrogation of the two captives taken after the ambush had established his reputation as a harsh enemy. The guard outside the door that day had heard the threats, seen the terrified faces of the prisoners.

Then they'd disappeared. No one dared question their fate.

Which recalled Lexi to her own dilemma. One she must handle alone. Poor Uncle Richard had no idea what she'd done, had been doing for some time. Melissande was about as useful as a peahen in a gaggle of geese. Dane, Geoffrey, even Brian might be her friends, but they were Cort's men first and last. Only Stefan, possibly, suspected the truth, or part of it, but she couldn't involve him in this coil. She would not force him to choose between love for her and loyalty to his new lord.

Her still-tender temple began to throb. If she didn't otherwise occupy her mind, she'd go mad. Vexed, Lexi drew one of her few remaining sheets of precious parchment from the small bedside table drawer.

By the light of a single candle, she drew from memory the bare outlines and tunnel system of the keep Cort planned. Assessing the sketch, she wondered if it might be possible to flare the upper walls outward. She amended it with light strokes of the charcoal. A good design. One that would prevent an enemy's scaling the structure.

Perhaps she'd show it to Cort. If he was nice to her.

A sharp rap on the door had her jumping. Her hand jerked, sending the charcoal flying against the wall behind her.

"Lady, I would speak with you."

Cort. The mere sound of his voice scattered her thoughts and sent her heart racing. Nerves jittered in her stomach, a mix of apprehension and desire.

"A moment." She set the sketch on the bedside table, then stood and straightened her skirts. "Come in, my lord. The door's unlocked."

The latch snicked, and the portal swung inward. Cort, handsome, serious, dangerous in the flickering shadows, filled the opening. Without a word, he stepped into her chamber, then nudged the door shut with his boot heel.

Lexi frowned, her anxiety escalating. "I'd prefer the door ajar, my lord," she managed through a tight throat. "'Tis not proper—"

"This will take but a moment." He strolled to within a foot of her. "I wish that moment to be private."

This close to him, she felt the heat of his body, saw the dark blond stubble along his jawline and the depths within those jewel-toned eyes. The firm line of that wide, sculpted mouth. Gaze steady on his, she tried to ignore the butterfly swoop of her stomach, the yearning in her blood.

And lost the battle when he closed the narrow distance between them, wrapped his fingers in her hair, and tilted her face up to his.

"Cort," he said. "I am Cort to you, not my lord."

"Yes." As naturally as a flower unfurls its petals to the sun, Lexi's mouth opened to his and drank in the moist warmth, the sweetness of wine, the dark undertone of man. Hands fisted in his tunic, she drew him in so that his hard body melded with hers.

Cort released her hair and wrapped his arms around her, taking the kiss deeper. When she moaned, he swept her mouth with his tongue, then left her wanting as his lips nipped and sucked their way down her throat to the pulse beating hard at its base.

"I've missed you," he murmured. "Missed the taste of you."

Confused, Lexi rested her head on his chest. "Then why, since the night you first kissed me, have you not spoken to me but as you must at meals?"

His muscles tensed. "I've been busy, as have you."

Lexi slid her hands over his shoulders, gathered his hair, and tugged. When he lifted his head, she studied the play of candlelight over his somber features, the intensity of his eyes.

"'Tis more than that." Voice flat, she felt her blood cool. "Why are you really here? What is it you want?" Heart aching, she released him. His arms fell away as she stepped back. "I do not think you have missed me or the taste of me."

"You are wrong there." His sensual, mobile mouth now set in a grim line, Cort gripped her upper arms with less than gentle fingers. "Right that I seek you for another reason as well. Truth, my lady." He gave her a gentle shake.

Fear choked her. He knew. But how? Stefan. Had her brother voiced his suspicions, thinking to protect her from possible harm?

"Tell me the truth," Cort demanded.

Lexi closed her eyes, opened them again to his probing gaze. While it might cost her dearly, she would answer him. "I told you I do not lie, my lord."

"Do you know who attacked me and my men the day we arrived here?"

She almost buckled with relief. Thank the Virgin and all the saints, his question did not touch upon her secret. "I do not. On my soul, I swear it."

"Will you swear, also, that your brother was not involved in any way?"

"Stefan?" Lexi huffed. "Of course not. What

could he possibly have to gain? Like me, he is here under my uncle's aegis and no more. He has no stake in Avonly. Amiton. My home, the estate my brother will eventually inherit, is in the North. Our loyalty lies there, not here."

Cort's fingers tightened for a moment before he released her. Then he lifted her chin with the side of his hand, forcing her gaze to his. "I trust you have not betrayed me in this, Lexi. Should I discover otherwise..."

"You will not," she swore.

He nodded, then looked beyond her to the open casement. A slight breeze lifted his hair and sent her sketch of the donjon fluttering beside her to the floor.

Cort swept it up, held it high in the meager candlelight. "Interesting. Brilliant, actually." He smiled at her for the first time in forever. "I'd not thought to lever the upper section outward. Excellent for defense—if Demming can manage to construct it so. I shall have to speak with him."

He reached around her to replace the drawing on the table.

"Kiss me again," she said before she could stop herself.

Eyes smoky turquoise in the shifting light, he took her face in his hands and kissed her hard and fast. "Brilliant," he repeated. His fingers skimmed her hair before he turned and left her.

Well. Lexi touched trembling fingers to her well-kissed mouth, willing her still surging blood to calm, her racing heart to settle. Her chamber felt suddenly empty and cold, as if Cort had taken all light and heat with him. Nonsense. She picked up the charcoal from the floor and the sketch from the table and climbed the double steps to her bed.

She'd felt alone before. But now, for the first time ever in her life, she was truly lonely.

With a heartfelt sigh, she stretched out on her stomach, flipped the parchment, and found herself idly writing Cort's full name in a variety of patterns. Like a lovesick girl. Dragging a soft pillow against herself for comfort only served to remind her she much preferred the feel of Cort's hard body. "Lizard livers!"

Just because he kissed her until her toes curled didn't mean he cared for her, not the way she'd begun to care for him. Nor did it take her any closer to the freedom she craved. Still, satisfied that her secret remained safe, she rolled up the drawing, secured it with the thin red riband she'd earlier pulled from her hair, and tossed it on the table. And drifted into healing sleep.

Snarling. Men-cursing. Booted feet pounding up the stairs.

Lexi jerked awake, disoriented by the weak light that filtered through her narrow bedside casement and the chaos beyond her door.

"Dear God!" She leapt to the floor, hardly aware of the cool wood beneath her bare feet. Were they under attack? Pushing tangled hair from her face, she rushed to the door, then thought better of opening it. Instead, she cast about for a weapon. Other than the sheathed misericorde at her waist, she saw only the pewter candlestick upon the mantel. Frantic, she raced to the hearth and gripped it in her fist.

Something slammed hard against the door.

"*Jesu*!" a man bellowed. Cort? He sounded more angry than threatened.

"Get it! She'll have my head." Definitely Cort.

What...? Muffled shouts, barking, sounds of men scuffling, bouncing off the walls. Then utter silence.

Lexi frowned, her ear pressed to the door as the words registered. It? And who was the she who'd have his head?

Curious at the prolonged silence, she inched open the door. And heard the tinkling of bells. Several men in various stages of undress stood frozen in the hall, staring at something she couldn't see. A low, rumbling growl sounded to the left. Lexi stepped into the passage.

Cort stood against the opposite wall, hands fisted at his sides. She followed his gaze to a shadowed corner, aware at first only of a large, dark shape. Then her eyes adjusted to the scant light, and she drew in a sharp breath.

Cort turned his head toward her, his glare accusatory. "Do something, dammit. Now." His voice was low and rough, like pin pricks against her skin.

Ignoring the sensation, Lexi focused on the corner tableau. "It's almost funny."

Cort's molten stare could have incinerated bedrock.

"Well, it is," she muttered, refusing to look at him again as she advanced with care toward the corner. An arm's length from her objective, she paused and slowly lifted her hand. A vicious growl issued from the huge, hairy beast before her.

Lexi lowered her hand and asked over her shoulder, "Has he a name?"

"Fen." Cort's voice was taut, abrupt.

"Relax, my lord," Lexi advised. "He senses your tension."

"You'll feel more than my tension if you don't—"

"Oh, hush. You'll make things worse."

"Easy, Fen," she crooned, taking a tiny step forward. "It's all right. Let me help you, boy. I won't hurt you. Promise."

The waist-high Irish wolfhound stood like a statue, his gaze pleading as she murmured reassurances. Poor thing, she thought, stifling a sudden urge to laugh. Rather demeaning for such a huge animal to be brought low by such a small creature.

Lexi had never considered Athene aggressive, but this was, no doubt, a case of self-defense. The ferret hung like a dead weight from the dog's face, her teeth buried just below Fen's right eye. His warrior instincts seemed to have deserted him at this unprecedented threat. His whine was pathetic.

"Athene, that's enough." Lexi kept her voice soft but stern. "No, Athene. No." The ferret hung on with the tenacity of a burr.

"Don't worry, Fen. I'll get her," Lexi whispered. "You frightened her, but she won't hurt you. Here now, Athene. Come to me. Be nice to the poor, terrified beast."

Fen remained immobile, though his eyes charted the movement of Lexi's hands as she slid one beneath Athene's stomach and the other under her rear legs. Secure in her mistress' palms, the ferret promptly released her death grip on the wolfhound's face and turned her own up to Lexi, who nuzzled her. Cradled in Lexi's arms like a baby, Athene crossed her tiny paws over her chest and gazed at Cort with bright, innocent eyes.

With a baleful glare, he assessed the two, then snapped his fingers. Fen moved at once to his side, though his wary gaze never left the pair facing his master. Cort dropped to his haunches to inspect the dog's face, grunting with relief at no sign of major damage.

His men exhaled a collective sigh of relief.

Before Cort could speak, Lexi asked, "Is Fen a nickname?"

Though his expression told her he was in no mood for another of her name games, she indulged the mischievous urge. "Don't tell me his full name is Fenris."

The instant spark in Cort's eyes was answer enough.

"Fenris. As in Thor's wolf. And your destrier is Tyr." She sighed with dramatic effect. "Named for the Norse god of war. How wonderfully...symbolic."

Cort's shoulders stiffened. His fingers curled into his palms. Lexi thought she should be frightened. His eyes told her he'd like to wring her neck, yet she thought she knew him well enough by now to trust he would not hurt her. Certainly not with his men looking on. She pushed a little further.

"Is your name symbolic as well, my lord? Cort." She paused as if reviewing her knowledge of Viking lore. "No." Lexi shook her head. "Perhaps Dornogard."

His thunderous expression said he'd forego strangulation for a direct sword thrust. Uh-oh. A step too far.

Discretion over valor, Lexi decided, and back-stepped out of his reach.

Cort took several deep breaths. Ignoring her implied question, he snarled, "Fen could have killed her."

"Athene could have blinded him," Lexi snapped. So much for discretion.

"He could have crushed her with his paw, bitten her in half."

Lexi intuited their argument had moved beyond Athene and Fen and answered accordingly. "But he didn't. Perhaps there's a lesson in that, my lord."

His furrowed brow challenged an explanation.

"She is able to take care of herself." Her gaze held his. "On a more mythical level, of course, one could cite what King Arthur learned to his sorrow: Might doesn't always make right." She gave him her sweetest smile. "And in the real world, as I'm sure you know, bigger is not always better."

Cort growled.

Lexi sniffed.

Fen whined.

Athene yawned.

****

He should have seen it coming.

The fiasco that morning with Fen and Athene had been an omen of dismal accuracy.

Determined to work out his frustration, Cort had stormed to the tiltyard—and done something he hadn't done since his early days as Uncle Will's squire. Knowing the absolute concentration required at the quintain, he'd allowed his mind to drift to Lexi, his conflicting desire and distrust. Lust over logic. And missed the target's center. The sandbag weight slammed him from behind, knocking him ass over head.

The handful of men in the yard had the good sense to pretend they'd not seen his callow error. Tyr, who had no such qualms, circled back and roughly nudged Cort's shoulder as if he thought his master an idiot. Cort loosed a string of curses. The girl interfered even here.

Still flat on his back, Cort found himself looking up into the sweating face of a runner from the castle site.

"The stonemason needs you," the boy panted. "There's a problem."

Why was he not surprised? Cort groaned as he rose and smacked the dust from his backside.

"Get a drink of water, lad," he said, pulling himself astride Tyr. "No need to rush back."

"Thank 'e, m'lord."

Cort returned a nod to the runner's quick grin.

Five minutes later he stood beside Demming. "A ledge o' solid rock," the stonemason explained, pointing a rigid finger at the obstruction. "It runs ta entire lengt' o' ta fountation on tis side."

Cort scowled and shoved a hand through his hair. Neither man spoke as each surveyed the granite wall.

"Leave it," Cort said at last.

"My lord?"

"Leave it," Cort repeated. "This side faces the manor, the least likely escape route. With tunnels on the sides facing the woods and the village, we don't need it."

"You are sure?" the stonemason asked.

"Yes. It's not worth the time it will take to remove that much rock."

"Den our problem is solved, *ja*?" Demming spread his arms wide, his smile reflecting the relief in his eyes.

"*Ja*." Cort clapped the man on the shoulder, then vaulted onto Tyr. Matching his rhythm to the dark roan stallion's as they galloped down the motte toward Avonly, he gradually relaxed. A minor problem now solved. Simple. His day was improving.

He should have known better.

Chapter Twelve

"I did not do it apurpose!"

"Carelessness is not one of your shortcomings, lady. If anything, you are meticulous to a fault." Cort drummed his fingers against the table edge and watched her from lazy eyes.

Cognizant of the serfs who were setting the hall to rights after the midday meal, Lexi tamped down her anger. "Athene often squeezes into tight spaces in my room and goes to sleep. I have yet to discover all her hiding spots. I could not find her to put her in her cage before I went to the solar last night, or when I returned."

She could not tell him how affected she'd been by his nearness. "Well." She swallowed and forced herself to look at him. "My mind was on other things. I forgot to replace the wood slat at the base of my door. It was an accident. I'm sorry."

Cort said nothing, simply waited.

He could wait until Doomsday. She'd told the truth, even apologized to pacify him, the tyrant. What more did he want?

When Lexi maintained her stubborn silence, Cort's eyes narrowed. "I'm to believe Athene can...slither...through that narrow space beneath your door?"

"She does not slither. And I don't care whether you believe me or not. 'Tis the truth." Disgusted, Lexi stood and snapped out her skirts.

Cort snagged her wrist and plopped her back onto the bench. "You haven't been dismissed."

"No, you have." Furious beyond the thought of

consequences, Lexi wrenched free of his hand and scooted out of reach, struggling to stand. Cort jerked the bench. It hit her below the knees. She teetered backward and screeched as she lost the battle for balance.

No one could move that fast, she thought, as Cort's arm snaked about her waist. He lifted her against him with seeming ease, her back pressed to his chest. Lexi froze. His hand spanned her ribs, warm and hard, mere inches below her breast. And despite her pique, wished desperately that he would touch her there again.

She heard him take a ragged breath even as she ceased to breathe, felt his grip loosen so that she slid down the length of him and at last found her footing. But he did not release her.

"Now we're even," he whispered into her hair.

In a flash Lexi recalled their first meeting, how she'd saved him when he'd almost toppled over the bench in his chamber.

"I did not smack you with the bench. Though perhaps I should have."

"God forfend you should do something so common. You prefer to talk to goddesses." Choked laughter rumbled from his chest. She felt the tremors through every nerve in her body.

"Please, my lord," she pleaded. "They're watching us."

Cort's head jerked up. She suspected he had forgotten the serfs. Though Lexi dared not look at him while he held her this close, she could imagine his expression. With amazing speed, the servants scuttled out.

"Now, lady." He turned her to face him. "We are alone." He drew a harsh breath. "Have you anything else to tell me?"

There was much she could tell him, nothing that she would.

Instead, she chose safe ground. "I swear what I've told you about Athene is true," she said, her gaze direct. "I was careless, and she escaped. You cannot think I would allow her to roam the manor house and endanger herself."

"No," he admitted without hesitation. "You would not. As I will not allow you to roam without protection."

Back to that were they?

In an instinctive bid to reach him, Lexi moved her hands to his chest. His muscles contracted at her touch. Interesting.

Unwilling to meet his intense aqua gaze, Lexi talked to his shirt laces. "My lord," she began, her voice far steadier than her nerves. "Cort. I know you mean well, but I find it difficult to be followed everywhere. I am used to my privacy. I enjoy solitude. The attack on me was surely an isolated incident motivated by temporary anger. It had been a trying day. "

Cort lifted her chin with his thumb. "Is it that important to you?" His warm breath fanned her cheeks as he searched her face.

"Aye." She nodded, and his fingers slid up her throat to her jaw.

Lexi's hands spasmed against his shirt. Cort's muscles leapt to meet them.

"Solitude. Freedom." He spoke the words as though he also yearned for those things. "Do you swear to me those are the only reasons you wish me to withdraw your guards?"

Lexi forced herself to meet his gaze, praying he did not see the shades of truth she skirted. "I swear it," she whispered.

Cort's soft smile had her stomach pitching. Though whether from guilt or desire she could not say.

"I shall think on it," Cort promised, snatching

away her assumed victory.

"Think on it?" Lexi shoved against his chest.

His fingers flexed around her waist, and she stilled. "Must we be always at odds, lady?" His voice sounded strained.

"I am not the one who set the tone, my lord."

Cort closed his eyes, seeming to accept her rebuke. When he reopened them, they danced with amused challenge. "Shall we see who sets the tone between Fen and Athene? He appeared properly chastened after their *introduction* this morning and would behave himself, I think, were they to meet again. What say you to a more controlled second encounter?"

Lexi felt the tension drain from her at Cort's unexpected overture to foster a friendship between their pets. The man did have his moments.

"This evening? In the solar?"

"Done." Cort's smile could have melted bone. It certainly melted hers.

The thorough, open-mouthed kiss he gave her before he strode away finished what his smile had begun.

****

Control. Patience. His father's voice.

The warning thrummed inside Cort's skull.

He'd thought his day was improving. Less than an hour ago he'd kissed Lexi and felt more lighthearted than he had in weeks.

Now, rage unlike any he'd known since Hastings shimmered just beneath the surface. The happy scene before him did nothing to assuage it.

Laughter floated around, but did not touch him. Conversation echoed from the beamed ceiling, cascaded off the walls. Cort could make sense of none of it. His awareness narrowed to the man lounging beside the mantel. His mantel, dammit. His hall. Cort's fingers twitched; his shoulder muscles bunched.

Control.

The visitor sighted him and straightened with languid insolence. "Ah, Dornogard," he called with barely veiled dislike.

Cort forced a marginal nod. "Bouchard." It was all he could manage without gnashing his teeth—or lunging for the bastard's throat. Much as he might wish it, Cort would not indulge himself in a public confrontation.

Almost five years since he'd seen Bouchard. Since Hastings. Since he'd taken pleasure in the thought of killing a man. Now, he could not afford that luxury. Not yet.

As Bouchard advanced toward him, a serf rushed forward to offer Cort a tankard of ale. He forced his fisted hands open and wrapped his fingers around the mug's handle. A poor substitute for Bouchard's neck, but better than nothing.

"Shall we sit?" Cort asked, surprised how civil he sounded. He moved to a trestle table near the center of the great hall, giving his unwelcome guest no choice but to follow.

Cort straddled the bench, then turned to face Bouchard, who sat across from him. Determined to maintain a casual facade, he quaffed deeply from his tankard before asking, "What's new in London?"

"I wouldn't know. I've not been there in several months."

Cort arched an eyebrow and waited for Bouchard to explain.

"My estate's kept me busy, what with planting and surly peasants and serfs." His voice dripped disdain. "But I intend to spend some time at court before summer is upon us."

While he talked, Cort assessed the changes in the man since they'd last seen each other. Still trim and tall, Cort supposed women found Bouchard attractive with his glossy brown hair and hazel eyes. At thirty-one, four years older than Cort, he was a seasoned fighter who loved war for its own sake, as Cort never could. On the eve of the Battle of Hastings, Bouchard had spoken of the coming fight with grisly pleasure. Afterward, Cort heard he'd regaled his men with detailed accounts of enemies' hacked limbs and broken bodies.

Poor King Harold. His death, some said, had been caused by an arrow through the eye; others swore he'd taken a sword thrust in the chest. Either way, his corpse had then been mutilated, a source of amusement to Bouchard. Cort had pitied the brave leader and been sickened by the brutality inflicted on his remains. Even King William had expressed dismay at the condition of the body and built a chapel at Hastings to honor Harold.

Cort doubted Bouchard's attitudes had softened since then. If anything, there was a hard arrogance now in his expression, a darkness in his hazel eyes that Cort did not remember. Not that he cared. The man could sink no lower in his esteem.

One moment at Hastings, forever seared into Cort's mind, branded this man as the one thing he despised beyond all else. A coward. And when he considered what the consequence of that cowardice might have been...

"Don't you? Dornogard? Dornogard!"

Cort refocused with a jolt. Bouchard regarded him with angry eyes, clearly unused to being ignored.

"Don't I what?" Cort offered a tight smile at the man's irritation.

"Plan to go to London?" Bouchard's voice was taut, his broad shoulders stiff with pique at Cort's obvious indifference to his temper.

"I prefer the country. I've no desire to spend time at court with mincing courtiers and toadies."

Bouchard's lips thinned, and his hands curled into fists at the implication Cort included him among them. "Your father spends much time there," he parried, his tone smug.

"At the king's request." Cort refused to be baited. "If given leave, he would be on the first ship back to Normandy."

"Perhaps. Though I cannot believe he'd so quickly relinquish the power he enjoys there."

Cort leaned across the table. "He does not enjoy it."

"All men crave power," Bouchard blustered.

"No, only ambitious men. My father has no need to play their games." He straightened his back and glared across the table. "Nor do I."

Cort watched the man's expression shift from testy to wary as he absorbed the veiled message. With a quick glance at the men gathered at a second table near the hearth, well out of earshot, Bouchard gave a curt nod.

"You play another game, though, don't you, Dornogard?" he drawled. "I see no point in it." He shrugged. "But, no tales from either of us, eh?"

Bouchard's superior grin raised Cort's hackles, but he forced himself to endure the man's complacency. For now. What he knew of Alaine was far more damaging than his own secret. He'd have the upper hand again.

A rush of footsteps drew the men's attention to the room's arched entrance. Lexi skidded into view, followed moments later by a sedate Melissande. Lexi's gaze skated over the room and settled on the two men at the center table.

The delighted smile that bloomed on her mouth took Cort's breath and curled around his heart. She was as happy to see him as he was her, and making no attempt to hide it.

She hurtled toward them on slippered feet, arms

extended. "Alain!"

Cort's heart plummeted as he swung his leg over the bench and surged to his feet.

Bouchard was already halfway to Lexi and reaching for her hands. "My lady," he murmured, placing a gallant kiss on her fingers. "It has been too long."

Stunned, Cort barely registered that Graham had arrived and now stood beside his daughter. "You know each other?" he demanded in a strangled voice, staring at Lexi and Bouchard. *His* Lexi. Stunning, responsive. Bouchard. Deceitful, bitter enemy.

"For two years, my lord." Her glad expression grew confused as she took in Cort's rigid stance. "Alain is a good friend."

"More than a friend, I hope." With a courtly bow to Lexi, he turned his back on Cort and addressed Graham. "I have come today with a special purpose in mind, sir." A bland smile on his mouth, he placed Lexi's hand, still held in his, on his arm. "With your permission, I would court Lady Alexis and take her to wife."

"Impossible!" The silence following Cort's roar was so absolute, he could hear his own heartbeat.

"Impossible?" Bouchard bristled, eyes dark with rage as he spun to face his enemy. "Why impossible?"

"Because," Cort grated, the veins pulsing in his throat, "the lady is betrothed to me."

Chapter Thirteen

She couldn't breathe.

It was a joke. At her expense.

No one was laughing.

The world tilted, then righted itself. With Cort the axis on which it spun.

He was waiting for her to say something, Lexi realized. She took a long, deliberate breath and studied him.

His face stark, his stance rigid, she was surprised not to hear the pop and snap of tendons. But one look at his beautiful, troubled eyes told her what he expected.

That she would challenge his word. Call him a liar. Even as he silently pleaded that she not expose him.

What was going on here? What lay between these two men? Both mattered to her. But she could choose only one.

Her response came, instinctive and soul deep. Without hesitation Lexi buried her confusion beneath a calm veneer and withdrew her hand from Alain's arm. Like the most demure maid, she dipped her head, then raised her gaze to Cort. "'Tis true," she whispered. "Lord Dornogard has so honored me."

Degree by slow degree, the tension ebbed from him. Relief washed over his face even as his eyes widened in surprise.

She lifted her shoulders in a tiny shrug. She had no idea why Cort had said they were betrothed, though she knew too well why she pretended it was true. He rarely did things without reason, and she could not humiliate him in public. Which didn't mean she wouldn't grill him over live coals as soon as she could drag him out of here.

Bemused, Lexi watched Cort extend his hand to her, the gesture tentative. A request, not an order. He was learning.

Her heart tripped as she closed the space between them. When she stood near enough to feel his body heat, Cort lifted her hand to his lips. They felt dry and firm against her skin. Then he turned up her palm and nibbled on her wrist. Lexi shivered and he grinned.

Damn the man! She was doing her best to carry out this absurd charade—for his benefit—and at great cost to herself. Giving him her sweetest smile, she stiffened her fingers as she withdrew her hand. And clipped him on the chin. She dropped a curtsy as his teeth clacked together.

An approving roar swept the hall, making Lexi aware of the absolute silence since Cort's announcement. She watched a blush suffuse his face and took satisfaction in the knowledge that he despised his inability to control the reaction. And that he had no alternative but to smile and take her hand as she rose. Though he was gripping it rather harder than necessary.

"Long live our lord and his lady!" someone shouted above the din.

Cort's men echoed the words. Bouchard's appeared less than enthusiastic. Alain himself looked on the verge of apoplexy. Or murder.

Lexi flinched at the lethal glare he directed toward Cort. These two were not new acquaintances. Alain's eyes now glittered with seasoned, long-term enmity. As if she could somehow protect him, Lexi pressed herself to Cort's side. While his gaze never wavered from Bouchard's, his arm curled protectively about her waist.

Unable to bear the malice swirling between the pair, Lexi turned her attention to her cousin and uncle. Graham's smile appeared forced. Melissande looked ready to drop. Of course, they must be as shocked as she by Cort's declaration. Oh, Lord. Had both, she wondered, harbored a secret hope Cort might seek *her cousin's* hand?

As if he sensed her thoughts, Graham pivoted toward Lexi. With a brusque hand motion, she directed his notice to his daughter. Eyes glazed, her skin shone pale as milk.

Placing an arm about Melissande's shoulders, her father rallied. "A small feast! Come, daughter, let us prepare a celebration." Without further ado, he swept her from the hall.

Lexi thought to follow them, but Cort shot her a warning glance. His fingers bit into her waist when she tried to move away. Swallowing her frustration, she forced herself to relax against him.

It was going to be a long afternoon.

****

He'd taken a foolish gamble. One that could well have blown up in his face. *I'm an imbecile.*

If Guy's shadowed expression was any indication, Cort thought his friend read his mind. Again. And agreed.

Offering a placating smile and light shrug, he trusted Guy to await a more appropriate time for his explanation. If he could come up with one.

The vow that now bound him to Lexi had been impulsive, not logical. Graham's feast cornered him with his enemy. Not a situation he'd have chosen, but it might—

"Lord Bouchard knows him," Stefan gushed, leaning over Cort's shoulder to pour more wine. "The Golden Dragon."

"I expect he does." Cort turned with hard-won calm toward Bouchard, seated several places to his right. The man's frigid grin goaded him to pursue the subject. "Both fought at Hastings."

The grin melted from Alain's face. Cort tilted his head in a silent touché.

"Aye." Stefan's excitement blinded him to the men's tension. "I asked him if the Dragon is like Dane, but he said Dane doesn't have the..." He'd said too much. A flush swept his cheeks. Concern and dismay colored the gaze he darted between the two lords.

Dane, seated at the head of the trestle table just below the dais, looked up as if summoned.

Cort heard Stefan swallow, felt him step back. His gut tightened. He could well imagine the unkind comment his *guest* had made, and his expression soured as he turned a hard gaze on the bastard.

"I spoke the truth." Bouchard's hazel eyes mirrored the defiant set of his jaw. He cast Dane a scornful look. "The Dragon's reputation is much exaggerated. But even I must admit the man is not...stupid."

The insult to his friend slapped Cort with the force of a thrown gauntlet. His father's voice whispered through his mind. *Control.* But even that could not prevent demanding satisfaction of Bouchard. It was Lexi's distraught look, and her hand, firm and warm on his arm, that stopped him.

Dane's questioning gaze said he either had not heard or did not understand Bouchard's slur. Cort gentled his expression as he looked at the giant. Loud enough for everyone to hear, he answered Alain's cruel contempt with honest praise. "Every lord in this land envies me Dane's loyalty and courage. The king himself has said so."

A proud grin broke over Dane's face before he shyly dipped his head.

Cort's men whooped and applauded, leaving Bouchard no choice but retreat. Cort ignored him.

Sunset shadows flickered across the few die-hard revelers.

Most had already taken themselves off, heads aching and bellies full. Graham ordered their guests settled on pallets or blankets in the bailey. The spring evening waned cool and clear.

Cort shifted and rotated his shoulders, relieved to see an end to the festivities. And Lexi's animation. For the last few hours, she'd bubbled like a porridge pot. Suspecting she would wait until they were alone before she boiled over, he groaned.

Draped over his cup, face sullen, Bouchard refused to surrender the field despite several overt hints. Forced to suffer the man's presence, Cort decided he'd make use of it.

"Well," he said, drawing the gaze of everyone at the table, "rather an eventful day."

Guy drilled him with a do-tell look, but his silence said he would follow Cort's lead.

Lexi's old-gold eyes promised retribution for the understatement.

"Full of surprises," Bouchard muttered into his wine.

Lexi's anxious gaze darted between him and Cort, seeming to evaluate each in turn. Which made Cort wonder if her exuberance today had been an honest reaction to his on-the-spur announcement of their betrothal or an act to disguise her alarm. He found the latter possibility bothered him far more than the former.

Cort forced his mind from Lexi. "We've a mystery you may be able to help us solve, Bouchard."

"What's that?"

"The day my men and I arrived, just over a month ago, someone attacked us several leagues from here."

"I heard." Bouchard did not so much as flutter

an eyelash. Innocence? Cort wondered. Old news? Or first-hand knowledge?

This would have been easier were the man half-pickled, but drinking to excess seemed not to be among his failings. He returned Cort's stare with clear, hard eyes. When Stefan reached to refill his cup, Alain waved him away.

"Have you heard any rumors, then, speculation as to who might have been responsible? Though I may never be able to prove it, I prefer to know my enemies."

"As does anyone with sense." Bouchard's gaze flicked past Cort's shoulder to Lexi.

She stiffened, her arm brushing Cort's. He felt her shiver, gently squeezed her hand to soothe her, but his concentration remained on Bouchard.

"Is that a yes or a no? Have you or have you not heard aught?"

After a long silence, Alain shook his head. "Only that you escaped relatively unscathed. A pity," he added with a brittle smile.

Lexi jerked upright, her soft gasp stirring the hair against Cort's shoulder. Guy's growl prefaced violence. Cort waved him to silence. "Care to explain that?" he asked with studied calm.

"Of course." His smile patently false, Alain said, "Had you been killed, you'd not now be betrothed to Lady Alexis. She would be mine."

Cort ignored Lexi's unladylike sniff. His stomach churned at the thought of this man claiming her, laying hands on her, making love to her. The cruelty he would undoubtedly inflict. When Mimir returned Odin's eye!

"If for no other reason, then, I must be grateful for my life," Cort said through clenched teeth.

Rage sparked in Bouchard's eyes. At last, an honest emotion. Perhaps the bastard could manage two in a row—if he could be caught now, off balance.

"A slinger saved us that day. A man of uncommon aim."

Bullseye! For the briefest second, something dark moved in Bouchard's eyes. He knew something, despite his muttered denial of "I'd not heard that."

Satisfaction surged in Cort's gut. Then curdled as he caught Lexi's hunted look from the corner of his eye. The suspicions he had tried to suppress since their first meeting raised ugly heads, demanding answers.

In the same instant, Stefan tripped and stumbled into the wall behind the dais. Careful, coordinated Stefan.

"Damnation!" The wine ewer flew from his hands, bathing a section of the bench and floor blood red.

Unwelcome tightness banded Cort's chest. "Damnation, indeed," he whispered.

An hour later, Cort shot out of the chair in his chamber as if slung from a catapult. *"What?"*

Stefan stumbled backward, eyes wide with fright and confusion. "I never thought about it." He cleared his throat around a bobbing Adam's apple. "That you didn't know where Lord Bouchard lives. Maybe two leagues northeast, my lord. An easy hour's ride from here."

A hard hour's ride from the site of the ambush at a gallop, though the horses would be near dead at the end of it. Cort towered above his squire a moment longer, then sank once again into his chair. He laid his head against its back and closed his eyes.

The fire sputtered on the grate, tossing shards of light and darkness across his eyelids. His chamber was silent but for the sounds of Stefan's restless feet and Guy's harsh breathing.

"Is that important, my lord?" The boy's voice sounded small in the heavy stillness.

Cort opened his eyes and turned his head

toward Guy. Their gazes locked in mute understanding. As his squire again shuffled his feet, Cort turned back to him. The lad looked tense, uneasy. “Do you trust me, Stefan?”

“Aye, my lord,” he said at once.

“Do you fear me?”

A brief pause. “Aye. Somewhat.” Stefan’s gaze held Cort’s for a moment, then dropped to study his new leather shoes.

“Good,” Cort said softly. “Fear is a healthy thing if wisely used.”

“As you say, my lord,” Stefan agreed, though Cort didn’t think the boy had any idea what he meant. He hadn’t, either, at that age.

“It can keep you safe,” Cort explained. “Prevent you doing something dangerous or foolish.”

“Perhaps you should have this talk with my sister,” Stefan said with a sly smile.

Cort hid a wayward grin. “Aye.” He swallowed hard, all humor gone as he recalled Lexi’s strange behavior that day.

“But at the moment I am having it with you. Do you fear me enough—are you wise enough—not to lie to me?” Cort hoped so.

Stefan bobbed his head, though his silver eyes shimmered with anxiety. As if he guessed the next question, and dreaded it.

“You know something of the slinger.” Statement not question. “Is he a friend of yours?”

Cort watched Stefan struggle to maintain eye contact. “No, my lord,” he whispered.

“But you know him.”

“No, I-I’m not sure,” the boy said miserably.

Cort drew a deep breath and stood, deliberately too close. “Is he you?”

Stefan’s head jerked up, his expression stunned. “Me?” Startled laughter escaped him. He met Cort’s stare with honest disbelief. “I’m sorry, my lord. But I never thought you might think me the slinger. I've never touched a sling, I swear."

"Just a guess." Cort shrugged, dropped back into his chair. "You're about the right height, slender, light eyes."

"As are a number of young men here and in the area." Guy sat forward on the bench beside the hearth and spoke for the first time. "But you admit, lad, that you might know the slinger."

"Not really. Just what I heard about the attack, and other stories from the village boys. Several are good with the sling." Stefan's voice lowered. "But they don't know a name, only that it must be someone who lives nearby. No one's sure. The slinger comes and goes. Hasn't been seen since your attack, they say."

Cort growled in frustration, hands gripped between his spread knees.

"If that's all, my lord?"

"Aye, lad. It's been a long day. Get some rest."

"Good night, then, my lord. Sir Guy." With a respectful nod, he left Cort's chamber, closing the door behind him.

"We've much to talk about, Guy. My betrothal. Bouchard." Cort grimaced and rubbed his temples. "I swear I'll explain all to you—on the morrow. I haven't the stamina tonight."

His second-in-command stood and stretched, then placed a heavy hand on Cort's shoulder. "Tomorrow, then." He turned to go, turned back. "Bouchard's estate little more than a stone's throw from here. How convenient. At a gallop... Do you think—?"

"You're the mind reader."

"It's good for your ego."

Guy read Cort's curious expression. "Two great minds share a common conclusion," he explained. His forced smile vanished as he added, "The conclusion being, we've likely found the head of the snake."

"It is his style." Cort's fingers curled into his palms. "Now, we need only to prove it."

Chapter Fourteen

"I want it. Now. All of it."

Lexi whirled on him, hands on hips, eyes snapping. "All of what?"

Cort stifled a groan. He thought he'd struck just the right balance between intimidation and wounded pride. It had taken the boiling porridge pot less than a second to dismantle that hope. Perhaps he'd been unwise to give her the night in which to simmer. "The truth," he barked, struggling to maintain the upper hand.

"About?" Her voice was soft, more wary than angry.

"Bouchard. Your good friend." Sickness churned in his gut.

Some of the tension seeped from her, as if she were relieved by the question. She clasped her hands at her waist and tilted her head to study him. "There's not much to tell, my lord."

The solar's tapestries whispered against the walls.

Use my name, he thought. *Cort*. "After two years of *friendship*? When he came here yesterday with the intent to court you?" Sarcasm would not help his cause, but he seemed unable to control it.

"Do you want the truth or not?" So much for her softness.

Holding Lexi's gaze with his own, Cort inclined his head.

"Two years ago, shortly after I came here, the king awarded Alain an estate north of Avon—pardon, Amiton. East of the river, He named it

Paix."

Paix. Peace. Cort grimaced at the combined irony of the name and the fact that the Conqueror had rewarded Bouchard for his services. If he only knew.

"Go on," Cort said, realizing Lexi had paused.

"Since then Alain has visited every couple months or so. Been a friend to us here. We spent several days at *Paix* last Christmas season."

"Even Mellie the Mouse?"

"Who?"

"Your cousin, Mellie the..." Blood rushed to Cort's cheekbones, and he dipped his head. "Hmmph." He coughed. "It's how I think of her."

"But she's beautiful, my lord!"

Lexi seemed to have missed the point.

"Mayhap. Guy thinks so. But she cowers and squeaks when she sees me."

"No, she doesn't," Lexi protested, though her mouth fought a smile. "Does she really, my lord?"

If she called him *my lord* one more time...

"She does," Cort insisted. "I've tried to speak with her, to assure her she needn't be afraid of me, but she sidles away like a cornered rodent and runs for the nearest hole. Had she whiskers, they'd twitch."

"Cort!" But her indignation dissolved in full-blown laughter, which he joined, glad she had abandoned *my lord* for his name, wondering if she realized she had.

He did not wish to resume their discussion, knew he must. "Does she fear Bouchard, too?"

"I don't think so." The merriment in her eyes faded. "She's somewhat shy, but they seem to get on well enough." Her shoulder lifted in an elegant shrug. "He'd always been a gentleman. Until yesterday."

She hesitated, gaze sharp as she searched his

face. "You knew each other before. And you weren't friends."

Cort tensed, unsure how much to tell her. She still knew more than she'd admit about the ambush. He hadn't the vaguest idea how she felt about their precipitate betrothal. About Bouchard. About him.

"Truth?" Cort summoned a tight smile. He could offer her a piece of it. "We sailed together from St. Valery, landed at Pevensey, fought for the king at Hastings." He swallowed, memory riding him hard. "We had a falling out there, went our separate ways. Haven't seen each other since."

"You're not going to tell me what that *falling out* was, are you?"

He was tempted. She'd never know how much. Whatever her kind sentiments toward Bouchard, the truth of his actions at Hastings would shatter them. Cort could destroy the man with what he knew. But he didn't want Lexi on those terms. On any terms—except her own.

Her choice.

"No point dredging up the past. It's done. But Bouchard and I will never be friends."

Motioning Lexi to a cushioned stool, Cort sank onto the one beside it. "There's something—no, two things I need to ask, lady. I pray you, be honest with me."

Expression once more cautious, a stillness settled on her. Cort smoothed a hand over her hair, then took her slender hand, watched her eyes as he spoke. "Had you any idea Alain meant to offer for you?"

"None." Her answer was immediate, hushed but steady.

He nodded. "Will you swear to me Stefan was not the slinger who saved my men, saved me, the day we arrived here?"

"Stefan again?" She blinked. "Stefan, your

slinger?" Her breathy laugh surprised him. "He'd sooner touch a viper than a sling. A knight, he once told me, would not lower himself to use such a weapon. He's very conscious of that sort of thing, you know. The noble code."

Something eased within him at her banter, an instinct that she had not lied on either count. Yet he had mistaken neither her startlement nor Stefan's last night at mention of the slinger. "Whatever made you think the slinger might be my brother?" Lexi's eyes danced with golden humor.

"Just a guess," Cort allowed with a half grin, raising her palm to his mouth. "A foolish guess."

She dropped her gaze to her lap. "My lord—"

"Cort," he corrected.

She gave him a brief smile, seeming unsure how to continue. "Cort." The pulse point at the base of her throat beat fast. "I think...that is, I would also like the truth. About yester—"

Footsteps pounded in the hallway. A sharp knock rattled the door. Lexi's hand clutched Cort's as the door flew open. Stefan gripped its edge, flushed and panting, his expression desperate.

"You must come, my lord," he gasped. "A cave in. At the castle."

****

The palfrey's hooves skimmed the ground despite its double burden. Dress hiked to her knees, Lexi clung to Stefan, who urged the horse toward the castle site. A small group milled about the east wall as they approached, but Cort was not among them.

Out of sight, men's shouts and women's cries, punctuated by the grate of shovels and the crack of picks on stone, carried on the warm spring air. Skirting the knot of onlookers, Stefan pulled the mare to a halt and leaped down. His hard hands grasped Lexi's waist, and he lifted her easily to the ground. When had he grown so strong? she wondered.

"Careful! You'll make it worse." Guy's voice.

Where was Cort? Lexi fought back the panic with every prayer she knew. Turning from her brother, she pushed through the line of men gathered along the north wall of the castle. And stepped into a nightmare.

Grit and rock dust all but obscured the sweaty men laboring atop a mountain of rubble. Shocked, Lexi guessed that almost a quarter of the north wall had collapsed. Judging by what remained, she could only be grateful it had not been more than six feet high.

"Move back! Everyone! Move!" Cort's voice, from the other side of the wall.

Lexi's knees nearly buckled with relief. *Thank you, God.*

The crowd scrambled backward. Behind the rubble, men grunted and cursed, wood groaned. A huge chunk of mortared stone reared up and crashed to the ground, bounced once, and settled scarce feet from the onlookers.

"Christ's bones." The man beside Lexi passed an unsteady hand over his face.

Heart racing, she returned her gaze to the ravaged wall.

Hands pressed to a huge split log, Dane appeared, visible from the waist up. Beside him, Cort said something Lexi couldn't hear. The giant nodded and flexed his massive shoulders. Cort bent down out of view and shouted, "Now!"

Dane's chest heaved as he bore down upon the end of the log. His arm and shoulder muscles swelled; his face purpled with strain. A great roar exploded from his throat as another section of rock broke free and tumbled to the ground.

"*Jesu* be praised!" Cort's exultant bellow was almost drowned in the screech of wood. A moment later he hefted a large timber and tossed it behind him. Sweat poured down his dirt-streaked face and chest, but the smile he shared with Dane glowed rich with satisfaction.

"We've got him!" Guy's head and shoulders appeared, his grin every bit as brilliant as his friends'.

"Gott im Himmel!" Disembodied hands lifted Karl Demming into view. Several men rushed forward to take him from his rescuers, ignoring his foreign curses as they reached over the jumble of stone and carried him to safety.

A touch on Lexi's arm diverted her attention from the stonemason. "Here." Stefan pressed her medicinal pouch into her hands. "You'll need this."

"And your help, brother."

With a hand on her elbow, he escorted her to Demming's side.

****

Dornogard was not about to give up, blast him.

But they'd done it! Against all odds, it had worked.

Hours had dragged by, yet organized crews still labored, spelling each other at regular intervals. Three men besides the stonemason had already been pulled from the wreckage. One to go.

Lexi, that traitor bitch, had set Demming's broken leg and ministered to the others' injuries, though one man had died just moments ago. Unfortunate. But the man had only been a common laborer, after all. An insignificant loss.

Dornogard's expression during his brief respites made it clear he was troubled. Poor man. Hah!

At present he sat off to the side, arm lax on a bent knee as he conversed with that ox, Dane. A shout brought his head around.

Guy Falcon, as filthy as the rest of them, raced toward him. With an angry gesture, Falcon threw something dark and misshapen on the ground beside his lord.

Dornogard picked it up, turned it in his hand. His face darkened with fury. Oh, to be closer. To hear what they said. No, too great a risk.

Dornogard surged to his feet. Yes! Come to me.

Carelessly retying his sweat-soaked hair with a leather thong, he strode without notice near those who had come to assist or to observe the rescue attempt.

"...whose presence would not be suspect!" he bellowed. Then, voice tempered, "Someone who saw the plans or has worked on the tunnels. Who knew precisely which timbers to burn."

He stopped dead, fist knotted around what, at close range, proved to be a piece of charred wood. "Where's ever-critical Donald?"

Guy turned toward his friend and shook his head, eyes bleak. "He's the one still buried in the tunnel."

Dornogard groaned. His chin sank to his chest.

How touching.

A pity, though. Donald would have made a perfect scapegoat.

Scapegoat.

What an excellent idea.

And I know one who may serve us as well as Donald. Perhaps better.

Chapter Fifteen

"Bright, as well as big and handsome."

Caught off guard by Lexi's compliment as he entered the solar that evening, Cort blushed. Then realized she was speaking to Fen.

Sprawled docilely before her, head on paws, eyes beseeching, his favorite wolfhound gazed at her with rapt fascination. No, not at her. At Athene, who sat on her mistress' shoulder and regarded Fen with a dark, unblinking stare.

Handsome? Only Lexi would think Fen... Loki's balls! "Jealous of a dog," he muttered.

With a light touch, he closed the door behind him and moved slowly into the room.

"Join us, my—Cort."

My Cort. He rather liked the sound of that, though he knew 'twas not what she'd meant.

Lexi looked at him for the first time, her smile deepening as she took in his flushed skin and seemed to intuit its cause.

"Another misconstrued compliment?" At his perplexed expression, she explained, "That first day, when you thought I called you Adonis."

New heat rose to Cort's face.

She relented. Sort of. "Oh, all right. You may share Fen's tribute. I've already told you you're comely, so you may add big and bright."

"Lexi—"

"Don't scowl. After the last two days, I thought a bit of humor in order." She patted the floor, where she sat with her legs tucked to the side. "Sit. Be at ease."

"Thank you." He could imagine her saying the same thing to Fen. "I think." With a wry grin, he dropped beside her and scratched the rough fur atop the wolfhound's head. Fen groaned his appreciation but did not remove his gaze from Athene.

Raising her hand to the ferret and making a soft clicking sound with her tongue, Lexi coaxed Athene onto her palm. With light strokes and the tinkle of bells, she settled her pet in her lap.

Fen whined and began to edge backward. Cort grabbed his collar. "Stay!" The command, quiet but sharp, halted the wolfhound.

"You are used to being obeyed, aren't you?" Lexi teased.

To prove to himself he could control his surging blood when what he wanted so badly was to take her, then and there, and show her—and arrogance aside, he had no doubt he could—how willingly he could make her obey him, Cort gave her his best glare. She laughed and returned her attention to the animals.

"So, lady and gentleman, how shall we proceed?" She cocked her head and raised Athene to eye level. "I think 'tis your move, Athene. You did this poor fellow an injury yesterday, and it's up to you to make amends. He's really quite friendly, you know."

She ruffled the coarse fur behind Fen's ears. "Be nice. If you are kind, he will be kind in turn."

Placing a kiss on Athene's head, Lexi raised her gaze to Cort's. Understanding leapt between them, and he smiled gently.

He watched her throat convulse as she hurriedly shifted her eyes again to Athene. "Behave," she whispered as she turned the ferret toward Fen.

He whined and tried without success to sidle away. "Can dogs flinch? Mayhap I should introduce him to Mellie the Mouse." Unable to control the amusement in his voice, Cort kept a death grip on the wolfhound's collar.

A ghost of a smile touched Lexi's mouth. Rather than answer, she set Athene on the floor in front of the dog, maintaining a gentle hold on her.

Athene sank to her belly, eye to nose with Fen. Neither moved. After long moments the ferret pushed herself up, whiskers twitching as she sniffed the dog's muzzle. Next she nudged him with her nose and flicked his mouth with her tongue. Fen stiffened beneath Cort's hand, then made the most pitiful sound his master had ever heard.

Amusement and chagrin warring within him, he eyed the dog with disgust. "I think his big brown eyeballs just rolled back in his head," he muttered.

"He's frightened," Lexi excused Fen's cowardice. "The near loss of an eye cannot be a pleasant experience."

"No. But how stupid can he be not to realize he need only open his mouth and swallow her whole?"

Lexi crossed her eyes at him, and Cort released the laughter crowding his chest.

"Look at them," Cort said when he at last regained his voice. "Fen must weigh more than you. Athene can't be more than two pounds."

"But she's afraid of nothing."

"Like her mistress," Cort noted as the ferret rose on her rear legs, a delicate paw braced on Lexi's knee for balance.

Fen's ears flattened as though they'd been sewn to his head. When Athene opened her mouth and emitted one of those airy screeches, Cort thought the dog might have breathed his last.

"Ah, brave Fenris," he mocked. "Companion of the gods, terror of the hunt. Coward of the manor."

Fen ignored Cort, closed his eyes, and played dead.

Athene dropped to all fours, then poked about the dog's square snout and burrowed into his stiff fur like an inquisitive kitten. Claws extended, she pulled herself along the side of his jaw, twisting and turning at the pleasurable sensation of his wiry hair against her skin. When he did not object, she climbed atop his head.

She pushed her funny little face into each ear in turn, then began to clean them with her curling tongue. Beneath Cort's hand the wolfhound relaxed. "I think he's purring," he whispered to Lexi.

Athene kneaded Fen's scalp as she worked and darted an occasional look at her mistress. Lexi gave her approval with a tapered-finger caress along her pet's back and soft words for both animals.

When Athene at last finished her ministrations, Fen surged to his feet and stretched. Graceful as a dancer, Athene leaped to his back. He swung his head toward her and met her unblinking gaze. Then, as if it were the natural thing to do, the ferret flattened herself along Fen's spine. Regal as any king, he paraded about the room.

"Incredible," Cort gasped, and collapsed onto his side.

Arms twined about her waist, Lexi joined her laughter to his. "It's all a matter of trust," she said.

Their amusement died as though it had never been.

"Speaking of trust." Lexi pushed her hair over her shoulders. "I think you've earned Donald's."

"I've never seen such a filthy, happy face in my life." Cort pushed himself back to an upright position.

"Nor I," she agreed on a shallow breath. "Though unhurt but for scrapes and bruises, he must have been terrified we wouldn't find him in time."

Cort nodded, his mind elsewhere. Long moments passed in silence before he straightened his shoulders and looked at her. "I can't help thinking it's all connected. The ambush. Your attack. Today.

The wall can be repaired. But a man died." His eyes clouded with regret. "And it was no accident. Someone set a fire in the tunnel that weakened the shoring timbers."

Lexi's stark gaze pinned him. "What you aren't saying is that you think Alain might have something to do with it."

"Bright lady." He dragged his hands down his face. "I know you're friends, but I have good reason to believe he will hurt me if he must."

Lexi gasped, her hand pressed to her throat. "No."

"Yes. His presence here today when the mishap occurred smacks of more than coincidence. One more day before we're rid of him."

"He wasn't here when I was hit on the head." Lexi skirted his previous remark. "How could he have been responsible?"

"He's not the type to work alone. Someone on the estate no doubt keeps him informed."

Her brow creased. "Much as you dislike each other, I can't imagine Alain—"

"I can." His jaw hardened. "Still, it's speculation without proof."

"Well over a hundred strangers have arrived here in the past two weeks. Any one of them might be guilty."

"True." Cort flexed his hands. "Guy and I had the same thought. We can't watch everyone. But your attack happened over a month ago."

"This is all so confusing. Mayhap my attack is not connected with the other two."

With a bare inclination of his head, Cort said, "Mayhap. But I've good instincts, and they tell me there's a common bond somewhere." He paused, weighing his next words. "Will you help us find it, lady?"

She blinked. "That you trust me enough to ask,

twice in the same conversation, both humbles and awes me. Of course I'll help," she whispered, her hand cradling his cheek. "Though I don't know how, or where to begin."

Cort curled his fingers about hers where they rested against his face, then pressed a kiss into her palm. Her eyes fluttered closed.

"I suggest we begin with us," he murmured. "Shall we discuss our betrothal?"

****

On her bed that night, gazing wide-eyed at her chamber ceiling, Lexi's heart trembled at the dreamlike memory of that discussion.

"We cannot avoid it forever, I suppose."

She'd already had two more days than she'd hoped for. Two days to pretend he was hers. Would always be hers.

But she'd known the truth the moment she saw her uncle's face. In the second before he masked it with feigned bravado, his shocked expression, his disappointment? announced he knew nothing of a betrothal.

Marshalling her reserves as they sat before the fire, Lexi had pressed her fingers to Cort's lips and continued haltingly. "I understand. All I ask is that you let a reasonable amount of time pass before you sever our imaginary betrothal. 'Twould otherwise provide more grist for gossip than it undoubtedly will."

She couldn't look at him as she withdrew her touch. Her eyes would give away the yearning, the love.

Yes, I love him.

Cort's voice came to her from far away. "Imaginary?"

God! Why didn't he just go?

"Lexi?"

"It's all right," she said, proud of her cool tone as

she forced her gaze to his. "I've had time to think about it, and now that I know how you feel about Alain...I believe your gesture was motivated by respect for me, and I appreciate that."

"Respect?"

Why did he keep repeating her words? And why must he look at her as if she'd grown a horn in the middle of her forehead?

"I'm a logical woman, Cort. You're an intelligent man. With my ties to and knowledge of Avonly, you can't want me married to your enemy. A feigned troth to me was the quickest, surest way to thwart Alain. As I said, I understand."

"You are, upon my soul, the most exasperating woman I've ever known."

What did that have to do with anything? Lexi blinked, confused.

"Are you always practical?" he asked, his voice gruff.

"I try to be."

"Why?"

"Why what?"

"Do you try always to be practical!" Cort's voice sounded strangled.

She shrugged. "It's my way."

"Were you practical as a child, too? While the other children played and ran, did you collect and distill herbs? As you grew older and those around you learned to dance and flirt, did you closet yourself with Arabic and Greek treatises on the medicinal arts? Did you have any friends?"

Stung by his mockery, she snapped, "Of course I had friends. And ran and played and learned to dance."

"But not to flirt?" he goaded, leaning toward her.

"I was never much good at it," she admitted stiffly. "I was always taller than the boys, and unattractive."

A choking sound escaped Cort as he stared at her, his eyes an opaque turquoise. "Unattractive?" He sounded bewildered. Then his voice drizzled over her like warm honey. "You aren't taller than I. But then, I'm not a boy."

"That's true," Lexi said around the lump in her throat. "However, it's a moot point." Then with false brightness, added, "Back to practical matters. We were discussing how best to end this betrothal-that-never-was."

"Were we?" Cort asked in a silky voice.

"Of course. You brought it up, remember?"

And I wish to Aphrodite you'd finish it!

"What I remember..." He held her gaze with eyes gone dark. "Is how you taste. And feel. How you make *me* feel."

He gave her no time to respond, but pushed to his knees and drew her against him even as he spoke. "You, like honeyed wine and silk roses." He sipped at her mouth while he gathered her hair in his fists and drew it to his throat. "I, like a drowning man who craves one precious drop of water."

Logical Lexi drifted away beneath the pleasurable onslaught of his hands and mouth. Cort's Lexi bid her a fond *adieu*.

When his lips strayed from hers to nuzzle a breast through her thin wool tunic, she moaned and pressed his head to her aching flesh. When his tongue laved her there, she arched against him. When his fingers constricted over her hips and slid to her spine, she melted into the haven of his spread thighs.

Then his mouth skimmed her shoulder, nibbled the length of her throat, and claimed her seeking lips once again. She opened to him like the rose he'd named her. His rough-satin tongue thrust and withdrew in a primal rhythm she knew, yet had never known, promising delights she had never dreamed.

Mind hazy with desire, it took Lexi a moment to realize Cort had withdrawn his mouth. His heart beat fast and hard beneath her cheek as he pressed her head to his chest, his other arm crossed over her shoulder blades.

"Not again," she muttered, recalling their first kiss.

Strained laughter rumbled beneath her ear. "You can't be any sorrier than I am, lady. But 'tis time—"

"To stop. Yes, I know. I wish..." She could have bitten her tongue at the careless words.

"That we really were betrothed?" Cort guessed.

She tensed, pain and regret like needles beneath her skin.

"I wish you had more faith in me," he murmured, strong fingers lifting her chin, guiding her face up so that she looked at him.

Trembling, Lexi gazed into warm, translucent aqua eyes.

"You missed mass this morning," he chided.

Now that was germane to the conversation.

"Am I to be damned as well as foolish?" she asked, hoping her flippancy disguised her anguish.

"Not likely," he said, stroking her hair. "But attending might have eased your mind. At least, I hope it would have. The banns," he explained when she continued to stare at him, unspeaking. "They were read this morn."

Lexi's stomach dropped to her toes, then catapulted into her throat. "Banns," she whispered, still unsure she'd heard correctly.

Cort's smile was as tender as his kiss. "The king promised me freedom in the choice of a wife. I choose you."

"Do I have a choice?"

His startled expression told Lexi her response

was not what he'd expected. "Do you want one?" Cort asked at last, voice husky.

"What of my freedom?"

He stared at her, clearly perplexed.

"My freedom, Cort. How willing are you to allow me the privacy, the solitude I knew before you arrived here? No escort, no supervision." She kept her gaze trained on his.

He threw back his shoulders, expression uncompromising. "It's for your safety. You're a—"

"What?" She pulled back, hands fisted on her hips. "A woman? Why do you insist my gender implies fragile, weak-brained? Incompetent?"

Cort looked taken aback by the barrage of questions as much as her defiance. "I will not risk your safety to satisfy your desire for privacy."

"And I will not sacrifice the freedom I have known all my life just to please you." Lexi's heart beat a painful tattoo in her breast. She wanted this man with every breath she drew, every beat of her heart. But she could not live in a prison, however well intentioned. Her love for him warred with her love of life.

She swallowed hard and waited. The decision was his to make.

"I could force you to wed me," he said, voice deadly quiet.

"Would you?"

Clearly, again, it was not the response he'd expected. His eyes widened, then narrowed. Silence hung heavy between them. After a seeming eternity, his features relaxed somewhat. "No," he admitted, though his beautiful eyes were dark with sadness. "But neither can I allow you to roam about unguarded. At least until this threat is removed. Then, mayhap."

He was as stubborn as she in matters of import to him. An admirable—and annoying—trait. He was asking her to trust him. Freedom. Trust. Love. They tore at her, unyielding and yet demanding compromise.

"When the threat no longer exists, I will demand more than a *mayhap*," she warned. "I will not live my life as a caged bird."

His curt nod was as close to agreement as she'd get for now, Lexi supposed. She bit the inside of her cheek at his unyielding expression and withdrew from further argument. The time to press her point would come. And she would choose it. Wiser, for now, to let him look *after* her than to have him look too closely *at* her.

A resonant snore drew their attention to the far side of the room. Sprawled on his back, legs extended skyward, Fen shifted in his sleep. Beside his huge bulk, Athene cuddled like a trusting child.

Turning back toward Cort, Lexi admitted, "I'd forgotten about them. Amazing how Athene knew just what to do to reach him."

"Any time you'd like to follow her example." Cort's fallen-angel grin settled somewhere below her waistline. "I'm open to suggestions."

Chapter Sixteen

Voices. Where there should be no voices.

Dane froze. Listened. Sidled closer to the door from behind which they came.

A single sconce just inside the manor's rear entrance provided more shadow than light. He slipped into a patch of dense darkness and pressed his back to the wall. Still, only snippets of dialogue reached his straining ears. "...goat. It's perfect." A female voice, too hushed to recognize.

Dane smiled and relaxed his shoulders. With their guests preparing to depart and Avonly's people occupied with cleaning the hall and kitchen, perhaps he had happened upon a young peasant couple who saw the chance for a few minutes alone. "I don't... He won't believe... scape... No such...perfect...goat." A male voice.

Dane frowned. A perfect goat? He hadn't seen any goats since—a misty memory of craggy, snow-capped peaks drifted through his mind. Rugged mountains and lush evergreens. A waterfall thundering into a raging stream. He'd been a child.

He shook his head to dislodge the image and concentrated on the hushed tones behind the door. "...tell you it won't... She's not...choice. He already...fair idea. Find anoth...good scape..." The man again.

What scape? Escape? Landscape? Dane's head ached. He jolted at the sudden anger in the man's tone. Though he could not hear the words, he knew that voice! Bouchard.

The only man his lord had ever truly considered

an enemy. That he did not understand why made no difference. Enough that he was Lord Thor—no, Dorn. Musn't forget that, Dane reminded himself. Lord Dorn's enemy.

And Bouchard should be in the bailey with his men. They'd had an early supper so that he and his retinue could make the trip home before full dark. Why was he here, then, inside the manor? Who was he talking to?

The woman's voice, still too soft to be clear, sounded distressed. Familiar. But he couldn't place it.

"How could...to me?"

Dane sensed their conversation had changed direction. The woman sounded choked, near tears. "...reasons. He mustn't know...mean to me... Trust...best for...love me, don't...?" Bouchard's deep, soothing voice penetrated the wood beside Dane's ear.

The woman sobbed once before silence descended.

Foreboding rippled along Dane's spine. Though what he'd heard made little sense to him, mayhap his lord—and Guy—could decipher it. Perhaps it meant nothing. The girl might be a servant with a tendre for Bouchard, the *he* her father or brother. Her identity might help them piece it together.

With a start, Dane realized time had passed while he considered possibilities. He slipped down the hall and through the rear door, leaving it slightly ajar.

He squinted against bright sunlight as the evening breeze carried the distant clink of harness and male voices from the bailey, but a quick glance assured him he was alone. Moments later, he heard the creak of hinges as an inner door opened. The wall sconce fluttered in a sudden draft and threw writhing shadows across the passageway.

With a whispered swoosh of fine wool, a slender figure stepped into the hall. Dane blinked against the uncertain light, his eye pressed to the narrow crack between door and frame. The woman turned back in the semidarkness. Face obscured by the hood of her cloak, she lifted one pale hand in a brief farewell before she hurried away down the corridor.

Framed in the open doorway, Bouchard watched her go.

Dane sprinted for the kitchen and swung inside just as the man shoved through the rear portal as though he had every right to be where he didn't belong. A smug smile edged his hard mouth. Long, arrogant strides carried him around the side of the manor and out of sight.

Oblivious to the startled expressions of the cook and scullions behind him, Dane ground his forehead against the cool stone of the kitchen wall and welcomed the pain.

He had to be mistaken. A trick of the light. What he'd seen made less sense than what he'd heard. Or he imagined danger where none existed.

Yet Bouchard was his lord's enemy, his meeting with the lady obviously a secret. She'd been upset at the end, but she'd waved when she left him.

Confused, ravaged by doubt, Dane closed his eyes. Could still see Bouchard and her. But he'd been some distance away, the light dim, her face mostly hidden.

The only thing he knew for sure was that he could not tell his lord or Guy. Not yet. If he was wrong...

He moaned aloud at the certain pain he'd cause if his suspicions proved true. But he dared not accuse her of treason without proof.

Treason. A death sentence.

****

"You're sure?"

That he wanted Lexi? "Yes." Less sure that he could truly trust her.

"Then you at last believe you can trust her," Guy said with obvious satisfaction.

Cort glowered at his friend. "You're trespassing in my head again."

"Does that mean I'm right or wrong?"

"Do you have a preference?"

Guy dropped onto the bench he'd dragged up beside Cort's chair and fixed his lord with a harsh frown. Cort wondered if that was how he, himself, looked to Lexi when she frustrated him past endurance.

"Then I'm right."

"I didn't say that."

Guy appeared in danger of imminent explosion. "If it's not too much trouble, could you tell me what the hell you are saying?"

"I wish I knew." Cort rested his head against the back of the chair. A low fire burned merrily in the grate beside them, warding off the late spring morning chill. "God knows I want to trust her. She's given me no reason to do otherwise. Yet I keep seeing her reaction that first day, when I questioned how she knew what caused my injury." His eyes narrowed in memory.

"Did you touch her?"

"I grabbed her wrist. But I didn't hurt her."

"Lexi didn't know you then. You likely scared the hell out of her. Let it go," Guy advised.

"I can't." Cort groaned. "It haunts me."

"One startled response, which you probably misread, weighed against everything you've since learned of her? Is that fair, Cort? Let it go," Guy repeated, his tone cajoling.

"What of her obsession with freedom and privacy?" Cort sat forward, his gaze fixed on Guy's.

"She's an independent spirit, my friend. If you're

determined to have her, you'd best accept that." Guy chuckled as though looking forward to the future contretemps Lexi's self-reliance would cause.

"You would not be laughing if it were Melissande and you were in my shoes," Cort said.

Guy's eyes clouded; his shoulders slumped. "True," he agreed after a moment's pause. "Though there seems little likelihood of that."

Cort damned his careless remark. "Sorry," he said quietly, a consoling hand on his friend's knee. He'd been so caught up in his own problems, he'd failed to notice how things progressed between Guy and Melissande.

"It's all right." Guy's shrug was careless, though his eyes reflected loss. "I'm attracted to her, but I don't love her." In a weak attempt at humor, he added, "At least she talks to me."

"Then you're one step ahead of this horse," Cort said with a grin. "But that was your point, I assume?"

"And what was your point in publicly announcing a betrothal to Lexi that didn't exist—at the time? Surely you could have denied Alain's suit some other way. If you don't trust her, what were you thinking?"

Amusement faded. "I wasn't. The words escaped before I realized I'd spoken. But I'm not sorry. I want her." His groin throbbed just thinking about Lexi. Earthy, ebony and gold, steeped in the scent of herbs and roses.

"So Alain just gave you a convenient incentive?"

Voice terse, Cort said, "He was the catalyst, not the motivation."

Guy held up his hands to let Cort know he understood the topic was closed.

Leaning back in his chair, Cort returned to their original subject. "We've been over this a hundred times, I know, but humor me once more. Since the collapse at the castle site, possibilities have been unraveling in my brain like twining threads. If we could grasp just *one* and pull it free."

Guy looked pained, but said gamely, "For you, one more time."

"We agree the tunnel mishap was not an accident."

Guy nodded.

"Bouchard's presence was more than coincidence."

"No doubt in my mind."

"He has the resources to have financed the ambush, and an estate close enough to Amiton to have served as a base before the attack and a refuge after."

"As well as good reason to fear you."

Cort's jaw muscles twitched at the memory of Hastings conjured by Guy's words. "Doesn't he realize that if I haven't said anything by now...? Damn fool. If we find proof he's involved in any of these *incidents*, he'll force my hand."

"If we're right, he's already tried to kill you once."

"And my men, who have nothing to do with our quarrel," Cort rasped, more angered by that than the possibility of his own death.

"He's not likely to play fair. Guard your back carefully, my friend."

"As always," he said with a tight smile. "But I'm not in the habit of fearing cowards. And I won't live my life worrying where the next attack might come from."

Guy shook his head. "Those words sound remarkably like your betrothed's. How can you fault her for her desire to live as you do, Cort?"

"Hanged with my own rope." Cort's gaze drifted to the fire.

"Speaking of which," Guy said, drawing his

friend's eyes back to his, "any new ideas about Lexi's attacker?"

Cort's fingers tunneled through his unbound hair. "None," he murmured. "You?"

Guy's expression mirrored his own frustration. "It could have been anyone in the manor that day. Not Stefan, of course. He's her brother and was still in the hall when it happened. Knights and men-at-arms, house carls, scullions. Too many to keep track of. Hell, even Melissande or Graham. In their rooms after the attack, but who knows where they were between then and the banquet."

Cort grunted his disbelief, lost in a mental maze that grew daily more complicated. In a bid for reassurance that his heart had not misled him, he asked, "You don't think Lexi's attack a blind, do you? A cover to make us think her a victim, when maybe...?" He could not bring himself to finish the thought.

Guy stared at Cort as if he'd lost his sanity. "That's the most ridiculous thing you've ever said."

Though hardly a compliment, the words relieved Cort, killing the doubts he'd not quite been able to destroy himself. "Thank you."

Guy's intelligent eyes glittered with understanding.

Needing to shake off the dark mood that had plagued him since yesterday, except for the time he'd spent with Lexi, Cort suggested, "Is it possible Lexi hit herself on the head?"

Guy's wry smile mirrored his own.

****

"You musn't worry," Lexi said, taking her cousin's small hand into her own.

"I guess." Mellisande gulped. "I'm so relieved he did not offer for me."

Lexi sighed. "*I'm* relieved you feel that way. I was afraid you'd hoped he would."

The girl's eyes widened in horror. "No. No. He's so...big."

"He is that," Lexi agreed, reveling in the reality. Recalling the heat, the hardness pressed against her. "But I believe Dornogard will be good to me."

"What of the rest of us?" Melissande's eyes rounded with anxiety.

In the week since Father David had read the marriage banns, Lexi had been too busy to give the girl more than a cursory thought. Determined to reassure her before another hectic day began, Lexi had followed her into the relative seclusion of the pantry.

"The rest of you? Look around, cousin. Look outside. In less than two months, the estate has grown into a small town. We're more prosperous now than we've ever been."

Lexi swept her arm toward shelves crammed with squat barrels of pickled eels, hogsheads of ale and wine, spice jars and butter tubs. Sacks of flour, barley, and onions rose to the ceiling.

"I don't deny the man's a workhorse, or organized and efficient. As you know, those are qualities I admire." Pain and something else moved in Melissande's eyes before she turned away to align several sealed jugs. "But he's claimed my home. Taken my father's place." Her shoulders heaved with low sobs.

Horrified at her insensitivity to her cousin's plight, Lexi took the girl into her arms. Melissande stiffened for a moment, then returned the embrace and wept like a child.

What could she say, Lexi wondered, to ease her cousin's loss? How would she feel if some stranger usurped her family home? Unhappy, angry.

Yet she was more practical than Melissande, and far stronger, she suspected. While she felt for her cousin, the greatest kindness she could offer was truth. "The spoils of war go to the victor," she murmured. "Amiton is luckier than most in its new master. He treats us well and fairly." Usually. "And your father seems not displeased. Though I think he wished Cort had chosen you."

"I know." Melissande's voice dropped to a whisper. "But Alain said Lord Dornogard is more than he appears. That there are things about him we don't know."

Lexi set the girl away from her, hands gripping her upper arms. "What things?" Lexi's heart pumped with anticipation.

"He didn't say, exactly. Something about his family. And what he did with the two men he took prisoner after the ambush."

Lexi dropped her arms to her sides and drew in a calming breath. Loyalty battered against suspicion as she sought to order her reaction to Mellie's words. She had no doubt Cort could be harsh when he felt it necessary. Or just when he felt like it. She grimaced at his despotic treatment of her.

And more than once she'd wondered about his family, his past. He never spoke of them, but she never spoke of hers, either. She must make it a point to ask him, to see how he responded. Their upcoming marriage would provide the perfect excuse.

That he and Alain were enemies stood as the one absolute. Cort had told her only his half of the story, and not much of that. Might he, rather than Alain, be the guilty party? Or did Alain attempt to sow seeds of unrest with vague innuendo?

Lexi couldn't think, not with Melissande watching her like a sharp-eyed robin. Not without time to find out what she could and evaluate it.

"I don't know whom to believe." Lexi rubbed her temples, admitting only to herself that she rather leaned toward Cort. "But when I've sorted it out, I'll share what I learn with you," she promised her cousin.

For the first time that morning, Melissande looked pleased. "If anyone can ferret out the truth, it's you," she said calmly, her tears apparently forgotten.

Lexi returned a wan smile. Whether the comment had been intended as a pun or not, it reminded her of Thene's mischievous nature and something she must do.

With a final reassurance to Melissande that all would be well, Lexi headed for her chamber. She had to *ferret out* Thene's newest hiding place if she meant to share her revised plans for the castle with Cort. Her sketch had disappeared.

Chapter Seventeen

"He doesn't love me," Lexi said with what she thought admirable nonchalance as she matched her step to Guy's the following morning. "But that's all right. We get on well enough together, and he's good for Amiton."

His gaze slid from her to the castle site across the meadow. "Give him time, lady. He has much on his mind." Guy's pained smile said he saw through her pretended indifference. "My lord likes and respects you, a better beginning than most marriages."

For a moment, she thought he meant to say more, but suspected Cort would not appreciate his interference. Instead, Guy fixed his attention on the cottage ahead and quickened his pace. Like Lexi, he appeared to have grown almost immune to the constant hum of activity in the fields and the more jarring cracks and thumps from the castle motte. This morning she welcomed their distraction.

Keeping pace with Guy's long, fluid stride, Lexi swept across the flowered meadow. Eyes half-closed, nostrils slightly flared, she absorbed the sights and smells around them. Beside her, Guy inhaled loudly, seeming to share her pleasure in the rich scents of new grass, gillyflowers, and fecund earth.

Until this moment, she'd never considered how much a creature of nature she was. But she loved the outdoors. Craved the caress of fresh air against her skin, the freedom to wander and absorb the sights and smells of each new day.

Though Cort's intent was to protect, not

imprison her, Lexi yearned for the independence and solitude she'd so taken for granted before his arrival. She would never be truly happy unless allowed to resume the unfettered life she'd lived before her attack. If she had a motive beyond that, well... Still, she enjoyed Guy and was not averse to his decision to accompany her to Demming's cottage this morning.

The stonemason reclined on a straw mattress in the shade before his home, his broken leg propped on a rough blanket. He waved as they approached, then pushed himself up on his elbows, attempting to sit.

"Lie down, sir," Lexi called. She hurried to his side and laid a restraining hand on his shoulder. "You know better than to stand on ceremony with me."

Her tart admonition drew a tight smile from the disgruntled man. "*Ja,*" he grumbled, "I know. Do not stand. Do not try to valk. Do not'ing. Be a slug. A wort'less...loot." He glowered at her.

Guy's mouth twitched when Lexi struggled to control her own mirth. "Lout, sir. A worthless lout. But you're no such thing. You must be patient, allow time—"

"Patient." Demming threw up his arms. "I haf no time for...dis." A broad, callused hand slapped his thigh above the wrapped splints. "Dey need me to show dem vat to do." He gestured toward the motte. "I vas not hired to lie here!"

Offering a sympathetic nod, Lexi knelt beside him and leaned over his broken leg. She cut through the top layer of bandages with her misericorde, then probed the limb with gentle fingers. With the exception of a brief grimace when she adjusted one of the slats beside his knee, Demming showed no signs of discomfort. Lexi sighed with obvious relief.

"Hal," she called, turning her head toward the cottage. "I need you." Instantly, a boy of nine or ten appeared in the doorway.

"Sir Guy," Lexi said by way of introduction, "this is Hal, one of Master Demming's apprentices." The boy bobbed his dark head to Guy. "He's caring for our patient until he can be trusted on his own."

Lexi's veiled warning and Demming's resentful glare stirred Guy to laughter. Wisely, he switched quickly to a cough.

"If you'll lift his leg just a little," she directed him, ignoring the stonemason's expression, "I'll remove these old bandages."

She gathered them in her hand as Guy knelt and did as requested, then looked toward Hal. "Bring me a bundle of fresh strips from the shelf, please."

The boy disappeared inside.

"You are doing very well, sir," Lexi said with grave satisfaction as she again focused on Demming. "And if you behave yourself," she whispered, "we may reach a compromise."

His eyes brightened with wary hope as Hal returned with the bandages. Lexi rewrapped his leg. Tying off the final strip of linen with a snug knot, she asked casually, "Now, what is so important at the castle that you feel you need to be there?"

"I must check ta construction of ta outer vall," he said, his face serious. "It must be built just so, in triple layers. An inner core of rough stone wit'in a t'ick shell of flint and rubble, an outer casing of chiseled stone."

"Ashlar," Lexi blurted.

Demming's eyes rounded in surprise at her knowledge.

"I read it on the plans Cort showed me," she said with some excitement. "I wondered if—"

"Vonder no more, my lady." Demming beamed at her, clearly delighted to discuss his craft. "Ta outer valls vill be several yards wide, proof against fire and all but ta most powerful var machines. My lord plans to slate ta roofs of ta buildings wit'in for ta same reasons, strengt' and resistance to fire."

"It's an expense Cort feels will pay for itself over time," Guy explained. "The extra cost now will limit future repairs and provide greater protection."

"I'm sure that's very wise, but I thought of some—"

"Ja, 'tis ta vise vay to build if one can afford it," Demming interrupted, seeming unaware of her frustration. "Your lord is a vise man."

When he winked at Lexi, she abandoned her attempted question with a graceful shrug and winked back.

"So, vhen can I go back to vork?" he asked, apparently hopeful she might weaken in this moment of accord.

"Don't think to cajole me, sir." But her smile belied her words. "Even before you winked at me, I'd planned to have you carried to the castle site. To watch," she qualified when he all but heaved himself off the mattress. "From a distance."

"Vatch!" Demming turned pleading eyes to Guy. "Who's in charge here?" he demanded, clearly hoping to rouse Guy's male pride.

"She is." Guy grinned. "At least until you're well."

"*Pferdsheiss*," Demming mumbled.

"Whatever that means, I'm sure it's not very nice," Lexi scolded. "However. Hal." She motioned the boy forward. "Go to the castle and have four men bring a small sled to carry your master to the site. I'll explain how they're to handle him."

"Yes, my lady." The boy's obvious relief before he raced away spoke volumes about how difficult a patient his master had been.

They spoke of progress in the town until the men arrived, dragging the sled behind them.

Lexi padded the leather bed stretched between stout poles with several blankets, then oversaw Demming's transport from the mattress to the sled. Hal produced two plump pillows from the cottage, which she told the men to prop behind the stonemason when they arrived at the site.

"Take your time," Lexi cautioned as they lifted the makeshift conveyance. "Try not to jostle him. And I don't care what he says," she added with fire in her eyes, "Master Demming is not to get up. For any reason. Nor is he to be placed in harm's way. If he argues with you," she said, her gaze on her patient, "you will bring him back here. At once. Lord Dornogard's orders."

Cort, of course, had ordered no such thing, and Guy's arched brow said he knew a blatant fib when he heard one. But he seemed to understand Lexi's reasons and did not contradict her.

"Perhaps your lord is not so vise after all," Demming muttered. "Vat a shrew. Poor man."

Lexi's laughter twined with the birdsong floating down from the trees as she waved the men off and started back toward the manor.

"What was it you wanted to ask Demming back there?" Guy spoke for the first time as they approached the wooden palisade.

Lexi stopped and tilted her head up at him. "You noticed? He didn't seem to."

"Too caught up in his own thoughts, I imagine. Is it a question I might answer?"

The fragrant breeze stirred her hair beneath its gossamer veil, catching sun-sparked glints as it fluttered over her sun-warmed cheeks. She brushed it back, again matching her stride to Guy's. The question she truly wanted answered was whether Cort would someday grow to love her—learn to trust her?

"Perhaps," Lexi said, forcing her thoughts back

to Guy's question. "But the night Cort showed me the plans, I made a sketch with some changes. He liked them. If I can find it." She shrugged, stymied by its disappearance, but not concerned. "Well, I suppose I can draw another if I must."

"You'd rather have his approval than mine," Guy guessed.

Heat flushed Lexi's cheeks, and he chuckled. "A perfect match," he said, shaking his head. "You blush almost as prettily as Cort does."

Lexi smacked his arm, and he laughed harder.

"That was a compliment, my lady," he advised with mock austerity. "I find a blush very human. And most endearing."

"That's me," she said with a droll smile, accepting the arm he offered as they strolled through the gate. "Sadly human, but endearing for all that."

****

She was with Guy.

That should have reassured Cort. It didn't.

From his chamber window, he watched them cross the meadow, pause outside the palisade, banter and laugh. And all he could think was that he, not Guy, should be with Lexi. Sharing her laughter, her smiles, her thoughts. Her touch.

He wasn't jealous, he told himself. Absurd to even think it. Guy was his best friend, Lexi his betrothed. And he didn't love her.

But he wanted her. As he had never wanted another woman.

Lust, pure and simple. Well, hardly pure or simple. He'd never experienced it before, not like this. Not so that he woke to it in the morning and suffered its torment into sleep. He'd always been able to control his physical desires. Until Lexi. Their first kiss, in her chamber, had enchanted him.

Their second and third had ensnared him.

Lexi's innocent but unfettered response had

been the most erotic experience of his life. Yet they'd barely begun when he'd forced himself to stop. Because he'd have taken her there, on the bed or the floor, without a qualm. And he wasn't proud of that. Still, even now he grew hard just thinking about it.

Oblivious to the noisy activity below, Cort watched Guy and Lexi enter the bailey and separate. His friend headed for the stables. Lexi disappeared around the side of the manor house.

But he had only to close his eyes to see her.

To remember how she felt. Lush, firm breasts pressed against his chest, heavy in his hands, soft beneath his mouth. Porcelain skin warm beneath his callused palms. Long, delicate bones and a slender frame that yielded readily to his hard strength. Hair of ebony silk that slid over his face and throat, sifted into clinging filaments between his fingers.

To remember how she tasted. Moist velvet lips tinged with honey. Tongue hot and slick as it tested his lips, darted in and out between them. Warm-silk throat, arched against his questing mouth. Nipples that hinted of musk and roses even through the fine wool of her tunic. And a taste that was uniquely, maddeningly Lexi.

Cort groaned and shifted his feet in an attempt to relieve the pressure in his groin. It didn't help. He'd been in a state of semi-arousal since yesterday eve, and his condition seemed unlikely to improve.

If he had any sense—which he apparently didn't—he'd grab the first willing wench he could find and slake his lust. He was lord here. He could do whatever he wanted.

He was lying to himself.

He didn't want just anyone. If he rutted with a hundred women, he would still ache. For Lexi.

"Damn her." Fists pressed to the sides of the window casement, Cort hung his head and breathed in the sweet morning air. But rather than the fragrance of freshly turned earth or yeasty bread, he smelled morning woodlands and honey. "Thor's hammer," he spat, the swelling in his chausses now painful. "I'll never last the two weeks until the wedding."

That he was still not positive he could trust Lexi no longer seemed to matter.

I'm losing my mind. But that no longer seemed to matter, either.

He wanted her. Craved her. Now.

Beneath him. Above him. On the floor.

In his bed.

****

"Is it my imagination, or has Dane been acting strangely?"

Guy turned in the direction of Cort's nod. Polishing the head of his flare-bladed ax, the blond giant sat alone beside the hearth in the great hall. His hands moved absently over the weapon, gaze distant and unfocused.

"I hadn't noticed, I've been so busy. But he does seem...preoccupied."

Cort frowned. "Withdrawn, almost. Like he used to be. Quiet and solitary. Something's wrong."

"Dane," Guy called. "Join us. We've all been so busy, we haven't had a chance to just sit and talk this past week."

If the man heard, he gave no sign.

"Dane." No response. "Dane!"

In the twilight flicker of firelight and wall sconces, every head in the room turned toward Cort and Guy, then toward Dane.

He remained oblivious to those around him.

Troubled, Cort swung his leg over the trestle bench and approached his friend. When he laid a hand on Dane's shoulder, the man jumped a foot, just managing to retain his hold on the ax as it slid toward the floor.

Startled blue eyes rose to meet Cort's concerned gaze. "Wh-what is it, my lord?"

"Are you well, Dane? We called you three times. Invited you to come sit with us. You didn't answer."

"Did you?" He sounded confused.

"Aye, we did." Cort dropped onto the bench beside the huge man. "Are you angry with me? With Guy? Has one of us somehow upset you?"

With a vigorous shake of his head, Dane said, "Nay, my l-lord. You've d-done naught."

"What is it, then?" Now that he thought about it, Dane had been acting strangely since Alain's departure. "Did Bouchard say something? Do something to you? You've not been yourself since he left."

Dane's gaze clouded, then shifted to the floor, but again he shook his head. "Nothing. I never sp-spoke with him."

"Dane?"

The man sat like a statue, his huge hands clenched about the haft of the lethal ax.

"Dane, look at me," Cort commanded softly.

With obvious reluctance, he raised his gaze to Cort's.

"Talk to me, my friend. If aught is wrong, I'd like to help."

"'Tis nothing." Dane straightened his shoulders. "Can I not...not have some t-time to myself, like other men? I...I am not a child. You do not b-badger the other men if they w-want time alone!"

Stunned by the outburst, Cort could think of naught to say. It had been almost eleven years since he'd found Dane in the woods on his parents' estate in Normandy. Beaten, half-starved, suffering from a severe head wound that had rendered him unconscious for nigh on a week, all he'd been able to say at first was "Dane." To this day Cort didn't know if that was his name, his nationality, or had something to do with the men responsible for his condition. But he had not objected when they called him Dane, and so the name had stuck.

Never in all those years, except in battle, had he been anything but kind. To Cort, ever respectful and loyal. Whatever had prompted this bizarre and uncharacteristic reaction to Cort's probing, Cort thought it best to leave him alone. Dane had a point. He was a man, not a child, and had a man's right to solitude. And to think through his own problems.

Torn between chagrin at his friend's unwillingness to share his troubles and pleasure at his show of spirited independence, Cort offered him a gentle smile and placed a hand on Dane's massive knee. "You're right. I've no call to interfere in your private life. But if you need someone to talk to, I'm here."

Dane's features contorted with regret and some darker emotion Cort could not identify. "I didn't m-mean—"

"Yes, you did." Cort rose. "And it's all right. Just don't forget what I said. I'm here. Anytime you want to talk, man to man."

"Thank y-you, my lord," Dane said with apparent relief.

"No thanks necessary. That's what friends are for."

True though that might be, it didn't make him feel any better. Dane was not one to keep secrets.

Dark premonition frissoned up Cort's spine.

Chapter Eighteen

Hair spilling over the floor beneath her bed, Lexi lifted her buttocks and rocked back on her hands. The sight almost dropped Cort to his knees. To imagine her thus was his fondest dream; to see her thus and be unable to have her, his worst nightmare. In what had become a habitual reaction of late, he leaned his head against the doorframe and closed his eyes.

When he reopened them, the view had not improved. Or improved too much, he thought with a tormented grimace. She'd levered herself back on her elbows to peer beneath the bed ropes, elevating her backside even more in the process.

Cort stifled a groan at the sudden heaviness in his groin, sure he was about to disgrace himself.

"Where could it have— Ouch!" The pained exclamation punctuated a sharp crack as Lexi's head connected with the bed frame. "Goat *gonos*." She rubbed her scalp as she sat back on her heels.

Amused by her rather inventive vulgarity, Cort released a bark of laughter and stepped into the room. She swiveled around with an injured expression.

"Your pardon," he managed, relieved that humor had somewhat allayed his passion. "I never heard that...phrase before. Are you all right?"

Delightful color rose in her cheeks as she touched tentative fingers to the bruised spot and winced. "Aye. My mother claims I inherited my father's thick Gaelic head."

It was the first reference she'd ever made to her

family. Cort thought now as good a time as any to indulge his curiosity. After he indulged his urge to tease. "Good thing, lady. You've certainly put it to the test several times these last two months."

Her tongue inched halfway between her teeth before she apparently reconsidered the gesture and withdrew it. Cort was tempted to tell her she was welcome to stick her tongue out anytime. As long as she used it on him. In any proper—or better yet, improper—way she chose. He shivered at the thought.

"Are you cold?" Lexi asked in her naiveté.

"Hardly." He had to force his voice through a throat grown noticeably thick.

She cast him a perplexed look, then rose and slapped the wrinkles from her sea-green tunic and ivory underblouse. "Did you want something, my lord?"

My poor, provocative innocent, you have no idea.

"Need I remind you again, it's Cort to you, lady, not my lord? Come here," he growled, forgetting for the moment his interest in her family.

Without demur she glided toward him, though her eyes reflected bewilderment at his tone. "Have I done someth—"

"No, but I hope you will." Cort swept her against him, uncaring that she must feel his arousal hard against her belly.

Lexi gazed up at him, translucent gold eyes startled. Then a shy smile started at the corner of her mouth and curved her full lower lip.

"What do you hope I will do?" she whispered.

"This." Making no attempt to disguise his desire, Cort took her mouth in a blatantly sexual kiss. Hungry, possessive, his lips flowed over Lexi's, demanding a response. But there was no need to demand. She yielded with exquisite sweetness, melding her generous mouth to his, then sought his liquid heat with every bit as much urgency as he did hers.

Her slender hands kneaded his shoulders, feathered up his neck, thrust into his hair, stripping away the leather thong that confined it. Loose strands teased his jaw, his cheekbones, drifted and held at the edges of their heated mouths.

Did she sense, he wondered, all that he offered, all that he was?

Muffled conversation from the hall below, distant jangling of harness and clank of swordplay from the bailey receded into oblivion. Cort knew nothing but the taste of her honeyed-almond mouth, the rose and woodland perfume of her incredible hair.

Well and truly lost. And glorying in every decadent moment.

The fingers of his right hand mapped the long line of her elegant back; the fingers of his left captured her jaw, pressing her head back against his shoulder. Sipping, nibbling, laving her now-swollen lips, he swallowed Lexi's pleasured sounds with his mouth. Moved on to her cheekbone, her temple, the porcelain perfection of her arched throat.

She whimpered as the arm that held her drew her into the cradle of his spread thighs. His fingertips roamed the taut fullness of a breast beneath her raised arm, descended along her ribs to her narrow waist, her buttocks. A soft cry broke from her, and Cort abandoned his exploration of the fragrant skin beneath her ear.

Raising his head, but as yet unwilling to face Lexi's distress, he kept his eyes closed and damned himself for a rutting boor. His mother would have his hide if she knew what he did to his intended. Young and untried, she deserved better. As amenable as she might be, she could not know where such love play would lead.

But he knew.

Reining in his desire, he at last gathered the courage to look at her. What he saw was not what he'd expected. Lexi met his gaze with dark, somnolent eyes, glazed with passion, not fear. Her fingers tangled in his hair, tugged his face down to hers. She whimpered again when he resisted.

Conscience fought desire, and lost, when she commanded in a fierce whisper, "Not again. Don't you dare tell me 'tis best we stop, Dornogard. Not this time."

His fate was sealed when she rotated her slender hips against the dire ache between his legs. A hoarse cry escaped him at the contact. He leaned into her lush, welcoming body.

Sliding his hand beneath her hair, Cort turned his wrist to wrap its wealth around his forearm. With unerring instinct, Lexi wound her arms around his waist and sought his needy mouth.

His tongue plunged and retreated in desperate imitation of what he yearned to do to her body. What he would do... He almost spent himself at the wave of heat that image evoked. What he would do if he didn't—

"Stop!"

At first he thought the command inside his own head.

"Stop! That's...that's enough!"

Enough? A lifetime with this siren would not be enough.

Sanity returned to him more quickly than it did to Lexi, who continued to cling to him like a limpet. Another enraged screech from the doorway jolted through him. He stiffened. Lexi sprang back as though bee-stung, her hair still twined about his arm, eyes dazed.

While he moved to block Lexi from view with his large body, he turned his head toward the unwelcome interruption and scowled.

"I...oh, I— My God," Melissande bleated, her normally blanched complexion almost purple with...what? Fury? Embarrassment?

Cort didn't know, didn't care. His only concern was Lexi and how she would respond to her cousin's horrified censure.

"Get out," he ordered, voice deadly quiet. "Get out now. And close the door."

Which he should have done when he entered the room, he realized now. But he hadn't planned to seduce Lexi, and then he'd become so absorbed in her, he'd forgotten it.

Cort wondered if Mellie the Mouse had any idea how much he wanted to throttle her. When he clenched his fists to suppress the urge, she jumped and fled.

Dreading Lexi's reaction, Cort forced himself to face her.

Head bowed, glossy strands of raven hair obscured her features and trailed over his arm and down her back. He drew her to him in wordless comfort, unsure what to say.

A fine tremor shook her shoulders, and he pressed his cheek to the crown of her head. "Don't cry, love," he implored. "You did nothing wrong. If anyone's to blame, 'tis me. She's just a jealous, nosy—"

"Mouse." Lexi choked on a laugh and lifted her face to his. Her eyes glittered with blatant amusement.

For the second time in a matter of minutes, surprise and relief spiraled through Cort. Rather than the guilty shame he had anticipated, Lexi gifted him with an insouciant smile.

"Don't apologize, Cort, please," she said, her expression all at once serious.

"I won't." His thumb grazed her cheek. "It would

be a lie."

Lexi set her hands on his shoulders and rose on tiptoe to kiss his chin. "I see now what you mean." She dipped her head toward the door. "Mellie does skitter when you speak to her." With a very Gaelic shrug, she added, "Prudy little mouse. Let her find her own cheese."

Laughter gusted from Cort's chest as he hugged Lexi to him.

Saved again.

****

"You think she's ready? Truly?"

"Aye, mistress. Follows the lure like an angel, she does." The falconer grinned at Lexi, then at the mottled peregrine balanced on his leather-strapped wrist. "Anxious to try her wings at the real thing, I'd wager."

Belled jesses seemed to tinkle the bird's agreement as it shifted from foot to foot on lethal talons. Lexi beamed with delight.

Three days of gusty rain had curtailed outdoor activity. But this morning's sun had already burned away much of the lingering mist over the fields, and the air blew sweet and cool against her cheeks.

"Shall we test her then, Daniel Hawkins?" Lexi asked the falconer before turning to Dane for confirmation. "May we? Please? It's such a lovely day."

No proof against her enthusiasm, Dane smiled. "I suppose. If we do not w-wander far."

"Oh, Grace," she cooed to the sharp-eyed peregrine. "We're going hunting!"

"You didn't."

Cort's deep, mocking voice spun Lexi around. Amid the shrieking chatter of the birds in the nearby mews, she had not heard him approach.

"Didn't what?" she challenged, fists on hips.

"Name her Grace." He eyed the bird.

"Why not, I'd like to know? She's beautiful, and graceful."

Cort dropped his forehead into his palm and groaned. "Of course. Athene for wisdom, Grace for graceful. And you ridicule my animals' names?"

He was right, of course. Not that she would admit it.

"You don't like her name?" Lexi neatly circumvented the question.

"It's not a matter of..." Raking his hair back from his face, he surrendered with a lopsided smile. "She's not a pet, lady. She's a bird of prey. You don't name—"

"Is there a law?"

"What?" Cort's eyes clouded with confusion.

"Is there a law against naming a hunting bird?" She enunciated each word as if he were a stubborn child.

Cort scowled. "No, there's no law."

"Then I can. Name her, I mean. Grace, meet Lord Dornogard." Smile impish, Lexi dropped her best curtsey. "My lord, Grace."

Cort relented with a hapless grin and tipped his head to the bird, which studied him with bright, dark eyes. "May I join you?" He kept his gaze on Grace as if asking her permission rather than Lexi's.

Dane, who watched their banter with undisguised interest, seemed to await a response as he turned his attention to the peregrine. When she cocked her head and sidestepped, setting the bells to jingling, he hooted with laughter.

"I think th-that's a yes, my lord."

"Let's go, then." Cort rubbed his hands together in anticipation of the hunt. "I'll see the horses saddled and meet you at the stables. Twenty minutes."

****

The men would hunt bear and stags come late

fall, wolves come winter. Now, in mid-May, boar, fox, pheasant, and deer were preferable targets. But theirs was a small party, more set on an outing than a serious hunt, and Cort had no intention of exposing Lexi to unnecessary danger.

"This is a trial excursion for Grace," he told her in no uncertain terms. "We'll but flush out some birds and see how she does."

"You'll get no argument from me, sir. Though I enjoy venison and boar steak, I have no desire to kill the creatures that provide them." Lexi guided her palfrey among the trees with an expert hand, eyes wide in the green coolness of the forest. "Besides, we're hardly equipped to deal with large game."

Cort glanced ahead to the falconer and Dane. Hawkins' only weapon was Grace, hooded to keep her calm as she rode perched on his gauntleted forearm. Dane's ever-present, flare-bladed ax hung suspended by a short thong from the left side of his wide leather belt; his sword scabbard bisected his broad back, the weapon's hilt jutting above his right shoulder.

"True," Cort said, feeling the pressure of the short bow wedged over his own shoulder, the weight of Deathwright against his right thigh. "No pikes or boar spears in sight. At this time of day near the river, there's little chance we'll need either."

"But if we should require additional protection, Fen will provide it. Right, boy?" Lexi asked the wolfhound trotting alongside his master.

With a resonant bark, the huge dog bounded ahead. When a chattering squirrel and flock of crows scattered at his approach, he stilled but for his proudly wagging tail.

"You can do better than that, Fen," Cort chided. "Grace needs a bird worthy of her station, not some flea-bitten old crow."

As if stung by his master's rebuke, the hound

bayed plaintively and set off in apparent search of more dignified fowl.

A bubbling freshet meandered through the woods beside them, its gurgle a cheery backdrop to the occasional quail's call of "bob white" and the more energetic warbles of thrush and starling. Damp moss blended its scent with the crisp tang of ash and oak. Pockets of wildflowers, crushed beneath the horses' hooves, offered up their own drugging sweetness.

Yet beneath it all Cort swore he smelled the seductive rose and honey of the woman who rode beside him. Eyes half closed, neck arched like a proud filly's, Lexi drank in the beauty of the day. Her dreamy smile reminded him of what Guy had said the afternoon he and she had visited Demming. "A creature of nature," his friend had called her. An apt description.

Clad in a hunter-green riding habit of heavy linen, which clung to her lithe frame and generous breasts, Lexi seemed a woodland fairy queen. Her raven hair was gathered into a snood of web-like cream threads, her slender hands and feet encased in matching leather. Even in the dappled light, her amber eyes glittered above cheeks flushed with pleasure. It struck Cort then that he had spent little time with her out of doors. Seeing her now, more beautiful and alive than she had ever looked before, he vowed to remedy that omission.

Better yet, he thought, head turned away to hide a secret smile, he would bring Lexi here after they were wed. And instruct her in the true meaning of *au natural*.

Lost in erotic possibilities, Cort did not immediately register the hiss of air that skimmed his right cheek. Lexi's shout snapped him back to his surroundings at the same moment a sizeable stone cracked against a tree inches from his head. Bark and grit showered his face.

Momentarily blinded, he jerked the reins. “Get down, Lexi! Down!”

Eyes streaming, Cort reached for her as he slid from his own mount. He blinked, attempting to focus on her wavering image. He could see enough, despite his blurred vision, to know she had not obeyed him. Crouched over the saddle, she jerked her horse’s head toward him, using herself and the animal as a shield. To protect him.

“Down!” he roared, lunging forward to drag her to the ground. “Get down, you little fool!”

With a wild grab at her sleeve, he yanked her sideways. She stiffened and screamed, then collapsed against his chest.

A metallic sweetness rushed into his nostrils.

He did not need to see. He could smell it. Feel it. The hand that clasped her to him was drenched with blood.

Chapter Nineteen

Christ's blood!

No. Lexi's blood. Warm and precious. Pouring through his fingers, down his arm beneath the loose cuff of his shirt. Dripping onto the vivid moss-and-grass carpet on which he knelt.

Whether he'd called to Dane and Hawkins, or they'd heard his previous shouts or Lexi's cry, Cort did not know. He had not heard them approach, but they were there, appearing as stricken and confused as he.

Dane's head snapped to the left at the distant sound of crackling brush. With a rage-filled glance at Lexi's inert body and a sharp nod to Cort, he swung his sturdy palfrey in the direction of the noise and spurred him forward. In seconds, his zigzag course carried him out of sight among the trees.

The falconer's horrified expression no doubt mirrored his own, Cort thought, then forced his gritty eyes to follow the path of Hawkins' stare. Cort's scarlet-stained sleeve and tunic blended with Lexi's now-drenched back and bodice. Blood pulsed thickly around the arrow shaft embedded above her right shoulder blade.

Though he had seen his share of wounds, the injured victim here was not a warrior. It was Lexi. Common sense said it made no difference. His heart disagreed.

Breath shuddered from his lungs. "Ride like hell, Hawkins. Tell Graham what's happened and that I'll bring my lady back as soon as I remove the arrow." He clenched his eyes at the necessary pain he must cause her.

Grace shrieked through her hood and hopped from side to side, her jesses' musical tinkle a mockery in this somber circumstance.

"Agitated by the scent of blood," Hawkins explained. "Easy, pretty girl. We're for home." He soothed the bird's ruffled feathers. "Can...can you do it yerself, milord?" He glanced quickly at the slanted arrow, then away. "I'll stay if y' need me."

"Dane will be back any moment," Cort assured, praying his confidence was not misplaced. "Go, Hawkins. Hurry." His voice was far steadier than his hands, which trembled at the prospect of what he must do.

Hawkins spun his mount and retraced the path they had traveled earlier.

Lexi moaned, the first sound she'd made since the attack.

"It's all right, wild rose. I'm here. I'm here," he murmured. If she heard, she gave no sign.

Dane's mount thundered back onto the track moments later and skidded to a halt. Dismounting before the horse had fully stopped, he gathered the reins in one large fist and looped them about a low-slung branch several yards from where Cort supported Lexi's crumpled form. For the first time, Cort noticed their mounts had wandered a short distance down the path, where they nibbled shoots of new grass.

He shot a vicious glance at the limp body slung in front of Dane's saddle. "Dead?"

The giant winced, clearly upset the man would be unable to provide answers. "I'm sorry, my l-lord. He turned at the l-last moment. Caught the edge of the blade, not the flat as I'd in-intended."

Cort nodded and levered himself away from Lexi. Carefully, he lowered her head and shoulders, face down, to his thigh. The arrowhead, dark with blood, had exited beneath her shoulder. A mercy, he knew. The thought of having to pull the barb backward to extricate it from her flesh made his stomach roil.

He looked up as Dane knelt beside him. "Just the one?"

"Only one I saw." Dane smoothed Lexi's dark crown. "A slinger. Still wearing the th-thong."

"The archer got away, then." Cold rage poured through Cort's veins. "Bastard," he hissed, gaze fixed on the arrow imbedded in Lexi's shoulder. "I'll find you, *canaille*. You're a dead man."

The silent woodland seemed to suspend its breath at the threat. The breeze stilled of a sudden. No bird sang. No creature moved.

He leaned forward and withdrew the misericorde from the sheath at Lexi's waist. The first, precise stroke slit her habit from wound to neck, the second from wound to shoulder. He peeled the wedge of fabric from her clammy skin, then sliced down the back of her dress and nudged aside the material bunched about the arrow shaft. The flesh was ragged and puffy, though the blood flow had decreased to a seep. "Bring the wine from the basket." Cort nodded toward the hamper strapped to the back of Lexi's hunter. They'd planned a picnic....

"The tablecloth, too," he called to Dane's broad back. "We can tear it up for wadding and bandages."

The giant returned at a run, setting the wine decanter aside as he dropped to his knees and ripped the sturdy linen cloth in two. One half he spread on the ground; the other he tore into strips and heaped on the clean square of fabric beside him.

The two men exchanged a hard glance. Then Cort unstoppered the wine jug and poured the burgundy liquid over his hands. "Guy told me the day we arrived of Lexi's obsession with clean hands." A bittersweet smile curved his mouth as he recalled his friend's recital of her treatment of Geoff. "She prefers wine to water, though I don't know why."

Dane gazed down at Lexi's still face, obscenely white against the deep gray of Cort's hosen. "When she's w-well, we must ask her," he whispered.

Cort gave a distracted nod and steeled himself for the first step in removing the arrow. His large hands felt clumsy as he gripped them close together around the thin shaft. He sucked in a deep breath. Exercising every ounce of self-control he possessed to keep them firm and steady, he snapped the ash in one quick motion.

Lexi's body jerked; a pained cry broke from her throat. Her lashes fluttered but did not open. Sweat sheened Cort's forehead and dripped down his temples as he hurled the fletched end of the shaft toward the trees.

At once, Dane sprang to his feet and ran to retrieve it. Cort blinked in confusion.

"The p-pattern of the feathers m-may lead us to the archer," Dane explained as he held up the piece of blood-stained, feathered wood and knelt once more beside Lexi. "Someone at Amiton may r-recognize it."

"Of course," Cort muttered, chagrined at his own stupidity. The one solid clue they had after almost two months, and he'd thrown it away. "Thank you, Dane. I'm not thinking."

"Our lady is hurt, my lord. You hurt f-for her," the giant stated with simple yet profound understanding.

"Yes, I do," Cort whispered. "We'll need that later." He glared at the offensive piece of evidence. "But for now, get the damn thing out of my sight."

Dane thrust the broken shaft into the back of his wide belt. Huge hands now planted on his knees, his patient expression said he awaited his lord's instructions.

"Move around by her head." When Dane had

done so, Cort continued, "Now hold her good shoulder and left upper arm as tight as you can."

Looking as if he feared he might crush her, Dane placed his hands as directed, then gradually firmed his grip.

Lexi's groan vibrated through Cort's thigh as she shifted, then opened eyes disoriented and dull with pain. "Cort." Her voice was a mere thread of sound.

"Yes, love, I'm here," he managed around the hard lump in his throat.

A grimace she'd probably meant as a smile tightened her mouth. "Too tall," she murmured.

Cort raised his eyes, not surprised to see his own bewilderment reflected in Dane's face. His friend sat back, his scarred hands relaxed on Lexi's arms as though reluctant to touch her now that she'd regained consciousness.

Able to make no sense of her remark, Cort attempted a wry smile when her gaze at last focused on him. "This is not the moment I would have chosen for you to awaken, wild rose."

"Pain," she rasped through dry lips. "My...shoulder."

"I know. But Dane is here, too, and together we'll help you." Strands of her lustrous hair had escaped their net, and he smoothed them away from her bloody shoulder.

"Dane." The name held a wealth of affection. "Where...?" Her torso stiffened as she tried to lever herself upright.

"Behind you, Lady Lex," Dane said softly, his blunt fingers pressed into her upper arms to hold her immobile. "You must n-not move."

She obeyed, and once more relaxed against his leg, repeated, "Too tall."

If she wouldn't cooperate by passing out again, Cort thought, perhaps he could distract her with conversation. Just for a moment, so she'd not see it coming and tighten her muscles in anticipation of the pain.

"What's too tall, my lady?" Though he spoke to Lexi, his gaze moved from Dane's face to his hands. At Cort's abrupt nod, his friend slid his fingers into position on her shoulder and upper arm and tensed.

Cort felt Dane's shudder ripple through his own arms and chest as Lexi mumbled, "Who, who," like a night owl. "You. Even off..." She made a small choking sound. "Off your horse, too tall. Easy target."

Her eyes drifted shut. Short, panting breaths parted her dry lips. Her face was blanched, her body limp, as if the short speech had exhausted her.

"So you became my human shield." He remembered thinking that at the time, did not now attempt to control the strangled guilt in his voice as he tipped her gently to her left side.

"My lord." Dane's urgent whisper snapped Cort back to what he must do.

"Couldn't let him." Lexi's words rustled from her throat like dead leaves.

Cort closed his eyes briefly. As his right hand pressed just below the entry wound in Lexi's back, his left gripped the arrow, which protruded from her upper chest.

Quick. Clean. Give me strength, he prayed.

A hard glance at Dane. "Forgive me, my brave girl," he whispered. The blond giant at once leaned forward, his considerable power braced against Cort's.

Cort ignored the sweat that soaked his shirt as he judged the angle, aware he must not bend or crack the shaft as he pulled it free. Now!

He yanked his left arm outward. Felt the pull of resisting muscle. Heard the obscene suction of wood through mangled flesh. Lexi's agonized scream as she jerked, then sagged like a discarded cloth doll. And the arrow came free.

Dane wadded two linen squares, doused them with wine, and pressed one to the hole in her back, the other to the exit wound in front. With a long strip, he secured them in place, then wrapped another over the first and tied it off at the shoulder.

"You're as p-pale as she, my lord," he noted when he'd finished. "I'll get the horses."

Numb with relief, Cort dried his sweaty palms on the ragged cloth Dane handed him, then swiped it over his face. Careful not to jostle Lexi, he turned her face-up across his lap. Sliding his arms beneath her, he rose slowly to his feet.

He did not recall mounting his horse, only the desperate refusal to let her go, even for a moment. She remained unconscious, for which he thanked God.

In scant minutes they were safe within the bailey. It had been the longest ride of his life.

****

"Cort." She surfaced by increments from dark-layered sleep. "Cort!" Lexi's throat and mouth were parched, and she feared her voice reverberated only in her head. But she must warn him! Protect him!

Her thoughts were muddied, jumbled. She felt disembodied, light enough to float, yet her limbs responded to her brain as though immersed in thick syrup. Drugged. She'd been drugged. Couldn't move. Couldn't help him. A hot tear seeped from the corner of her eye and dripped into her hair.

"Cort!" A mere croak, not the forceful scream she'd intended. With supreme effort, she raised her eyelids a fraction and flexed her fingers.

A strong, warm hand enveloped hers. Not Cort's. The crown of a dark head, bent over their twined fingers, came into view. Stefan.

"Hello," she whispered with a weak press of her

palm against his.

"You're awake." His voice sounded strained yet relieved as he lifted a misty silver gaze to Lexi's face. Fatigue shadowed the skin beneath his eyes, the hollows beneath his cheekbones.

When she attempted to lift her hand to touch his cheek, pain lanced from her shoulder to her breast. She gasped, confused as her eyes took in the bulky bandage under her nightdress. And then she remembered.

Panicked, she gasped, "Where is—"

"Don't move," Stefan ordered, reaching for the ewer of water on the bedside table. He poured half a cup and held it to her lips. "Take small sips, but drink it all."

She smiled at his concern—at least, she thought she did—then savored every drop of the tepid liquid. "More," she said, her voice a bit stronger.

When she'd finished the second cup, Stefan replaced it on the table and turned back to her. "Where is Lord Dornogard? I assume that's what you started to ask?"

Lexi nodded, uncaring that her heart was in her eyes and her brother no doubt saw it. Surely he would not tease if Cort was hurt.

"Right here," said a rich baritone from the doorway.

Whole and hearty and handsome as Apollo, Greek god of the sun. Or Balder the Beautiful, god of spring, sunlight, and joy. Yes, Balder. Huge and golden, most beloved of the Norse deities. Killed by Loki's treachery.

Premonitory chills racked Lexi's limbs, slithered through her stomach and twisted about her heart like insidious snakes. No! she vowed. Cort was not Balder. She would not let him die.

"You're cold." Cort drew the coverlet snug about her as Stefan stepped back and relinquished his place to his lord. "But awake at last, thank Odin."

He looked much as he had the day after she'd been hit on the head, Lexi thought. Features finely drawn, aqua eyes blurred with sleeplessness, wide mouth taut with concern. Less boyish, but no less appealing. "At last? How long have I been here?"

"Two days." He settled himself on the stool Stefan had vacated. "Dane treated your wound." His relieved gaze shifted to her bandaged shoulder. "You've taught him well, it seems. No more bleeding."

"He's an apt pupil. Absorbs what I say like an ocean sponge."

"I'll tell him," Cort promised. "He values your praise more than he does mine."

A warm flush stained her throat and cheeks, and Cort chuckled. But his expression sobered as he asked, "How much do you remember?"

There was no doubt to what he referred. Lexi closed her eyes, relived the scene. "A stone ricocheting off a tree near your head. The bark blinding you. A sharp pain, burning in my right shoulder." She opened heavy eyes. "That's all."

"And after?" he prodded.

"When you removed the arrow, you mean?"

His face blanched; a shiver passed through his shoulders. "I'm sorry," he whispered, gaze fixed on his tightly clasped hands. "I hurt you."

Ignoring the twinge of pain, she covered his fingers with her own. "You had no choice, my lord. I'm glad it was you, not someone else."

"I'm not," he mumbled with an arched eyebrow.

Lexi understood. She'd been in his place. "So, everyone else is fine?" she asked.

"Except the slinger. He's dead. As will be the archer when I find him."

His expression fierce and distant, Lexi prayed she would never be on the receiving end of his fury.

Surely not, even when she revealed—and she must, soon—the whole truth. Foolish fear.

She shook herself free of it as a wide yawn took her unaware.

"You must rest." Cort smoothed the hair from her temple with a tender hand. "Your poor body scarce has a chance to recover from one wound before it's dealt another."

"Mmmph," Lexi said in true Gaelic fashion. Eyes already closed, she murmured, "Never had that problem before..." Her voice trailed off, then resumed quietly. "Never fainted before, either."

She heard Cort rise, sensed him hovering over her. Warm lips brushed her forehead, her cheek, lingered for a moment on her mouth. "I'll be up later to see you. Sleep well, wild rose."

Wild rose, wild rose. He'd called her that in the forest. Dared she hope the pretty phrase more than an unconscious endearment? Acknowledgement, mayhap, of her need, her *right* to flourish untamed, unfettered? To fly.

But she did not fly safely home. Nightmare sucked her into a netherworld of distorted faces, voices familiar yet garbled. On the verge of recognition, they bled together like melting wax, warped and hideous.

Cort was gone. Lost to her. Lost.

Swirling mist tumbled and spun her into a void of formless menace.

Chapter Twenty

Lexi's parting words haunted him. Though he did not believe she'd intended them to replay in his head with damning frequency.

She'd never been attacked. Cort finished the thought she had not: before he'd arrived at Amiton.

He smashed the side of his fist into the wall at the foot of the stairs. A knot of serfs scattered and disappeared. Ignoring them, he began his slow ascent, aware only of the urgent need to unmask the perpetrator of the attacks. The same man, he had no doubt, who'd engineered, if not himself set, the fire in the castle tunnel. When the estate itself had been violated, Cort realized, he should have heeded the warning. Immediately.

Bouchard. He sensed it with that gut instinct that had saved his life on more than one occasion. How like the man to play sadistic games and enjoy others' pain in the process.

Alain had not been surprised to see him the day he'd come uninvited to Amiton, despite the last name Cort now used. He'd heard, probably through servants' gossip, of Cort's imminent arrival—surely with sufficient time to plan the ambush and recruit an informer. Though why that person, if that's who it had been, had attacked Lexi remained a mystery. And Bouchard's presence during the castle fire seemed far too coincidental. Last but not least, the man had motive: Cort could destroy him with a word.

And what of Graham? While he seemed generally amenable and helpful, he could not but wish Cort had chosen Melissande rather than Lexi. Numerous benefits would have flowed from the new overlord's marriage to his daughter, not the least of which would have been his heirs' inheritance of Amiton. Was the man's cooperation sincere, or sly deception?

Then there was Dane, whose withdrawal and now almost-constant guard of Lexi had originated with Bouchard's visit. Yet if Dane knew something, why remain silent?

Cort's mind spun with confused speculation—and frustration. He didn't have a shred of proof. As a last resort, he was tempted to tell the king of Bouchard's cowardice at Hastings. While it would be his word against Alain's, he didn't doubt the outcome. And if it came to a contest of arms to vindicate his honor, he would welcome it.

Still, this was a matter of pride as much as honor. Bouchard had made it personal. Cort knew he must remove the threat to Lexi, prove to himself and his enemy, if no one else, that he could protect her. The knowledge that Alain was undoubtedly laughing at him counted as but a minor annoyance, for he'd not be laughing long. While threats against himself he could handle, Cort would not allow his enemy to jeopardize Lexi's life.

The irony of the situation struck him as absurd. His reputation in battle was formidable, yet he seemed unable to guarantee the safety of his woman. His. Her bravery three days before made his heart swell with pride, then constrict with dread. He'd come so close to losing her.

Heavy treads on the landing scattered his musings and drew his gaze upward. Guy stood at the top of the spiral stairs, face creased in a smile when he caught sight of Cort. They'd not seen each other since breaking their fast that morning; it was now early afternoon.

"How fares your lady?" he asked as Cort stepped up beside him.

"Mending. If she weren't still weak from blood loss, I fear I'd have to threaten, again, to tie her down."

"Think you'd have any better luck this time than last?" Guy's mouth quirked.

"No, but I figure the odds are with me. Sooner or later, she'll have to obey something I say."

"Mayhap by the time that gold hair turns silver." His friend flicked the gilded ends from Cort's shoulder.

"I can only hope." Falcon fell into step beside him. "Were you looking for me?"

Guy's expression darkened. "The news isn't good. Dane hung the slinger's body outside the bailey wall yesterday as you instructed. The men gathered up everyone on the estate and paraded them by. Despite the reward offered, no one claims to know him. It's been two days now. If someone were going to come forward..."

Cort slipped the latch to his chamber and followed Guy inside. Raking his hair back from his face, he spat one harsh expletive after another, then kicked the door shut behind them.

"What of the arrow?" he demanded. "Each archer's fletching is unique."

"We're still checking with both our men and the new arrivals, though those who've lived here all their lives seem the most likely to recognize it." Guy hesitated, clearly unhappy with his next thought. "Of course, even if we find the man who made the arrow, there's no guarantee he's the one who loosed it."

"By Odin's ravens! Proof or no, you ken as well as I that Bouchard's behind this. After what happened to Lexi, I'm tempted to go after him and drag his balls up through his throat."

Hands shaking with cold rage, Cort lifted the wine jug from the table and poured two goblets. Guy raised his brow in question. "I know it's early," Cort growled. "But I'm in need at the moment."

"To the bastard's relocated balls," Guy said with aplomb as he took the proffered cup.

Cort drained his own in one long swallow.

****

"He's protective by nature, you know that," Guy grumbled an hour later, the depleted jug lying on its side near his foot. Apparently aware from Cort's mood that it promised to be a long afternoon, he'd stretched out on the hearthrug, hands behind his head, clearly mellowed by the third goblet of wine.

"Aye." Cort reclined on the bed in a position that mirrored Guy's. "No one is more loyal to those he cares for than Dane. Mayhap the fire at the castle made him nervous. And he knows I despise Bouchard, though not why. Now that we're betrothed, it would be like him to feel a special responsibility toward Lexi."

Cort felt too mellow himself to hide his dreamy smile. "She's been good for him, hasn't she?" he mused.

"Aye. Good for us all. I sometimes wonder how we did without her."

"We will not have to worry about doing without her." Cort jerked upright at the thought. His fingers clenched the edge of the mattress. Though his vision was somewhat blurred, his words came fierce and lucid. "He came too close, Guy. My luck cannot hold out forever."

"Luck?" Brows drawn together, Guy rolled to his side and propped his head on his hand. "It was luck that Lexi was shot rather than you?"

Cort shot him a you're-an-idiot look and shook his head. "Of course not, you dolt. I wish it had been me. I meant it was pure luck she was not fatally wounded."

"The archer lacked the *uncommon aim* of our mysterious slinger?"

"Not at all." Cort scowled, dark emotions swirling through his gut. "I was too caught up in Lexi at the time to think about it, but I realized later that if I...I hadn't grabbed her when I did and pulled her from her horse, that arrow would have taken her in the back. Perhaps punctured a lung." He shuddered. "Or caught her at the base of the neck." He swallowed the bile that threatened to choke him but was unable to obliterate the image.

"You were right behind her," Guy said, his voice hushed and thoughtful. "And the more likely target, I expect. If she hadn't moved in front of you..." He pushed himself up on his elbows. "With your height, the arrow might well have caught you in the upper chest or throat."

Cort nodded, then fell back onto the pillows.

Guy dropped back down and sucked in several deep breaths before he continued. "When the time comes, my lord," he said, his voice as stiff as his body, "take me with you to confront Bouchard. You are welcome to his privates. I want his head."

****

Not lost to her, she thought. Here. Cort perched on the edge of her bed like a golden bird of prey, one powerful thigh mere inches from her hip, the other leg extended to the floor for balance. Gentle turquoise eyes smiled at her sleepy expression. Warm knuckles caressed the hollow beneath her cheekbone.

Lexi closed her eyes to better absorb the delicious sensation, then turned her head toward the long, narrow casement. Weak sunlight drizzled like melted butter across the smooth wooden floor and brightened the wool rug's flowered border. Tiny particles danced like gilded fairy dust in the cool, fresh air that blew through the unshuttered opening.

"Good morn," she whispered.

"Is that a greeting or a guess at the time of day?" Cort asked lightly.

Lexi shifted her gaze to his amused countenance and smiled. "Both."

"Then good day to you, wild rose, and yes."

"I slept the day 'round again?" She frowned.

"Your body knows better than you what it needs. Your color is almost normal today."

"What did it resemble yesterday? A rotted fish belly?"

Cort chuckled, her tart reply seeming to assure him she was well on the mend. "Not quite that bad. But if you didn't look much improved this morning, Herr Demming suggested we feed you blood sausage."

"I've never felt better," Lexi blurted, determined to ignore the dull throb in her shoulder. She was, bless the saints, young, strong, and healthy. Time and Dane's excellent care of her would heal the wound. "Tell Herr Demming *danke,* but to stuff his saus—"

"Lexi." Cort drilled her with a warning glare.

All wide-eyed innocence, she said, "I only meant to suggest he stuff it down his own throat, not mine."

"I'm sure," he muttered reprovingly, though she saw his mouth twitch before he lowered his head and cleared his throat.

Lexi pressed her palms against the mattress to lever herself higher against the pillows and gasped. Tears of pain and frustration sprang to her eyes.

"Here, wild rose," Cort said, all sympathetic concern. "Let me help you." Big hands almost circling her waist, he gently lifted her and propped several pillows behind her back. "Better?"

She nodded and fought to keep her tears at bay.

"Did I hurt you?" Remorse glittered in his aqua

eyes.

"No," she whispered. "It's just so annoying. I'm not used to feeling helpless. And I hate being confined to bed."

Cort searched her face as though assessing the true state of her health. Apparently satisfied with what he found, a slow smile turned up the corners of his wide mouth. "Tyr could use some exercise. If I run him a bit, he'll be satisfied to walk later."

Confused by the seeming change of topic, Lexi canted her head in question.

"Give me three-quarters of an hour," he said. "To work off the worst of Tyr's energy and cool him down. Then I'll take you out for a bit of fresh air."

"Really?" Lexi made no attempt to conceal her delight.

"Really." Cort's gaze met hers, then drifted down to her mouth.

Lexi's lips tingled with remembered heat and moisture. Next to his eyes, she liked his mouth best. Though his hands were rather incredible, too, and his shoulders magnificent.

There isn't one inch of him I don't crave.

Leaning forward, Cort braced a hand on either side of her and brushed his lips over hers. She sighed and lifted her hand to the side of his throat. The pulse beneath her fingers beat strong and steady, the tendons like corded iron.

"Hmmm," she murmured as he sucked on her lower lip, then laved it with his tongue.

He groaned, withdrew from the kiss, and straightened. "I'll send one of the girls up to help you dress."

Most of the time she could handle her own toilette and refused to have a personal maid. She preferred her solitude. Now, until her wound healed, she had little choice. "Thank you," she murmured.

The backs of his fingers brushed the top of her

breast as he swept her hair back over her shoulder. She felt the contact all the way to her curling toes.

Cort slid off the bed and strode toward the door, turning back as he opened it. “We’ll stick to the open meadows. Still, I’d better invite Dane and Brian to go with us.” He wiggled his eyebrows suggestively. “I can’t trust myself alone with you.”

Though she forced a smile, Lexi knew better. Taking Dane and Brian with them had naught to do with Cort trusting himself, everything to do with protecting their backs.

Chapter Twenty-One

Tyr plodded across the open meadows with his double burden, pausing occasionally to crop what he seemed to consider a particularly tempting patch of grass. Supported by Cort's hard chest and arm, Lexi breathed in the promise of early summer. Primrose, goldenrod, and gillyflower rioted across the fields, their blended scents a heady perfume. The green-clothed branches of elm, oak, and alder swayed and dipped like elegant dancers in the fitful breeze. Meadowlarks and thrushes swooped among the trees, their melodic songs sweet and distinctive.

Beekeepers, busy with the inspection of their hives, hailed the small group as it passed and expressed their concern for Lexi's health. Everyone they met, whether cotter, villein, or knight, offered their lord and his soon-to-be lady a warm greeting. Lexi was more pleased for Cort than for herself. He'd accomplished so much, garnered such trust in the two months he'd been at Avonly. No, Amiton now, in truth. A good-sized, friendly village. With far-flung acres of wheat to be harvested come late summer, a thriving hillside vineyard, and communal vegetable plot.

Halting at the foot of the castle motte, Cort observed the construction with a critical eye. Within the low rings of mortared stone that would eventually form the inner and outer bailey walls, the keep had begun to take shape. Tawny gold in the rich, early-summer sun, Lexi imagined how impressive it would be when completed.

"It will be impregnable," she murmured, looking

up at Cort. "The progress you've made is amazing."

He snorted. "It will be another year and a half or more before it's done."

"But worth the wait," she guessed with an admiring glance in the rising donjon's direction.

"Aye," he agreed and tightened his arm around her.

She ached to pull his mouth down to hers, but resisted, unsure of his response to such a public display. Suddenly uncertain, Lexi dipped her head and fidgeted with the side lacings of her bliaut. "The night you showed me your renderings of the castle and I drew that one of my own," she said, voice strengthening as she gathered courage. "The one you saw. I wondered..." She glanced up to find Cort's gem-like eyes focused on her. "That is..." She stumbled to a halt beneath his perusal.

"You wondered." His encouraging smile bade her continue.

"It was just an idea. But you seemed to like it. Did you ever mention it to Herr Demming?"

"I did."

Discomfort heated her cheeks. "He scoffed, no doubt. Said it's impossible."

"No, actually." Cort tapped the tip of her nose. "Difficult and time-consuming, but not impossible. When we return to the manor, we can look at the sketch again if you're not too tired." He dropped a light kiss on her mouth. "There's more than enough time, though. We're months out from that section of the donjon."

"I can't find it. That's what I was searching for when you found me looking under the bed." Her blood hummed at memory of the heated kiss that followed. His huge, hard body molded to every inch of her own, soft and yielding. At where it might have led had Melissande not interrupted... She shook off the distracting image. "I left it on the table in my chamber, but it's gone. Thene's mischief, I expect." Her grin self-deprecating, she added, "At the very least, I would need to touch up the sketch, but I think Demming more likely to follow your suggestions."

For a moment Cort's expression closed, his eyes vacant as if his mind were far away. Then they filled with curiosity, and Lexi might almost have sworn she'd imagined his brief withdrawal. "Why?"

"Why what?"

"Why do you need to touch them up?"

She had not imagined his odd tone. Seeming to sense his master's tension, Tyr tossed his head, flaxen mane like rich buttermilk against the deep red coat. When he began to skitter sideways, Lexi felt Cort tighten his knees against the stallion's belly. Tyr immediately subsided.

Cort's face gave nothing away as she explained, "They were hastily done, and the light was poor. Also, and alas," she continued with dramatic honesty, her fingers caressing his strong jaw, "though it bruises my pride to admit it, my artistic skill does not begin to rival yours. But after I've had a chance to look at the sketch in daylight, I'll show it to you. When I find it."

Cort's abstracted nod tempted Lexi to tighten the hand that lay against his face. But before she could, he turned his head and pressed a soft kiss into her palm.

"I have to be better than you at some things." His intimate whisper blew warm across her wrist. "Besides, you show great promise at other, more important, skills."

****

"He didn't tell you?"

Lexi stared at her brother and thought she might be sick. The deepening shadows of dusk seemed to swirl around her, pressing her down beneath the mound of light covers. Only this afternoon he'd kissed her in this very bed, then taken her riding on Tyr, teased her, kissed her palm.

"Lexi, what's wrong?" Stefan bolted to his feet from where he'd been laying a fire in the hearth and hurried to her side.

"Nothing," she managed.

His expression said he didn't believe her. "You're being a goose," he chided.

"A goose?" Surely her brother knew, at least in general, how she felt about Cort.

"It's for your own good. He's only being considerate. You could at least appreciate that. Friday's wedding is off, and there's an end to it." The tilt of his chin was so painfully reminiscent of his lord's, Lexi groaned.

"The wedding is off," she whispered, feeling the outer darkness flow into her and burgeon like a night-blooming flower. *Off.* So that Stefan would not see the tears that flooded her eyes, she turned her face toward the window.

"What difference this Friday or the next?" a deep voice inquired from the doorway. "You need another week to heal and regain your strength."

Lexi's head whipped toward the open portal. Blinking furiously to contain the moisture that threatened to spill over her lower lids, she was at last able to focus on the imposing figure silhouetted there. Though unable to distinguish his features with the hall's dim light behind him, she at once recognized that voice, could not mistake the long, gilded hair or the ax-handle width of those shoulders.

"Cort." It was an almost breathless sigh, but he must have heard it, for he approached the bed with that sweet smile that never failed to curl around her heart.

Stefan's "My lord" reminded Lexi of his

presence. Before he could step away so Cort could sit beside her, Lexi fisted her left hand and slugged him in the arm. "Lout!" she accused, overriding his startled yowl. "You tell me half the story, then wonder why I..." But her relief was greater than her anger, and she shook her head at Stefan, then laughed softly. "Get out of here before I slap you inside out, little brother."

Assuming what little dignity he could beneath his lord's inquisitive eye, he bowed stiffly and strode from the room.

Cort retrieved a smoldering twig from the edge of the fire. Blowing on it until it burst into flame, he touched it to the beeswax taper on the bedside table. His shadow leaped across the wall, then followed him down as he settled on the mattress beside Lexi.

The candle's glow accented the hollows below his high, strong cheekbones and the firm, chiseled contours of his mouth. Golden lights sparked in his hair as he shrugged it behind his shoulders, were reflected in the depths of his clear aqua eyes.

For long moments, they simply stared at each other. Finally, voice soft, he asked, "Why would you think I'd cancel our wedding?"

Feeling shy and somewhat foolish, Lexi dropped her gaze. "I d-don't know," she stammered. "I'm not sure why you arranged it in the first place." She looked up, hoping for an answer, but his bland gaze told her nothing. "But when Stefan said..." Her fingers fidgeted with the bedclothes. "Well, I didn't know what to think." Her gaze strayed self-consciously to her bandaged shoulder. "I'll have a scar. It's healing well enough, but the skin there will be red for some time, and it will always be puckered and—"

"A wound taken in defense of me," Cort murmured. Lifting her chin with his finger, he brushed her lips with his, sank in for more. "A scar of honor. A reminder to me of your loyalty and courage." His mouth widened in a slow smile. "I'm giving you a weapon here, wild rose. Something to bludgeon me with if I become too... arrogant, was it? Stubborn? Unreasonable?"

Though she laughed at his teasing and squeezed his hand, her question was serious. "You aren't marrying me out of gratitude, I hope?"

"Hardly. Besides, you'd only been hit over the head then. It was after that you were skewered." In a flash, Cort's features turned fierce, slowly softened as he added with a wry smile, "I've more than my own share of scars, as you know."

"But you're a man, a knight. 'Tis expected."

"I suppose." He studied her in the flickering candlelight, his expression at once warm and serious. "Forget the scar, lady. You could never be anything but beautiful to me."

"Hah!" With a vehement shake of her head, she said, "I'm not—"

"Yes, you are." His mouth moved over hers in a slanting kiss. "Don't argue," he whispered against the corner of her now-moist lips, "with your lord and soon-to-be husband. Word is he's a stubborn ogre."

"Mmmm," she agreed, sinking her teeth lightly into his bottom lip. "Stubborn, arrogant. Delicious."

But rather than claim another kiss as she'd hoped, Cort pulled back and raked his hands through his loose hair. Lexi frowned. He frowned right back. "I'm already regretting my concern for your injury, lady. If I must wait another week for you, I'd prefer to make it as painless as possible."

When he shifted his long legs in discomfort, Lexi understood. "You don't have to wait," she murmured, eyes downcast, heart drumming. "I mean, no one would stop you. You have the legal right—"

"Damn legal right!" Cort gritted his teeth and drew a hissing breath. "Don't tempt me, lady. There is nothing I want more than to strip away your bed robe and gown and lose myself in the taste and feel of you. I dream of my mouth on you, my hands all over you, what it will be like to be buried in your wet heat."

Oh, Lord. At his words, moisture pooled between her legs. Her breath hitched. Her breasts tightened as desire swarmed in her blood.

"But I can wait. Will wait." He pressed taut fingers to his temples. "I'll not dishonor you that way. Or my mother. Not to mention she'd strip my hide if she ever learned of it. Which brings me to why I've come."

"Because of your mother?" Lexi's eyes widened. "She's here?" She tossed back the bedcovers. "I must—"

Hand on her good shoulder, Cort held her in place and pulled the blankets back up. "Relax. As far as I know, she's overseeing my father's estate in Normandy while he's in London with the king. But I thought you might tell me of your family, and I might tell you of mine." He raised his hands, palms up, in a Gallic gesture that lifted his shoulders. "It seems appropriate to know something of each other's family if we're to wed, don't you think?"

"I'd like that," she answered, canting her head. "More than once I've wondered about your parents, if you have brothers and sisters."

"Do I." He sighed, rolling his eyes skyward. "I'll stop when you tire of hearing about them. Or I hear you snoring. Whichever comes first."

Lexi grinned and settled back comfortably into the mounded pillows.

While her wounded shoulder ached from fits of uncontrollable laughter during Cort's sometimes rambling, interspersed with kisses, always humorous accounts of his boyhood adventures and sibling rivalries, Lexi discounted the pain. She could almost see him as he'd grown from child to youth to adult, could place him now within a family and better understand the man he had become. Neither tired nor bored, she delighted in his willingness to share his memories and obvious affection for his parents, brothers, and sisters.

"So, now you know what to expect." Stretching his arms above his head, he grimaced, then groaned with apparent relief as cramped muscles loosened and joints popped.

"Three brothers and three sisters," she said in wonder. "Let me see if I can recall their names. You're the eldest."

He nodded. "But don't worry about the order of the others."

She closed her eyes in concentration and ticked off the names on her fingers. "Etienne, Britta, Eric, Nicola. Ummm, Leif, and...one more girl." Lexi cracked open an eye. "A Norman-French name, right?"

Cort grinned. "Right."

Lexi screwed up her face and reviewed the list again in her head. "Julianna!"

"Well done, wild rose." He bent to kiss her forehead.

Lexi shifted, wincing as she attempted to ease the ache in her shoulder.

Cort frowned. "Are you all right?"

"Just a bit stiff."

"Should I call Dane to look at your wound?" His gaze shifted from her face to her shoulder as if checking for fresh blood.

"Nay." Lexi shook her head. "He was in before you came and will change the dressing again before he retires. There's no infection, and it itches like a bedbug's haven, so I know it's on the mend. The muscles will ache for some time. It's natural."

"As you say," he conceded, though his eyes

remained clouded. "Mayhap you should rest."

"Trying to worm your way out of hearing about my family?"

"Nay." Expression earnest, he took her hand. "But you must not overtax yourself. Our ride—"

"Wonderful and invigorating. Just what the healer ordered," she teased. "I've missed being outside more than anything."

"More than me?" His mouth smiled, but his eyes were serious.

"Never that," Lexi whispered, lifting his hand to her cheek. Yet even as she said the words, she doubted she could ever be happy, ever relinquish her freedom. Even for him.

She buried her qualms as Cort smoothed the hair from her temples. "All right, then. If you're sure."

Rubbing the pad of his thumb over her knuckles, which did nothing for her concentration, Cort again relaxed on the edge of the bed.

"My upbringing was tame compared with yours," she began. "Just Stefan and I. My father, who's Irish, inherited my mother's parents' estate in the North when they died. It's small, but lovely, and I grew up with far more freedom than I'd have had on a large estate or at court. Each day I roamed the hills and woods, and Stefan often trailed behind me. When he left to come here to serve Uncle Richard, it seemed odd to me at first to wander alone. But I've always been happy by myself, and I learned to value my solitude."

"I've noticed," Cort muttered, dark blond brow arched.

Lexi huffed but otherwise ignored the comment. "My mother's gift for healing appears to have passed down to me, as your father's artistic skill has to you. She taught me all she knew as I grew up. Before my parents sent me here."

She heard the wistfulness in her own voice and knew Cort had, too, when his hand stilled on hers. "They sent you from home? Why? How long ago?" His tone was as gentle as his touch.

"At the start of the Northern Rebellion two years ago. My mother is English, and her sentiments ran with the rebels. But both she and my father understood the futility of opposing the Conqueror. And they were right." Lexi sighed. "When they refused to take an active part in the uprising, they feared our English neighbors would consider them traitors. And there was always the chance that your Norman army would not believe them neutral in the struggle. So," she concluded with a fatalistic shrug, "they sent me here to Uncle Richard, out of harm's way."

Cort pulled a face at her, and Lexi surmised he shared her thoughts on the irony of that. Out of harm's way, indeed.

"Graham seems a good man," he said, though his brow furrowed.

Lexi soothed the lines with her fingers. "He is what he seems," she assured. "I love him dearly."

His nod of acceptance was not altogether convincing, but he said only, "And Stefan was already here, so you were together again."

Convinced Cort would come, in time, to recognize her uncle's true nature, she smiled at mention of Stefan. "I'd seen him but once a year since he left home at the age of seven. Now he's fourteen, almost grown. My parents miss him, I know."

"And you, also, no doubt."

"I hope so."

"As you miss them."

"Aye." For the second time that night, she closed her eyes against impending tears. "Perhaps they might come for a visit later this year?" Lexi opened her eyes and gazed hopefully at Cort.

"They will always be welcome at Amiton, love. You need not ask."

Love. She remembered now that through the haze of agony after she'd been arrow-shot, he'd called her love. Sweet yearning suffused her to make it so. To make him love her enough that she need keep no secrets from him. That he might come not only to accept who she was, all that she was, but to value it. Embrace it.

And he would, she vowed. In time. "Thank you." She lifted his hand to her lips and kissed his knuckles. "I shall write at once and invite them to come after the wheat is harvested. 'Twould be an ideal time."

"Whatever you wish." He sealed the vow with a hard, too-brief kiss and slid from the feather mattress.

"Now, 'tis time for a wild rose to rest." His arm about her waist, Cort eased Lexi under the covers and arranged several pillows beneath her head. "I'll send Dane to you," he said before claiming her mouth for a sweet, final kiss. "Sleep well."

"Friday next," she murmured, eyes closed, lips curved in a dreamy smile. "Then you'll not have to leave me."

"Shameless girl," he breathed against her ear.

"Do you mind?" Peering through one half-opened eye, she delighted in the eagerness in his dark aqua gaze.

"That you lust for me?" Cort asked with a sinful grin.

Blood rushed to Lexi's cheeks. His chuckle told her he saw it despite the guttering candlelight.

"You're a wicked man," she accused.

"You have no idea, sweetheart. But come Friday next, 'twill be my pleasure to show you."

Lexi's heart beat fast at the prospect. "I look

forward to it, my lord." She met his hungry look with a bold one of her own. "As a man of honor, I expect you to keep your word."

With a strangled laugh, he bowed from the waist. "I'll do my best, lady. Or my wicked worst. As you prefer."

Yawning hugely behind her hand, Lexi allowed her eyes to drift shut. "Hmmmm," she murmured. "Wicked would be nice."

Chapter Twenty-Two

"We've found him!" Expression triumphant, Guy slammed the broken arrow shaft onto the table at which Cort sat in the great hall. "One of the English archers recognized the fletching."

"He's sure?" Cort surged up from the trestle bench, both hot excitement and cold rage churning within him.

Guy nodded, then turned toward the archway. Cort had not noticed the figure standing there. Donald. The man-at-arms who'd harassed him at supper the day he'd arrived, the man whose life he'd saved after the cave-in at the castle, the man who'd avoided him ever since.

Cort motioned him forward, wondering at his hesitance. "Come here, Donald. What do you know of this?"

"I...that is, if I may say something first, my lord?" Posture rigid, he stopped several feet from Cort and cleared his throat, his gaze focused well to the right of Cort's shoulder.

"Relax, Donald," he said with a wry smile. "I haven't beheaded anyone all day."

The man's shoulders eased in response to the jest, and he at last shifted his eyes to Cort's face. "I owe you an apology, my lord, for my behavior the eve of your arrival here. And my thanks for helping dig me out of the tunnel. 'Tis long overdue, but I was too—"

"Apology and thanks accepted, Donald. I appreciate both. Now, what know you of the man who identified this arrow and the archer who made it?"

He appeared relieved at the interruption. "Our man, James Lang, is knowledgeable and honest. He'd not have spoken if he wasn't sure. Known the archer who made it for several years, so 'twas difficult for him to reveal."

"I understand," Cort said, tamping down his impatience. "Lang is trustworthy, and positive he's identified the right man. What else?"

"I'm not sure, even then, he'd have named the archer, 'cept the arrow was used against Lady Alexis. But he said he don't believe Hal Robbins would shoot a woman. 'Twas either an accident or someone else what loosed the arrow."

"Hal Robbins," Cort said softly. "In my experience, most archers make and use their own arrows. Why would someone else shoot his?"

"Lang don't know for sure, my lord. But Robbins has six children, and Lang says how he recalls the man often trades new shafts he's made for cloth or leather goods or food."

"It's possible." Guy's gaze shifted from Cort to Donald. "More than possible if he has that many mouths to feed."

"Aye," Cort agreed wearily. Though he could not refute the reasoning, it frustrated him to have found the source yet be unable to make use of the information.

"Or the arrow might have been stolen," Donald said. "A man what's willing to kill somebody ain't likely to quibble about bein' a thief."

"Damn!" Cort slammed his fist on the table. "If what Lang says of Robbins is true, 'tis not likely he's our man." Frustration knotted his muscles. "Unless he was forced to it."

Hands flattened on the table, he leaned across it. "What if his family was threatened? The safety of his wife and children? He might not commit murder to save himself, but to protect his family?" Eyes sharp with speculation, Cort regarded the two men before him.

"Every man has his price," Guy responded.

"Could be." Donald nodded. "I've heard his lord can be hard when he wants somethin'."

"His lord?" A headache brewing at the base of his skull, Cort pinned the man-at-arms with a hard stare. "Stupid of me not to have asked sooner. Let me guess." His breath hissed through clenched teeth. "Robbins is Bouchard's man."

"Aye, m'lord." Eyes wide, Donald bobbed his head. "Lord Bouchard's."

"May he roast in hell," Cort whispered, remembering Lexi pale and bleeding, hearing again her cry of agony as he'd pulled the arrow from her body. Knowing the pain she still suffered from the wound.

Shouts from the gate tower, echoed by excited cries from the bailey, shattered the vision. Guy and Donald turned toward the sounds. Cort rounded the table and bolted toward the doors. The two men pounded up behind him.

"What now?" he muttered, scowling as he brushed his hair back over his shoulders. "Everything at once."

Chaos reigned in the inner bailey. Knights and men-at-arms scurried in every direction, tripping over weapons and frantic squires. Serfs and peasants gathered in tight knots, their expressions a blend of awe and fear. Geese honked; chickens clucked and dashed about within their pens. Amid all the noise and confusion, it took Cort a moment to understand the tower guard's shouts.

He stopped dead, heart lodged in his throat. Guy bumped him from behind. Donald swerved just in time to avoid them both. Cort barely noticed. He closed his eyes and swallowed hard.

No. Not now. Not yet.

He'd meant to tell Lexi the truth this past week or more, but seemed unable to find the right words, the right time. A quick glance at the open doors and crowded courtyard confirmed she wasn't there. He prayed she would remain in her room, give him time to speak alone with—

Trumpets blared even as the manor gates swung wide. The ground beneath Cort's feet trembled with the rhythmic impact of the approaching troop, half a hundred horses strong. An occasional clink of metal and creak of leather was audible above the driving hoofbeats as the entourage gained the rise and thundered toward him.

A scarlet silk banner snapped crisply above the heads of the forward guard. Its gold-embroidered design reflected the light like a rippling sun. Twin lions *passant*, regal and erect.

The knights slowed their mounts to a canter as they breached the gates, then reined them to a stately walk. The odors of sweat and horse hung heavy in the air. Destriers and palfreys tossed their heads and snorted; harness jingled and saddles groaned. Then, for an instant, utter silence, as though all living things held a collective breath.

From the corner of his eye, Cort glimpsed movement within the manor's shadowed doorway. Hoping against hope, he angled his head just in time to see Dane lower Lexi from his arms to her feet. Damn!

Still, if he was careful, if he didn't say the wrong thing, he might yet salvage the situation. Might yet have a chance to tell her the truth in his own way. Pretending he had not seen her, he squared his shoulders and descended the steps.

All about him women curtsied and men dropped to their knees, heads bowed. Those who responded too slowly were shoved down by more quick-thinking neighbors. Cort's gaze scanned the front rank of horsemen and found the figure he sought. He sank to one knee as the man removed his helm and tossed it to the mounted knight beside him.

"Up, man. Get up." The deep voice boomed across the distance that separated them, rich with humor and affection.

"Welcome, sire," Cort said as he rose to his feet. "Though we are ill prepared to properly receive you. Had we known of your arrival—"

"What?" bellowed William, King of England. "And ruin the surprise?" His broad grin gave way to a hearty laugh.

Sweet Jesu, Cort thought. *I do hate surprises.*

But he smiled gamely and nodded to Guy, who, along with Sir Richard, at once moved toward the king's entourage to arrange billets and see to their comfort.

With the sun in his eyes, Cort could not see whether Dane and Lexi remained within the doorway. If he was lucky, she had returned to her chamber. If not, he might still manage a brief introduction and escape unscathed. Five minutes alone with his liege was all he needed.

"How could you think I would not come?" William asked as they mounted the stairs.

"You've much to do, sire. In the scheme of things, my marriage is surely of minor importance."

As they stepped from bright sunlight into the dim entryway, it took Cort several seconds to discover luck had not favored him. Face pale, eyes wide and dark as smoky topaz, Lexi leaned against the arch leading into the great hall, Dane beside her.

Before either could move, William the Conqueror blinked at Cort, clearly astonished. "Minor importance?" he demanded as though offended. "You're my oldest godson. And above and beyond that..."

Cort saw it coming. But there wasn't a thing he could do to stop it.

"You rank among my most valued knights."

Cort's breath snagged in his throat at the brief reprieve. He shook his head sharply to deter further speech. Either the king did not notice, or he chose to ignore the gesture.

His hand on Cort's shoulder, William chided, "Think you I would miss the wedding of my Golden Dragon?"

****

When Lexi'd had time to sort through the jumble of emotions that swamped her, what rose to the top most was an odd combination of awe and guilt. The Golden Dragon. A romantic, fantastical figure. Larger than life, indomitable, ruthless—whose reputation had been earned on the battlefields of England during the first months of the Conquest.

The legend inspired respect, and fear. The reality demanded bleak honesty.

Lexi stared at the ceiling with blind eyes, trying to equate the man she knew with the savage tales told of him. Unbidden, Cort's conversation with Stefan the night he'd shown her the castle plans surfaced in her mind. He'd scoffed at her brother's stories—called them exaggerated—said that heroes were more often made by chance than by design. He'd warned Stefan that all men were flesh and blood and prone to mistakes.

And he had been talking about himself.

But all the wisdom and humility in the world could not give back the lives he'd taken—English lives. Yet she believed to the marrow of her bones he was not brutal by nature. Rather, a warrior by profession, as befitted his rank, in a world where war seemed an inescapable evil. Would she condemn him for his extraordinary skills were he an English knight who'd killed scores of Normans? The answer was obvious.

She thought of all the good he'd done at Amiton. His work ethic, his sense of justice. His apparent affection for her. That he could be a fierce soldier did not make him an evil man. Look at Dane. Given the choice, she believed he preferred gentleness to cruelty. But reality demanded that he live in both worlds, be both builder and destroyer.

The irony tweaked her conscience, and Lexi sighed. She could not condemn him for the dual role the world forced him to play. She'd been gifted with the ability to heal, a skill she valued because it allowed her to help others. Yet circumstance and necessity, fate, perhaps, had forced her hand—and she, herself, had once chosen to kill. Thinking back to that pivotal moment, she could not be sorry.

A sharp rap on her door interrupted her musings. Before she had time to reply, the portal swung inward. Cort stepped slowly into the room, eyes guarded, and closed the door quietly behind him. Lexi watched him, unspeaking. Cort's gaze met hers for a long, uncomfortable moment, his body tensed as though for battle. She wondered if he expected her to physically assault him.

"I'm sorry." His voice was gruff, remorse as evident in the tone as in his bleak turquoise eyes.

"Hmmm." She would not allow him to see her surprise. A direct, simple apology, the last thing she'd expected from him. "Not as sorry as you'd be if I whipped something at that thick head of yours."

Cort's eyes widened, a clear indication he was unsure how to take her remark. Lexi wasn't sure how seriously she took it herself. The thought more than tempted. But she'd never been a throwing-things sort of person, and what she wanted now, most of all, was to have Cort explain himself. Be honest with her.

The moment it intruded, she cut off the thought that she had not been wholly honest with him, either. But that she felt justified in withholding information from him made her rather more willing to listen with an open mind.

"I half expected you to," he admitted with a sick smile. "Should I take it as a good sign that you haven't?"

"I'm not sure," Lexi admitted. "I suppose that will depend on why you've come and what you have to say."

Obviously relieved she had not condemned him out of hand, he took a tentative step toward the stool that sat beside the narrow casement window. He hadn't fully settled on it when he changed his mind and pushed himself to his feet. Restless steps carried him to the hearth, then back to her bedside. For a long time, he stood and stared at his boots.

"The words don't have to be pretty, my lord," Lexi murmured. "They just have to be true."

His troubled gaze at last rose to meet hers. "I'd meant to tell you, you know. Since our betrothal, I've thought to tell you a hundred times. But I couldn't seem to find the right moment. And the more I delayed, the more I feared your reaction. Then you were injured, and I didn't want to add..."

Cort closed his eyes, long fingers tunneling through his loose golden hair. "But I should have told you, whatever the consequences. I never meant you to find out this way."

"Something of a shock," she said. "The king must think me a featherhead, buckling at the knees as I did."

Cort shook his head. "Not at all. I didn't go into detail, but told him you'd been hurt in a hunting accident while protecting me. He was quite impressed, actually."

"I'll be satisfied if he doesn't think me foolish."

She paused. "But I don't really care about the king's opinion of me right now. I care about why you hid the truth from me. From everyone here." She flung her arm wide to encompass the entire estate.

Holding her gaze with his, he settled on the edge of the bed but did not touch her. "It seemed a good idea at the time. Now, I'm not so sure."

Uncertainty from this strong, confident man pierced her heart, but she needed to know the reason for his silence. "Go on."

Cort cleared his throat. "I heard enough stories about the Golden Dragon to know he could not be a popular figure among the English. Though I tried to counter the exaggerations—even denied some of the tales that were pure fabrication—my reputation grew. Absurd, but there seemed naught I could do to stop it."

Lexi nodded.

Clearly impatient with his own legend, he continued. "My own countrymen have encouraged the fantasy. To instill fear in your people, I suspect. And I must admit it worked well during the first months of the Conquest and while I supervised castle construction for the king. But now, on a more personal level, it's created more problems than solutions."

Cort cracked his knuckles and stretched his legs, brow furrowed in concentration. Lexi waited while he sorted out his thoughts.

Finally, gaze direct, he explained, "When I petitioned the king for Avonly, I feared the people would distrust me, hate me even, if they knew I was the Dragon. Before they ever had a chance to meet me, accept or reject me for myself, they'd have marked me as ruthless and conscienceless. I knew the transition from Graham's stewardship to mine would not be easy for most of them. Overt hostility and preconceived notions might have destroyed any possibility of my success here. I couldn't take that chance."

Understanding better than most the danger of taking chances, Lexi's heart softened further. "And then you were ambushed on your way here," she said quietly.

"You are a quick one," Cort approved. "The attack killed any doubts I might have had about disguising my identity. Until I knew the who and why of the attack, it seemed far from wise to admit the truth."

"But if the attackers had known, your reputation as the Golden Dragon might have prevented further trouble."

"Perhaps." His brow furrowed. "The other side of the coin, of course, is that the truth might have goaded them to try again, to prove I was not invincible. Unless our assailants already knew my identity, which I now suspect was the case." Expression dubious, he admitted, "I don't know."

"Nor do I," she admitted. "And I have to admire the way you've looked at the issue from both sides. Whatever other tales of you may have been exaggerated, 'tis clear you are an excellent strategist."

"You aren't angry?" Cort asked when Lexi offered nothing more. His eyes begged her forgiveness.

"For a brief time, I thought I was. But it was guilt."

"Guilt?" He cocked his head, gilded hair sliding forward over his chest, confusion evident in his aqua eyes.

"For caring about you as I do. Inflated or not, there must be some truth to your feats on the battlefield. You've killed more than your share of my countrymen."

Cort nodded agreement, though he did not seem

happy about it. "I expect that's so. But I took no joy in it. Being a knight is part of who I am. Not necessarily the better part, yet I will not apologize for doing it well."

"The world is a hard place." Unable to resist, Lexi sifted fingers through his thick golden hair. "I suppose we all must do things we'd rather not."

Taking Cort's hand, she studied the long, tapered fingers, then traced the callused palm.

"Most of all, I guess I was hurt," she said. "That you did not trust me enough to tell me the truth."

He winced, but did not look away from her. "I meant to."

"There is something else I would like to know." She shoved her own guilt aside, unable to resist the opportunity, hoping he'd answer to compensate for his subterfuge.

Encouraged by his wary nod, she asked, "Will you tell me the cause of the enmity between you and Alain? If I'm to be your wife, I would know why he is your enemy."

For several painful heartbeats, Lexi thought Cort would deny her. Then he exhaled loudly and said, "If you wish. But not now. The king wishes to meet you."

"Of course!" She'd almost forgotten about him.

"I'll send a maid to assist you if you say I'm forgiven." The corners of his mouth curved just slightly.

"You're forgiven. None of us is perfect, certainly not me." With a deliberately enigmatic smile, she added, "So who am I to throw stones?"

Chapter Twenty-Three

"I must tell them," Cort said when he came to escort Lexi to supper an hour later. "Tonight. Before Uncle Will blurts it out again."

She didn't pretend to misunderstand him. "I think that would be best." With a puzzled frown she asked, "Uncle Will?"

In the dim hallway, a blush crept up Cort's throat to color his cheeks. "That's what I call the king when we're alone or with family. He's my godfather, not my uncle, but he and my father are very close. Long before he fostered me or became King William, I knew him as Uncle Will."

"You fostered under the king?" she asked, impressed despite herself.

"Aye. From the time I was eight until I earned my spurs."

Lexi preceded Cort down the narrow stairs, determined to make a good impression after the afternoon's debacle. Dane, who'd carried her to her room when she'd almost collapsed, now stood beside the king at the hall's entrance. Beside the blond giant, William looked even shorter than his just-average height.

Lexi crossed the stone entryway and dipped into a floor-sweeping curtsy before him. "Your majesty. We are honored you've come for the wedding."

"The honor is mine." His tone as warm as his hand, he raised her to her feet.

"My betrothed, sire—Lady Alexis Fallon." Cort bowed.

The Conqueror studied her carefully before he

spoke. "Not only lovely, Lady Alexis, but brave, as well, I hear. My thanks for risking your life to save my Gol—godson," he corrected.

Cort must have warned him of the deception after Dane had taken her upstairs. While his bland expression revealed neither approval nor disapproval, he had obviously agreed to play along.

Still, he was a blunt man, and as Cort feared, had almost blurted out the truth.

Cort smiled at the king, then turned to Lexi. "She is a most unusual woman, sire. Much like your Matilda, if I may be so bold."

William raised an amused brow. "When have you not been bold and plain spoken?"

Cort winced, avoiding Lexi's eyes. The lie he had perpetrated since coming here weighed heavily on him, no doubt. As she had good cause to know, secrets made uncomfortable companions.

"You're a lucky man, then, sir," the king continued. "The queen sends her best. She is sorry to miss the wedding, but young Rufus is ill, and she would not leave him."

"Nothing serious, I hope?" Lexi asked.

"Just mild fever and a cough, but my lady is devoted to her children. She will not leave them in another's care when they are unwell." William's voice warmed with pride.

"Tell her I miss her, sire, and love her, as always," Cort said.

"Of course."

Like a true courtier, the king extended his arm to Lexi, and she laid her hand upon it. As he escorted her to the dais, she looked to her right and barely controlled the urge to laugh. Lined up like stair steps, tallest to shortest, were Dane, Cort, herself, and the king. Though regal in bearing, William the Conqueror was stocky. As he walked beside her, the crown of his head came even with her nose. If anyone else in the hall noted the disparity, he wisely kept it to himself.

The king took his proper place at the center of the high table, Cort and Lexi to his right, Guy and Dane to his left. Lexi smiled down the table at her uncle Richard and Melissande, both of whom looked sober and respectful. They nodded in unison. Then, her cousin signaled the squires to serve the wine, the scullions to distribute platters.

For Lexi, the meal was reminiscent of Cort's first evening at Avonly. Torches flared along the walls, their smoke drifting in lazy spirals among the rafters. Though close enough to summer that no fire blazed on the hearth, the clean scent of beeswax tapers permeated the air about the dais. Shadows leapt against the walls, and thick tapestries undulated like colorful waves, driven by the brisk evening breeze that wafted through the high, narrow windows.

But the knights and men-at-arms gathered tonight looked far more relaxed than they had been that evening over two months ago. Englishmen and Normans now sat together, conversed easily, shared cups and trenchers. An atmosphere of harmony rather than hostility reigned among them.

Lexi glanced over at Cort, wondering if his thoughts paralleled her own. Despite his satisfied smile, his eyes reflected the uncertainty he felt at what he must soon tell them. She took his callused hand and pressed it in silent encouragement.

As the meal drew to an end, Cort leaned close to the king and whispered something Lexi could not hear. Then he straightened his shoulders and rose to his full, commanding height. Those who had not noticed were elbowed by those who had, and within moments the hall fell silent.

"A toast to King William, who honors us with this visit," Cort began, his goblet raised. Several of the English appeared reticent, but all complied and drank. Cort lowered his cup with care as he looked out over the men seated at the tables below.

"I've something to say which should have been shared long since. The men I brought with me to Amiton have always known it, as has the king. Lady Alexis learned of it earlier today. 'Tis time you know as well. I can only hope you will understand why I have withheld this truth until now."

Puzzled faces and curious whispers greeted the statement. Cort held out his hands in an oddly vulnerable gesture. "I hope you have come to trust me. That you believe I care for you and this new town we are building together."

Enthusiastic cheers rocked the hall.

As quiet descended once more, he continued, "By wedding the lady Alexis, I commit myself to you as well as to her. Amiton is my home now, the most precious place in the world to me. As my lady is more precious to me than any other."

Lexi's eyes blurred with joyous tears as Cort turned to her. The hall erupted with earsplitting "Hear, hears," the slamming of dozens of tankards on scarred wooden planks, and the stomping of booted feet.

Once more Cort extended a hand for silence and faced the diners. "I do not apologize for who I am or what I have done in the service of my country. All soldiers understand what war demands of a man. We have all done things in the name of victory that we would never otherwise do."

The men below him murmured their accord.

He paused, expression sincere as he leaned forward, strong, tanned hands dark against the snowy linen cloth. "Do you recall my words to you the night of my arrival? That you did not know me, nor I you, well enough to judge each other?"

Heads bobbed in assent.

"I think we know each other well enough now," Cort said, his rich, quiet voice carrying to the far corners of the hall.

"Aye!" thundered from a hundred throats.

"If 'tis so, then I trust you know that much of what's said of a warrior's battle feats is exaggerated, that the way he lives his life day to day is the true indicator of the man."

Lexi watched the men's faces as Cort spoke, noted their expressions of interest, confusion, or wariness. Saffron velvet skirt gathered in her damp palms, she bit her lower lip and prayed that the loyalty and respect they felt for her betrothed would survive the truth.

As if he knew the moment had come, that little more could be said in his defense, Cort took a deep breath. "My surname is not Dornogard. I feared my true identity would provoke distrust and anger among you before we ever met and so chose to conceal it. My real last name is Thorssen."

The Normans smiled, many with obvious relief that the charade had ended. Lexi guessed it had not been easy for them to sustain the ruse, especially in their first days at Avonly when met with many of the English soldiers' and tenants' surly attitudes.

A number of Graham's former men gasped or scowled; others appeared awed or intimidated. The remainder looked from Cort to their fellows with blank confusion, clearly unfamiliar with the name.

Cort straightened from the table. His gaze met theirs with unflinching honesty. "I am the man they call the Golden Dragon."

****

Silence thrummed around him like the buzzing of a thousand bees. Dark, vibrant, it settled in his soul and told him the price he'd pay for his deceit. Though a handful of the English appeared willing to withhold judgment, a select few to comprehend his motivation, the majority looked angry, wary, or disappointed. No more than he deserved, Cort admitted to himself. In their place, he might well feel the same.

Yet if he could go back, he would not change what he had done. There was no way to know what difference the truth might have made, how Avonly's people would have reacted had he told them his real name from the outset. He and Guy had discussed the problem in depth before their arrival. Despite the setbacks he might now encounter, he still thought their decision a sound one.

These people knew him now, had lived and worked with him. He had to believe their better sense would, in time, overcome whatever reservations they felt at the moment. Though he had not considered it before, he now recognized the boon his marriage to Lexi would be. Amiton's residents loved and respected her. Much as Cort had sensed when he arrived that they would follow Graham's lead, he now prayed they would follow hers. And Lexi, bless her, gazed up at him with pride in her eyes for all to see.

Displeased she might be with his lie of omission, unhappy with the hard fact that he'd killed scores of English soldiers without a qualm. But she was, inimitably, Lexi: practical, fair, tolerant of others' failings and perceptions. She might not like what he'd done, but she had not condemned him out of hand. Rather, she'd listened and appeared to understand and accept his explanation.

She trusted him. Perhaps the time had come for him to trust her, as well.

The king placed his hand on Cort's arm, drawing him back from his ruminations. As William nodded for Cort to sit, he, himself, rose.

Despite his short stature, his shoulders were broad, his brown eyes sharp as he surveyed those before him. The powerful aura that had raised him to his present position as supreme ruler of both England and Normandy seemed to shimmer around him.

"The Golden Dragon sits high in my esteem," he proclaimed, his deep voice resonating from the walls and rafters. "Disloyalty to him is disloyalty to me." The warning rang clear. "But one man's commitment to another should not rest solely on necessity or fear. Strong bonds require the heart and soul. Lord Thorssen has pledged his to you this night. I pray you are wise enough to pledge him yours in return."

He looked to Cort, who, even seated, was eye level with him, and smiled. With an innate, noble grace, he bowed to Lexi. "I think I'll retire now."

Not for the first time, his gaze shifted to the hall entrance. A puzzled frown creased his brow. Then he cast one final, stern glance over the assembly and motioned his squire to accompany him to his chamber.

Every eye in the hall followed the king's departure. Heavy silence hung over the gathering for several long moments after he'd gone. Cort could think of nothing to say to ease it. Some chastened, some indignant, the men began to file from the room.

A loud voice halted their exit. "I be one of you—and un'erstand how you feel."

Cort watched in amazement as Donald leaped onto a trestle table. One foot planted beside an oval pewter platter, the other dead center of a soggy bread trencher, he addressed his fellows.

"You know I do not pander to others, so what I say be spoke in truth, not for gain. Lord Dor—Thorssen knows as well as us that we got no choice but to serve 'im. Like it or not, we swore an oath, and that's an end to it."

One by one the men turned to look at Donald and listen. "No one were more set against our new lord's claim to Avonly than me."

Most remembered his remarks that first evening and nodded.

"I don't like that he lied to us." Donald's gaze on Cort unwavering, his bold words overstepped the boundary of respect. "But his reasons make sense. There ain't one among us who wouldn't ha' judged him afore we seen him."

Feet shuffled among the rushes. Several men cleared their throats and looked away.

"It weren't easy to say what Lord Thorssen just said. He didn't have t' explain himself to us at all." Hands on hips, he scanned the faces of those about him. "I can't tell you what t' think. But I know what I know. He's been fair. He works hard. Lady Alexis cares for him." He paused, eyes once more focused on Cort. "And he saved m' life."

Seeming suddenly embarrassed by his monologue, Donald lowered his head and scrambled off the table. Pushing his way through the throng, he disappeared through the archway.

For a minute, the men stood frozen. Then, in utter silence but for the swish of cloth and tramp of feet, they followed Donald out into the night.

Guy and Dane grinned. Lord Graham looked thoughtful. Melissande sat rigid as a poker. Lexi, coin-bright eyes alight with hope, leaned against Cort's arm and kissed his cheek.

"Was that Donald?" she asked with an impish grin. "Doubting Donald? I believe, my lord, that you've found yourself a most unlikely champion."

****

Cort looked more tired than she'd ever seen him. Not even after his all-night vigil at her bedside, or at the end of days spent in exhausting physical activity, had he appeared so fatigued. But this was a weariness of the soul, she suspected, not the body, and far more draining.

He stared at the empty archway a long time after the men left, his eyes bleak. While Lexi believed his candid speech to the men and Donald's defense of him would, in the end, win them over, it would take time to regain their trust. In general, they were simple men with simple needs and strict codes of honor. No doubt Cort understood their attitudes better than she. They'd been honed on similar battlefields, their stake in this issue both professional and personal.

And unlike her, they didn't love him.

She still felt guilty for having forgiven Cort so easily, then felt even more guilt for feeling guilty. She couldn't like the fact that he had deceived her, yet couldn't fault his reasons. He'd done what he had to do as a warrior.

The Battle of Hastings was almost five years past. For most of the time since, he'd been constructing castles, not fighting. She'd been friends with Alain for two years and never thought to judge him for his Norman heritage.

Should she condemn Cort simply because he was more skilled than most? As a healer, her own talents were often suspect. More than once, she'd heard behind-the-back whispers of witchcraft when she'd cured someone of an oft-fatal malady. Should she let people suffer or die to escape such superstitious nonsense?

Lexi sighed. To do less than her best was foreign to her nature. As she suspected it was foreign to Cort's.

Excited shouts from the battlements snapped her from her musings. Cort pressed her back down to the bench when she began to rise.

"Stay here, wild rose. Guy, Dane." He cocked his hand in a signal to follow him and swung his legs over the bench.

Irked at his command to her, she nonetheless

obeyed. He had enough on his plate without her quibbling.

Carts rumbled and horses' hooves clattered on stone as the three maneuvered among the barking manor hounds, trestle tables and refuse scattered about the floor. Greetings, muffled but clearly friendly, reached Lexi's ears. Relieved and curious, she sat forward, anxious to learn the identity of their visitors.

Quick, light footsteps sounded on the outer stairs. Then a blue and gold whirlwind swept across the entryway and through the arch.

"Cort!" Without so much as a pause, the feminine form stretched out her arms, and Cort stepped into them with the fluid grace of a dream figure. His arms encircled her, hugging her as tightly as ever he had Lexi. He lifted her, then twirled her about until her skirts floated about her calves. He kissed her face as she kissed his, happily, indiscriminately. When Cort at last lowered her to the floor, he loosened his hold but did not release her. She made no attempt to move away.

Lexi sat stunned, her throat and chest constricted with shock. Guy and Dane looked on like proud parents, faces split in idiotic grins. Then they moved to the still-entwined couple, laughing and hugging them both. Isolated and confused, Lexi could almost feel herself shrinking as her usual self-confidence evaporated like mist.

His mistress? Torn by rage and sorrow, she barely noticed when the girl kissed Guy and Dane in turn, then shooed them back. Slim white hands slid from Cort's neck to his chest to grip the front of his deep red tunic as she leaned back to study him. The hood of her cloak dropped to her shoulders, revealing a wealth of thick auburn hair.

Cort smiled like an imbecile. "God, I've missed you, Jewel. You've grown into a beauty."

Shaking her dark red curls, Jewel grimaced. "What did you expect?" she asked tartly. "A harridan?"

"Nay. But in truth, I was not expecting to see you at all."

Neither was I, Lexi thought grimly, angered anew as she was forced to admit Cort's words were true. Though bigger boned than Lexi and almost as tall, her hour-glass figure, large blue eyes, and full red mouth would tempt any man.

"Nor did we anticipate you'd look like a fairy princess," added Guy. The traitor.

Lexi feared she might be sick. Instead, she cleared her throat in a bid for attention. No one seemed to notice.

Jewel pushed away from Cort, her smile blinding as she turned to Guy. Pulling his head down, she gave him a lusty kiss.

Lexi gasped. Cort scowled.

When she at last released Guy's mouth, he drawled, "Your time at court has not been wasted, I see."

"Did I do it right, then?" Her innocent pleasure at her success drew uproarious laughter from the men.

"Right enough," scolded a gruff voice from the shadowed archway. "Do it again, and I'll warm your bottom."

In that instant, Lexi realized she'd just witnessed play, not passion. Whoever she was, Jewel posed no threat.

Duly chastened, the girl lowered her eyes, though an impish smile tugged at her mouth.

Focused as she'd been on the group before her, Lexi had not noticed the pair who stood framed in the great hall's entry. But as they moved into the light, she realized at once who they must be. Cort's resemblance to the older man was striking.

"Father!" Cort's shout confirmed Lexi's guess. He closed the distance between them to wrap the man in a bone-crushing hug.

"When you did not respond to my missive about the wedding, I thought you must be away and unable to come."

"Isn't William here?"

"Yes. He arrived this afternoon."

"He didn't tell you to expect us?"

Cort shook his head. "We had little time to talk alone. It's been a somewhat difficult day." He frowned. "When he did not mention you or *Maman*, I did not press him. If you were away on the king's business, I did not want him to feel responsible that you couldn't be here."

"I was away—but only after your letter arrived at court. I sailed home to bring your mother here. Etienne can supervise my estates for a time. Good practice for him—"

"All that can wait for later," Cort's mother interrupted. "It's been too long since I've held my eldest son."

"Hello, *Maman*." Even from where she sat, Lexi could see the shimmer of tears in Cort's eyes. "Three years since I've seen you. Much too long."

As she rose on tiptoe to kiss her son's cheek, Cort's arms pulled her close. She wrapped her own about his waist, weeping unashamedly as she pressed her head against his chest.

"Welcome to Amiton, my home." He rested his chin on the dark braids coiled atop her head.

The movement brought his gaze in contact with Lexi's. She watched his eyes widen and a blush seep into his cheeks.

"Thor's hammer!" He groaned, gently disengaging himself from his mother's embrace. "I forgot abou—"

"What's all the commotion?" William asked with

gruff good humor as he strode into the hall. "About time you arrived, Eric. Lady Rosalind." He brushed the back of her hand with his lips. "What kept you? I'd begun to worry."

"Broken axle," Eric Thorssen replied succinctly. "I could use some wine."

"After you meet my betrothed, Father."

Cort grinned as he skirted the long tables, then cleared the stairs to the dais in one leap.

"Forgive me, wild rose," he whispered as he helped Lexi to her feet. "My sister's entrance distracted me, and her greeting, as usual, was hardly proper."

"Oh?" She arched an eyebrow. "I thought it most proper." Her mouth curved in a cat-that-got-the-cream smile. "'Tis the way I'd prefer to greet you."

"And I you." Cort chuckled, his hand at her waist as he led her toward his family.

"Father, *Maman*," he said, his face serious as he made the introductions. "This is Alexis. Alexis, my parents, Lord and Lady Thorssen."

"Such formality," Rosalind chided. "I hope you will call us *Maman* and Father as Cort does, my dear."

Lexi marveled at the woman's graciousness. Cort's mother didn't even know yet whether she'd like her soon-to-be daughter-in-law.

As if she'd read Lexi's mind, the woman smiled archly. "If Cort's chosen you, you must be special. I look forward to our visit."

Lexi returned the smile, already sure they would get on well together. Though Cort resembled his father, his more refined features and turquoise eyes were surely a legacy from his mother. Fair skinned and dark haired, she possessed a lithe, classic beauty. Lexi suspected her son's candid, familiar manner was also a gift from his mother, and felt immediately at ease.

Eric Thorssen took Lexi's hands in his and studied her with a sober mien. Seeming satisfied at last, his mouth curved in a slow grin. "Like father, like son. We do have a talent for choosing extraordinary women."

Lexi could not imagine what he'd seen to prompt such a comment, but she dropped a shallow curtsy and murmured, "That's one of the reasons you are extraordinary men."

Deep, appreciative laughter enveloped Lexi as Cort's father's gaze met hers. He squeezed her hands lightly before turning toward the others.

"Come, lady wife, for wine and conversation with the king before we seek our own bed. Jewel?"

"Let her stay with us awhile, Father," Cort suggested. "It's been a long time—"

"Aye, son. Enjoy your visit." With warm smiles, his parents bid them good night and followed William up the stairs.

"They're wonderful," Lexi breathed.

"Usually," Jewel said with a slight grimace. "Though there are times when Father can be—"

"Too much like a father?" Cort teased, leading his sister up the dais steps.

Jewel sniffed, though her eyes twinkled with humor.

"If you do not m-mind, my lord, I'll retire now." Dane, who stood at the foot of the steps, yawned hugely.

"Of course," Cort agreed.

The others settled themselves along the bench as Dane departed.

"So, Julianna," her brother said as he poured wine into a silver goblet. "Tell me. What news of home?"

Julianna, Lexi realized. Of course. J-u-l-e. Not J-e-w-e-l.

"Not a thing," the girl replied with blithe

unconcern. "And I'd much rather hear about you. Father told me and *Maman* all about your work on the castles but naught of what you've done here. Has aught exciting happened since you arrived?"

"Talk about putting your foot in it." Guy's gaze met Cort's, and for a moment they stared at each other. Then Cort's eyes began to simmer with unholy amusement. His laughter, deep and rich, infected Guy, and Lexi's lips twitched until her merriment joined the men's.

"Oh, my." Julianna appeared dumbstruck at their response. "What did I say? I don't think I'm making a good first impression on Lady Alexis."

"Lexi," she corrected.

Cort merely laughed louder at the look on his sister's face. She rounded on him with flashing eyes, having found a target on whom to vent her obvious embarrassment.

"How dare you laugh at me, you great oaf!" she chastised, ignoring the fact that he had not laughed alone. "Teasing is one thing, Cort Golden Dragon Thorssen, but I'll thank you not to make me look the fool." Jaw thrust forward in a show of temper, Julianna seemed to have already forgotten her concern with first impressions.

"Irrepressible as ever," Cort said without one ounce of remorse. "All right, *petit soeur*, I surrender."

He grinned as he fended off a well-aimed fist. "Your visit to court may have taught you how to kiss, but it failed to tame your temper. I did not mean to hurt your feelings. It will take time for me to accept you're no longer a little girl."

Acknowledging the warm sincerity in his voice and expression, Jule relented and blew him a kiss. Then she turned to Lexi. "So, you've really agreed to marry this vandal?"

"Well, yes, I—"

"Tell me all about it," she urged, blue eyes

bright with curiosity.

"Actually—"

Cort stepped in. "It's rather a long story, *ma fille*. Let's just say that we find we suit very well. Our pets suit very well. Our interests suit—Ooof!"

Air exploded from Cort's lungs as Julianna's fist connected with his solar plexus.

"Men can be such noddleheads." Unconcerned, she turned to Lexi, who fought hard to control her amusement. "Are you sure you want to marry this?" Jule jerked a thumb in her brother's direction.

Lexi nodded, unable to tame her grin at the girl's outrageous antics. "Though I'm not sure why. Such an impossible man."

Raising innocent eyes to her future husband's, Lexi watched with burgeoning delight as his fierce expression softened and a dimple creased the corner of his sculpted lips.

"Impossible?" he mouthed, leaning so close that his warm breath tickled her nose. His thumb rose to caress her nape. "Shall I demonstrate how impossible I can be?"

Lexi gulped as Cort grinned knowingly into her eyes. "You're a devil dragon, my lord. No gentleman would—"

"Agreed." He planted a swift kiss on the tip of her nose. "Devil, perhaps. Dragon, when I must be. But certainly no gentleman, not with you."

Lexi blushed but answered honestly, "I would have you no other way."

"I'm glad, wild rose." He pitched his voice so low only she could hear it. "For you will. Soon. Any way you want me."

"Cort!" She slapped him lightly on the chest.

"So, are you glad we surprised you?" Jule interrupted their banter.

"Of course, I'm glad," Cort said. "Though I'm not usually fond of surprises, your visit is an exception."

"I rather thought you might expect us. Being my big, older, genius brother," Jule cooed with mock admiration.

Cort scowled, then muttered, "Well, I didn't. But I'd have been sorry if you'd missed the wedding."

"I'm glad your taste has improved since you were in Normandy. You can be sure I'd have missed your wedding if you'd chosen anyone like that...that prissy Fitz-whatever you were so enamored of that summer—"

"That was almost eight years ago!" Cort defended himself.

Guy chuckled, and Lexi grinned as a telltale blush crept up Cort's neck.

"Damn!" Taut fingers tunneled through his hair.

Oblivious to her brother's reaction, Jule concluded in her forthright manner, "But I think Lexi is an excellent choice, though more, I'm sure, than you deserve."

"Quarter!" Cort shoved his sister's wine goblet toward her with a quelling stare. "Have a drink. Your throat must be parched."

She obeyed with a sweet smile, and he huffed out a breath. "Still brutally honest, aren't you? And right on every count. Shall we sign articles of surrender, so we can enjoy a last cup in peace before we retire?"

"Good idea." Guy refilled Jule's cup and his own. Eyes green as new grass sparkled with his obvious appreciation of the give-and-take between brother and sister.

"Won't you tell me even a little of the long story you mentioned earlier, Cort?" his sister pressed.

"I'm not sure where I'd begin," he mused. "Would you settle for one word until I can sort it out?"

"One word?"

Cort nodded. "Chaos."

Lexi clapped her hands to her mouth at his too-accurate summation.

Julianna looked from one to the other, her consternation clear.

Slumped sideways against the table, Guy drawled, "Oh, I don't know. I rather think of it as a web. An ebony strand here, a gilded strand there. Aqua eyes ensnared by golden ones. Woven together by the swish of a magical dragon's tail. Yes," he stated with quiet and absolute conviction. "For the Golden Dragon and his lady, nothing less than a golden web."

Chapter Twenty-Four

As if stirred by fairies' fingers, the low-lying morning haze dipped and swirled in the hollows, then rose in wispy ribbons to catch among leaf-thick branches. But the early June sun burned strong, aiding the warm breeze's attempt to sweep away the mist. Within the hour it would be no more than a memory.

Like his bachelorhood, Cort thought. Yet he regretted its loss no more than he did the dissipation of the mist. With his commitment to Lexi, he'd vowed to bury his suspicions. Marriage to her would be like moving from fog into sunlight, the natural exchange of one kind of beauty for another.

His mouth curved in a purely male smile. Lexi burned brighter than any sun at his touch. He couldn't wait to feel her heat, to taste the fire of their passion until they both went up in flames.

When Cort's manhood stirred at the thought, he groaned. *Wise Freya, give me the strength to get through this day.* He'd been in a state of semi-arousal since the moment he'd met his betrothed. Just a few more hours, he prayed, without disgracing myself. Nightfall seemed impossibly distant.

****

Guided by age-old tradition, Cort stood before the open door of the village kirk and watched Lexi, escorted by Stefan, approach across the greensward. Behind them, young and not-so-young maidens scattered wheat chaff and flower petals, symbols of fertility and happiness. Their offerings fluttered on the breeze before drifting to the emerald earth like a vivid cloak.

At Cort's request, everyone on the estate was present. After the ceremony, the workers would enjoy their own celebration and a day of rest. He fervently hoped this union would be a step toward restoring him to their good graces.

His parents and sister, King William, Guy, and Dane were aligned at the forefront of the gathering, looking proud and pleased. Graham and Melissande stood beside them. Cort acknowledged them with a quick, nervous smile as the crowd parted with hushed whispers to allow Lexi's passage.

Stefan, serious and handsome in black velvet, kissed his sister's cheek before assisting her up the four steps to take her place beside Cort. Then he joined his lord's family.

Hundreds of eyes bored into Cort's back as he and his bride turned to face Amiton's priest. After that, the world faded to nothing, and he was aware only of Lexi.

A thin, riband-plaited braid graced each side of her face; otherwise, her hair swayed unbound almost to her knees, as it had the first time he'd seen her. A deep-gold bliaut hugged her generous breasts, its side laces drawn taut to emphasize her long, narrow waist. A sheer-silk underblouse, shot with silver and gold threads, fluttered about her slender arms. Around her neck she wore the pendant he'd sent her that morning as a bride gift. A feminine version of his personal crest, the rampant dragon of solid gold embedded in a sapphire sunburst was a miniature copy of the design embroidered on his azure tunic.

She looked more beautiful than he had ever seen her, and not because of the finery she wore. As they exchanged vows before God and man, Lexi's magnificent golden eyes brimmed with hope and joy...and a more intense emotion he could not identify. Her voice as she committed herself to him was soft but steady, her expression serene. Cort wondered how she saw him at this moment, if she were as pleased with her choice as he with his.

When Father Edgar at last blessed their union and turned them to face the crowd, Cort thought he might explode with pride. Lexi's fingers warm in his, he raised their joined hands to her cheek and took her soft mouth in a devouring kiss. The resounding cheer that greeted the gesture boosted Cort's hopes that all might yet be well between himself and his subjects. Still, he was honest enough to admit that William's presence no doubt encouraged their enthusiasm.

His family, the king, and a small group of knights followed the priest and newly married couple into the tiny church for the wedding mass. The rest of Amiton's people hastened back to the manor to complete preparations for the wedding feast or set up tables on the common for the townsfolk.

At Father Edgar's nod, Cort and Lexi knelt before the altar. Behind them, Cort heard the others file into the wooden pews, their comments properly hushed. Slanting a glance at Lexi, he saw her shiver in the cool air. He slipped his warm fingers through hers and squeezed gently. Her lips curved in a tremulous smile.

Hidden within the folds of her skirt, his thumb traced seductive circles against her palm. This time when she shivered, Cort hoped the cause had nothing to do with the temperature.

An irreverent grin pulled at his mouth as he whispered, "Wanton."

"What?" Lexi mouthed, breath shallow.

"Wanton," he repeated, voice low and husky. "Hold the thought. It will warm you through the day."

"I don't need—"

"Don't you?" he murmured as she shivered once again.

Color bloomed in her cheeks as she shot him a behave-yourself look.

With an elegant shrug, he assured her, "No matter. I'm more than warm enough for both of us."

Pretending not to have heard her gasp, the priest continued, but his words registered as naught but the droning of so many bees. Poor, saintly man. Cort wondered how he'd react if he knew Cort could see nothing but the woman beside him, smell nothing but her fresh, spring-warm scent, still taste nothing but the drugging heat of her mouth. And sacrilege or not, wanted naught more than to strip her down to naked skin and take her. Here. Now. Through the afternoon, into evening, and long into the night.

****

Marvelous as the day had been, Lexi thought it would never end. When Cort's mother offered to help her ready herself for the night, she gladly agreed. But Cort looked up at his mother, who stood behind his shoulder, and shook his head.

"Not tonight, *Maman*, though I thank you for the offer. I'll see to my bride myself."

She laid her hand on his gilded hair and nodded her understanding. "As you wish. Your father and I will stay here and keep the men belowstairs, then, shall we?" Rosalind's eyes danced with mirth.

"An excellent idea," Cort agreed. "If your glares and Father's threats fail to convince them to stay far from our chamber, tell them any man who defies the order will meet me tomorrow in hand-to-hand combat. If my reputation means anything, that should suffice."

His mother leaned down to kiss the top of his head. Eyes on Lexi, she whispered, "God bless. If this barbarian isn't good to you tonight, he'll have *my* reputation to fear." With a playful tug on Cort's unbound hair, she slipped away and settled again beside her husband.

Cort rose and drew Lexi up beside him. With a warning glare at the men seated at the trestle tables, he swung her into his arms to the sound of ribald cheers and pounding tankards. Only after he'd climbed the stairs and kicked his chamber door closed behind them did he dare to breathe again.

Alone at last, Lexi thought. Cort threw the bolt, then lowered her feet to the floor, but did not release her. Her body, pressed along the length of his, was all too aware of his arousal. She felt her eyes widen and a blush stain her cheeks, but she held Cort's heated gaze with her own. How foolish to feel shy now, when they had the moral and legal right to consummate their clearly mutual desire.

Neither spoke. They simply looked at each other, alone, together, for the first time as man and wife.

"We've had company," Cort said softly, looking beyond Lexi's shoulder.

She followed his gaze and sighed with pleasure. The large bed's dark green coverlet had been turned down, revealing snowy linen. On one pillow lay a small cluster of gillyflowers and goldenrod tied with a light blue riband. On the bedside table rested an oak bucket in which stood a sealed, glazed jug.

"Guy's idea, I suspect." Cort strode to the table and lifted the jug. "Father brought me some of my favorite stock from Normandy. Falcon's as fond of it as I. Will you try some, wild rose?"

In response, she reached for the pair of heavy goblets. Cort slit the seal with his misericord and twisted it free. Pouring each of them half a cup, he returned the wine to the bucket, then moved to stand before her.

"What shall we toast, Lady Thorssen?" His eyes leaped with aqua flames in the glow from the hearth and the candles set upon the mantel.

Though she rarely indulged in spirits of any kind, this was a very special moment. One to share and savor. Heart thundering with anticipation, Lexi swallowed.

"Our marriage. Our future." Her mouth curved in a warm smile. "Our happiness."

She ached to add "our love," but hesitated to presume that he shared the soul-deep affection that burned in her for him. She'd not now chance destroying the mood.

"Amen," Cort agreed reverently.

Their cups touched with a sharp metallic *clack*. Arms entwined, they sipped from each other's goblet.

Cort removed the vessel from Lexi's fingers and set it on the bedside table. Turning to her once more, he studied her in the flickering amber light.

"You're beautiful," they said in awed unison.

Cort's laughter washed over Lexi, more intoxicating than the rich red wine. Her answering smile faded as she gazed up at his strong, vivid features. Cort's stunning eyes reflected her own burning need to touch.

Hands trembling, lips meshed in an open-mouthed, unrelenting kiss, they undressed each other with awkward but tender haste. Lexi pushed at Cort's tunic until he was forced to release her to pull it over his head. It dropped unheeded to the floor and was swiftly joined by his full-sleeved shirt. His fingers searched out the pins that held her floral coronet and sheer veil in place. Slipping them free, he dropped them carelessly to the woven rug and wound his hands in her hair. When he drew her head back for a hard, carnal kiss, she moaned low in her throat.

Lexi leaned back so Cort might unlace the sides

of her bliaut. His normally deft fingers clumsy, he swore steadily under his breath, but at last drew the garment over her head to reveal the gossamer underblouse.

Her breasts swelled against the sheer fabric, nipples ripe. Cort dipped his head to nuzzle the flesh beneath the thin layer of fabric. His tongue, warm and wet, laved the sensitive peaks through the erotic friction of sliding silk. Then he suckled each gently, grazed with his teeth. Lexi grasped his head and arched backward, offering herself freely. Cort's growl of pleasure almost sent her over the edge.

His hands slid up from her waist to her breasts, dragging the fragile fabric with them. "Nothing between us, Lexi, ever again," he rasped as he stepped back to strip off his chausses and boots.

Her heart stuttered as momentary guilt lashed her. She must tell him. She must. But not now.

Mind dazed with passion, it took her a moment to comprehend he waited for her to finish what he had begun. Swaying with need, she pushed all thought away and divested herself of her underblouse even as Cort reached for her once more.

For the briefest moment, she glimpsed his naked form and recalled the day they'd met. If possible, he appeared even more magnificent now. Every inch of him sleek muscle, taut sinew, long, elegant bones. Every mouth-watering, masculine inch, hers.

"The rest is mine to do." The words fluttered a sensuous whisper against her thighs as he dropped to his knees to remove her slippers.

He ran his hands up her silk-clad legs to her bare hips and pressed his cheek to her flat abdomen but did not remove her stockings as she'd expected. Rather, he lifted her in his arms, gently laid her on the bed, then followed her down.

Their combined weight tipped the pillows toward the center of the mattress, and the fragrant bouquet rolled against Lexi's cheek. She smiled hazily. "Lovely."

"I'd hoped you'd like them."

"These are from you?" Lexi asked, stunned that he had thought to do such a thing.

Clearly self-conscious, Cort nodded. "The goldenrod matches your eyes, and the others are just...pretty. I know how you love the woods and flowers."

"Oh, Cort," Lexi breathed, heart overflowing. "They are the most precious gift you could have—"

"No," he whispered, fingers to her lips. "They are but a token. You are the most precious gift."

Eyes liquid with tears, fingers trembling with love, she touched Cort's face, traced his eyebrows and cheekbones and mouth as if seeing him for the first time. She was beyond speech, but he seemed to understand.

"Sweet wife," he whispered against her ear. "Heart and soul of this golden web."

The rending of fragile silk as he ran his hands beneath her stockings might have been a harsh counterpoint to the soft endearment, except that Lexi trusted Cort would never hurt her. Rather than contradictory, his words and actions simply blended the savage and gentle facets of his nature.

His need for her tonight seemed manic and matched her own. They would take each other with equal ferocity this first time, she thought. His mouth swooped to her throat, downward to breasts grown heavy with desire. Her nails dug into his rock-hard back, and all thought fled.

She knew only what she sensed in him. Power. Danger. Control. Tenderness. His hands were a fever upon her skin.

"I would not end this sweet torment so soon. Patience," he murmured as Lexi shivered in delight.

He slowed the pace. Rolling from atop her, he

pulled her with him so they lay face to face.

So, so slowly, with absolute reverence, he traced every plane and hollow of Lexi's body with callused fingertips and hard palms. In the webbed moonlight that bathed the bed, Cort watched her. Her own eyelids drooped, and she pressed toward him, glorying in his touch. His lips skimmed her hair, tested the moist skin of her forehead, her eyelids, drifted across her cheekbones and downward to claim her mouth in a cherishing kiss.

His wine-sweet mouth brushed lightly over hers, barely touching. His teeth nibbled at her lower lip. His tongue slid between her panting lips and traced the sensitized contours.

With subtle finesse, Cort altered the kiss. His mouth slanted across hers and sucked her more deeply into the vortex of his passion. His hands slid from thigh to buttocks, drawing her tightly against him.

Lexi strained for that contact, every nerve, every muscle in her trembling body attuned to Cort's hands and mouth.

"Now, my dragon. Now!" Her voice rode on a thready, erratic breath, barely audible despite the absolute silence that cocooned them.

He shook his head as he slid down her body, the caress of his hair against her stomach a negation of her plea. His fingers skimmed her inner thighs.

"Not yet, my darling wild rose." Voice husky, he raised his head until his gaze locked with hers. "Not yet."

"But I'm ready now." Tone petulant, her hands fluttered moth-like over his face.

"No, sweetheart," Cort whispered. "You only think you are."

"Cort—" she pleaded.

"Hush, my lovely Alexis." He slid up beside her to stroke her hair. "Do you trust me?"

Eyes clouded, Lexi managed a bare nod.

"There is so much more, lady wife." His hands resumed their worship of her. "Trust me. So much more."

Unable to resist his compelling stare, the lean fingers that cradled her face, Lexi said, "As you wish, husband."

"An obedient Lexi?" His mouth quirked. "No, sweetheart. What you wish. There are many ways of loving, and I would teach you all of them."

Lexi's mouth opened to Cort's gentle kiss while desire roiled through her like dense smoke.

"Love me," she whimpered at last against his now-teasing lips. "Do anything you wish with me, only love me."

"Higher and higher," he promised, his mouth moving lower and lower. "Better and better yet."

"What...should I..." Lexi gasped.

"Not a thing, wild rose." His fingers settled on her trembling lips. "This night is yours, and your pleasure, mine."

A harsh breath shook him. "Let me show you how it feels to die and be born again, to visit a world where only dreams exist, where the spirit is shattered only to be made whole."

When Cort levered himself away from her, she closed her eyes and whimpered at the loss. Until a liquid chill touched her breast, followed by warm breath that sent a shudder through her. Opening her eyes, she watched dazedly as Cort propped himself on an elbow beside her and dipped the fingers of his left hand into the wine goblet cradled in his right.

"Guy had no idea what a special gift he left us. It would be a shame to waste it." His wine-drenched fingers lingered over her breasts and ribcage, tracing cool patterns on her skin, which he heated with his breath and wet with his tongue.

Gaze unfocused, Lexi watched Cort's eyes gleam

with savage satisfaction at her restless movements, the erratic catches in her breath as he stroked her from shoulder to toe. Clearly encouraged at her reaction, he followed the tingling path of the wine with butterfly kisses, nipping teeth, and swirling tongue.

"Such a strong yet delicate body," he whispered. "A feast fit for...a dragon." His gaze moved to the pendant he'd given her, its gold and sapphire image a bare glimmer within the valley between her breasts.

Lexi absorbed his touch as her skin absorbed the wine. "What are you...doing?" Her word slipped out in tortured gasps; her body writhed beneath Cort's knowing fingers and mouth.

He ignored the question and buried his face in the hollow of her throat. "How lovely you are, wife. Velvet and satin, smooth and firm. Every inch of you beautiful, sweet. And mine."

Lexi gazed at him through desire-blurred eyes.

"As to what I'm doing... Only what you asked of me. Loving you. Can you hear me, Lexi?"

Her hands slid upward into his thick mane, vagrant and insistent. Lost in gauzy layers of sensation, she heard herself moan, which was apparently answer enough.

Cort kissed her jaw, her throat. His tongue tasted her shoulders, her collarbone, her breasts. Lexi's nipples responded the instant he moved down to suckle. Then, he continued the sensual journey, laving her sides, her hips, the taut inner thighs which opened to him of their own volition.

Lexi's heels, dug deeply into the down tick, thrust her hips mindlessly against his hungry mouth. Cort melded his fingers with that motion, slipping them in and out of her as he nibbled and stroked the sensitive crest of her sex.

The rapture surged, taunted, then crashed

through her with blinding force. She screamed with the raw power of it.

"Sweet God! Cort!" She sobbed and went on sobbing, "Cort, Cort, Cort."

With her body shattered, Lexi floated, shimmered. Strong arms drew her against a smooth, hard chest. Warm lips soothed her sweat-slick brow and temples. Gentle fingers smoothed damp hair from her face. For a long time he merely held her. And Lexi, even had she wished to, could not have moved. She was more than content to allow the pieces of herself to gather together again in their own time.

Steeped in lethargy, when at last she stirred, her limp hand landed with a smack against Cort's neck.

"How?" Her voice shook with reaction. "What?"

She felt Cort smile against her hair. "Hush, lady." He caressed the line of her hip and waist. "It's all right, you know. Superbly right. Loving as it's meant to be."

"But I..." Tears spilled from Lexi's eyes. She'd never anticipated the emotional storm and seemed unable to control it.

Cort's eyes widened in horror. "Christ." He frantically wiped at her tears. "I've made you cry. You never cry. I'm sorry. I didn't... Don't cry, my rose—"

"Oh, Cort." She offered a watery smile. "Don't be sorry. I just never expected... It was incredible. Wondrous."

"You're certain?" he asked, sounding anything but.

"I'm certain." She hiccupped, and they both smiled.

"You are my wife, Lexi. If I hurt you, you must tell me. But what we do behind closed doors, how we choose to love each other is our affair. Yet I would not make you cry. Ever."

"I'm done." She swiped at the final vestiges of moisture. Then bolted upright. "Oh, my lord! You didn't... Would you have me do for you what you did for me?" Eyes level on his, she stroked her hand down his stomach to his rock-hard arousal.

He arched off the bed at the contact. Need and hunger leaped in his eyes.

"My poor dragon," she crooned. "You have delayed your own satisfaction to guarantee mine."

Rather than respond, Cort closed his eyes and undulated against her seeking fingers. She smiled to herself when his back bowed off the bed.

"Is this the right—"

He peered at her through slitted eyes, his throat sounding clogged. "Move those delicate fingers again and I'll explode."

In a lightning-fast move, he grasped her shoulders and flipped her onto her back. "Another moment of that," he warned through clenched teeth, "and we'd have missed this. I shudder to think how devastating you'll be with a little experience."

Lexi felt him nudge at the entrance of her womanhood. "Experience is usually a good thing," she purred.

"With you, I think, it will be more than good. I swore not to hurt you," Cort whispered. "But the first time—"

"I want you more than I have ever wanted anything in my life." She smoothed his tangled golden hair behind his shoulders and thrust herself against him. He drove into her.

The momentary pain gave way to the wondrous sensation of him filling her.

"Sweet heavens." Cort's initial, slow strokes escalated until he was moving frantically within her. His heart hammered against her breast like the bellows of hell.

"You'll kill me, wife." Arms straining, powerful neck arched, sweat slicked his chest. "Enough...torment."

"Torment?" Lexi rose to meet another thrust. "Nay, my husband. Do you not feel it? Hear it?"

Her body convulsed about his even as she felt his hot seed flood her. "'Tis the swish of the dragon's tail weaving yet another strand into our web. Oh, Cort, 'tis the dragon's song."

Chapter Twenty-Five

A deep contentment settled in Cort. Marriage to Lexi was a far more pleasurable reality than it had been a fantasy. She brought her passion for life with her to their bed and seemed daily more vibrant, witty, and generous. His family and the king appeared to love her almost as much as he did.

He stilled, the truth of it all but stealing his breath. He loved her. Every spirited, intoxicating, edible inch.

When had it happened? The night she'd been hit over the head? The first time he'd kissed her? The day she took the arrow meant for him? Their wedding night, when he'd made love to her—several memorable times? Perhaps from the very moment he'd looked into her extraordinary eyes and read the humor, intelligence, and challenge there.

When seemed hardly important now. What mattered was that his impetuous decision to claim her had been the best choice he had ever made. Still, he hesitated to tell her. Though they exchanged endearments freely in the privacy of their bedchamber, Lexi had never said she loved him.

To reveal his own emotions when he was unsure of hers would make him vulnerable. While he'd buried his doubts about her personal loyalty to him, he retained his gut belief that she knew something about that first ambush. Innocent as that knowledge might be, until she trusted him enough, cared for him enough, to reveal it, he dared not trust her with his heart.

He swore beneath his breath. *Too late for that,*

Dragon. She already owns it. True. But she didn't know that, and he wasn't about to tell her. Yet.

As his wife stirred beside him, Cort breathed in the sunshine scent of her hair and smiled. Afternoon light spilled like liquid gold through the open casement, across the floor; occasional birdsong drifted in on a light breeze; the sounds of bailey and tiltyard rang sharp within the otherwise silent room. Every soul on the estate was no doubt busy: farming, building, cooking, hunting, training. Everyone except he and Lexi.

He should be ashamed of himself. But he wasn't. He'd been up since dawn, checking on the new castle's progress, conferring with Guy, practicing with Deathwright.

He hadn't planned this interlude with his wife. She'd just happened to be here when he'd come to change clothes, and he'd made the mistake of touching her. As if he didn't know where that would lead, he thought with a wicked grin. Cort glanced down to find the cause of his truancy watching him with clear topaz eyes.

"Slugabed," he teased, smoothing her glorious, tangled hair with one hand while he traced her narrow waist with the other. "You've diverted me from my work. Again."

"Have I?" She didn't sound at all sorry as she smiled lazily up at him, then lifted her mouth to his.

"Hmmmm."

Fighting the arousal that threatened to once again distract him, he gave her a hard, final hug. "I asked Stefan to join us when he finished sword practice with Philip. As that was some time ago, I expect him momentarily." Cort winked. "I rather think he would prefer to find us dressed."

Legs entwined, bedclothes rumpled, they looked at each other and grinned.

"Seeing his sister naked would not faze him, I

think, one way or the other." Lexi stroked Cort's hair from his cheeks. "But responsible youth that he's become, I fear my brother would be scandalized to find me whiling away the day in such a frivolous manner."

Disentangling herself from Cort and the damp sheets, Lexi climbed over him and down the steps of the high bed. Whisking her simple cotton dress from the floor, where she'd tossed it in her haste to make love, he remembered with smug satisfaction, she shook out the wrinkles.

"Stop."

Brows raised, Lexi turned toward him.

With a deliberate leer, he sat up and perused her body from her long, slender feet to the top of her lovely head.

"What?" she asked, coloring beneath his appreciative stare.

"I was just thinking," he said, "about names—how they've played a part in our lives from the moment we met."

She gazed at him, clearly puzzled. "Yes, and...?"

"Mine has no significance. Well, Dornogard does, and I'll explain that when Stefan joins us. But our pets, my destrier, my sword. All their names have special meaning."

"May I dress while you continue this game?" Without waiting for permission, she began to pull the garment over her head.

"Not yet."

Disgruntled, Lexi lowered it, her arms still in the sleeves.

"All right." He gave a stifled laugh. "I just wondered if you know what *your* name means."

"My name?" Brow creased, she shrugged. "I never thought about it."

"You should," he advised. "Your parents' choice was perfect."

Piqued by his amused tone, she approached the bed and narrowed her eyes at him. "And why is that?"

"Just look at you," he said, his voice a husky, reverent whisper. "Every beautiful, slender inch."

Lexi cocked her head, a tentative smile softening her mouth. "My name means beautiful and slender?"

"Depends on your perspective." Cort's long fingers reached out to caress a firm thigh. "To me it does."

Lexi trembled at his touch. "Which means that's not—"

His hand trailed over her hip and down her leg. "Which means that when I watch you walk or dance, it's all I can think of, wild rose. And when you're wrapped around me in bed, it's heaven."

Lexi smacked his wide, muscular chest with the loose end of a sleeve. "Tell me what my name means, you impossible Norman."

Laughter rumbled from his chest. "Besotted Norman," Cort corrected, his gaze traveling from her waist to her feet. He raised his eyes to hers, making no attempt to disguise his desire.

"Alexis," he murmured, "means all legs."

She leaped on him then, though she hadn't a chance against him with her arms imprisoned in her dress sleeves. "It doesn't!" she snapped as he pulled her across him and wrestled her to her back. "You made that up."

"Why would I do that?" A roguish grin split his face.

"Because *Cort* means horse's behind."

He choked. "I think you made *that* up."

"True," she admitted. "But it fits."

"Oh?" His mouth quirked. "I'd take offense, but I rather appreciate your quick wit. Better yet, I'd rather you prove it's true." He tugged the dress from her arms and tossed it over his shoulder. "Show me it fits, wife. Wrap all of your legs around this horse's behind."

They'd barely dressed and straightened the bed when Stefan arrived. If he noticed Lexi's swollen lips and Cort's lazy, sated expression, he gave no sign. Running a brush quickly through her hair, Lexi plaited it in a single, thick rope that draped over her shoulder as he and her husband carried the bench from the hearth to position it opposite Cort's chair.

Studying her husband's pensive features, Lexi found it difficult to believe him the same man who'd romped with her in bed mere minutes before.

"I promised to tell you of the cause of the friction between me and Bouchard." His sober turquoise gaze found Lexi's as she sat. "I think it only fair, and equally important, that Stefan knows as well."

Lexi nodded, glad he trusted her brother enough to reveal the truth. Warmed to her soul that he trusted *her* enough.

Cort's eyes shifted to Stefan. "You are my squire. As such, I trust you with my confidences. And my life."

Stefan's chest literally swelled with pride. His expression sobered.

"Until now, only Guy and I have known the full extent of what I am about to tell you. But I feel 'tis imperative you both understand the depth of Bouchard's treachery—and why I do not trust him."

Cort scrubbed his face with his hands, then rested them on his thighs. "I worked with the master of horses at Hastings when first we landed. Most of the destriers were uneasy after the channel crossing. We had to ensure they settled before we rode into battle. Tyr, barely four then, was accustomed but to me, and except for minor skirmishes, untried in combat. Alaine's horse was older, used to several riders, and seasoned in warfare. At the time, before the fighting began, the difference did not concern me. 'Twas only later..."

Mouth tight, Cort drew a deep breath and squeezed his eyes shut as if pained by the memory he conjured. When he again opened them, Lexi shivered at their dark ferocity.

"When the king jumped off his ship, he insisted he be the first to touch English soil. In his haste, he tripped, which many soldiers took as a bad omen. Ever resourceful, William sank to his knees and kissed the sand."

"As though he meant to do so all along," Stefan offered.

"Exactly," Cort said. "Only those nearest him ever knew for certain. But the gesture reassured the men, and they cheered him.

"During the course of the battle, however, his mount was wounded and collapsed beneath him." Cort's fingers flexed and slid down to grip his knees. "When he disappeared among the knights and foot soldiers surrounding him, our forces faltered. Many thought him dead, the fight lost. It was, I think, the most crucial moment of that day."

"Could you not have signaled in some way, or called out that he was well?" Stefan blurted, eyes wide as an owl's as he listened to his lord's account of the fateful conflict.

Cort smiled without humor and shook his head. His golden mane now scattered over his shoulders and chest, he continued. "Except for those nearby, it would have done no good. The field was chaos—men shouting and cursing, horses snorting, some of both screaming with pain."

His eyes dull and distant, Lexi knew Cort's mind had retreated into the past.

"Lances jabbing, swords slicing and clashing. And everywhere, the smell of blood. So deep in places, it pooled and ran like a river. Footing was treacherous."

The word seemed to snap him back to the present. He started, gaze once more hard and focused. Stefan watched him with the fascination of an acolyte for his master. Hands knotted in her lap, Lexi held her breath in anticipation. Behind her the fire sizzled and popped as the flames consumed pockets of sap.

Cort shot to his feet to pace the length of the chamber, seeming unable to remain still as he relived what had happened next. Lexi and Stefan followed him with their eyes. "Things happen so fast in battle," he muttered. "Split-second decisions are oft the difference between victory and defeat."

He raked his hair back, then held their gazes with his as if to convince them he spoke the truth. "A horse raced by, but I was unable to catch its bridle. I was little more than a yard from William, Bouchard within striking distance behind him. Dane and Guy had become separated from me and were encircled by a group of foot soldiers. My father had ridden to the far side of the field minutes earlier to fight back a wave of Harold's reinforcements." Stance rigid, he said, "Choices were few, and we had to make one—the right one—quickly."

Cort strode back to his chair and sank into it. His head dropped forward, the gilded curtain of his hair obscuring his face. Neither Lexi nor Stefan moved.

At last Cort raised his head and said quietly, "To give Bouchard his due, he killed an axman who charged the king. But without a mount, William's breaths were numbered. I read that awareness in his eyes. Just as I read it in Bouchard's and he in mine, I'm sure. The English closed in like a pack of wolves for the kill. Christ." Pinching the bridge of his nose between thumb and forefinger, he expelled a loud breath.

"As I'd feared, Tyr had been skittish all day.

Even the melees we'd fought had not prepared him for the reality of war. And again, he was accustomed to no one save me."

"But Alaine's horse was seasoned," Stefan said, brows raised. "If he was that close to the king, he could have reached him and given—"

"He refused." Cort's voice was thick with scorn, his eyes dark with anger.

Stefan's gasp echoed Lexi's.

"I signaled him to surrender his mount, that I would take him up with me. We could have found him another. A score were riderless by then."

"What did he do?" Lexi could manage naught more than a hushed tone.

"Did the king not see him refuse?" Stefan asked on the heels of her question.

"William was fighting for his life. And he was facing me." Cort's gaze shifted to Lexi. "Bouchard wheeled his horse and rode away. Never even looked back." His jaw clenched. "'Twas the last I saw of him that day."

Lexi sensed her brother's shock ran as deep as her own. For a moment she could not form a coherent thought. Cort sat as still as a granite statue.

"What did you do?" Lexi whispered.

"Gave him Tyr." Cort shrugged. "Despite the risk that Tyr might not respond exactly as he'd been trained, I had no choice. It was imperative the men see at once that their king was safe. No time to capture another horse. And he had to have his own. To command, to move freely about the field."

"Which left you—"

"On foot." He spread his hands with casual unconcern. "Better me than the king."

Lexi gaped at him with pride, and more than a little outrage. Though she understood the honor that had motivated him, she could not agree with his final comment. Better for William, no doubt. Certainly not for Cort—or her.

"What happened then?" Stefan urged.

"Guy heard the commotion and fought his way back to me, Dane close at his back. He took me up behind him until I found another mount."

He spoke of the incident as matter of factly as Lexi might mention which herbs she'd harvested that day. She didn't know whether to hug or strangle him.

"Did Tyr behave for the king?" her brother asked.

"Rather well, actually. Better than I'd expected. Afterward, William told me they had one contest of wills early on, then managed fine together."

"They say the king removed his helmet during the battle," Stefan said. "Is that true?"

"Aye." Cort nodded. "One of the most courageous, foolhardy gestures I've e'er seen."

You should know, Lexi thought, biting her tongue to prevent speaking the words aloud.

"As soon as he was seated on Tyr, William removed his helmet so the men could see 'twas really he. Our forces rallied at once, took new heart in the certainty he was hale. I'll ne'er forget how he looked at that moment, how the men cheered and fought with new ferocity. Had I not already committed to him, he'd have earned my undying loyalty then." Cort's eyes glittered with admiration.

"William is *Uncle Will*, isn't he?" Stefan asked.

"Aye, lad. Not by blood, as I told your sister the day he arrived, but by affection."

"Then, Deathwright was a gift from the king," Stefan whispered in awe. He frowned. "But if Deathwright is the Golden Dragon's sword," he murmured, "*your sword*—why does the hilt not look like the one told in stories of you?"

Cort chuckled. "The description you'd repeated

to me that first evening you polished the blade was exaggerated, Stefan. But if you'll bring it to me, I'll show you something that might help ease your disappointment."

Needing no further encouragement, her brother raced to where Deathwright hung beside the hearth and took it at once to Cort. Lexi watched in surprise as her husband slipped a knife from his boot and sliced through the oiled-leather grip. The night he'd showed her the castle plans, he'd been adamant Stefan take care not to damage the hilt. Why was he now—

Cort grinned like a proud father as he peeled back the soft leather and tossed it aside. Arms extended, he offered the blade to the butter-rich light that poured through the casement beside him.

The hilt glittered in the sun, a finely wrought, gold-plated dragon with turquoise eyes, its tail wrapped up and over its back to form a perfect curve for a man's hand. The furled wings rested upon an azure starburst.

Stefan's hand trembled as he touched it with reverent fingers. Lexi's own unconsciously strayed to the pendant at her breast.

"It is magnificent, my lord," Stefan said, voice breathless with wonder.

Lexi's gaze locked with her husband's. "Like owner, like sword."

"Like wife," he mouthed back.

They met halfway, lips touching in a brief but telling kiss.

Absorbed in Deathwright, Stefan ignored them.

Cort arched a brow at him. "Take it, lad."

As if afraid it would shatter, he cradled it in his hands, then sat on the floor and laid it across his lap.

"One last thing I must tell you." Cort leaned forward and took Lexi's hand.

"May I ask you something first?" she ventured, unsure of the wisdom of her question, yet compelled to seek the answer.

"Aye. Anything."

Convinced from all she knew of him, especially that he abhorred war's savagery and needless brutality, Lexi gathered her courage. "What became of the two prisoners?"

His brow creased in confusion. "Who?"

"The two prisoners you captured after the ambush and brought here. They disappeared after you questioned them and were never mentioned again." She paused. "No one dared inquire about their fate."

"That was my intent," Cort admitted. "Guy loves me as vicious warlord." He grimaced. "I could not allow Amiton's people to believe treachery against me would go unpunished. They knew the men had been involved in the attack. I had no choice—"

Horrified, Lexi gasped. "You killed them?"

"Nay!" Cort's sincerity eased the sudden tightness in her chest. "I let them go."

"Let them go?" she breathed.

"They were instruments, not the villain who planned the attack. Neither one knew anything useful. Both have families who depend on them. I frightened them near to death, I think, for which I will not apologize, but in the end Guy and I sent them on their way unharmed." He shrugged broad shoulders and squeezed her hands. "No one here was the wiser, and my point made. Satisfied?"

Relief swamped her. "Very."

"Now, to this last thing I wish to tell you." He cleared his throat. "Why I chose to call myself Dornogard."

Recalling their earlier conversation and its aftermath, heat rose in Lexi's cheeks. Cort's wolfish grin said he read her mind.

"Fond as you are of names, I half expected you'd have unraveled it by now."

"I've not given it much thought." Not since the night when, engaged in fanciful daydreams, she'd toyed with the letters on the back of the castle sketch she'd not seen since.

Cort tapped her nose. "Think about it. Rearrange the letters."

Brows furrowed in concentration, she and Stefan looked at each other. For a minute she could think of nothing except Melissande's comment that Alaine had said there was more to Cort than they knew. In that, at least, her husband's enemy had spoken the truth.

She dismissed the memory, now unimportant, and let the letters in *Dornorgard* tumble about in her brain like wind-blown leaves.

"Aren't you the clever one," Lexi said in awed delight when part of the solution at last clicked into place. "The last six letters, reversed, spell dragon." She laughed softly. "All this time, I never saw it."

Stefan grinned. "But d-o-r or r-o-d...o-r-d? o-d-r? They don't..." His pleasure slid into puzzlement.

"Ah, but they do," Cort said. "I suppose 'tis only fair I tell you I eliminated the apostrophe."

Which tells me nothing, Lexi thought, exasperated. Apostrophe or not, the letters still made no sense.

When neither she nor her brother was able to unravel Cort's clue, he at last relented. "D-'-o-r, in French, means gold or golden. Golden Dragon is *dragon d'or*. I reversed the last set of letters, moved the first three to the beginning, and dropped the apostrophe. So, wife," he teased, "you are quite right. I am clever."

Lexi smacked his arm. "And fortunate that *Dornogard* sounds so...Norse."

"Pure luck, wild rose." Grin smug, his eyes went

dark and hot.

Lexi's heart tumbled when he skimmed his knuckles down her cheek. "Like finding you. Pure luck."

Chapter Twenty-Six

Pain unlike any he'd ever known almost dropped Cort to his knees. He closed his eyes, pleading with gods both Norse and Christian that he misunderstood. That he hadn't seen what he knew he'd seen.

Knowing his pleas were futile.

He forced his eyes open, made himself look again at the smoke-and-dirt-smudged sketch he now pressed flat on the bedside table in Lexi's chamber. The literal black-and-white proof he'd sought, prayed for… He all but choked on the devastating irony. To steady himself, Cort gripped the table's worn wooden edge. Air pumped in and out of his lungs as though he'd run for miles.

It's not true. Sweet Christ, let it not be true.

He spread his palms over the wrinkled parchment, no longer able to bear the sight of the evidence of Lexi's guilt. Her words that day he'd taken her up on Tyr for a ride mocked him.

The night you showed me your renderings of the castle and I drew that one of my own... I can't find it... left it on the table in my chamber, but it's gone. Thene's mischief... at the very least, I would need to touch up the sketch.

Clever girl. She'd have had to do more than *touch it up*. How she must have enjoyed her veiled taunts. How convenient the sketch was *lost*—and to blame its disappearance on Athene. She'd never mentioned it again, and between their wedding and company, he'd forgotten it.

Cort straightened slowly, his gaze now riveted to

the bold, elementary lines of the donjon, the curtain wall. The passages beneath. They seemed to leap off the page, mutely scorning his hope. His trust. His love, goddamn it. For at the base of the sketch, smeared yet all too clear still, a heavily circled *X*. In the very spot where the tunnel timbers had burned and caused the collapse.

Pure luck...pure luck...pure luck. The words he'd spoken to Lexi two days before pounded like hammer blows within his skull.

Nay. Cruel fate—Wyrd—his forbears would say, to snatch from him the greatest joy he'd ever known, the all-consuming love he'd just discovered. The dream of his own home and family.

But it was *pure luck* he'd found the drawing. Pure, cursed luck.

For the first time in his life, Cort understood the meaning of agony. Tears burned his eyes. Rage choked him. Shock waves, alternately hot and cold, racked his body. Bitter, guttural laughter he could not control poured from his throat.

He crushed the drawing in his fist, then turned it over as if doing so could somehow erase the truth. Feminine scribbles on the back drew his attention. With rigid fingers he once more smoothed the parchment.

His assumed surname, written in varied patterns: downward, sideways, crosswise, circular, covered the page. Had Bouchard hinted about his true identity to Lexi, implied he was other than he seemed? Had she figured it out, known all along who he was and only feigned her response when she'd overheard the king?

Did it matter?

Athene, stretched out now atop her cage, watched him with black, unblinking eyes. Thene, who had unwittingly dragged the drawing from a crevice beside Lexi's old bed and begun to bat it around as he entered the room. Thene, whose ironic betrayal of her mistress threatened to unleash in Cort another burst of irrational laughter.

Thoughts and suspicions spun and clashed in his head. Loyalty could indeed be a two-edged sword. Because he had wanted so badly to believe, he'd not questioned Lexi's seamless transition from faith in Alaine to faith in him. And then there was Dane's odd behavior of late, his withdrawal, his constant shadowing of Lexi. Cort had simply assumed the man overprotective since she'd taken the arrow intended for him. Now, Cort wondered if Dane was torn between loyalty to his lord and the woman he'd come to admire and adore. Had he seen something, heard something that might implicate his mistress in the ambush, the fire?

Cort groaned. Too many uncertainties, which he'd chosen to ignore. Because he'd let his heart rule his head. No more. Before his eyes, black-and-white proof he could *not* ignore, of his wife's guilt.

He'd been blindsided, all his defenses stripped away. A week of heaven, he thought with sick disillusionment, for which he would pay with a lifetime of hell.

But not alone, he vowed. Before he was done, Lexi, too, would understand the meaning of perdition.

Cort stormed into their chamber and slammed the door shut with his boot. Garbed in only a sheer linen underblouse, Lexi whirled to face him. "What—"

"Recognize this?" He hurled the wadded parchment so hard and fast, she had no time to react. It struck her breast before dropping to the floor.

Stunned, Lexi stared at her husband, then shifted her gaze to the crumpled paper at her feet.

"Pick it up," he snarled.

She could not seem to make herself move. "I don't know—"

"Pick it up, *lady wife*," he said too softly. "Or by Christ and Odin, I'll pick it up for you and ram it down your throat."

Dazed, Lexi understood nothing—except that he was deadly serious. For the first time since they'd met, she truly feared him. Realized that until now she'd never seen him roused to more than irritatation or annoyance. Recognized, without having to be told, that this Cort was the one his enemies faced on the battlefield. Brutal, ruthless, single-minded, and without conscience.

Here, then, was the Golden Dragon.

A frisson of terror skittered up Lexi's spine, intensifying her confusion. Eyes locked with Cort's, she bent, fumbled with shaking fingers for the crumpled parchment. When at last she managed to grasp it, she straightened, her gaze never leaving her husband's hard face.

"Open it. Look at it."

Lexi almost wished he would yell at her. His quiet, controlled fury unnerved her more than his glacial stare and frozen stance.

The parchment crackled as she stretched it taut between her hands. His name leaped out at her in the fanciful patterns she'd scribbled that night over a month ago. But why would that upset him? She'd never unraveled the letters, and he'd since explained, so...

"I was thinking of you," she murmured. "Romantic, mayhap foolish—"

"Far more than foolish. More name games, wife?" Cort whispered, voice silky with menace. "Courtesy of our *friend* Bouchard?"

Was he saying...? Fury stained her cheeks.

"How touching you can still blush with guilt after all you've done. A man died in that tunnel." His tone whipped over her skin like tendrils of fire.

"Guilt?" He'd mistaken the cause of her reaction. What did he think she'd done that would make her—

"My name doesn't matter now." Cort's hand cleaved the air in a violent arc. "Turn the paper over, lady."

Lexi did as ordered, having forgotten until she saw it what was on the other side. "My sketch!"

"Then you don't deny it's yours?" For a moment, he appeared bewildered, his anger tempered by surprise.

"Of course I don't deny it. Why should I?"

Lexi took in his shuttered gaze, the skin stretched tight over high cheekbones.

"Look at it," he ordered from between clenched teeth. "Look at it closely. Then, you tell me."

Lexi dropped her gaze to the crinkled drawing. Brow furrowing when she noted the inexplicable dirt and soot smears, she followed the original, lightly flared lines of the donjon, the outward curve she'd later added to the curtain wall. Her eyes tracked lower.

For a moment the significance of the circled *X* did not penetrate. When it did, her fingers tightened convulsively. Her eyes snapped back to his. "Where did you find this?" she demanded, as furious as he. "The original sketch is mine, but I never marked the spot—"

He sneered. "Most convincing, Alexis." That he had distanced himself from her was clear in his use of her formal name. "Such credible outrage. You are either mad, or the best liar I have ever known."

Lexi swallowed his verbal assault, determined he answer her. "Where did you get this?" She shook the parchment now clenched in her right hand.

"Not that it matters," he said, "but Thene dragged it out of a crack in the wall beside your old bed. I'd stopped in to put her back in her cage at the very moment she pulled it free."

"Where's the riband?"

"What riband?"

"The red one I tied it with."

"There was no riband. And what the hell difference does it make?" He scowled with impatient ire.

"All the difference," Lexi insisted. "I told you the day we rode to see the castle that I suspected she'd stolen it. Her eyesight is poor, but she's drawn to bright colors. That must be why—"

Cort's harsh laughter cut through her explanation. "Did she hide it before or after she'd altered it?" he asked, tone scathing.

Lexi bristled at his mockery. "Of course she didn't. Someone else must have found—" She stumbled to a halt, aware of how far-fetched that sounded. Equally aware it was the only explanation. Which meant someone within the manor, someone whose presence within her chamber would not be remarked, was a traitor.

With that incredible speed she'd come to expect from him, Cort closed the gap between them and grasped her shoulders with remorseless fingers. "Who else knew of it? Who but you, Demming, Guy, and I?"

Her uncle's brief appearance in the solarium the night Cort had shown her the new castle plans flashed through her mind. But she would not believe him guilty of treachery. And he had not known of the sketch. Had he? "No one." The truth, of course, only further implicated her. Lexi winced but refused to buckle when his fingers dug deep enough to bruise muscle.

"You neither planned nor executed the deed alone. You could not risk being caught in the tunnel." An unholy light blazed in her husband's eyes. "Who helped you? Bouchard, of course," he answered himself. "He had both motivation and opportunity."

But not access to her chamber, Lexi thought. Again, from Cort's perspective, *she alone* provided the link between the perpetrator and the fire. Since denial would earn her naught, she called upon reason.

"You dare think I've betrayed you? What of Geoff?" she demanded. "Did I save him to amuse myself? Did I defend you at table and then hit myself over the head?"

Her mind rebelled at his lack of trust. Her thoughts raced with all the arguments she might summon to convince him of her innocence. "What of the day you announced our betrothal and I did not gainsay you? The aid I offered when the tunnel collapsed?" Her breasts rose and fell in agitation. "The arrow I took in your stead? For the love of Mary, our marriage? Our lovemaking?"

Lexi's heart ached far worse than her shoulders at the knowledge that he could so easily discount all they'd shared. Her acceptance of who he was, the humor, the affection.

Face mere inches from hers, Cort's eyes paled to icy shards, his breath blew hot on her trembling mouth. "I haven't yet had time to fit all the pieces together. But I will."

"Let me know when you do," she dared, no longer caring how he would react. He could not hurt her any more than he already had. The physical pain was but an irritation. 'Twas the fear of losing him—fear she'd already lost him—running parallel with love that drove her. "I'd like to hear it myself."

He ignored her. "You had to at least pretend to help me, didn't you? Assuage my doubts, as it were."

Lexi sensed him falter. His eyes widened, and for a heartbeat revealed vivid pain. Then they darkened once more before he closed them against her.

"By Christ's Holy Rood! I have no one to blame but myself. I fell for it. For you. Every witty barb, every lying smile."

Lexi backstepped as he reopened his eyes and slid his hands down to manacle her upper arms with vicious force. If he meant to intimidate her, he succeeded. The sheer size and strength of him all but overwhelmed her, yet she would not let him see it. The injustice of his accusations burned like acid in her blood and shot bile into her throat.

She swallowed hard. And kicked him.

He thrust her against the wall and pinned her there with his massive body. "Oh, you were good, lady," he purred, ignoring her resistance. "All those heartfelt sighs and throaty moans, your pure-as-truth gold eyes."

Without warning, Cort's left hand snaked out, tangled in her unbound hair, and yanked her head back. It cracked against the wall. Her mew of pain was muffled as he ground his mouth over hers. Stars shattered behind her eyelids, and she tasted blood.

"This is what you want, isn't it?" he growled. "Proof of my...affection? Surely, if you prefer Alaine, my shows of lust thus far have been much too tame."

Lust? Lexi thought, her mind reeling from Cort's verbal and physical punishment. Was that all he felt for her?

Nay. She would not believe it. He'd treated her with kindness and concern from the first, and far more tolerance than she'd deserved. He might not love her, but—

The sound of rending fabric jerked her back to the present. Left hand still snarled in her hair, Cort had bunched her shift in his right and torn it to the waist.

Hot gaze fastened on her bare, upthrust breasts, he swore, "No other man will ever see you like this.

Touch you like this." He raised his eyes to hers as he cupped one heavy globe and squeezed just short of pain. "Certainly not Bouchard."

"He... I never..." She could barely hear herself above the blood thundering in her ears. "Bouchard is—was—a friend. Nothing more," she insisted in a thready voice.

"Loyal to the end," Cort murmured, aqua eyes bleak and distant. "One of the things that drew me to you." His laugh was brief and bitter. "But you must learn to choose your loyalties more carefully."

Lexi longed to tell him the truth about what she knew of the ambush, what she'd done. In the end, pride held her mute. If all they'd shared, all they'd been to each other was not enough to convince her husband of her commitment to him, her secret would hardly do so. Perhaps it was too late anyway. He was clearly unwilling to listen. And might not believe her even if he did.

"You are *my* wife, lady, whether you wish it or no," Cort whispered against her throat. "On our wedding night, 'twas to *me* you gave your virginity. Was it a noble sacrifice, a black necessity of your scheme? When the plots against me failed, was marriage to me the single alternative?"

He raised his head, gripped her jaw in clenched fingers. "Should I die now, as my widow, you would inherit Amiton. I am one of the king's favorites, and he seems taken with you. He would likely allow you to remarry whom you wish. Bouchard's treachery would remain a secret. And should you choose him, William would not object."

As if that final thought shattered what remained of his tenuous control, Cort released her hair and surged forward, crushing Lexi between his iron-hard body and the wall. Some small part of her admired his reasoning, absurd as she knew it to be. The larger part despised him for thinking so little of her, and for abusing—worse, destroying—the tenderness she'd so cherished in him.

His right hand plunged between them, then fumbled with the leather points of his chausses. Nay, she thought, panicked. He would not...could not... Dear God.

She kicked and squirmed, nails clawing at his arms and face.

The large hand still clamped about her jaw tightened until pain shot through her temples and she feared the bones would crack. Her arms fell to her sides when his other hand tore away what remained of her shift, then returned to work free the fastenings at his waist.

His fingers—which she'd once thought an artist's, tapered and elegant—moved down to her throat, their solid pressure threatening to choke her. "Open for me, lady wife." Cort's voice drifted to her, strained and dark.

The edges of her vision blurred, Lexi forced her gaze to his. Her heart beat like a trapped animal's. And she said what she had never thought to say to him. "No."

"No?" he panted, eyes narrowed. "You would deny your husband?"

"You are not my husband," she managed, despite the press of fingers on her throat. "My husband is kind and gentle—"

"Your husband, Alexis, was a trusting fool. *This husband* is not. Our *marriage*," he sneered, "shall be as *I* dictate henceforth. You will warm my bed and do as I say. No more."

His hands spanned her waist and slid her up the wall, careless of the random splinters that tunneled into her back. Damned if she'd let him see her pain, she swallowed the cry filling her throat. While she did not believe he'd done it apurpose, his intent to rape her was clear. More than enough pain in that to last a lifetime.

As her face came level with his, Cort's gaze fell to her right shoulder, the arrow scar just newly healed. He turned his head away, and her throat convulsed at the memory of that afternoon, her husband's tender care of her in the days that followed. Memories, Lexi thought. All she would ever have now.

Unless she could prove her innocence.

Cort's hips ground into hers as he gripped her thighs and tried to force them apart. Against his superior strength and without leverage, resistance was futile. Still, she would fight him to her last breath.

"If you do this," she vowed, "I will hate. You. Until the day I die."

"Is that supposed to stop me?" One fair brow arched.

His golden hair had slipped free of its thong during their struggle and was as tangled as her own. Absurd that, even now, she longed to smooth it from his face, wrap her fingers in its silken length, kiss the gossamer strands that clung to his wide, sensual mouth.

Lexi shook her head slowly, wretched tears blurring her eyes until she could no longer see him. "No," she choked. "Nothing, no one can stop you. Just as after it's done, neither you nor I will ever again be the same."

The tragic truth of that settled in her heart and drained the last of her resistance. If Cort took her now, in anger and without consent, even proof of her innocence could never repair the damage done. He would break her spirit in a way she could not explain. As nothing else in life ever could.

Her body went limp at the thought, boneless as a cloth doll's. Her senses dimmed as her mind closed in upon itself, unable to bear the death throes of the only love she had ever known. The only love she would ever want.

When Cort thrust against her once more, her legs parted like lifeless sticks. He pulled them around his muscular waist and held them there.

Lexi closed her eyes, hot tears seeping beneath her lids to trickle down her cheeks. Shoulders pressed painfully to the wall, hands hanging at her sides, she accepted her utter vulnerability. And ceased to care.

Long moments passed before she realized Cort had stilled, the only sound, his harsh breathing. Then, he stepped back. Lexi would have collapsed to the floor had he not caught her. Face blank, he lifted her in his arms, turned, and tossed her upon their bed.

Without a word or backward glance, he adjusted his clothing and strode from the room. Lexi heard him move to the top of the stairs and call out, her mind too numb to register the words. Booted feet beat a rapid tattoo up the spiral steps and stopped beside the door. Low voices filtered through the opening.

Lexi wiped her tear-stained face and, racked with chills, pulled the light coverlet around her.

The door snapped shut. A key grated in the lock.

Chapter Twenty-Seven

"Where is she now?"

"Locked in our chamber. Dane's standing guard." In the deepening shadows of the solar, Cort made no attempt to disguise his devastation.

"Is that wise?" Guy asked. "He's devoted to her."

Cort raked unsteady fingers through his unbound hair and sank onto the bench beside the blazing hearth. An unseasonably chill wind had picked up in late afternoon; storm clouds massed on the horizon. Conditions well-suited to both his thoughts and mood.

"I told him we had an argument." Cort frowned at the vast understatement. "That she threatened to leave. He thinks he is protecting her from the hazards of running away, alone, at night."

Though Guy nodded, Cort had never seen him look so harried.

"Something's not right," he muttered, settling on a stool opposite Cort. "Our instincts have always been good. One or the other of us has erred on occasion, but both? Never."

"You would defend her?" Cort asked, voice dangerously soft.

"I'm trying to reason this out," Guy shot back. "I'd have staked my life we could trust—"

"Here's your trust, *mon ami*!" Cort tore Lexi's sketch from inside his tunic and tossed it in his friend's lap. "Look at it." He surged to his feet to pace the chamber's width and back.

Guy smoothed the crinkled parchment across his knees, then studied it, front and back. His breath whistled through his teeth when he at last looked up. "Where did you find this?"

Lexi's question. Lexi's protests of innocence. Lexi's liquid gold, guileless eyes. Even now, his love and need for her pumped through him in hot, heavy waves. Damn her.

"She had courage if no sense," he mumbled, thinking of what she'd risked by defying him. Had he chosen to, he could have crushed her.

"What?"

"Nothing." Cort rubbed his forehead and returned his attention to Guy. "You asked...?"

He tapped the parchment.

"In Lexi's chamber. Thene wriggled backward out of a space between the boards just as I entered. She dragged that"—he jerked his head at the sketch—"out with her."

Guy's expression grew pensive. "This is the sketch Lexi mentioned the day you rode to the castle site? The one that disappeared?"

Cort nodded, unsure of Guy's point.

"You know she never locks her door, that anyone who needs her wanders in at will."

"Your point?"

"Someone could have found this and tampered with it." His second-in-command raised the bedraggled sheet. "Returned it later."

Cort sneered. "A lot of things *could* happen. How much coincidence do you expect me to swallow?"

Guy shrugged, though his demeanor did not ease. "Foolhardy, even dangerous, to keep the sketch. It could do naught but incriminate her."

Vague unease slithered down Cort's spine. If he were wrong... "Unless she spoke the truth, at least in that it disappeared. Thene *might* have hidden it."

"Possible," Guy conceded. "What about writing your name in these designs on the back?"

"She was thinking of me." Cort glowered. "I bet

she was."

"Is that so difficult to believe?" Guy asked, eyes hooded. "If she cares for you—"

Cort's hand slashed the air. "We're speaking of Lexi, my friend. Prosaic, pragmatic Lexi. Am I to believe she'd play romantic games with my name?"

And wasn't that precisely what she'd said?

"She's a woman, Cort. All women dream of romance."

Guy's defense of his wife was wearing on Cort. "Other than the arrow, that drawing's the only hard evidence we've had these two months to provide proof against our attackers. She's involved somehow."

"Which reminds me. Right before you summoned me here, I had word of Hal Robbins, Bouchard's archer," Guy interrupted. "Donald spoke with Lang earlier today. Robbins didn't make it home that day. Told his wife he was going hunting. Never returned."

Cort could well imagine what had happened. Whether he'd failed or succeeded, Robbins was a threat to Bouchard. No doubt, the man was dead, his corpse buried, never to be found.

"Another convenient coincidence," he muttered in disgust. "But that does not absolve Lexi."

"Perhaps we should begin from the day we arrived. With the king gone back to court, we needn't dine for several hours. If we talk this through, we may see aught we've missed."

Cort drew in a calming breath, returned to the bench, and dropped his head back. He massaged the headache raging in his temples, resigned to sort through every remembered detail.

An hour later, the overwhelming pain and fury he'd felt when he discovered the sketch and confronted Lexi had receded to a controllable simmer. His headache, however, beat inside his skull like Thor's hammer.

The storm had arrived full force, battering the shuttered casement and pounding the wooden roof in slashing waves. Restless, he'd paced the solar while he and Guy reviewed every fact they could recall, then stirred and stoked the fire against the damp, invasive chill.

As he sank once more onto the bench, Guy ignored him, concentration centered on the notes he'd made on the heavy linen paper. Cort closed his stinging eyelids in hopes the powerful storm and the hissing flames might soothe his raw nerves. And heart. They didn't.

Lexi, he thought, a fresh wave of pain cresting within him. So witty, so bright, so lovely. So clever, so treacherous. Her betrayal pierced him to the soul, stripping him of every dream he'd ever cherished. He'd ignored his gut suspicions, handed her his soul, much as he had the castle plans, on a platter. No one but himself to blame.

He thought of his sister, his parents, who were to leave in two days' time. They musn't discover what had happened. His parents must depart believing his marriage would be as fulfilling as theirs. They'd taken Lexi to their hearts as surely as he had. To reveal her perfidy would destroy them.

A bitter smile ghosted over his mouth. How right he'd been that his mother would love Lexi.

"Almost finished," Guy muttered, severing Cort's musings.

The quill scratched over the stiff linen as his friend made some final notations, then clicked the hollow, feathered shaft as he laid it aside. Cort cracked open one eye to peer at him. He appeared far too satisfied.

Because he knew from experience what that look signified, Cort groaned. Guy loved the role of devil's advocate, but Cort was in no mood tonight to humor him.

"Yes, my lord," he said with infuriating resolve, dark brow arched. "One last time. For continuity and objectivity."

Cort stretched, felt the welcome pull of tendon and muscle, and glared at his persistent companion. "All right."

Guy leaned forward, elbows on knees. "On our way here," he began, "we were attacked."

"Ambushed."

"As our two captives verified. "

Cort grunted assent at the memory of the men's terror.

"I met Lexi before you did. I told you then, I tell you now, her treatment of Geoffrey was careful and competent. He recovered well, did he not?"

"Don't bait me, Guy," Cort warned. "Present the facts and see what we can make of them."

"So, in her favor—"

"It would have been most unwise for Lexi to do other than heal him. Since I arrived basically whole, her cause was better advanced by gaining my trust."

"True, but what of Dane? Why go out of her way to befriend him?"

"Mayhap she believed his friendship would benefit her in some way." More slowly, he added, "Or she felt sorry for him." Pity clutched at his heart that Lexi might have used Dane for her own ends rather than from any true affection for him.

Guy winced, clearly unable to argue the point. Instead, he proceeded. "She treated your injury shortly after that. Again, was gentle and competent."

With sharp pain, Cort recollected their initial meeting: those first moments when he'd thought her mad, his introduction to Thene, the laughter in Lexi's sane, coin-gold eyes. And after, her veiled comment that she meant him no harm—her trembling body when he'd questioned how she knew the cause of his wound.

Eyes stark, Cort focused on Guy once more. “She knew—*knows*—something, Guy. I felt it that afternoon, and I feel it now.”

“We’ve discussed this. I’m not saying you’re wrong. Remember, you deceived her, but not for nefarious purposes. Even if she’s hiding something, it doesn’t mean—”

“Then why not divulge whatever it is when I confronted her with the sketch?” Cort all but shouted. “It might have stopped me from—”

“You hurt her!” Guy accused, stunned.

“She’s my wife,” Cort snarled, unwilling to acknowledge the guilt that lashed him at what he’d almost done. “I may do with her what I wish.”

Guy glared his condemnation until Cort lowered his gaze. “Not really.

“Her arms may be a bit bruised. I grabbed her. I couldn’t think, I was so...” He closed his eyes, and saw Lexi’s opaque stare, felt his own agonized rage.

Guy’s expression softened with compassion. “You are like a wounded bear, my lord, that lashes out against its torment. Your anger is spurred by pain, and all the more anguished for it.”

Cort turned away, again wondering if Guy’s ability to read him was gift or curse. He breathed deep as his heart twisted. Voice gruff, he asked, “What’s next on your damn list?”

Guy glanced at the parchment clenched in his fist. “Lexi’s defense of you that first night, the assault on her afterward.”

“Again, her defense of me might have been a ploy to gain our trust. But why would...” A disturbing thought resurfaced. “Guy.” Breath clogged his throat. “What if her assailant was someone who suspected she planned to betray me? Someone who feared her scheme might jeopardize Amiton’s people, that my anger might be turned against them? To call her ‘traitor’ would take on a whole new meaning."

Guy blanched but rallied quickly. "Supposition. My instincts still insist she's innocent, my lord."

Cort suppressed another groan. His second-in-command could get a rise out of the Virgin Mary.

He could not bring himself to say that his own instincts had, until now, done the same. Since Lexi's advent into his life, he'd no longer been sure of anything.

Guy cleared his throat. "Next, Bouchard's arrival."

Cort's jaw hardened. "On that our instincts agree. He is the source of all that's gone awry."

Guy nodded. "Lexi's reaction to his intentions was as stunned as her response to your declaration of betrothal. You were busy watching Bouchard," he said at Cort's skeptical look. "I watched her. I swear on my soul, she was totally unprepared for either offer."

Cort considered that, aware for the first time the rain had abated and the wind died down. "Even so, surprise does not mean she's not in league with him. Had I not intervened, their betrothal would have allowed them to spend time together without raising suspicion. Had she accepted—"

"Or rejected," Guy blurted.

"Or rejected," Cort spat, "it would not necessarily have affected their intrigue. They'd managed well enough before."

"Assuming they were working together at all."

"One more word, *mon ami*, and you'll be searching the floor for your teeth."

"Just trying to maintain our objectivity," Guy said, unperturbed.

With a baleful glare, Cort moved on. "During Bouchard's visit, the tunnel collapsed. Which brings us back to Lexi's sketch."

Guy's expression sobered. "It looks damning, I

agree. Yet, again, why would Lexi keep proof of her treachery? She'd have destroyed it. Immediately. You would have, Cort."

"Unless Thene hid it before she had the chance. Stupid not to leave it to burn in the fire." Doubts and probabilities rattled around in his brain like carelessly thrown dice. He could not refute Guy's logic, longed to believe him as desperately as he longed to be in his wife's arms again, secure in her warmth and affection. As desperately as he wished things could be as they had been.

Yet she'd admitted the drawing—most of it, anyway—was hers. To accept someone had stolen, then replaced it, only to have Thene hide it, strained credibility.

If innocent, why had Lexi not revealed what she knew of the ambush when he'd threatened her this afternoon? If there'd ever been a time to speak up... .

"What of the arrow Lexi took, meant for you?" Guy's voice reverberated in the strained silence.

Cort's gut tightened at the memory of her lunging toward him, deliberately placing herself between him and their would-be assassins. The arrow in her shoulder. The blood. Her agonized scream when he'd pulled it free.

She'd risked her life to save his. Or had she?

When Cort did not reply, Guy said, "That leaves only three unknowns. Our mysterious slinger, Lexi's assailant, and the inside informant."

Cort was only half listening.

"If *you're* right, the first two could be the same person. And Lexi," Guy added quietly, "could be the third. But I don't believe it. I won't."

Cort raked back his hair, mind still wrestling with Lexi's behavior the day they'd gone hunting. Would she have sought him out had he not happened by? Known they'd be followed?

"What if she knew?" His heart pounded. "What

if it was an accident?"

Cort surged to his feet. Guy rose to face him, green eyes dark. "What do you mean?"

"Lexi could have expected the attack. She had sufficient time between our meetings at the mews and the stables to tell someone of our outing." The possibility turned his gut to stone, his heart to a shriveled knot.

"When the slinger missed and she moved between us, it looked like a courageous attempt to protect me. But she never expected the archer to fire. Don't you see?"

Guy stared at him, expression incredulous.

"She never dreamed he'd shoot *her*. Thought to pretend to save me without risk to herself." A muscle in his jaw ticked painfully. "I think—"

"What *I* think," Guy grated out between clenched teeth, "is you're twisting everything to suit your tortuous reasoning. Why is that? To justify your cruel treatment of her earlier?" He smacked one fisted hand into his other's open palm. "Your conjectures are absurd. And far more devious than your lady ever thought to be."

Guy mirrored Cort's aggressive stance. Fury flashed in his sea-green eyes.

"You would put our dreams at risk to defend her?" Cort demanded. "Our friendship?"

"Nay." Guy's voice vibrated with anger as they faced off like snarling wolves. "You would."

"Had we not been like brothers for so long, I would call you out for that." Cort regretted the words even as he spoke them.

For a long moment, Guy simply stared. Then, his mouth thinned with a hard, mirthless smile. "Would you?" he taunted. "As 'tis clear you're set on your own path, choose the time and place. I'm at your service, *my lord*." He snapped a brief, insulting bow and stalked from the room.

Chapter Twenty-Eight

Cort sensed his dream crumbling around him and could see no way to save it. He felt as he had as a five-year-old when his brother Etienne, only a toddler, had stumbled into the castle he'd built of carved wooden blocks. He recalled the vivid panic as he'd scrambled to prevent the destruction of his prized donjon and battlements, the aching sadness when the blocks tumbled and scattered in ruin around him.

For a young child, that mishap had been the greatest tragedy of his life. How trivial now in comparison to the disaster his world had become.

And if Guy was right...

Cort shuddered. Lexi might never forgive him for what he'd said, what he'd done and almost done. For his lack of trust in her. Just as his best friend might never forgive the insult he'd just dealt him.

A light knock drew his gaze toward the door. While he had no desire to speak with anyone at the moment, he welcomed the diversion from his black thoughts. "Come!"

Dane edged around the thick oak portal and closed it behind him. His gaze skittered from Cort to the fire to the tapestry undulating against the wall in the sudden draft. Huge hands opening and closing at his sides, shoulders hunched, he looked as tentative as Cort had ever seen him. Pale blue eyes pleaded. For what? Twice the giant attempted to speak, but seemed unable to form coherent words.

Despite his impatience, Cort forced a gentle tone as he asked, "What is it, Dane? Why do you not guard my lady's door?"

He was not so much concerned Lexi would escape as surprised Dane would abandon his post. "Is aught amiss?" Oh, sweet Christ, had something happened?

The man's throat worked as he again tried to speak. "I... It... There's s-something I must t-tell you," he blurted at last. "I saw."

Every nerve in Cort's body snapped to attention. Still, he maintained a calm façade so as not to unsettle Dane.

"What did you see?" Cort coaxed. "Something to do with Bouchard's visit? 'Tis why you've been so quiet, why you've stayed so close to Lady Lex." Certainty stirred within him. Certainty and a formless dread.

Dane jerked a nod, clearly relieved his lord understood that much. Blood thudding in his temples, Cort waited for the rest.

"The d-day he left, B-Bouchard...I saw him meet a w-woman, alone, near the b-back of the manor."

Despite his resolve to remain calm, Cort stiffened.

Dane paused, eyes downcast. "I only heard p-part of what they s-said. No sense. A perfect g-goat and a scape." Brow ridged in concentration, he lifted his troubled gaze to Cort's. "I didn't want t-to get her in trouble. If I'm wr-wrong..." He stammered to a halt, fists clenched.

"I understand," Cort assured him, nausea roiling in his gut. "But if you're right, it could be important. We might discover the truth behind the ambush and the tunnel fire. And the attack that day in the woods."

Dane's blue eyes went glacial. "Lady Lex was crying," he growled. "I came down to t-tell you, and you were arguing with Guy. That's when I knew I h-had to tell you about Bouchard, wh-what I saw and heard."

What he'd heard. *Perfect goat. Scape.* The words made no more sense to Cort than they did to Dane, circling in his head like a spinning mace. Then they clicked into place with sickening clarity. One word, not two. *Scapegoat. The perfect scapegoat.*

"Oh, God. Oh, God, what have I done?" *Lexi.* Cort's breath hitched in his throat. But was *she* the scapegoat, or had she planned to incriminate someone else before her plan went awry?

"Who, Dane?" He wanted desperately to know. And not to know. "Whom did you see?" He felt as if his very life hung upon the knight's response.

Looking as though he might choke on the answer, Dane swallowed, then blinked and swallowed again. "L-lady Lex—"

"Christ's blood, man!" Cort's control snapped. He slammed his fist on the small table, cracking it in two. "Just say it!" *Say it, and condemn me to Hades.*

Dane's lips quivered in an effort to finish the thought. "Guy was wrong about h-her," he said at last, voice strangled. "And your lady will b-be angry with me when sh-she finds out I told. B-but I had to—"

"My lady? Lady Lex?" The awful truth curdled his stomach, sent tremors down his arms and legs.

Eyes confused and anxious, Dane nodded and shuffled his feet. "Lady Lex won't like th-that I got her in trouble. She's... It's her—"

Cort had heard more than enough. He was no longer listening. Striding to the door, he flung it open and pinned Dane with a commanding stare. "Find my father. And Guy. Tell them Lexi's the traitor and I've gone after Bouchard. And make sure *my wife* stays in our room. I'll deal with her when I return."

"W-wait!" Dane stood transfixed, palm pressed to his forehead, eyes clenched shut. They reopened slowly, bewildered and anxious. "What did I… I can't r-remember what I…"

"It's all right," Cort assured, wanting nothing more than to be gone. "Hard though the truth might be"—*hard* didn't begin to describe the agony that ravaged him—"you were right to tell me."

"Pain." Dane ground his head between his hands. "The lady a t-traitor. No…" Dane moaned as though his head might explode.

"I must go!" Cort slammed his fist against the open portal. "Guard Lexi's chamber. I'll speak with Guy."

"Only meant to h-help. L-listened to voices since that day. Had to be s-sure," Dane muttered.

"Guard Lexi!" Cort shouted over his shoulder, pounding down the stairs. His boots thudded against the slate entry as he bellowed for Guy.

Legs pumping, his friend plunged through the back door from the rear yard and down the central corridor. He skidded on the worn slate foyer, slammed his shoulder into the wall, and dashed after Cort into the fire-lit great hall.

"What's wrong?" His heart leapt into his throat at Cort's obvious distress.

Stefan stared, owl-eyed, from the bench before the hearth. "I couldn't sleep and came down for—"

"Wake my father," Cort ordered.

The lad scrambled from his seat and out of the hall.

Cort, took a deep breath, wiped at the sweat that seeped down his temples, and turned his attention to Guy.

"Dane just came to me." He swallowed. Hard. "Though I wish to Christ I didn't, I know now what's been troubling him. He saw Lexi and Bouchard together. Overheard a most damning conversation."

Tears gathered in his eyes, and Guy's heart constricted. "Tell me what you need, Cort. What do you plan to do?"

"I wanted to be wrong, Guy. I really did." His throat convulsed before he corralled his anguish.

"'Tis past time to confront the *canaille*. I'm going after Bouchard."

"I'm with you, of course." His shoulders slumped. "Odin's eye. Lexi."

"What's amiss?" Cort's impressive sire strode through the archway. His casual attire of braies and a dressing gown did not in any way lessen the impact of his presence.

No way now to keep his parents in the dark. Cort's terse summary of events drew a growl from the older man. "I'm sorry, my son." His eyes clouded. "Guy and I will rouse the men." He laid his hand on Cort's arm.

"I'm your squire. I'll go," Stefan said from the foot of the stairs. Gaze anguished, he added, "I would not believe my sister could betray you, my lord. But my loyalty is to you."

"You will not go." Eric Thorssen stared him down. "Whatever your sister has done, she may need you here." He strode over to ruffle the lad's hair. "This time, you must trust us to take care of your lord."

Expression mutinous, Stefan gave a grudging nod and met Cort's gaze directly. "I will bring down your armor, my lord."

Cort almost bowled him over as he pushed past his father and thundered up the stairs, then back down moments later, his helm, shield, and Deathwright in hand. "Catch up with me!" He threw open the front door.

"Damn, Golden Dragon. You will wait..." Thorssen spun toward the stairs, stripping off his robe as he took the spiral steps two at a time. "Saddle our mounts," he shouted back over his shoulder. "Quickly now."

Cort stepped over the threshold, Guy on his heels before he paused and turned back. Stefan remained frozen midway up the stairs. "Tell Cort's mother what's happened and take her to Lexi. Mayhap your sister will speak with her and..." He shook his head. "I'll roust the men on my way to the stables."

"Aye." The boy dragged himself up the stairs.

"Guard my lord's back, sir. Guard it well," he called down from the shadowed landing.

"With my life," Guy swore. Tyr burst from the stables, Cort crouched over his back as they hurtled through the gate. "If I can get to the damn stubborn ass in time."

****

Lexi tensed at the sound of the key in the lock. When a massive silhouette filled the doorway, her shoulders slumped with relief. Even Cort wasn't *that* big.

"Dane," she croaked, throat raw from crying.

"Our lord's lady m-mother's with me." He stepped into the room, Rosalinde close behind. "Stef will tell you b-both what I ex-explained to him." He wrung his hands, remorseful gaze fixed on Lexi. "I m-made a mistake. Said the wr-wrong thing, and your huband d-didn't wait to hear what I m-meant."

They listened without interruption, Cort's mother perched beside Lexi on the bed. No questions, no comment by any of them on her puffy eyes or tear-stained face, bless them. Shocked one moment by her brother's quick recounting of Dane's revelation of *Melissande's* involvement with Bouchard, the next at the realization Cort would soon know *her* innocent, Lexi's mind whirled.

She lost the thread of the conversation until she recognized 'twas Dane, not Stefan, speaking. "...gone to kill him, I th-think."

Every muscle in her body contracted with fear.

Rosalinde gasped, and Lexi at once relaxed the unconscious death grip on her fingers. “Sorry, Mother,” she murmured, her thoughts flown to Cort.

“Alone?” she demanded. “He’s gone alone? How long ago?”

“Just before we came up,” Stefan said. “Mayhap a quarter of an hour.”

“His f-father and Guy are riding after h-him w-with the men. I must go.” He turned toward the door.

The storm had passed, but thin wracks of clouds played hide-and-seek with the half-moon visible through the arrow casement. Full darkness had descended while they spoke.

Lexi gave her mother-in-law’s hands a reassuring squeeze, then scooted to the far edge of the raised bed and dropped to the floor.

“Lexi.” Rosalinde’s odd tone stopped her progress toward the wardrobe on the far wall. Turning, Lexi followed the direction of the woman’s stare.

“Frog warts!” She’d forgotten she was clad only in her shift—what was left of it. Gathering the tattered linen across her breasts and stomach, she glanced at Dane and her brother. Eyes now averted, both, she was sure, had gotten an eyeful. No help for it. And modesty was the least of her concerns at the moment.

Cort had gone after Bouchard. Alone, unless the others caught up with him in time. And as she’d seen Cort ride, that was unlikely. He would discover she was innocent. If he lived.

“Stefan, go. Make sure Cort’s troop is on its way.” Her voice echoed from the depths of the oak cabinet as she stretched to reach the far left recess. “Dane, stay.”

“But I m-must join them.”

“No.” She backed out of the wardrobe, checked to

make sure Stefan had left. "You are going with me."

Dane shifted from foot to foot, clearly agitated. "I m-must—"

Hoping the wadded garments she clutched provided an adequate shield, Lexi stepped in front of him. "I need your help, my friend. Cort may need mine. I'd rather ride with you than alone, but either way, I'm going after him."

Rosalinde's mouth gaped.

"I'm going," Lexi vowed with quiet intensity. "I saved Cort's life the day of the ambush, and I didn't even know him then. Now that I love him, would you have me do less?"

Rosalinde's blank expression said she had no idea to what Lexi referred. But Dane's gaze widened in disbelief, slid from her face to the mottled clothing in her arms, back to her face.

"The... You... You're the sl-slinger?"

She smiled, then mimicked the salute she'd given Cort months ago in the clearing.

Dane shook himself like a waking bear and returned her smile. "I'll t-tell the ostler to ready a mount for you, l-lady, and be r-right back."

While Lexi pulled on the green-and-brown hosen and tunic and braided her hair, she gave Cort's mother an abbreviated version of events from the day he'd arrived to the present. The afternoon unpleasantness she omitted all together, save to mention the sketch and Cort's belief she had betrayed him.

"I've not had a chance of late to practice," she admitted with a frown. "Your son has had me guarded. For my own protection. Hah!"

Rosalinde's tone mirrored Lexi's pique. "Thorssen men do tend to be protective."

Lexi's gusted out a frustrated breath. "Yes, well, let's hope his *protective* instincts haven't badly impaired my skills." She arched a brow. "Which, I might add, are considerable."

Despite the dire cirmcumstances, Rosalind smiled. "Two modest warriors married to each other. I can't wait to see your children."

Lexi's heart flip-flopped against her ribcage. Children they would never have if Cort...

She wound the three-foot-long braid atop her head and crammed the floppy hat over it, refusing to complete the thought. Last, she jammed her feet into calf-high black boots.

Feet thundered on the stairs. "Come on, l-lady," Dane's voice boomed through the door. "Your palfrey's s-saddled."

Lexi snatched up the sling from the bed and snapped the wrist thong over her hand. Stones rattled within the deerskin pouch Rosalinde handed her. She tied it to her wide leather belt, then opened her arms when Cort's mother stepped in for a hard, brief hug.

"I cannot like sending you into danger, daughter. But I understand your need to go. Bring your husband and yourself back safe." Rosalinde's warm lips brushed her forehead. "Godspeed."

"I'll see him safe if it kills me," Lexi swore.

And one way or the other, it just might.

Chapter Twenty-Nine

He didn't want to die tonight. But an eerie sense of *deja vu* settled around Cort as he watched the approaching riders gallop over *Paix*'s plank bridge.

He appreciated the exquisite balance of Deathwright's grip in his left hand, the solid weight of his shield on his right arm. The differences between and similarities to that first ambush and this encounter elicited a grim smile.

Day rather than night.

Clarity rather than swirling mist.

Armor, then, but no helmet—the reverse of his present attire.

And this time he had warning.

The odds of four to one were about the same, as was the source of the attacks.

And, again, he had only himself to blame.

He'd been twice foolish, allowing impulse to guide his actions. If he hadn't known then, he knew now that Bouchard was a conscienceless bastard. Why had he ever thought his enemy would act with honor and meet him in equal-odds combat?

Betrayal slapped like acid through his veins. Fate, he suspected, would not be so kind a second time. It had spared him once through a minor miracle—when he'd believed in miracles. He no longer trusted his instincts, and logic warned his uncanny luck had run out. As absent this night as his mysterious slinger.

Muffled hoofbeats vibrated through the turf beneath him. A fog-shrouded moon sparked occasional glints of light from armor and weapons as his opponents closed in on him.

Cort back-stepped Tyr to the edge of the encroaching woods. Valiant Tyr. He must be exhausted. Despite Cort's intent not to overtax him on the ride here, he'd pushed him harder than was wise. Yet Tyr whinnied and tossed his head at the group thundering toward them as if to assure Cort he was willing and able to confront the approaching danger.

Cort whispered brief encouragement and praise even as he tightened his knees and gauged his enemies' strategy.

They cantered to the far side of the glade, then fanned out in a semicircle. Heavy ground fog settled about their destriers' hooves and powerful legs. The man on the far right nudged his horse forward, lost in, then emerging from the distorting mist like a nightmare figure. Just out of Cort's reach, he reined in his mount.

"At last." His voice was a hollow whisper in the thick air.

Bouchard.

"You are a fool, Alain," Cort scoffed.

"Who's the fool? I'm not the one who came alone."

Cort ignored the jibe. "Had you left things as they were—"

"I couldn't do that, Thorssen. Too much at stake."

"If I'd intended to tell the king of your cowardice at Hastings—"

"Cowardice?" In the flickering moonglow, a tight smile hardened Bouchard's mouth. "I prefer to think of it as self-preservation."

Cort's derisive laughter echoed in the treetops. "You would." Then, as if Bouchard had not interrupted, he said, "If I'd meant to tell, I'd have done so long before now."

"Perhaps." Alain canted his head and shrugged his heavy shoulders, chain mail clinking as it reflected light like metallic fish scales. "But I could never be sure of that, could I?"

"Certainly not now," Cort replied. "When you attacked my men, my home, you forced my hand. Whether I live or die, several of my men know the truth. If for no other reason than to protect Amiton, they'll tell William what you've done."

"Without proof?" Bouchard sneered.

"Loath though I am to mention it, the king will not be pleased to receive my corpse. It may be all the proof he requires."

Even in the uncertain light, Cort saw the color leach from Alain's face. Then Bouchard cleared his throat, gauntleted hands worrying his stallion's reins. "Your body, if it is found at all, will be far from *Paix*. It will be my word against theirs, should it come to that. There's more at stake here than you understand."

A light breeze lifted Cort's hair from his shoulders and set the fog spiraling upward. For the several seconds the space between himself and his enemy cleared, he studied Bouchard's intense expression.

More at stake? What was he missing?

Guessing Alain would enjoy the chance to gloat, he said, "If I'm to die—" an unwelcome but likely prospect "—I'd first have my curiosity satisfied. What *is* at stake? Other than my life, of course." Guy would be proud of his cold-blooded warlord face, Cort thought.

A soft, steady wind had begun to blow. It ruffled the mist, dragged it back and forth in ever-thinning bands. The horses stamped and curvetted, obviously spooked by the twisting fog. Armor and harness jingled, the sounds magnified by the cloying moisture.

"What else is at stake?" Cort demanded when Bouchard hesitated.

"Amiton," he said at last.

"Amiton?" Cort didn't know what he'd expected, but it hadn't been that.

"It should have been mine. It was the estate I wanted when the king gave me that one." He swept his arm in the direction of *Paix*'s manor. "But William was holding it in trust for you because you'd expressed an interest in it. When I heard you were on your way there—I knew it had to be you—this spring, I thought to rid myself of you before you had a chance to claim it. And her."

So, he'd been right, Cort realized. Bouchard had deduced who he was, despite the spurious last name. Then his heart tripped, took up a dull, painful rhythm. Her. Lexi. He'd sworn not to think of her, remember her, ache for her.

"Too late for that," he murmured, unable to prevent the catch in his voice. "For either of us."

He glared at Alain, willing the man to understand his fury at their treachery, his satisfaction in their downfall. "She's another problem for you, Bouchard. We caught her, I'm afraid. Sooner or later, she'll break, and when she does, I'll wager she exchanges her neck for yours."

Despite his confident tone, Cort had serious doubts about that. Whatever Lexi's faults, she was loyal to the bone. Sadly, her loyalty did not belong to him. The truth pierced his heart, try as he might to pretend he no longer cared. Could not afford to care.

"...stronger than I thought," Bouchard was saying as Cort refocused on his enemy. "She set the tunnel fire, you know. Said it was almost too easy. After all, who would ever question her presence there? She watched you that day, too, furious that your successful rescue attempt made you a hero to your people."

For a long moment, silence reigned. Then, as if struck by an errant thought, Bouchard narrowed his eyes. The soft wind had begun to dissipate the mist, and Cort could see quite clearly for several yards in all directions.

"You say you caught her?" Alain demanded. "It was the sketch, wasn't it? That damn sketch. I told her to leave it alone, that it was too dangerous. Things were going well. We didn't need a scapegoat."

Cort stilled as Dane's words replayed in his mind. They niggled at him, prompted a vague sense of unease he could not explain.

"Well, I'll think of something." He frowned in apparent concentration. Then the corner of his mouth lifted. "She's far better at pretense than I ever anticipated, but this time she'll listen to me. With a little guidance, who knows." Alain's smile blossomed into full-blown nasty. "I do believe she'll make me a most satisfactory and biddable wife."

"Biddable?" Cort almost choked. "If you believe that, she's better at pretense than even I imagined."

Bouchard's obvious confusion at the remark set Cort's nerve endings tingling.

"I can think of a number of words to describe Lexi," he said, "but *biddable* is not among them."

"Lexi?" Alain blinked like a sun-blinded owl.

Cort's heart stopped. His breath stilled. His chest and throat constricted as vague unease coalesced into dread and awful certainty. "Oh, God. Not Lexi."

As impossible as it seemed, there was only one other woman it could be. Dane's final, unfinished sentence rang in Cort's ears. *It's her*—cousin. That one word would have saved a world of grief. Saved his own life, perhaps. But he'd been too impatient, too tunnel-visioned to listen, to either Guy or Dane. Seen only what he'd convinced himself was true.

Remorse. Fury. Love. Tangled emotions twisted

his insides until he thought he might strangle on them. He heard the despair in his own whispered, "Lexi was the scapegoat?"

Bouchard's harsh laughter scraped along Cort's already raw nerves. "It worked?" His mirth smoothed to a vicious smirk. "We'd thought to convince Lexi to relinquish Amiton after your death. If unsuccessful, mayhap have her suffer a fatal *accident*. That won't be necessary now, will it? Mayhap I've not given sweet little Melissande due credit. You actually thought Lexi had betrayed you? That's rich, Thorssen."

With unmistakable malice, he added, "Too bad you'll not have the chance to tell her how sorry you are. I'll tell her for you, if you like. Or perhaps, instead, I'll tell her you died cursing her name."

Hot rage slammed through Cort's body. The cool, beaded moisture on his face warmed and ran in sweaty rivulets down his cheeks to drip from his chin. He was aware of nothing save his desire to kill Bouchard.

Not to salvage his own honor. It was too late for that. No, he'd do it for Lexi. To compensate her in some small measure for the harm he'd done, his lack of trust. Not that she was ever likely to know. But he'd know. And if God was good, she might in time realize that, doubts and all, he had loved her more than life. At the least, he prayed she would eventually forgive him. However little he deserved it, she was good at forgiveness.

"Come, *batard*," Cort hissed. Gaze riveted to Bouchard's, fingers melded to Deathwright's familiar grip, he kneed Tyr forward.

I love you, Lexi.

****

The clash of steel, the destriers' gusting breaths, the guttural curses reached them long before they saw the men. Lexi's heart plummeted in fear, then soared with hope as she and Dane reined in at the edge of the clearing. Hopelessly outnumbered Cort might be, but he was alive. And fighting.

During what had seemed an interminable ride, she and Dane spoke not at all. He'd followed her lead without question as they raced through the night, his face as grim as she suspected her own must be. Even the shifting mist had not hampered their pace. She knew this land as well as she knew her herbs and simples.

In the two years since she arrived at Avonly, she'd ridden out countless times alone to practice with her sling. She had but to keep the River Avon on the left until she reached the huge granite boulder that marked *Paix*'s southern boundary. From there she'd cut through the oak and alder forest that bordered Alain's land, a quicker route than that of field and meadow, which Cort had no doubt traveled.

Still, she'd prayed his progress would be slower, that he might lose his way. Or bypass the manor entirely in the concealing fog.

Lexi gave an unladylike snort. Too much to hope. The man had the instincts of a spawning salmon.

A harsh cry and the clang of swords echoed around her as she sidestepped her mount so that Dane might move up beside her. In the luminous fog, their horses' coats glistened with lather as the poor beasts' bellies puffed and deflated with their labored breathing. But she had no sympathy to spare at the moment.

With a practiced eye, she assayed distance and angle and quickly guided her mare several yards to the right. Dane followed, his anxious gaze shifting to the combat in the glade, then back to Lexi.

"Hurry, my l-lady," he urged. "My lord's in t-trouble."

Lexi dared not glance toward Cort for fear of what she might see. She pulled her feet from the stirrups and settled her hand on Dane's shoulder for balance. Drawing her legs up under her, she stood on the hard, flat saddle and reached for an overhanging branch.

Dane surged upward, feet planted in his stirrups. "Up you g-go," he said as he gripped her waist in his huge hands and boosted her onto the limb as though she weighed no more than a kitten. Not surprising, Lexi thought as she wedged her back against the tree trunk and splayed her feet at the sturdy base of a forked branch. More than once she'd seen Dane tote his in-excess-of-a-hundred-pounds armor in one hand.

The instant she was settled, he dropped back into the saddle. He slid her a hard smile and his flared ax from its sheath. "Aim true," he growled, then spun his destrier and charged into the clearing.

A spine-chilling battle cry rent the night as the great ax's blade circled his head and swept down on its first victim. Lexi shuddered as steel cleaved through armor and bone. Blood sprayed upward. She swallowed hard, closed her eyes, and blocked all from her mind save the task at hand.

Pulling open the drawstring of the pouch hanging from her belt, she chose a stone by touch. Smooth and cool, the size of a walnut in her clammy palm. Mere threads of fog still hung upon the surrounding branches, not enough to impede her aim, thank God. The widely spaced tree limbs allowed adequate room to maneuver.

To the left, Dane was engaged in battle with two knights, neither of whom seemed willing to come within reach of his lethal blade. Heart thudding as if it would burst from her chest, Lexi forced herself to focus on her target. Bouchard.

He was turned slightly sideways, perhaps ten

yards away. Cort sat between them, his back to her, the awkward angle at which he held his shield a sure sign he was injured. Again.

Despite all her husband had told her of Alain's treacherous nature, not until this moment, when she realized he would kill Cort if he could, had Lexi truly accepted the dark truth of those accusations. This man she had once defended, once called friend, was intent on taking from her the only man she would ever love.

Cort's distrust of her cut deep, but she could not let him die because of it.

Move! she urged him silently. *Move aside, just a little.*

Deathwright swooped through the air, driving Bouchard back. The hard line of his mouth bespoke frustration. Lexi suspected Cort was smiling. Dane's presence had evened the odds, and his own deft, left-handed swordplay had reduced Alain's to choppy, jabbing motions. As though he'd read her mind, Cort sidestepped Tyr to parry Alain's next thrust.

Lexi sighed with relief. Resolve washed through her like a soothing tonic. Eyes narrowed, hand steady, she slipped the stone into the leather cup attached to her wrist thong and straightened away from the tree's supporting trunk. Raising her arm, she circled it above her head. Within seconds the weapon sang with a smooth, natural cadence.

Whoosh, whoosh, whoosh. Lexi whipped her wrist as it came parallel with her right shoulder.

Snap! The stone whistled through the damp air.

A sharp, metallic crack reverberated across the clearing, drowning any sound Alain might have made. She'd missed. Hit the nasal of his helmet.

Despair shivered through her. The tree shuddered beneath her. Reflexively, she stepped back and wrapped her left arm about the tree. Steady thunder beat up through its trunk.

Heartsick, Lexi shifted her gaze from the clearing to *Paix*'s walls. Moonlight glittered on chain mail and raised swords as a sizable troop galloped over the bridge toward the glade.

Dane, who had at last dispatched both his adversaries, now turned to the new threat. But Lexi realized even he could not defeat a score of men, even with her help. How many could she hurt or injure before they discovered her position and either captured or killed her? Too few. Eyes blurred with hopeless tears, she fumbled in her pouch for another stone.

One last look, she thought as she dropped the large stone into the sling. Her heart cried out for her to call to Cort, to let him know before they died that she loved him, had come to save him. Common sense stilled her tongue. He might feel honor-bound to protect her then. When he must concentrate on protecting himself.

Though it seemed forever since she'd slung the first stone, Lexi knew it could have been no more than a few seconds. Swallowing the sob that choked her throat, she forced her gaze back to the clearing.

Cort's face was turned toward her, his eyes searching the perimeter of trees. Beyond him, Alain leaned back in the saddle, his sword lax at his side. Even as she watched, it slipped from his fingers and fell to the ground. His head canted suddenly to the side, as if the weight of the helmet were more than he could bear.

Lexi stiffened in disbelief. Outlined in the icy moonlight, Bouchard's nasal jutted above his nose at a straight ninety-degree angle.

Arms limp at his sides, he toppled from his mount. Mail clinked as he slammed to the ground in a graceless heap.

The din of hoofbeats slowed. Clearly confused about what action to pursue now that their lord was defeated, the leader raised his hand and halted. Cort turned to face them as Dane moved up beside him.

Lexi held her breath. She would never know what *Paix*'s men might have decided.

A single, distant cry warbled through the night, was joined by the full-throated roar of a contingent. Her heart surged into her throat as she snapped her gaze to the crest of the hill that marked the estate's Western border.

An aura of misty light seemed to pulse about the troop of horsemen who poured down the slope, blades and maces slicing the air. As they raced nearer, Lexi was at last able to discern their words. "The Dragon! The Dragon!"

Knees like aspic, she sagged against the tree and whispered, "Thank God."

Without even token resistance, *Paix*'s men retreated. In moments, Cort's men flooded the clearing, his father and Guy at the fore.

"Well met," Cort called as he sheathed Deathwright and walked Tyr toward the tree in which she hid. Face streaming sweat, he grinned with boyish enthusiasm. "Thank you, Dane." His gaze shone warm with gratitude. "Your timing, like theirs, was perfection."

Dane responded with a modest nod.

"Almost too perfect." Erik Thorssen swung his horse into position beside his son's and scowled, though his eyes glimmered with relief in the stark moonlight.

Guy moved to flank Cort on the other side. In an almost simultaneous gesture, the three removed their helms.

The branch beneath Lexi dipped in a sudden gust of wind. With a startled cry, she lost her balance. Three sets of eyes watched her plummet downward, derriere first.

Cort's arm snatched her from the air. She

landed in his lap with a painful thud. Her hat tumbled off, freeing her long braid. It whipped across her face, then flopped over her shoulder to her thighs.

"Bouchard's alive," Brian called from behind them. "Out like a snuffed candle, but he's breathing."

"Umph," Cort grunted. His veiled gaze never wavered from Lexi's upturned face. Silence thrummed around them.

"Well," Guy said at last with characteristic amusement, "I think we've found our slinger."

Cort arched a censorious brow. "Have we?"

Lexi scrambled for a tart reply to disguise her anxiety. "I'm not admitting to anything while you have that expression on your face."

"What expression?" Cort asked softly.

"The one that's drawn up tighter than a miser's purse strings."

His arm tightened about her as his features relaxed, though his eyes shimmered with anger. "You could have been killed."

"So could you."

"I'm a warrior."

"I'm a woman."

"I believe that was my point."

"Exactly. And the very reason I did not tell you the truth, at first or later. You'd have forbidden me to protect those I love." She huffed out a breath. "At the mere hint of danger, you had me guarded closer than a tick on a goose. What would you have done had I admitted to being the slinger?" she demanded.

"I don't consider being slammed in the head and called traitor a *mere hint of danger*," Cort shot back.

Lexi sniffed. "You're avoiding the issue. Freedom is at stake here, husband. My freedom."

"Your safety was—is—also at stake, and far more important than your freedom."

"Not to me."

Lexi tore her gaze from his, furious at his implacable attitude. She'd just saved the horse's behind, again, yet as she'd feared all along, he meant to curtail her movements even further. Deprive her of the privacy, the solitude she so cherished.

Her eyes focused on his sword-slashed upper right arm. Long but not deep, the cut's blood flow had slowed to a trickle. Still, she needed to examine it more closely to determine if it required stitches.

"What of me, my wild rose?" Cort's thumb beneath her chin forced her gaze back to his. Features strained, voice husky, he continued, "What would become of me should something happen to you? How could I live knowing I should have protected you and did not?"

Tears blurred Lexi's eyes at his gentle expression and heartfelt tone. But she could not let him win. Not this time. "Listen to yourself," she whispered earnestly. "Do you not think I feel the same? Does being a woman mean that I am forbidden to protect those I love? Life offers no guarantees, my lord. I could fall from a horse and break my neck. Die of lung fever or in childbed. Any number of things could happen to me." She swept her arm toward the men scattered across the meadow. "To any of us. But if you wrap me in security, deny me the right to wander the woods and fields, you will kill my spirit, destroy who I am." She paused, desperate to make him understand. "I would rather die than live so."

"Do you?" he whispered.

"Do I what?"

"Love me."

She felt the accelerated rhythm of his heart against the side of her breast, heard the subtle shift in his breathing. And knew, at that moment, that despite the risk of making herself vulnerable, she could not deny him the truth.

Nothing more between us. Ever, he'd said on their wedding night. No more secrets. No more walls. Still, Lexi wondered if he'd heard one word of what she'd said just now.

"I've always loved you. Foolish, stubborn man."

Vaguely, Lexi realized the others had tactfully retreated. Pain frothed in Cort's eyes the moment before he closed them. "Enough to forgive me?"

Before she could respond, he continued in a raw whisper, "I would have understood if you'd betrayed me for love of your people. I wouldn't have liked it," he admitted, eyes now fixed on her like glittering gems, "but your loyalty to them I could have accepted. Even forgiven, in time. It was..." He swallowed hard; anguish moved in his eyes. "It was the thought that you loved Bouchard, that your passionate response to me was pretense that I could not bear."

His tormented gaze tore at Lexi's heart.

"God, I am so sorry, Lexi."

She smoothed the damp hair along his temple. "I know. I will forgive you only if you forgive me." She could barely speak for the tears clogging her throat.

"For keeping your secret so long?" His eyes were as gentle as a caress. "I would forgive you almost anything, wife. You destroy me. I love you."

His admission was all the more precious for being freely given. But would he give her the freedom she desired, needed, to be happy? Lexi touched his face with trembling fingers, then clutched his tunic to pull herself up and placed a tender kiss on his hard mouth.

She sighed and gave him an impish smile. "I'm glad. More than glad. But if you love me, you must also forgive my poor aim."

Cort frowned. "Poor aim?" He glanced behind him to a still-inert Alain.

Lexi peered over her husband's shoulder and wrinkled her nose in self-disgust. "I was aiming for his throat. Or maybe yours."

For a moment she thought he would laugh. But his expression sobered as he met her gaze and said, "That's what comes from lack of practice. You must remedy that."

She eyed him warily, almost afraid to hope. "Must I?"

His response neatly circumvented the issue. A wry chuckle rumbled from his chest. "Oh, my parents will love this. We've never had a slinger in the family. And there's nothing my mother loves more than an unconventional woman." His voice dropped a sensual octave. "Nothing *I* love more." He would not distract her, Lexi vowed, with his sweet words and golden allure. Still, something within her melted at the warm promise in his voice.

She forced herself to pull away from Cort's strength and heat, willed his gaze to hers as she prepared to take the biggest gamble of her life. If she lost, she would gain her precious liberty, but naught else.

"I will not barter my freedom, husband. Not even for you."

The air crackled between them. "Will you not?" he asked too quietly.

She shook her head once, hard. "Are you not grateful I came here to aid you?"

With a scowl, he tossed his hair back over his shoulders. "Aye," he admitted grudgingly.

"Well, I don't want your gratitude. I want your admission I could not have done so without my freedom."

"Lexi," he warned in a tight voice.

Undeterred, she insisted, "Nor could I have routed the troop that ambushed you and your men that day on the way to Avonly."

"Enough!"

"I saved your life."

"Not another wor—"

"Twice!"

His jaw cracked as he ground his teeth together.

"Don't think to threaten me with your temper, Golden Dragon Thorssen. I've seen it at its worst and survived."

She almost hated herself in that moment as pain and guilt crested in his eyes, stark evidence he was reliving his unjustified distrust, his harsh treatment of her earlier that day. But her arsenal of weapons was meager, and she would use what few she had.

"After I was shot with the arrow, I dreamt you were lost to me," she murmured, smoothing the hard planes of his face with unsteady fingers. "Are you lost to me, Cort? Will you deny me the very essence of what I am and have me lose myself?"

Epilogue

"I'll never again be so quick to dismiss coincidence," Cort admitted with a grimace.

"Or your instincts?" Guy guessed with a wry smile.

"As usual, my friend, you've read my mind."

My friend. Cort savored the truth of that, the readiness with which Guy had forgiven him. Like Lexi, he possessed a loyal and generous spirit.

It had been a long, difficult month for all of them. Cort missed Richard Graham, but Melissande could not be allowed to remain at Amiton. Lexi's compassionate pleas had resulted in the girl's exile to a Shrewsbury convent—a far kinder fate, in Cort's opinion, than she deserved. But he'd allowed it for her father's sake. The man had been decimated by his daughter's treachery. Still, he loved her and had chosen to rent a property near the convent.

"Your parents and sister arrived safely at court, I hear," Guy said.

"Aye. A letter arrived today from *Maman.* William has agreed to allow my father to return with her and Julianna to Normandy and to stay until fall. Perhaps next year he will be able to remain for good. England will never be home to him, and he misses my mother."

Guy shifted on the bench, then sipped from the goblet cradled in his right hand. "What news of Bouchard?"

Cort gusted an impatient sigh. "Uncle Will hasn't yet made a final determination. For now, Alain remains in The Tower."

Guy's gaze grew distant, and quiet settled around them. Evening shadows darkened the corners of the great hall. The hushed sounds of dusk wafted through the casements on summer-soft air. A nightjar's fluid song rippled through the clarion call of a shepherd's horn, was answered by the bleating flock. Men whistled as they wandered home, and mothers called their children.

"Coincidence." Guy's voice whispered through the deepening gloom. "Some might call it Fate."

"Another abstract in which I never put much faith." Cort's smile was deliberate, slow and gentle. "Until now."

"You're not always quick, my lord, but sooner or later you come around."

"It's hard to ignore the truth, my friend. That I chose Avonly out of all the available estates in England, that Lexi should live here, that by mere chance she had been practicing when and where we were ambushed. Add to those, Lexi's thieving ferret, Bouchard's chance proximity, and Dane's overhearing the bastard's conversation with Melissande,"—whom he would never again think of as Mellie the Mouse—"and I'd be a fool to discount coincidence."

With a wry smile, he admitted, "Mayhap I'd have benefited more than Lexi from a knock on the noggin." Thoughts of his wife warmed him, as they invariably did, with humor and love, laced heavily with desire. "She saw the pattern far sooner than you or I."

"Her knowledge of our slinger's identity no doubt helped her cause." Guy's mouth twitched with amusement. His gem-green eyes twinkled.

"Aye," Cort agreed with mock solemnity. "Even so, her instincts are as good as ours. She loved me from the first."

Guy's laughter echoed through the room.

Cort shook his head. "I can deny her nothing."

"You'll get used to it in time, my lord. Have you ever seen her happier?"

"Nay." Cort slanted him a pained grin. "At least she has compromised somewhat. Wanders only on our land, no longer wears men's garb when she practices. And she's given up climbing trees."

"There you have it. A demure, biddable wife."

Cort snorted.

Both men laughed.

"Speaking of which." Cort gave an exaggerated yawn and stretched his arms high above his head. "My lady awaits."

"And you sit here talking to me?" Guy asked. "Be gone, man."

Anticipation spiraled through Cort as he bid Guy good night and descended the stairs to the hall. If all had gone as planned, the gamekeeper would be waiting with the *present* Cort had requested.

He shook his head and smiled. He was probably the first husband in history whose wife would thank him for such a gift.

****

"What have you there, husband?" Lexi could not disguise her curiosity as Cort's long saffron tunic jumped and writhed against his thigh. "Surely you've more control over yourself than that."

Blushing no longer seemed to bother him as it used to. He laughed at her bawdy comment. "Not where you're concerned, love. And I fear the condition will not improve with time."

"I hope not." She pressed herself to his side so he might take her mouth with his. "Now, what do you really have under your tunic?"

"Zeus."

"Wishful thinking, my lord."

He gave her a fierce scowl. "Enough denigration of my anatomy, wife. I've brought Thene a gift."

"Athene?" Surprise and pleasure jolted through Lexi.

Dipping his hand to the pouch concealed beneath his clothing, Cort yanked on the leather thong that held it closed. "Do you think she'll like him?" he asked as a cinnamon-furred, triangular face popped into view. "He'll need to be trained."

"What man doesn't?" Lexi gave him an impish smile. "But I think Athene will love him."

"They're like us, fair and dark," he explained as Zeus clawed his way up Cort's fine wool tunic to his shoulder.

"The gamekeeper found a nest in the forest and trapped several. The other male is twice this one's size, so we think Zeus must be young. A good mate for Athene, eh?"

Lexi nodded assent as the ferret slid-clawed its way down her husband's back, then bounded to the floor to investigate its new home.

"Why *Zeus*? I'd have thought you'd choose a Norse name."

"If they're to begin a dynasty, it seems appropriate he have a king's name. A Greek name to complement hers. Odin doesn't sound right."

"But Athene sprang from Zeus' head," Lexi said. "She was his daughter. I mean—"

"Nonsense. She is the goddess of wisdom. As king of the gods, Zeus is omniscient, isn't he? A match made on Olympus."

He looked so smug, Lexi could not resist a response. She shrugged her shoulders in apparent defeat and released a dramatic sigh. "I suppose it's as true in the animal world as it is in the human one."

"What?" her husband demanded when she said no more.

"Women know everything. Men think they know everything."

"Drew me right in on that one, didn't you?" He growled as he grabbed her around the waist and pulled her close.

"Did I?" she asked, all innocence. "You did ask, my lord."

"Are you saying I got what I asked for?" Cort's tone was pure silk.

Lexi laughed into his eyes. "Not if you'll give me what I'm asking for." She finger-climbed his chest and caressed his neck before tunneling her hands into his thick gilt hair.

"I think I know what that is," he whispered, quirking a fair eyebrow.

"Trust me, my Golden Dragon," she murmured. "I'm a woman. I know you do."

Allowing herself a secret smile, Lexi thought of the babe she carried, the dynasty she and Cort had already begun. She closed her eyes and imagined their children tumbling about in the meadows, heads both fair and dark, eyes flashing gold or turquoise. A tiny girl with her mother's raven hair and father's aqua eyes, a miniature sling dangling from her wrist.

She must tell Cort. Later.

Now, with the finesse of a master spinner, he drew her to him. Lured her with his dragon's heart, his promises of heat and tenderness and forever love. Wove her into the fabric of his days with threads of trust and passion. Ensnared her willingly, body and soul, in his intricate golden web.

And she would, from now until forever, cherish the knight.

A word about the author...

With a lifelong love of reading and writing, becoming a high school English teacher was a natural segue for Diane O'Key. She so cherished her students and coworkers and values that many over the years still keep in touch.

Publication is a dream come true for her.

She and her husband divide their time between SW Florida and upstate South Carolina.

She would love to hear from readers at:

dianeokey.com.

Thank you for purchasing
this publication of The Wild Rose Press, Inc.
For other wonderful stories of romance,
please visit our on-line bookstore at
www.thewildrosepress.com.

For questions or more information
contact us at
info@thewildrosepress.com.

The Wild Rose Press, Inc.
www.thewildrosepress.com

To visit with authors of
The Wild Rose Press, Inc.
join our yahoo loop at
http://groups.yahoo.com/group/thewildrosepress/

9581484R00181

Printed in Great Britain
by Amazon.co.uk, Ltd.,
Marston Gate.